DARK MOON

A MEDIEVAL HISTORICAL ROMANCE

BY KATHRYN LE VEQUE

A DARK SONS NOVEL

KATHRYN LE VEQUE NOVELS

Medieval Romance:

The de Russe Legacy:
The White Lord of Wellesbourne
The Dark One: Dark Knight
Beast
Lord of War: Black Angel
The Iron Knight
Dark Moon

The de Lohr Dynasty:
While Angels Slept (Lords of East Anglia)
Godspeed (Lords of East Anglia)
Rise of the Defender
Steelheart
Spectre of the Sword
Archangel
Unending Love
Shadowmoor
Silversword

Great Lords of le Bec:
Great Protector
To the Lady Born (House of de Royans)
Lord of Winter (Lords of de Royans)

Lords of Eire:
The Darkland (Master Knights of Connaught)
Black Sword
Echoes of Ancient Dreams (time travel)

De Wolfe Pack Series:
Warwolfe
The Wolfe
Nighthawk
ShadowWolfe
DarkWolfe
A Joyous de Wolfe Christmas
Serpent
A Wolfe Among Dragons
Scorpion

Dark Destroyer
The Lion of the North
Walls of Babylon

Ancient Kings of Anglecynn:
The Whispering Night
Netherworld

Battle Lords of de Velt:
The Dark Lord
Devil's Dominion

Reign of the House of de Winter:
Lespada
Swords and Shields (also related to The Questing, While Angels Slept)

De Reyne Domination:
Guardian of Darkness
The Fallen One (part of Dragonblade Series)
With Dreams Only of You

House of d'Vant:
Tender is the Knight (House of d'Vant)
The Red Fury (House of d'Vant)

The Dragonblade Series: (Great Marcher Lords of de Lara)
Dragonblade
Island of Glass (House of St. Hever)
The Savage Curtain (Lords of Pembury)
The Fallen One (De Reyne Domination)
Fragments of Grace (House of St. Hever)
Lord of the Shadows
Queen of Lost Stars (House of St. Hever)

Lords of Thunder: The de Shera Brotherhood Trilogy
The Thunder Lord
The Thunder Warrior
The Thunder Knight

The Great Knights of de Moray:

Shield of Kronos
The Gorgon

High Warriors of Rohan:
High Warrior

Highland Warriors of Munro:
The Red Lion
Deep Into Darkness

Time Travel Romance: (Saxon Lords of Hage)
The Crusader
Kingdom Come

The House of Ashbourne:
Upon a Midnight Dream

Contemporary Romance:

The House of D'Aurilliac:
Valiant Chaos

Kathlyn Trent/Marcus Burton Series:
Valley of the Shadow
The Eden Factor
Canyon of the Sphinx

The House of De Nerra:
The Falls of Erith
Vestiges of Valor
Realm of Angels

The American Heroes Series:
The Lucius Robe
Fires of Autumn
Evenshade
Sea of Dreams
Purgatory

The House of De Dere:
Of Love and Legend

St. John and de Gare Clans:
The Warrior Poet

Other Contemporary Romance:
Lady of Heaven
Darkling, I Listen
In the Dreaming Hour

The House of de Garr:
Lord of Light
Realm of Angels

Sons of Poseidon:
The Immortal Sea

The House of de Bretagne:
The Questing (also related to Swords and Shields)

Pirates of Britannia Series (with Eliza Knight):
Savage of the Sea by Eliza Knight
Leader of Titans by Kathryn Le Veque
The Sea Devil by Eliza Knight
Sea Wolfe by Kathryn Le Veque

The House of Summerlin:
The Legend

The Kingdom of Hendocia:
Kingdom by the Sea

Note: All Kathryn's novels are designed to be read as stand-alones, although many have cross-over characters or cross-over family groups. Novels that are grouped together have related characters or family groups.

Series are clearly marked. All series contain the same characters or family groups except the American Heroes Series, which is an anthology with unrelated characters.

There is NO particular chronological order for any of the novels because they can all be read as stand-alones, even the series.

For more information, find it in **A Reader's Guide to the Medieval World of Le Veque.**

TABLE OF CONTENTS

Chapter One...1

Chapter Two 15

Chapter Three...23

Chapter Four...43

Chapter Five..60

Chapter Six..70

Chapter Seven 92

Chapter Eight..115

Chapter Nine 120

Chapter Ten 139

Chapter Eleven 156

Chapter Twelve...177

Chapter Thirteen 193

Chapter Fourteen 207

Chapter Fifteen...227

Chapter Sixteen 244

Chapter Seventeen..253

Chapter Eighteen..264

Chapter Nineteen 280

Chapter Twenty...289

Chapter Twenty-One...304

Epilogue...317

About Kathryn Le Veque 325

AUTHOR'S NOTE

Another book that readers have been begging for. Welcome to Trenton de Russe's novel!

Trenton is the first son of Gaston de Russe (THE DARK ONE: DARK KNIGHT), a product of Gaston's marriage to Mari-Elle, his first wife. Trenton was just a little boy in that book, about eight, and he had suffered through a horrible mother who had poisoned him towards his father. Gaston spends a good portion of the book trying to mend that relationship with Trenton, who really just wants to be loved. In re-reading the passages with Trenton in them, he's such a sad little boy with a very manipulative mother and an absent father, although Gaston tries hard to make good with him. Still, Trenton is a sad boy who turns out to be very brave. That bravery carries out into his adult life.

Several things about this book are firsts for me – firstly, it is the first book I've written with Henry VIII involved. Things were changing with Henry, including the coming Church of England, formal forms of address (Medieval kings were referred to as "my lord", and in this age, we start seeing forms of "your highness"). We are essentially now in Tudor England and have passed from Medieval times around 1500 A.D., but there is still a blend of the late Middle Ages entering into the Tudor period.

In my research about Henry VIII, I learned many things about him. Of course, we all know about his six wives and his quest to have a son and heir, but there are several things about Henry that I didn't know – for example, he was an accomplished musician and singer. He composed many songs, including Pastime with Good Company. You can listen to it here on YouTube:

www.youtube.com/watch?v=_q4sclrHTtg

Henry was clearly more than the despot we are commonly led to believe – a man of great intellect and reading, of poetry and music, so it was interesting reading in breaking the stereotype of Henry VIII in my mind.

And – and you'll love this – I read that it was Henry who came up with the idea of getting paid every time someone used his songs, hence the term "royalties". I couldn't confirm this, as different sources said different things, but if it is true, then that term suddenly makes a lot of sense.

As I sometimes do, I have provided a phonetic pronunciation guide because of the interesting names in this novel –

Lysabel – Liss-a-bell (sometimes she is called "Lys", pronounced "Liss")

Cynethryn – Sin-ETH-renn

Brencis – basically like Francis, except "Bren" instead of "Fran"

Alixandrea – Alex-on-DRAY-uh (not Alex-ANN-dree-uh)

Troyes – Twah (think the French word for "three")

I've also attached a family tree of sorts, listing the children from both the heroes and secondary characters of THE DARK ONE: DARK KNIGHT and THE WHITE LORD OF WELLESBOURNE, since those two stories are so closely intertwined. Even if some of the brothers and sisters of Gaston and Remington, or Matthew, aren't mentioned in this novel, I have listed them anyway just for reference.

Meanwhile, this is quite a story, and a very powerful love story, but it brings up many of the questions that arose in THE DARK ONE: DARK KNIGHT. Is love more powerful than anything, morality be damned? Or do things like honor supersede it? Unfortunately, Trenton is facing his own moral dilemma, and these are all valid questions, to which I tried to find some answers. But one thing is certain – in the case of Trenton, much like his father, love is never a simple thing.

Enjoy Trenton and Lysabel's story!

Hugs,

Kathryn

DE RUSSE AND WELLESBOURNE FAMILY TREE

Children of Gaston and Remington de Russe

Trenton (Gaston's first marriage to Mari-Elle de Russe)

Dane (Remington's first marriage to Guy Stoneley)

Adeliza

Arica

Cortland (Cort)

Matthieu

Boden

Gage

Gilliana

Children of Matthew and Alixandrea Wellesbourne

Lysabel

Rosamunde

James

Thomas

Emeline

Daniel

William

Children of Nicolas and Skye de Russe

Robert

August

Milo

Laria

Children of Jasmine and Antonius Flavius

Mary (Jasmine's daughter)

Sophia

Celestina

Gisella

Viola

Children of Mark and Caroline Wellesbourne

Sebastian

Quentin

Lucius

Children of John and Lizbet Wellesbourne

Adam

Joyelle

Cecily

Luke

Stephen

De Russe motto: *Et est spes est virtus*

"In Valor there is Hope"

CHAPTER ONE

July, 1518 A.D.
Stretford Castle, Dorset
Seat of Benoit de Wilde, Sheriff of Ilchester

T HEY COULD HEAR screaming.

It was dark this night, a moon so dark that it was barely seen hovering over the shadowed landscape. It was an omen of what was to come, that dark moon, a harbinger of ends and the gateway of beginnings. In truth, it was a night of great foreboding and the screaming of the woman didn't help matters. It simply complicated them.

They couldn't take the screaming into account.

They had a job to do.

Slapping sounds and more screaming. Four men, heavily armed and dressed in black, were on the darkened grounds of Stretford Castle, which was more of a manor house than an actual fortress, and the sounds coming from the second-floor window above their heads were distressing. A woman was being thrashed; that much was clear. She was being beaten within an inch of her life and they'd been listening to the sounds since they'd made their way across the clogged moat on a raft they'd brought with them.

The sounds, however, had worked to their advantage because the soldiers on duty were also distracted by the noises. Lured by them, in fact. They'd seen one man on the wall walk, his attention turned towards the window where the screams were coming from as he'd rubbed at his groin, stimulated by the sound. That stimulation had been the last thought on his mind before a silent arrow had slammed into his back, taking him down as the four men used a grappling hook to pull themselves over Stretford's sand-colored walls.

With the wall sentry out of commission, the men had stowed their raft and slinked across the side yard, through the garden, and to the walls of the manor itself. They were prepared to enter any window in order to reach their target, but they suspected their target was the very man beating the woman on the second floor. Rumor had it that de Wilde was a brute, a nasty bastard that the king despised, so they rightly assumed that their best option in finding this man was directly over their heads.

Follow the sounds of the screaming woman and they would find him.

"I shall go first."

A very big man with smoky gray eyes and a square jaw hissed the words. Clad in black leather from head to toe, he was protected against weapon strikes for the most part, but the nature of his job prevented him from wearing the technology of the day, the heavy plate armor that knights currently wore. In fact, he preferred the outdated chain mail, which he wore around his neck and shoulders. For this job, he needed to move swiftly and silently, and he couldn't do that in clanging plates of steel.

Crouched next to him was a younger man in much the same dress. He watched the big man gather the rope on the grappling hook they'd used to mount the wall.

"Why should you go first?" he whispered. "Let me go in first and catch him off-guard. Then you can come in after me and capture the man while I have him occupied if, in fact, this is the man we are looking for. It could very well be someone else, you know."

The man with the gray eyes cocked a dark eyebrow. "The man up there is in that room beating a woman to death," he said. "You know de Wilde. You know his brutality; we have all heard rumors of it and, now, we hear the reality. The world will be a better place without him, so shut your lips and let us get on with it. Henry is waiting for him."

But the second man shook his head. "Trenton, listen to me," he said, grasping him by the arm as if he were about to tell him something life changing. "Let both of us go up at once. He cannot fight off both of us at the same time. Timothy and Adrian will bring up the rear."

Sir Trenton de Russe eyed the young, eager knight who had been his partner in crime for the past six years. Sir Anthony de Witt was a brilliant egotist who sopped up glory and excitement like most men sopped up gravy from a trencher – the man literally fed off of the thrill of an operation like the one they were in the process of performing. As agents for the king, this was their vocation – the king commanded, and they fulfilled. If the king told them to remove an enemy, that was exactly what they did.

And they did it without an army.

Only their wits, skill, and cunning.

Like tonight. They'd been sent to capture Benoit de Wilde, the Sheriff of Ilchester and a strong opponent of the king's agenda. De Wilde held his position by legacy, meaning his father and his father before him had held the post, and de Wilde had been a thorn in Henry's side long enough. He made it no secret that he thought the King of England to be a vile piece of work, and Henry had enough of the man when de Wilde had stolen a mistress away from the king.

Literally, spirited the woman away so Henry couldn't get to her.

Perhaps that didn't seem like a deadly offense to most, but to Henry VIII, it was a clear sign of disrespect and disrespect would lead to retaliation. At this time in his life, he was almost ten years into his reign and he'd already established himself as a strong king who didn't tolerate opposition.

That was where Trenton de Russe came in.

God, but he was deadly.

A deadly man from a long line of deadly men, his father being the deadliest of all. At least, that was the general opinion until Trenton grew into adulthood and came into his own. Because his father, Gaston de Russe, had served Henry VII for many years, Trenton and Henry's son, the future Henry VIII, had grown up with one another. Trenton was several years older, but young Henry looked to Trenton as the older brother he'd never really had – powerful, intelligent, respectable, and talented. He'd long admired the man and when he became king, Trenton had been offered a most special post—

The Crown's Own Agent.

It meant that whatever Henry needed Trenton to do, the man did. He and his team of three specialized knights could do it all, and they often did. They were masters of many trades, and most of them deadly, as Benoit de Wilde was about to discover. When Trenton de Russe was on a scent, nothing short of God's intervention could prevent him from completing his mission.

In fact, that was the very thing Trenton was thinking of as Anthony begged him to alter his plans slightly. Instead of Trenton going in head first and alone, he and Anthony would go in together and create a distraction. That meant that one of them could surely capture de Wilde, with Timothy and Adrian backing them up. It was a safer plan, but not nearly so fun. Yet Trenton suspected Anthony had suggested it so he could share in some of that glory that seemed to follow Trenton around.

Whatever the case, it was time to move.

"Then get up there, you glory whore," Trenton growled, picking up his iron grappling hook and preparing to throw it to the window above. "Move when I move. And watch out for the guards when you climb."

Anthony nodded eagerly. Taking the second grappling hook, he moved down the wall, his gaze fixed on the large window overhead, emitting both light and screams. The screams were growing weaker, however, and now there were growling words intermingled with them. A woman was sobbing. Trenton caught Anthony's attention and nodded, once.

The grappling hooks flew up and hooked onto the edge of the stone windowsill.

There was no time to delay. The sentry with the arrow through his torso hadn't been discovered yet, but it was only a matter of time. Trenton and Anthony heaved themselves up the wall, deftly climbing the rope until they both reached the windowsill at nearly the same time.

Unfortunately, they were met with an obstacle. Because the windows were set back from the sill, they hadn't a clear view of them until they were upon them. Now, they saw that the windows were made from crown glass, cylinder shapes in a pattern that comprised the window itself. The windows in the center were fixed, but smaller side windows were open for ventilation. This meant they would have to go through the glass, which was heavy and imperfect, and secured with wood or iron braces. They really couldn't tell. All they knew was that they had to get through it.

Trenton released his grip and slid down the length of the rope until he was on the ground, followed by Anthony a split second later. As Anthony and the others watched curiously, Trenton dislodged his grappling hook, gathered it up, and swung it again, this time harder. It sailed up at the edge of the broad window, lodging itself in the top of the windowsill now. Without pause, he began to haul himself up again.

Anthony, puzzled at what he was doing, followed suit and, soon enough, he had his grappling hook wedged into the top of the stone window frame, too. But Trenton was already halfway to the window. Not to be outdone, Anthony followed eagerly and recklessly. He was grunting, making some noise, as Timothy and Adrian looked around the grounds, concerned that they were going to be discovered.

But preserving their secrecy fled when Trenton suddenly took a big swing on his rope and broke through the window, creating something of a racket. As Anthony sailed in behind him, and Timothy and Adrian began to swiftly make the climb, Trenton's main focus was on the man who was now standing near the blazing hearth.

From his periphery, Trenton could see the woman on the bed, which was an elaborately carved vessel of dark oak and a heavy entablature supported by the posts. It was rich and extravagant. In fact, the entire chamber was rich and extravagant, but Trenton wasn't much looking at his surroundings. His focus was on the man at the hearth who, startled to see two men bursting through his window, rushed to pick up the fire poker that was leaning against the wall.

There was panic in the air now, the shock of armed men hurling into the chamber. Anthony was closer to the hearth than Trenton was, purely from the sheer momentum that had taken him through the window and into the room. He was still running, his booted feet falling on the chunks of the thick, heavy glass he'd just come flying through, and he was still running as he tackled the man who had just managed to grasp the fire poker.

Bodies crunched against the stone wall, grunts of pain in the air. Now, it was a fight as Anthony and the man grappled for control of the poker. As Trenton headed to the pair to snatch away the poker, Timothy and Adrian leapt into the room. Timothy ran straight for the door to ensure it was bolted while Adrian, heading for the fight, slipped on the chunks of glass and landed on his knees. But he was up in a flash, reaching the struggle just as Trenton grabbed the poker and tossed it aside. Now, it was Anthony and Adrian subduing the struggling man.

"What do you want?" the man demanded, his voice cracking in terror. "Why are you here?"

Trenton stood back, coolly observing the man. "Benoit de Wilde?"

The mention of the name caused the man's face to turn shades of red. "Do you have any idea what I can do to you?" he snarled. "This will not go unanswered. Who has sent you?"

"*Are* you de Wilde?"

"This is my home, idiot. What do you want with me?"

"It would behoove you to give me a direct answer. I do not wish to punish the wrong man."

"*Punish* me?" the man exploded. "For what? Let me go!"

Trenton didn't reply. He had his answer, even if it was via clues and assumptions. So he turned to Timothy, who was now standing beside him and waiting for orders.

"Bind him and gag him," he commanded quietly. "Make it so the man cannot move a muscle."

Gleefully, Timothy's young face was full of delight as he went to separate the rope from the grappling iron over by the window. But as he did, he noticed that the sentries below had heard the noise and were coming to the side of the manse to investigate. Quickly, he grabbed both ropes and pulled them through the window, removing any external evidence.

"My lord," he said to Trenton. "We have little time. Men are moving below."

Trenton glanced at him. "They have heard us?"

Timothy nodded. "They have heard something. We must hurry."

Trenton understood. They hadn't exactly been discovered, but their scent was in the air. The crash through the window had created noise, and the grounds were alerted. He flicked a hand at the struggling prisoner.

"Then quickly bind him," he hissed. "We must depart before his men grow wise."

Swiftly, Anthony and Timothy and Adrian did as they were told. De Wilde struggled and fought, and the four men eventually ended up on the ground, with Timothy sitting on de Wilde while Anthony and Adrian bound the man hand and foot.

It was a snarling, nasty mess of men – the captors against the captive. At one point, de Wilde ended up with his foot in the fire and Timothy had to put out the flames as his hose began to smolder. Then, de Wilde began to howl until Anthony quickly shoved a gag into his mouth, fabric torn off of de Wilde's fine silk tunic.

As this was going on, Trenton rushed over to the window, seeing men gathering in the garden below, pointing up at the broken window as if wondering what should be done. Trenton tried to stay out of sight as he watched them. He was pressed against the wall next to the window, straining to see if the men were going to make their way into the manor and up to their lord's chamber. There seemed to be some indecision about it because with de Wilde's well-established history of violence, no one wanted to be the first to charge in and risk their lord's anger.

And that was where Trenton would capitalize.

"Adrian," he muttered, motioning to the young man, who came on the run. "I want you to get to the first floor of this structure and create a diversion. I do not care what it is; start a fire if you have to. But we must move these men away from the window if we are to escape unseen and unscathed."

Adrian nodded swiftly. He was tall, and strong, with wavy dark hair and flashing dark eyes. Women adored him, and he had an aura of greatness about him, and Trenton knew that Adrian Levington had a bright future. Smart and resourceful, he would go far. As the young knight dashed to the chamber door and put his ear against it, listening, Trenton was about to turn back for the skirmish near the hearth when he heard soft whimpering on the bed.

The woman that has suffered the brunt of de Wilde's brutality was on the bed. She was sitting on it, hunched over, her hand on her face. She'd made no noise at all during the entire time de Wilde was being captured, and Trenton could have very well fled the chamber without saying a word to her.

But he didn't.

He'd heard her screaming, and he'd heard the body blows that de Wilde had delivered, and it had been a brutal beating. Although Trenton wasn't one for compassion, or kindness, something made him eye the woman and pause in his haste. He may have been a ruthless man, but when it came to women, he didn't approve of a man taking a hand to them. It was savage and ignoble, he thought.

As a child, he'd witnessed the unspeakable horrors of it.

Therefore, he took a moment to speak with her, if only to reassure her that de Wilde wouldn't be around to harm her again. It was a brief act of compassion in an otherwise compassionless night. Moving to the bed, which was against the wall and shadowed in the dim chamber, he stood over her.

"What is your name, my lady?" he asked in a voice that could only be described as deep, quiet, and raspy.

The woman kept her hand over the left side of her face, trying to ease the side that had been bruised.

"I am Lady de Wilde," she whispered.

Trenton eyed the woman. She had long, bronze-colored hair, tied in a braid that was now mussed as a result of the fight with her husband. She was wearing a fine robe, which had been torn and tattered. But beyond that, he couldn't really see much.

"We are taking your husband," he muttered. "Do you understand that?"

She nodded, but then she turned to look at him. "But why do you take him? Who are you?"

Trenton didn't answer right away because there was something oddly familiar about the woman. She had a fine-featured face, full lips, and enormous eyes that, with the flames reflecting in them, looked like undulating pools of blue. A liquid color that was both mesmerizing and beautiful. In fact, the woman was stunningly beautiful in spite of the fact that one side of her face was red and swollen. But it didn't detract from her magnificence.

Christ, he thought. *I know that face!*

He peered closer.

"What is your family name, my lady?" he asked, puzzled. "I have seen you before."

She was eyeing him warily because he seemed quite interested in her. Her expression conveyed terror with what had happened to her and what was happening in general. But as she started to turn away, it must have occurred to her that he looked familiar to her, too, because she began to peer at him the way he was peering at her. She stared at him, starting at the top of his head and then ending at his cleft chin.

Her eyes widened.

"*Trenton?*" she gasped.

Trenton's dark eyebrows lifted. She certainly knew him, but he still couldn't place her. As he wracked his brain, her familiar features suddenly became clear to him, and his mouth popped open in surprise.

"Lysabel?" he said. "Lysabel Wellesbourne?"

She nodded eagerly, her entire face lighting up. "Aye," she breathed. "Oh, Trenton, it *is* you!"

Trenton's could hardly believe it. "Christ," he hissed. "Lysabel Wellesbourne, as I live and breathe."

She smiled, her swollen lips revealing straight teeth and a big dimple in her chin. "It has been such a long time."

"A long time, indeed," he said. "But… Lysabel, *you* are married to Benoit de Wilde?"

She nodded, the joy on her face wavering. "Aye," she said hesitantly. "I have been for twelve years. Trenton, what are you doing here? What in the world is happening?"

As Trenton looked at her, he found himself overcome with the reality of the situation; to find the daughter of his father's best friend here, being savagely beaten, filled him with rage such as he'd rarely experienced. He'd grown up with Lysabel Wellesbourne, although she was eight years younger than he was, but still, he'd known her since birth. He'd served her father as a squire for a few years and had even been knighted by Sir Matthew Wellesbourne.

Lysabel was the eldest daughter of the man he'd served as a young knight, a lovely girl who was sweet and kind, and she'd been a favorite at her father's home. But he'd lost track of her when she'd gone away to foster, and he hadn't heard much more of her after that, not even that she'd married.

And now, this.

Anger and disgust didn't quite encompass what he was feeling.

"Henry wants de Wilde," he said. He couldn't even bring himself to call the man her husband. "Lysabel, does your father know of… *this*? Of what the man does to you? Good Christ, we could hear the screaming outside."

Lysabel's smile faded and tears pooled in those big eyes. "He is my husband," she said tightly. "He may do as he pleases. It is his right."

Trenton frowned. "That is nonsense," he said. "Answer me. Why have you not told your father?"

Lysabel's gaze trailed to the man she'd married, now trussed up and gagged, and the only emotion on her face was that of clear and present fear.

She was terrified even to look at him.

"He can do nothing," she finally said, looking up to Trenton. "Please, Trenton… do not tell him. I beg you. And if you are taking my husband, then I should go with him. He will want me with him."

Trenton cocked an eyebrow. "You are *not* going with him," he said. "You will remain here, far away from him. Where he is going, there is no return."

Lysabel's eyes widened. "Why do you say this?"

"Because it is true. Henry wants your husband. He will not return."

Before Lysabel could reply, Anthony was suddenly standing next to Trenton, edginess in his manner. "We must leave now," he said quietly. "There is no more time to delay and Adrian is prepared to create the diversion."

Trenton nodded, but he returned his attention to Lysabel, who was gazing up at him rather anxiously. He felt an odd stab to his gut because of it, but there was no time to explore that sensation. Anthony was correct; there was no more time to delay.

"I wish I could remain and catch up on the many years we have not seen one another," he said, "but I must go. You will not tell anyone that you saw us. For all you know, you were asleep and when you awoke, your husband was gone and you do not know where he has gone. Do you understand?"

Lysabel's eyes started to fill with tears again and she shook her head, fearfully. "I cannot," she said. "If I do not summon his men, he will become angry."

"He is not returning, Lysabel. He cannot hurt you again. I will make sure of it. You must believe me."

Lysabel moved to stand. It was clear that she didn't believe him in the least, conditioned after years of abuse on how to behave with her husband. Terror fed her actions. But the moment she tried to stand on her feet and straighten up, she crumpled back onto the bed, her hands on her torso. As she gasped in pain, Trenton bent over her with concern.

"He has hurt you badly, hasn't he?" he growled.

She shook her head, struggling to swallow away the agony she'd experienced many times before. "It is nothing," she said. "You cannot help."

Trenton was a man of little emotion, but he did have a temper. When it was unleashed, there was no stopping it and, at this moment, he could feel the spark of temper rising in his belly. It was bad enough for a man to beat a woman, but in seeing how injured Lysabel was, an old friend, it was more than he could take.

"It *is* something," he said in his low and raspy voice. "He has badly injured you and I would be willing to bet my life on the fact that this isn't the first time."

Lysabel had her left arm wrapped around her torso. She knew from experience that Benoit had broken a rib or two, and she knew her eye would be bruised come the morrow from the heavy blow he'd dealt her earlier. Trenton said her husband wasn't coming back, but how could he be so sure? Fear kept her silent.

"You must go, Trenton," she whispered. "Please, go before my husband's men come."

Trenton didn't push her. He could see how frightened she was and that stab to his gut was only growing worse. Heavily, he sighed.

"Do you at least have someone to tend you?" he asked, rather kindly.

"Aye," she whispered, turning away. "Please go."

"I will," he said. "But first, I want you to tell me the truth. Has he always beaten you?"

In spite of attempting not to push the subject, he was. He couldn't help it; that odd stabbing in his gut was sparking something more than his temper. It was sparking the first true experience with compassion and sympathy that he'd had in a very long time. He watched her as she forced herself to stand up straight again and pushed herself off the bed. But in doing so, she lifted her right arm, which was heavily bandaged. Trenton caught on to the wrapped arm and he pointed at it.

"Did he do that?"

He was asking her through gritted teeth, an angry sort of question, and Lysabel looked him in the eye, showing him dignity he hadn't seen before. She was standing strong, holding her bandaged arm against her cracked ribs, facing him regardless of the anguish she was feeling. Benoit had beat on her for years. But in spite of that, he hadn't been able to crush her spirit or destroy her nobility.

The Wellesbourne strength was still there.

"Go, Trenton," she said, more forcefully. "If you remain any longer, I am afraid you will not make it out at all. I will not tell you again."

He could see in her face that she meant it. She wasn't going to answer any of his questions, no matter how much he asked them, and the truth was that it wasn't any of his business, anyway. That pretty little girl he remembered from his youth had grown into a magnificent woman who had ended up in a horrific situation. It wasn't her fault. But the truth was that he couldn't leave her, knowing her situation and not doing something to help. That wasn't in his nature. In that moment, Trenton made a decision that, in hindsight, was going to affect him for the rest of his life.

But it would be one he would never regret.

For an old friend, he knew what he had to do.

Turning away from Lysabel, he gave silent orders to his men. A hand signal had Adrian rushing from the chamber and into the darkened manse to create a diversion that would allow them to complete their mission. Another hand signal had Anthony and Timothy rushing for the one grappling hook they had left, wedging it into the windowsill on the inside and then waiting several long and anxious minutes until the men below began running towards the kitchen yard to the north side of the manse.

A fire, they were saying, and the faint scent of smoke could be smelled on the cold night air. Adrian had evidently created quite a distraction and as the garden below cleared of de Wilde's men, Anthony and Timothy bailed over the side of the window, shimmying down the rope and waiting for their prize, which Trenton would lower from the window.

But Trenton didn't lower Benoit at all. As Anthony and Timothy watched, Trenton simply tossed the man from the window, head first.

He was dead the moment he hit the ground.

CHAPTER TWO

The Palace of Greenwich, London
One month later

"I T IS NOT like you to make a mistake, Trenton. But all things considered, it was a blessing."

Trenton stood in the private solar of the king, a room that faced out over the River Thames. The ceiling of the chamber was a masterpiece of Gothic architecture with intricate patterns. Small panes of square glass made up an enormous window that presided over the bucolic landscape beyond. In all, it was a room built to impress, and impress it did. Imported woods and the smell of leather from the furniture built by Savoy artisans in France ensure that all who entered the room were properly awed.

But Trenton wasn't impressed by his surroundings. He hadn't been for a very long time. To him, it was a room just like any other. He leaned against the windowsill, gazing at the blue waters of the Thames as it meandered to the sea, thinking on how he would reply to the king's statement.

It hadn't been a mistake.

He'd meant to do it.

"We were rushing to remove him from his chamber and in the haste, he slipped from my grip," he said after a moment. "I explained to you the sequence of events, Your Highness, so it was simply an unfortunate happenstance."

Henry VIII, King of England, was sitting near the open window, with the river breeze infiltrating the room. Being that it was in the dead of summer, the humidity in the air was nearly unbearable and Henry's entire court was preparing to move to Penhurst Palace in Kent, where it was considerably cooler and away from the moisture of the river. But Henry preferred Greenwich so that he never left the palace unless it grew intolerable, and it was quickly reaching that state.

Still, he had business to conduct, and important business with Trenton de Russe. He sipped on watered wine, cooled because it was kept in the vaults below the palace where it was dry and downright cold at times. Trenton had been offered some, which he had refused. He wasn't much for drink like this during the day. He didn't like the fog of alcohol in his head so early in the day. Henry sat near the open windows, sipping his refreshing drink, while Trenton leaned against the wall and watched the traffic on the river.

"As I said, it is for the better," Henry said, a slight lisp evident when he spoke. "De Wilde has been a thorn in my side for years. Now that he is gone, the Ilchester title reverts to me to do with as I please. In truth, I am not dissatisfied with this outcome."

Trenton glanced at him. "You would take the Ilchester inheritance from de Wilde's heir?"

Henry shrugged. "He only has two daughters that I am aware of," he said. "Legitimate children, I mean. Who knows how many bastards the man has running about? In fact, I have half a mind to grant you the Ilchester titles, Trenton. You have rid me, and England, of a sour excuse of a man. You have done us all a great service."

Trenton was shaking his head before the king even finished speaking. "Nay, Your Highness," he said. "As honored as I am that you should think of me, I already have a title that I have little time to tend, with homes and lands that I must leave to subordinates to manage. If there is any real trouble, then my father must see to it. I have no time."

Henry glanced at him at the mention of the almighty Gaston de Russe. "And how is your father these days?"

Trenton smiled, though it was without humor. He moved away from the window. "My father and I have not spoken in some time," he said. "I still hear from my mother on occasion, so my father is in good health. She would tell me otherwise."

Henry nodded. "And I am sure we would have all heard," he said. "But I am sorry to hear that you and your father have not spoken. It seems to me that you have not really spoken to him since you came into my service those years ago."

Trenton shrugged, hunting for a chair to plant his bulk into. "You know he did not want me to accept your position," he said quietly. "My father believes what I do for you is less than honorable."

"Coming from the man who betrayed Richard at Bosworth and allowed my father to come into power, that is an ironic opinion," Henry sniffed. "Clearly, he does not realize how important you are to me, Trenton, and if you did not believe this to be important work, then you would not have accepted the post. Does he not realize that?"

Trenton sat in a cushioned chair near the darkened hearth. "My father told me that he'd always hoped I'd have a better reputation than he did," he said. "He does not think that special missions for the king are the way to achieve that. As it is, I have men's respect mostly because they fear me. It is terror that causes them to obey or fall at my feet, not genuine admiration. I suppose I never really knew what my father meant until I started undertaking some of your more... questionable directives. Now, it is too late."

Henry didn't particularly like to hear what he perceived to be a condemnation. "Regrets?"

"Never," Trenton shook his head firmly. "What should I regret? That I have helped a king hold fast to his crown in a country where vipers abound? I should never regret that. But I do regret that my father views me as a disappointment."

Henry was feeling some guilt for that, as if the rift between father and son was some of his doing. He'd pushed hard for Trenton even when Gaston had come to visit him and asked him not to offer Trenton this position. But in the end, it was Trenton who had made his own decisions. Nothing had been forced upon him.

At least, that was the way Henry viewed it.

He always got his way in the end.

"So the great Duke of Warminster finds you a disappointment," he muttered, scratching his head. "You, his eldest son and heir. You hold the title of Earl of Westbury, a courtesy title for the heir of Warminster, and Westbury is a wealthy holding. You are a man with some independent wealth, Trenton."

Trenton shrugged. "As I said, I cannot properly administer the lands I have and must leave it to subordinates."

"Do you want less responsibility? Do you want to return home and make amends with your father?"

It was the first time in almost ten years that Henry had even remotely offered him some kind of respite from the constant missions he undertook on the king's behalf. Trenton's first reaction was to deny he needed any time away, but he stopped himself. Perhaps, time away from his usual dirty dealings was a good idea. But as he considered it, he realized there was a particular reason why he was, indeed, thinking about it.

Lady de Wilde.

He hadn't been able to stop thinking of Lysabel since that night. His thoughts weren't lustful, or those of interest in the sexual sense, but more of great concern. If Henry sent him out on another mission right away, which was usual, then there was no knowing when he'd be able to return to Dorset to see how Lysabel was coming along.

He'd left her almost three weeks ago, damaged and broken, and it had haunted him. That sweet, lovely woman had been so badly damaged, and no one had known – not her father, and certainly not his own father, because between the two of them, they would have done something about it. If Trenton hadn't killed Benoit, then he was fairly certain that the old knights would have. But Lysabel had kept her secret, and bore her burden, without telling a soul of the hell she'd been going through. What was it she'd said? She'd been married to de Wilde for twelve long years.

Twelve long years of hell.

For the sake of an old family friend, Trenton very much wanted to return to see how she was faring. Therefore, he found himself nodding to Henry's question even though he had no intention of visiting his father.

He had other destinations on his mind.

"That would be in order," he said after a moment. "Mayhap... mayhap, it would do me good to see my father. He and I have shared a complicated relationship over the years."

Henry gulped the last of his watered wine and set the empty cup down. "You could also visit your wife," he said. "When was the last time you saw Adela?"

The mere mention of the name was like mud in Trenton's ears. It was an ugly, dirty word as far as he was concerned and he abruptly stood up, feeling the familiar agitation that the mention of his wife brought.

"I do not remember the last time I saw her and I do not care," he said flatly. "She lives as if she has no husband, and I am happy to let her do it. I care not for anything about her."

Henry snorted; he probably shouldn't have spoken on Adela de Montfort de Russe, but it was a pathetic situation Trenton had gotten himself in to. All of London knew it, if not all of England.

Trenton's record with women was not a good one.

"God's Bones, Trenton," Henry said, feeling the slightest bit tipsy from the watered wine. He stretched out on the chair, lazily. "You have had terrible luck with women, my friend. For your first wife, the lovely Alicia, to die in childbirth, and then the second wife to be murdered by her own father. I remember that event very well. What a shock it was to hear that Lord Atwell murdered his daughter because his coffers were empty and she would not help him gain your money as he'd hoped. Horribly shocking."

Trenton was well aware of his history with women and he didn't need a slightly drunk king to remind him. It was an embarrassment, and probably more disappointment to his father than his service record for the king ever could be.

He didn't want to dredge up old shame.

"No need to revisit this, Your Highness," he said evenly, but he meant it as a warning. "It is all in the past."

But Henry wasn't hearing his tone; he continued to muse about Trenton's marital history. "And then you let your father talk you into marrying that French duchess," he said. "You married Adela of Brittany, the illegitimate daughter of the Duke of Brittany, because your father thought it would bring you great wealth and support from the French. What he did not know was that Adela was a whore and had no intention of giving up her whoring ways."

Trenton looked at him. "You will not speak of my wife so," he said, his threatening tone more evident. "Regardless of her behavior, she still bears the title Lady de Russe and is due all respect, even from you."

Henry eyed him, unmoved by the hazard in his voice. "She took your home, and your money, and now you are not even welcome at Penleigh House, your seat." He sat up and lifted a frustrated hand. "She has even banished you from her bed. Have you not gone to the church with this, Trenton? Surely you can gain an annulment based on the fact that she will not allow you to touch her. I have told you this before, Trenton. You must do something about this woman."

By this time, Trenton was growing weary of the conversation. He didn't want to discuss his father, and he certainly didn't want to discuss his three marriages, including his current wife. Henry didn't know when to shut his mouth sometimes.

"The arrangement is an agreeable one, considering I have no desire to touch her, either," he snapped softly. "As you have so eloquently reminded me, much of my life has ended in utter failure. I will leave well enough alone when it comes to my marriages. Three failures are enough."

Henry's brow furrowed as Trenton's mood became apparent to him, now realizing that his words had been careless. He respected Trenton too much to offend him, but he could see that he'd done precisely that.

"You have a great many things to be proud of, Trenton," he said, trying to make up for his tactlessness. "I have always been proud of you. Your reputation in battle and in service is unparalleled."

"But my private life is in shambles."

Henry had a twinkle in his eye. "As if mine is perfect."

He had a point. Henry's marriage to Catherine of Aragon was anything but problem-free. Still, Trenton would not be soothed. He didn't like the comparison to the king's rather lusty and imperfect private life, because he wasn't like that at all. He was an introspective man and he had tried to be careful with his marriages. He'd tried to pick women of honor, he thought, or women he was attracted to. He wanted what his parents had, an excellent union for many years. Unfortunately, the universe had worked against him, and that was a bitter pill for him to swallow.

He was not to have what his father had when it came to love.

But he didn't want to think about that at the moment. Henry's idle chatter had put a great many things on his mind, and now he was feeling depressed and moody. God, he hated that he couldn't shake feelings like this. He'd never been able to. On the surface, he was a man of stone, but inside, he was weak and emotional. Therefore, it was best to simply end the conversation before he said something ridiculous.

He'd been known to.

"I have decided to accept your offer of time away," he said as he turned to Henry. "I shall also tell Anthony, Timothy, and Adrian that they may also take some time for their leisure as well. They have earned it."

He was suddenly on his feet, heading for the chamber door. Henry watched him go, rather quickly, he thought.

"Wait," he called after him. "Are you going to your father's home? Can I reach you at Deverill Castle?"

Trenton put his hand on the door latch, pausing. "I will send you a missive from wherever I decide to go," he said, not wanting to give him a firm answer because the truth was that he didn't have one. "You have my thanks, Your Highness. Time away is exactly what I need at the moment."

With that, he yanked the door open and passed through, slamming the panel in his wake. He half-expected Henry to come running after him and was mildly surprised when he didn't. Perhaps, even Henry realized it would be better to let him go, especially in light of the touchy conversation they'd just had.

With instructions that they were to meet up in three weeks at The Horn and The Crown tavern in the village of Westbury, part of Trenton's properties, Anthony, Timothy, and Adrian found themselves granted eighteen days of leisure time, nearly unheard of in their profession, but something they gratefully accepted. As they gleefully went on their way, Trenton went on his, collecting his big black steed. The green, rolling hills of Dorset were calling to him.

He had to see an old friend.

CHAPTER THREE

Stretford Castle

"PICK IT UP, Cissy! It will not bite you!"

It was late on a sunny day, warm with a summer breeze, as Lysabel sat in the kitchen yard of Stretford and watched her daughters as they tried to corral the chickens for the night. Her words of encouragement were directed at six-year-old Brencis because was afraid of the chickens. She didn't want to be pecked. But her elder sister by two years, Cynethryn, didn't seem to fear the chickens at all. She was grabbing them two at a time to put them back into the coop.

"Pick them up around the body, Cissy," Cynethryn said impatiently. "They cannot peck you if you hold them like that."

But Brencis wasn't certain at all. In fact, she watched her mother and sister gather up all of the chickens to put them back in the tall coop so the predators couldn't get to them overnight. She felt rather useless, but it was better than being pecked.

"What else can I help with, Mama?" Brencis was eager to help but reluctant to do half of the things she was told. "Can I bolt the door to the coop?"

Lysabel stood next to the open coop door, wiping at her forehead with the back of her hand. She looked down at her youngest child, with huge blue eyes and curly blond hair. She looked so much like her grandfather, Lysabel's father, that it was frightening.

"Of course you can," she said. "That is the biggest task of all."

Brencis beamed as she shut the door and threw the bolt. "Is that all?" she asked. "What else do we have to do?"

"Nothing, sweetheart," she said, putting her hand on her daughter's shoulder. "We may go inside and prepare for the evening meal now."

The sun was beginning to set, and the smell of baking bread and roasting meat wafted upon the warm summer air. It had been a beautiful day in a line of beautiful days, because every day for the past thirty-six days had been the best day of Lysabel's life.

The only days in the past twelve years where she'd lived without fear.

Aye, the sky had never looked so blue, nor the grass so green. Cynethryn and Brencis were starting to come out of their shells a little, no longer living in fear of their father and his violence. Cynethryn still screamed at loud noises and Brencis still wept every night as she was put to bed. But for the most part, Lysabel could see the beginnings of healing in her girls. She knew it would take time. But with Benoit gone, they had nothing but time to heal lifelong wounds.

It was a hope she genuinely thought she'd never have – a hope for healing.

Crossing the dusty yard as the servants began to prepare for the coming night, their paths were crossed by a running dog and three growing puppies, which immediately lured her daughters like the call of a siren's song. Brencis captured a puppy with long legs, hugging it, while Cynethryn petted the mother dog. Lysabel continued towards the manse, watching her children with a smile on her face.

It was so very good to see them happy.

A dream, she thought. *I'm going to wake up and this will have all been a dream.*

Lysabel had the same thought every day since that dark night when four men had burst into her chamber, trussing up her husband and then throwing him from the window. In truth, it had been Trenton who had tossed Benoit out of the window because she had seen it.

She'd seen everything.

Trenton had thrown Benoit to the ground two floors below and then informed her that her husband's neck had been broken in the process. He had been quiet and unemotional about it, as if he had been discussing nothing more than the weather, and then he'd climbed from the window and disappeared into the night. The last she saw was the four men crossing the manor's moat on a small raft before fading into the darkness, all the time carrying her husband's body with them.

And that had been the end of it.

It was the night that had quite literally changed her life. For several days following that event, Lysabel still couldn't quite figure out if she'd imagined it or not. But as the days passed and Benoit didn't show himself, finally, she began to believe. She prayed that it was true. She didn't know where her husband's body had ended up and she surely didn't care. All that mattered to her was that for nearly the first time in her adult life, she wasn't living in daily fear.

All thanks to a childhood friend.

As she called the girls into the manse, leaving the dogs behind, Lysabel's thoughts turned to the eldest de Russe son. Her father was Trenton's father's best friend, and had been since they were children, so the de Russe and Wellesbourne families had always been quite close. Lysabel was her father's eldest child, but when she was born, Trenton had been at least eight years of age. She remembered him from her childhood, seeing him on holidays and other occasions when the families converged. And when he'd been fourteen years of age, he and his brother, Dane, had come to serve her father and the Wellesbourne war machine.

Trenton had been as big as a full-grown man at that age, very tall, a quiet and somewhat intimidating young man whom her father had taken under his wing. There had been something inherently sad about him and she'd heard her parents whispering about his past, about a birth mother who had been a whore and a father who had stayed away because of it.

But neither Lysabel's father nor her mother had ever told her anything directly about Trenton's past, and all she'd ever heard were the whispers or rumors. Some of the old knights used to say that his father had betrayed King Richard at the battle of Bosworth, and that her father, Matthew, had saved Gaston de Russe's life. Matthew had lost his left hand as a result. Lysabel didn't know the entire story, and she probably never would, but none of that mattered. She was simply grateful to a very old friend who had saved her from a life that had become hell on earth.

She wondered if she'd ever be able to thank him for it.

But thoughts of Trenton faded as the great hall of Stretford Castle spread out before her. The hall was on the ground level, with hard-packed earth as the floor and a ceiling that was supported by great arched beams. Lysabel took her daughters into the great hall to help the servants set out the coming meal. It was their usual behavior at mealtime, considering Benoit liked all of the women around him to serve him one way or another, including his daughters. They'd been a great disappointment to him when they were born, being that they weren't male, and he made sure to let them know every chance he got. Brencis hadn't been beaten down by it yet but, at eight years of age, Cynethryn was starting to show signs of it.

Another behavior that Lysabel hoped she could help her daughters forget.

As the sun began to set, the servants built a large fire in the hearth that was tall enough for a man to stand in it. Brencis was over by the hearth where a heavyset male servant was positioning the fire, taking kindling from the little girl because it wasn't too heavy for her to lift. Cynethryn was in the servant's alcove, watching them prepare the trenchers that would be delivered to the family and also to the soldiers, men who ate at their own tables. There was one table for the family, at the head of the room, and then two longer, well-worn tables where the soldiers ate. Benoit had been welcoming to his men at mealtime, and liked for them all to eat in the hall, mostly because he wanted to preside as lord and master over them. It had made him feel important.

The reality was that Benoit's men weren't fond of him because he was irrational and heavy-handed, but they respected him simply because he put a roof over their heads and food in their bellies. Benoit's men were mostly from the surrounding area, with very few from outside of Dorset, and their loyalty to him was bought and paid for. Nothing more than that. The night Benoit had died, Lysabel told her husband's one and only knight exactly what Trenton had told her to say – that she'd been asleep and when she'd awoken, he had been gone. When asked about the broken window in the master's chamber, it had been easy enough to explain that Benoit had broken the window in his rage.

It wasn't as if everybody in the entire castle hadn't heard it.

Benoit's men, for the most part, were numb to the way their lord treated his wife, but there were some who were sympathetic. There were also some who fully supported Benoit's right to do as he pleased and even enjoyed her pain. For the past month, Lysabel hadn't made any changes to her husband's small army, or sent anyone away, simply because they were under the impression that Benoit would return. So everything was just the way he'd left it. For the time being, Lysabel was satisfied with that. But she knew, at some point, the men were going to start asking questions.

She'd deal with it when the time came.

For now, however, she was happy. So very happy. She didn't want to think about what tomorrow would bring, only what her life was like at this very moment. She was safe, her girls were safe, and that was all that mattered.

Bliss.

Much like her daughters, however, she still fell into the old habits that Benoit had instilled in her. *You will serve me, you whore, with all that you are.* Lysabel was so accustomed to supervising the kitchens so that the meal would be perfect, and Benoit would be satisfied, that behaving as the leisurely lady of the manse wasn't something that ever entered her mind. She wasn't one to sit when there was work to be done, simply because that was what her husband had expected of her. It was years of conditioning that saw her go into the kitchens to supervise the progress of the meal as her daughters continued their small tasks.

When nighttime finally fell, and the land beyond the warm kitchens was dark, the cook brought in the fowl that she had been roasting outside over an open flame. It was time to serve the hungry who had gathered in the hall, and Lysabel made sure the bread and butter were sent to the tables. Servants were moving into the great hall as the soldiers gathered around the feasting tables, and the buzz of conversation could be heard.

Lysabel collected her girls from where they'd been completing their duties and pulled them over to the master's table, which was now for only the three of them. Lysabel never thought she'd know the day where Benoit wouldn't be sitting at the center of the table, arrogantly surveying all beneath him. Now, that chair was empty and it would remain so. The first time Lysabel had realized that, she broke down in tears. No one had noticed, thankfully, but for her, it had been a pivotal moment in her life.

No more pain.

More men entered the hall and the trenchers were put out. The conversation grew louder as Lysabel and her daughters sat at the dais, served by a serving wench who was young and sweet, and often liked to play games with Cynethryn and Brencis. The girls were excited to see her, trying to coerce her to sit with them, but the servant girl shook her head and whispered words that instantly quieted them.

Lysabel liked the young servant, Cassie was her name, because she was not only attentive to the girls, but to Lysabel herself. Trenton had asked her if she'd had anyone to tend her wounds, and it was Cassie who did it. A well-bred young woman whose father had owed Benoit a debt, she had served at Stretford for the past two years to pay off that debt. Now, as Lysabel looked at her, she realized that she could send

Cassie home.

Benoit wasn't around to stop her.

As she pondered that possibility, she noticed someone entering the great hall, a large figure who had moved into the shadows once he came through the door. The light from the hearth and the numerous candle banks weren't enough to reach to the entry door, which was tucked into the northeast corner of the hall.

With the dais being at the opposite side, Lysabel couldn't see very much of who had entered. In fact, she was turning back to Brencis to help the child cut her meat away from the bone when, abruptly, she took a second look at the figure now moving into the hall and into the light because something about him was vaguely familiar.

It took her a moment to realize that it was Trenton.

Shocked, Lysabel turned the meat cutting duty over to Cassie, who was still hovering near the table, and quickly stood up, rushing to greet Trenton. When their eyes finally met, Lysabel couldn't help the smile that was so easily on her lips.

"Trenton," she gasped. "You... you have *returned*."

She sounded incredibly surprised and Trenton smiled at her, an awkward gesture, as if he hadn't smiled in years and had forgotten how. It all came out like a grimace.

"Indeed, my lady," he said, oddly uncomfortable. "I apologize if I am interrupting anything, but I came to see how you were... faring."

Lysabel was deeply touched. More than that, she was glad to see him, the rush of excitement one has when seeing someone to whom she owed a great deal. Trenton appeared much different than he did the last time she'd seen him, as he'd been dressed for the serious task he'd been undertaking. But this time, he was dressed for travel, with black leather breeches, boots to his knees, a few layers of tunics, and a heavy leather vest that acted as protection against weapons, including arrows that might be fired upon unsuspecting travelers.

But there was more to her observations, something she hadn't really noticed until now – Trenton was easily as tall as his father, who was the tallest man Lysabel had ever seen, and he had his father's nearly black hair and smoky gray eyes. But his father had a long, angular face from what she remembered, and Trenton had a square-jawed appearance with a big cleft in his chin.

He was handsome; there was no question about that. The man was quite beautiful as far as men were concerned. But she'd never considered anything about him beyond that; to her, he was an old friend and nothing more.

Lysabel was shaken from her observations when it occurred to her that he might want to speak to her alone. He seemed rather ill at ease, looking at the men around the hall as if unnerved by their mere presence. Lysabel came to the conclusion that, perhaps, he had something to tell her that he didn't want others to hear. He seemed reluctant to say anything more than what he'd already said. No conversation, no idle words of chatter. Simply... silence.

Nay, she didn't like that thought at all – he'd returned when he never said he would, and now he seemed... nervous.

Oh, God...

"Please," she said, suddenly feeling sick to her stomach. "Come... come with me. We may speak elsewhere."

Trenton didn't say anything, but he nodded, and Lysabel led him out of the hall, fighting off the panic that was growing in her heart. She took him down a small flight of stairs and into a section of the manse that contained several rooms, all darkened at this hour whilst everyone was in the hall.

Trenton trailed after her in the darkness until they ended up in a room that smelled heavily of smoke and dampness. Lysabel shut the door behind him and he stood there, in almost complete blackness, listening to her moving around in the room. Suddenly, a flint sparked and a small flame on the tip of a taper pierced the dark. As she moved to find another candle, he spoke.

"I did not mean to take you away from your meal," he said in his deep, raspy voice. "We could have just as easily spoken on the morrow, my lady."

Lysabel lit two more candles, these in an iron candelabra, and with those additional tapers, the room lit up sufficiently to show that they were in a solar of some kind, with expensive furniture and wood-paneled walls. The darkened hearth had an elaborately carved mantel, with images of saints and scenes of great saintly battles. As Trenton glanced around, Lysabel set the candelabra on the cluttered table in the center of the room.

"You did not take me away from my meal," she said. "Clearly, you have come for a reason and I would not be so rude as to put you off. Trenton... has something happened with Benoit?"

Weary from four very long days of travel, Trenton realized that his appearance had frightened her. It had been unexpected, and abrupt, and now the woman was spiraling into panic. He could hear it in her voice and see it in her expression. Feeling foolish that his appearance had been so clumsy, he hastened to reassure her.

"Nothing has happened," he said quickly. "I am sorry if you thought I have come to tell you otherwise. De Wilde is dead, my lady, and I have only returned to see how you were faring since his death. I swear to you that is the only reason."

Realizing her momentary panic had been unfounded, Lysabel exhaled heavily and closed her eyes, leaning against the table for support. She couldn't describe the relief she felt and even if she tried, she would have burst into tears before the words left her lips. Therefore, it took her a moment before she could recover her composure enough to face him again.

"It was kind of you to think enough to return," she said, though her voice was still quivering. "In fact, I am glad that you did. It gives me the opportunity to thank you for what you did."

Trenton gazed at the woman in the pale light; the night he'd abducted Benoit, she'd been beaten and harried, but she'd still been surprisingly lovely. Standing before him now, she looked relaxed and content, her face smooth and unmarred by a bruised cheek, and her hair was gathered at the nape of her neck, revealing the swan-like feature and graceful shoulders.

In truth, it made him wonder why he'd never looked at her twice in the days he'd know her, because Lysabel Wellesbourne was a genuinely stunning creature.

"There is no need to thank me," he said. "I was on an errand for the king."

Lysabel shook her head. "Truly, Trenton, you have no idea…" She paused, thought carefully on her words, and began again. "Suffice it to say that my children and I have experienced peace for the past thirty-six days, peace as we have never known. I was thinking this evening, in fact, of how my daughters seemed to have blossomed in just the short time their father has been… away."

Trenton regarded her carefully. "I heard you had daughters."

"Aye," she nodded. "Two. Cynethryn, whom we call Cinny, and little Brencis, known as Cissy."

So she has children who were subject to Benoit's horror, he thought grimly. "And they only believe he is away?"

"Everyone does."

He understood, mostly because he'd told her to convey that very thing to the people of Stretford. "For now, that is all you can do," he said. "But at some point, it will be known that he is dead."

"Why must it be known?"

He shrugged. "Do you truly wish for everyone to believe that he could come back at any moment?" he asked. "Forgive me for being blunt, my lady, but I heard what he did to you the night I was here, and I saw the results. You were bandaged and broken, so it seems to me that it is no secret how de Wilde treated you. Would it be incorrect of me to assume that?"

Lysabel averted her gaze. After a moment, she let out a hiss. "I have spent such a long time suffering in silence and denying what was really going on that it is difficult for me, even now, to respond to your question," she said. "You and I have not seen one another in years and although we were never close, our families were. Our fathers are the best of friends. My father must never, ever know what has happened here, Trenton. Will you swear to me that you will never tell him?"

"I swear."

That seemed to ease her a great deal. "Thank you," she whispered sincerely. "Truly, it is of little matter now, anyway. Benoit is dead and he shall never return, thank God."

Trenton could hear the emotion in her voice when he spoke. Wearily, he searched for a chair and, spying one, he pointed to it. "May I?"

She nodded quickly. "Please."

Trenton moved to the chair and lowered himself down into it, feeling his exhaustion to his bones. But his interest in this conversation was stronger than his fatigue.

"You are correct when you say we've not seen each other in many years," he said. "I was trying to think of the last time I saw you and your family, and I believe it was during the Christmas holidays nearly sixteen years ago."

She smiled weakly. "At least."

"I was twenty years and four, I think," he said. "Your father sent me to London on an errand to the king's father, also Henry, and I never returned. Somehow, the de Russe name meant a great deal to Henry Tudor and the man would not let me leave. But I digress… it was a very bad winter when last I saw you and your family, although I've seen your father periodically since that time, but it has been a few years. How is Matthew faring?"

The subject of Lysabel's beloved father always brought a smile to her lips. "Well," she said. "Papa is as old as dirt now, and he surrounds himself with his grandchildren and grandnieces and nephews, but he is still the same. The White Lord of Wellesbourne will never change."

"And your mother?"

"My mother is very well, thank you. She writes to me frequently to tell me of what is happening at home."

He nodded. "I am glad to hear that," he said. "It is strange, really. I was so much older than my younger siblings, and older than you and your siblings, and I fear that you were all much closer to each other than I was. I always felt as if my brother, Dane, and I were off on our own, being that we were so much older."

Lysabel's smile broadened at the thought of Trenton's brother, Dane, who was a year younger than Trenton. Dane was his mother's firstborn, and Trenton was his father's firstborn, and when the pair came together, Trenton and Dane became instant brothers. That bond was something that had only strengthened over the years, or so Lysabel remembered. Trenton de Russe and Dane Stoneley, who took the name of de Russe after the passing of his father, had been inseparable, and she remembered that well.

"And how is your brother, Dane?" she asked.

"He is well. I saw him a few months ago and he was prosperous and happy."

"I see," she said. "I suppose it is safe to tell you that I was madly in love with him in my younger years. I vowed to marry him someday, in fact."

Trenton grinned. "That swill-headed lout?" he scoffed. "What makes him so special? What does he have that I do not?"

Lysabel laughed, something that sounded like the chime of angels to Trenton. "God's Bones, Trenton, you were too frightening for a delicate young lady," she said. "Dane would at least speak to me."

"But you never spoke to *me*."

"I was afraid of you!"

He pretended to be miffed. "So Dane received your undying love," he said. "I shall have to punch him the next time I see him."

"Why?"

"Because all adoration should have gone to me, as the most handsome."

Lysabel began to giggle uncontrollably. "Take heart, my fine lad," she said. "My sister, Rosamunde, professed her undying love for you. At least she did until the next young man caught her eye."

Trenton rolled his eyes. "Fickle woman," he said. "Do you mean to tell me I could have had a Wellesbourne daughter all this time?"

Lysabel snorted. "Mayhap," she said. "But you would have had to go through my father to get to us."

Trenton cocked an eyebrow. "That would not have been difficult," he said. "Benoit certainly did."

That brought the light mood of the conversation to an instant halt and Trenton immediately regretted his words. He wasn't the most tactful man, and he wasn't very good when it came to gentle conversation with a woman, and that lack of finesse was readily evident at that moment. He cleared his throat softly.

"I am sorry," he said. "I did not mean to say that. I simply meant..."

Lysabel lifted a hand, cutting him off. "I know what you meant," she said, though she didn't seem angry. Simply depressed. "It is true, you know. Benoit charmed my father to the point where my father was his biggest supporter. In fact, Benoit was very charming in the beginning, and very kind. Everyone thought so. He came from a great legacy, the Sheriffs of Ilchester, so his pedigree was strong. When he asked for my hand, my father had no reservations and neither did I. It was only... afterwards."

Trenton suspected something like that must have happened, because the Matthew Wellesbourne he knew would never have allowed his daughter to marry a man with anything less than a stellar character.

"So he pretended to be something he was not until he got what he wanted," he said quietly.

Lysabel nodded. "Aye," she said. "He very much wanted to be married into the House of Wellesbourne. As my father's eldest child, I have a considerable inheritance due, and he wanted it. He wanted it before my father passed away and when it became evident after a year or so that my father would not relinquish what Benoit felt belonged to him, that was when the trouble started."

Trenton had heard tales like that before, but never to someone he'd known. Wealthy women married by greedy men, only to be treated lower than a dog when the inheritance or money wasn't produced. Already, he could feel the disgust upon his tongue.

"And your father never knew?" he asked, almost in disbelief.

Lysabel shook her head. "Nay," she said firmly. "Benoit made it very clear that if I told my father, he would kill me. I did not believe him, of course, because should he kill me, he would not get my inheritance, but even if he would not kill me, he made sure I wished I was dead. There were times when I hoped I would die."

Trenton was watching her seriously, feeling the impact of her hopeless and sorrowful words. "But you never thought to ask your father for help?" he asked. "Surely he could have protected you."

Lysabel shrugged. "I belong to my husband," she said simply. "My father had no say in how he treated me, so why tell him? It would only make him miserable. It would make him commit murder. How could I do that to my father, to have such a thing on his conscience? Killing my husband and knowing he did it because the man… because of what he did to me. My father is a sensitive man, Trenton. You know this. He is emotional about things."

Trenton knew Matthew well enough to know that what she said was true. "Then you did not tell him to protect him?"

"Aye. I love my papa too much to make him realize that he condemned me to such a terrible life. That is not fair to him."

Trenton understood, somewhat. It was an extremely noble attitude, protecting her father while she suffered so terribly. Not that he agreed with it, but he did understand her.

"When was the last time you saw your father?" he asked. "You are not too terribly far from Wellesbourne Castle. Does he come to visit?"

She nodded. "He and my mother visit about every year or so," she said. "Of course, Benoit was always on his best behavior. Papa never saw anything wrong."

"So he never knew?"

"Never."

Trenton couldn't imagine a world in which a father wouldn't see the miserable existence of his daughter, but he didn't pry anymore about it. He'd probably already pried too much.

"That is all over with now," he said quietly. "Had I known this was going on, I would have come for de Wilde much sooner than I did. Mayhap you fear for your father's soul in killing his daughter's husband, but I have no such fear for my soul. I was happy to do what was necessary to protect you."

She looked at him, hearing a chivalrous declaration. *Simply kind words from an old friend*, she thought, but she was touched nonetheless. It had been a very long time since she'd last heard anything chivalrous.

"Why did Henry want my husband?" she asked.

Because the man stole a mistress away from the king, Trenton thought. But he didn't say what he was thinking; the woman had suffered enough indignity at the hands of Benoit de Wilde. He didn't want to add to it.

"That was not made clear to me, my lady," he lied. "All I knew was that Benoit de Wilde was my target. Henry wanted him, and as an agent for the king, it is my duty to carry out the king's command."

Fortunately, Lysabel seemed to believe him. She lifted her eyebrows in resignation. "Benoit had many dealings that were less than ethical," she said. "I am not surprised he attracted the king's attention."

"Indeed."

"I will not ask what you did with him, Trenton. But I hope you threw his body in a river and let the fish eat him."

It was a rather strong thing to say coming from a genteel lady. "You do not wish to know what I did with him?" he asked.

"Nay."

There was coldness to her answer, something he was pleased to see. He'd seen some women, even after being beaten by their husbands, still have some feeling for them, but not Lysabel. It was clear that she held nothing but contempt for the man who'd made her life a living hell for so many years. But her excuse for not letting the world in on that shame was because she wanted to protect her father's honor. It wasn't because she was weak or afraid – it was simply to protect the man she loved.

Strength.

The woman had strength that was rare. Trenton had noticed it the night he'd come for Benoit, that even beaten and broken, Lysabel still had a dignity her husband couldn't take from her. That was the Wellesbourne breeding, but it was also something more. Quite simply, Lysabel was just a strong woman in general. To be married to the devil de Wilde for all those years, she had to be.

How on earth did he not notice this strong woman those years ago? Or perhaps, it was simply something that developed after years of abuse – perhaps, she'd had to learn to be strong. In either case, Trenton's respect for her grew.

In truth, Trenton knew a little something about abused women. The woman he called his mother wasn't the woman who gave birth to him, but she was the woman who married his father and treated Trenton as if he were her very own son. Trenton had been eight years of age when he'd first met Lady Remington Stoneley. Although his father had tried to refrain from telling him too much about her past, and of her first husband, Trenton knew several things that her son, Dane, had told him – mostly that Dane's biological father had been an evil bastard who had abused Remington and her sisters terribly.

The man had been an enemy of the crown and had ended up in prison in the Tower of London, only to escape and try to return to the life he had before he'd been imprisoned. That meant reclaiming his wife, and Trenton remembered well the events leading up to the showdown between Gaston de Russe and Sir Guy Stoneley. Being young, but determined to help save Remington from the clutches of her evil husband, Trenton and Dane had set out to protect her, only to be captured by Guy himself.

In the end, Guy had been killed, and Remington had married Gaston. She'd been happily married to the man for many years now, and he treated her with the respect inherent to a man deeply in love, but Trenton still remembered witnessing some of what the woman had been forced to endure at the hands of an abuser.

Therefore, it made him more sympathetic to Lysabel than most, simply because he understood something about the abuse of a woman.

"Then I will not tell you what became of him," he said after a moment. "You need not be troubled over it."

Lysabel nodded, in appreciation he thought, and she didn't seem willing to linger over the subject. "I will not be," she said with some courage. "It is over and done now, although I will admit that I can still hardly believe it. I keep thinking that I shall wake up and this will all have been a dream."

He smiled wryly. "It is no dream, I promise. I was there."

"I know. I saw you."

He snorted. "And I do not make it a habit of appearing in women's dreams," he said. Then, he sobered unnaturally fast. "Unless I have appeared in your sister's dreams. Did Rosamunde ever dream of me?"

Lysabel burst out laughing. "When she was fourteen years of age, mayhap," she said. "But nowadays, I do not think her husband would like it very much."

He scoffed. "I fear no man," he said. "Wait – who did she marry? I may have to amend that statement."

Lysabel continued laughing. "Leo de Lara," she said. "He is from the great Marcher Lords of de Lara. Do you know of them?"

Trenton nodded. "I do," he said. "I did not know she married into that family."

"She did."

"And the rest of your siblings? Don't tell me they are all married away, too."

Lysabel shook her head. "Not all of them," she said. "Rosamunde is married, but my brothers, James and Thomas, are not. My other sister, Emeline, is married, as is my brother, Daniel. But my youngest brother, William, will probably never marry. Papa says he has too much of my Uncle Luke in him. Luke was killed at Bosworth right before I was born. Did you ever know him?"

Trenton shook his head. "Regretfully, I did not," he said. "But I well remember your brother, William, with his red hair and loud voice. I can remember your father trying to tame his wild streak, even when he was a young lad."

Lysabel grinned. "He still has that wild streak, so I am told."

"He will outgrow it."

"According to my mother, my father does not think so. God help us, we shall have a wild Wellesbourne on our hands."

Trenton smiled, gazing into the woman's eyes and feeling a jolt when he did. Like a spark, a hint of something that made his belly quivery, just a bit. He wanted to continue staring into her eyes, but something about her big blue eyes made him feel like she was sucking him right in, dragging him into that blue oblivion. He almost couldn't look away, and it was an effort to do so.

"Even if that is true, he has the Wellesbourne soul, and that means his character is inherently good," he said, tearing his gaze away because he was starting to feel strange. Unnerved... *giddy*, even. "And, mayhap, this has been enough of a conversation for one night. Thank you for speaking to me, my lady. Again, I am sorry to have taken you away from your meal, but I am glad we have had this time to speak in private. When I last left you, it was under stressful conditions. I hope you understand that, as someone who has known you your entire life, I simply couldn't walk away. I had to return to make sure you were well."

Another declaration she could have construed as chivalrous. Caring, even. God's Bones, Lysabel hadn't experienced a man's caring in years and had no idea how to respond to it. It was sweet, and endearing, but there was also something strangely uncomfortable about it. Years under Benoit's abuse had left her wondering if she was good enough to even be cared for in such a way.

"I am well," she assured him. "Thanks to you, I am well and so are my children. What we owe you, Trenton, I fear I can never repay."

Trenton was starting to feel very strange as he looked at her, something he'd never experienced before. The more he looked into her eyes, the more his gaze drifted over the curve of her face, the lines of her figure... something was happening inside of him that he didn't recognize. His initial discomfort at it had turned into something else, too, something that made his insides feel quivery. If he hadn't known any better, he would swear there was some interest in the lady on his part.

But, no...

It is fatigue, he told himself. He'd ridden hard the past few days, so it was logical that his body was starting to revolt. All he needed was rest.

But all he wanted to do was stay and talk to Lysabel.

He had to get out of there.

"I do not expect you to repay me," he said. "I would not want you to. What I did, I did because the king ordered me to do it. I did it because it was the right thing to do. But returning to make sure you had fared well in the wake of everything was my own idea. I owe your father too much to have behaved any other way."

Lysabel smiled faintly. "Mayhap someday, when he is very old, we shall tell my father what happened with Benoit," she said. "But until that time, I will tell him what I have told everyone else – that my husband left Stretford one night and never returned. Promise me that is all you will ever tell him, too."

Trenton nodded. "I already swore I would," he said. "You needn't worry, my lady. Your secret is safe."

Lysabel gazed at the man, feeling more comfort than she'd ever known in her life with his massive presence. It was true, he'd been a terrifying and intimidating young man, but she didn't feel that way about him any longer. He'd saved her and all she could feel when she looked at him was comfort.

Safe.

"Thank you," she said quietly. Then, she took a deep breath, her manner brightening. "Now, I am sure you must be famished. Will you join my daughters and me for a meal? I would very much like them to meet an old family friend."

Trenton thought that sounded rather attractive. A naturally solitary man, who ate and slept alone except when he was working with his team, the thought of sharing a meal with Lysabel and her daughters did not distress him. In fact, his inclination to leave the woman, to get away from her, because of the odd feelings she seemed to be stirring in him was weakened by her invitation. Trenton wasn't a weak man by nature, but when it came to any kind of emotion, something he kept very closely protected, he wasn't as adept at controlling it as he should be.

He could feel himself slipping.

"I would be... honored," he said after a moment. "I should like to meet Matthew's granddaughters."

Lysabel was pleased. "Good," she said, leading him towards the chamber door. "Cissy looks just like him, but Cinny takes after her father's side of the family. She is quiet, more reserved. I am sure they will be very happy to meet you."

Very happy to meet the man that killed their father, Trenton thought. Of course, they wouldn't know it, and probably never would, but he realized as he followed Lysabel back towards the hall, listening to her chatter, that he didn't accept her invitation to sup to meet her daughters.

He did it to be around her.

He was slipping further...

CHAPTER FOUR

I T WAS DAWN and he was awake.

He was always awake at dawn, simply because years of training as a knight meant there was no sloth or laziness involved. Men went to bed late and rose early, always to go about their duties, always to ensure their world, and the world of their lords, was safe and prepared for anything.

Therefore, he was always awake before the sun rose, as if his mind knew exactly when light was about to appear in the eastern horizon. He would get up, wash his face, throw water on his hair, and dress, and by the time he was finished, the horizon was turning shades of pale blue and pink.

But the trouble was on this day that he had no real duties to attend to. He was away from London, away from the king, and at a location where he had no responsibilities. He felt rather useless, but rather than wander around aimlessly and look like an idiot, he decided to head to the stables and tend to his horse. At least then, he'd be doing something.

The stable was dark at this hour, but the moment he entered, the animals began to shift around, knowing that human presence meant food in their bellies. When Trenton had arrived, he'd requested that his horse be put in the farthest stall from the door because the animal was quite excitable, and vicious, and people coming in and out of the stable would agitate it.

While most knights traveled on horses that were designed for travel, lighter-weight animals that were swift, comfortable, and agile, Trenton didn't hold to that philosophy. He traveled on his destrier, a massively heavy-boned warhorse that he'd taken into battle many times. The beast had been a gift from his father as a yearling, fifteen years ago, and was perhaps the smartest and most experienced battle horse in all of England.

Trenton was rather particular about the horses he rode on, and owned, resulting from a bad experience when he'd been a young lad, riding an old nag halfway across England because it was the only horse available. He and his brother had been forced to share the animal, and since that time, Trenton only rode horses that could accommodate his bulk easily and didn't crush his manhood. That meant he didn't ride on small or even medium-sized horses. Of course, the saddle had a good deal to do with that, too, and he had the finest saddle made, one he could ride in comfortably for hours on end.

His preference for horses and saddles was peculiar, indeed.

At the end of the row of tied-up horses stood his enormous warhorse; he could see the outline of the horse's back, taller than all of the other horses, when he approached. He whistled low to the animal to let him know he was approaching. The horse's massive head shot up, eyeballing Trenton in the darkness, nickering softly to him. A horse that could bite off men's hands or stomp them to death had a definite fondness for his master.

Trenton slipped into the stall, rubbing the big, black head affectionately. Dewi was the horse's name, named for the Welsh dragon god, simply because the horse was the closest thing Trenton had ever seen to a fire-breathing dragon. Dewi's big lips pulled at Trenton, nipping at him playfully, and Trenton avoided the seeking lips as he untied the horse's tether and backed him out of the stall.

Leading the animal to the front of the stables and tying the lead rope around his muzzle to prevent him from trying to snap at anyone, Trenton proceeded to check over the horse to ensure the rough travel hadn't done any damage. Dewi seemed well enough, now swishing his big tail at Trenton, as he was hungry and trying to prompt his master into procuring his food. Trenton slapped the big, black butt of the horse, grinning because the horse was doing everything it could to try and force him to go and get his morning meal. When Dewi started to lift his hind leg, as if to kick out at Trenton, the man laughed softly and decided he should hunt down a stable servant so his spoiled glutton of a horse could be fed.

The very subject of a meal had him thinking about the previous night's feast with Lysabel and her daughters. The children had been adorable and delightful for the most part, with their mother's sweet face. At least, he thought so, although the youngest girl did look a good deal like Matthew. It had been a long time since Trenton had lingered on thoughts of a woman, but he'd gone to sleep with thoughts of Lysabel on his mind and even now, visions of her lovely face and tinkling laughter filled his head.

In fact, he'd been unable to really sleep well because of it. He kept thinking of that long-limbed little girl he'd known; one who would run and play and jump with her siblings, and one who would sit on her father's lap and listen to him tell stories until she fell asleep. Of course, Trenton hadn't really been part of the family – he'd been a squire for a few years before Matthew knighted him, but he was always there, always around the family, and always watching. He remembered well the mostly-blond Wellesbourne children, except for Lysabel and Rosamunde, who had their mother's glossy bronze hair, and then William, who inherited red hair. He remembered them all, but he'd never given any of them much thought.

Until now.

Now, he was thinking of one of them in particular.

God, he was insane for doing it. This was all so foolish and confusing. His conversation with Henry came to mind, the one before he'd come to Stretford, where Henry reminded him what a terrible record he had with women. It wasn't untrue, and a terrible record was putting it mildly. But there was so much more to it.

It wasn't as if he'd been careless...

His first wife, Alicia, had come through his father. Gaston knew the woman's father and he'd brokered the agreement, which had been a good one until Alicia had died trying to push forth an enormous son, who died also, but that was something Trenton tried not to remember.

He'd been young, and he'd loved Alicia, and her death had been devastating. Memories of the pretty girl with the silly laugh only made him ache for what could have been. He remembered their marriage, of falling in love with her, and of the good life they had together. She was patient with him, and he appreciated that. Then came her pregnancy; they'd both been thrilled. When the day of birth arrived, he remembered the anticipation of waiting for his son to be born – two days of waiting – before the physic came to tell him that his wife had died and the child with her.

In disbelief, he'd run up to the chamber where she'd been laboring, convinced the physic was lying, only to find Alicia dead upon their bed with her legs splayed and the child stuck between them, halfway out. He remembered seeing two little legs emerged from her womb and after that, he didn't remember much else. Somewhere in the chaos, he remembered vomiting as the physic scolded him for even looking upon his dead wife.

He'd learned his lesson.

He would never look again.

He didn't look when his second wife, Iseuld, had been murdered by her father. She was dead; everyone told him she was dead, so he took them at their word. They'd been visiting her father's home shortly after their marriage because her father, a greedy baron, had demanded the meeting. He wanted money from Trenton, and some of the de Russe fortune, because he felt entitled to it now that his daughter was married into the family.

Trenton had sent word to his father to come and help him negotiate something that had confused him, because the demands for money had come directly from the father. Never Iseuld. Finally, when the father evidently couldn't get Iseuld to cooperate with him, he threw her out a window and told everyone that she had killed herself, but servants who had heard the arguing told otherwise. It had been murder.

Another wife dead.

And then came Adela...

He sighed heavily as he thought of his current wife. If ever a mistake had been made, he had made it with her. Another marriage brokered by his father had seen him wed Adela of Brittany, the illegitimate daughter of the Duke of Brittany. In theory, it should have made a fine marriage, but in practice, it was a horror. Adela was petty and spoiled, and had male "friends" who had followed her from France. Henry had alluded to her whoring ways and it only upset Trenton in the sense that Adela had sullied the de Russe name. She spat upon it every chance she got, and she hated the very sight of Trenton because she liked to pretend she wasn't married at all. It was a horrific situation but one that he couldn't do anything about.

But it also made it impossible to find any happiness of his own.

That included the daughter of his father's best friend.

Slapping his horse on the rump again, he realized he'd been lost in thought. The sun was starting to rise because the horizon was growing lighter, and Dewi was still swinging his tail around, deliberately trying to hit Trenton with it. At least, that was Trenton's belief. His horse was smart enough to do such a thing.

With thoughts of Lysabel still on his mind, he headed off in earnest to procure feed for his pig of a horse.

HER MOTHER WAS looking for her, but she didn't want to be found.

Brencis Alixandrea de Wilde was up and running. She liked to wake up early and rush to the stables to help the stable servants feed the horses before her mother or her nurse could corral her and make her go back into the manse, where her nurse would commence with lessons on language or art. Lately, she and her sister had even been subjected to writing their names, at the insistence of their mother, though they weren't to mention such a thing to their father. He evidently didn't like it that girls should learn to write.

But Brencis' love was first and foremost with horses. If it had four legs and a long face, she was in love with it. She'd been begging for a pony for two solid years, but her father never listened to her and her mother could only say that her father would "think about it". That wasn't good enough for Brencis; if she couldn't have a pony, then she simply wanted to be where the horses were. She wanted to smell the hay and the horsey smell of the stables.

So, she slipped from the manse, across the kitchen yard, and over to the stables. Since the sun was rising, she knew the stable servants would be feeding the horses and she very much wanted to help them. She ran the last several feet, entering the stable in a flash. Although the servants weren't anywhere to be found, she could hear them. She was about to turn and go look for them when a new horse standing right inside the stable caught her eye.

Even though it was dim in the early morning light, Brencis could still see what a beautiful animal he was. He was very big, with a flowing black mane and a flowing black tail, something that delighted her. He looked like a horse from one of the stories her mother told her, stories of knights on fine chargers who would ride to save their ladies fair. Surely this was the charger of a great knight, because he certainly looked like one.

She was intrigued.

Brencis made her way towards the horse carefully, inspecting his muscular legs and fat butt. And he was shiny, so very shiny; even the weak light reflected off his black coat. When he sensed her approach and his nostrils began to flare, she began to speak quietly to him.

"Pretty horse," she said softly. "You are the prettiest horse I've ever seen. Do not be afraid of me. I only wish to pet you."

She kept repeating the words, over and over, crooning to the horse in her soft little voice and completely unaware of the danger she was in. The horse was probably forty or fifty times the body weight of a six-year-old child, and absolutely gigantic next to her, but Brencis held no fear. All she knew was that she loved him already.

She moved closer.

In her sweet little voice, she continued to talk to the horse, wisely staying fairly far away because the horse's nostrils were flaring and he was craning his neck around to look at her. Close and closer she came, however, speaking softly, finally holding out her hand to him so he could see that she was approaching. The horse snorted when she came close and laid his ears back along his skull, baring his big teeth. Brencis came to a halt.

"You are very mean," she said sternly. "I came to be friendly with you, but you are mean. I have brought treats with me, but I do not think you deserve one. Well? Why are you so mean?"

The horse continued to bare his teeth at her but he couldn't do much more since he had a lead rope tied around his muzzle. But that didn't seem to deter Brencis; she began to dig in the pockets of the little apron she wore.

Out came a small pear, one she held up to the horse.

"If you are polite, I shall give this to you," she said. "Well? Are you going to be nice?"

The horse's ears perked up when he caught sight of the pear. It was enough of a gesture that Brencis carefully held the pear out to the horse and he sniffed at it, promptly sucking it up with his big lips and chomping down on it. Brencis pulled out another pear.

"See?" she said. "If you are nice, then I shall give you a treat. Here is another one."

She held out another pear, and the horse snatched it from the palm of her hand. As he did so, she was able to get in a scratch or two on his velvety muzzle. He continued to chew, and his aggression had died down, so she patted him on the nose again.

"You are a very big horse," she said. "But I fear that someone has been mean to you. Is that why you are so mean?"

Trenton chose that moment to return to the stable, a bucket of dried grain in his hand. When he looked over and saw Brencis standing in front of his horse, the bucket hit the ground and he ran to her, faster than he'd ever moved in his life, and grabbed her around the body, pulling her away from the horse in the same motion. As Brencis yelped in fright, Trenton put himself in between his horse and the little girl.

"What were you doing?" he demanded. "Did he hurt you?"

Brencis found herself wrapped up in Trenton's iron grip. "Nay!" she insisted. "He's my friend!"

Trenton set her on her feet, making sure to keep himself between her and his man-eating horse. "*Him?*" he repeated, confused and just the least bit terrified. His heart was still beating up in his throat. "You must be mistaken. This is my horse."

"He is? He's very big."

"And very mean."

"I know, but I told him if he was nice, I would give him a treat. He was nice, so I did."

Trenton had no idea what she was talking about. "You… you gave him a treat?"

"Aye."

"When?"

"Now."

His confusion grew and he stood straight, hands on his hips as he looked between his horse and the little girl. He peered closer at the horse, who did, indeed, seem to be chewing on something.

"What did you give him?"

"A pear."

Trenton didn't know what to make of it. He had the meanest horse in all of England, so he thought, so this made no sense to him at all. He eyed her.

"Show me your hand."

Brencis complied, holding out her right hand.

"The other hand," he said.

Two hands were produced. Trenton touched them, just to make sure she wasn't missing any fingers, before sighing heavily and struggling to calm his beating heart. He was still worked up about what he'd seen when he'd entered the stable – Lysabel's youngest daughter standing close to his gnashing, thrashing warhorse, an animal who had been known to kill men outright. He scratched his dark head.

"Didn't he try to bite you?" he asked.

Brencis shrugged. "Nay," she said. "But he did show me his teeth."

"He was warning you away."

She looked around him, at the big horse that happened to be looking at her, too, perhaps looking for another treat. Trenton could hardly believe it. Taking the little girl by the shoulders, he turned her back towards the bucket he'd dropped.

"Go pick up the bucket," he told her. "Bring it over here."

Brencis did as she was told. She scampered over to the bucket and picked it up, lugging it back over to Trenton. He'd spilled very little when he'd dropped it, because it had fallen upright, so there was virtually none missing. He took the bucket from her.

"Thank you," he said. "Now, you will please do me a favor. Do not go near my horse. He is very aggressive and I do not wish to see you injured."

Brencis cocked her head curiously. "He will not hurt me," she said. "See for yourself."

With that, she pulled another pear from her pocket and held it out to the horse, who stuck his big neck out to claim it. Trenton went to pull her back but he couldn't help but notice that Dewi wasn't showing any signs of aggression to her. The animal simply slapped his big lips against the pear and ate it right up.

"See?" Brencis said. "He likes me."

Trenton was at a loss. Scratching his head again, he didn't know what to make out of any of this. Putting the bucket of grain on the ground in front of the horse, he loosened the lead rope muzzle and Dewi began to eat heartily.

"I am not sure what has come over him, but he is not a pleasant horse," he told the child. "In the future, please do not come around him when I am not present. I fear what he might do to you."

Brencis wasn't happy about it. "But… but he likes me."

Trenton nodded. "I can see that," he said, realizing that she was hurt that she couldn't count the horse among her "friends". "And you are a very nice lass, but all the same, just be careful with him. He is a dangerous animal."

Brencis watched the big, black horse as he chomped on his grain, snorting and blowing out the dust from the bucket. She sighed sadly.

"Does he have a name?" she asked.

Trenton nodded. "His name is Dewi," he said. "That is the Welsh dragon god. He is a very fierce animal, I assure you."

"Dewi," Brencis repeated. "Have you had him a long time?"

"A very long time. He is sixteen years of age."

Brencis looked at him. "He is older than my sister."

"I know."

Her gaze lingered on him a moment before returning it to the horse. "I have always wanted a pony," she said. "When do you suppose I will be old enough to have one?"

Trenton could hear the longing in her voice, wanting something so badly. It was rather sweet. "I am not sure," he said. "What does your mother say?"

Brencis started to move towards the horse to pet it, thought better of it, and stopped. "She tells me that my father is thinking about it," she said. "He has been thinking a very long time. I do not know why he will not let me have a pony. I have promised him that I will take very good care of it, but he has told me that ponies are for boys. Is that true?"

Trenton shook his head. "Nay," he said. "That is not true at all.

Ponies are for boys and girls."

"Then you think I can have one someday?"

He smiled faintly. "I am sure that is a possibility."

It was an encouraging answer, but not enough of one. Brencis was very disappointed that she didn't have Trenton's full approval.

"When did you have your first pony?" she asked.

Trenton had to think about it. "My father gave me my first horse when I was eleven years of age," he said. "His name was Lightning, but he didn't move very fast. He was rather old."

Brencis was listening closely, hoping he'd give her a clue as to how she could coerce a pony from her own father.

"I will name my pony Pegasus," she announced. "My mother told me a story about Pegasus. He was a magical horse."

"Indeed, he is," Trenton agreed. "That is a fine name."

Brencis was losing herself in dreams of her future pony. "And he shall be white," she said. "I want a white pony and when I ride him, he will be able to jump things. Lots of things. Like this!"

With that, she began to run in circles, pretending to jump invisible barriers. Trenton watched with some amusement, seeing the innocence of life through the eyes of a child. That wasn't something he ever got to witness, so it was a rarity. His life was full of espionage and death, things that were the worst society had to offer, so to spend a few minutes with a little girl whose biggest dream was owning a pony was something of a sweet experience for him.

Something few and far between.

It also made him think of the child he had lost, the little boy that Alicia had died alongside. That had been ten years ago, so his son would have been a little older than Brencis. In the beginning, right after Alicia's death, he used to wonder what his son would have been like and what traits he would have had. He hadn't thought of the boy in some time but in speaking with Brencis, he was reminded again. It was difficult not to long for a son who never had a chance in life.

"Did you see me jump high?"

Brencis was standing in front of him, tugging on his hand. Jolted from his train of thought, he smiled weakly.

"I did," he said. "You did a very good job."

Brencis beamed. "I can jump higher!"

To prove her point, she rushed around and began jumping again while Trenton watched. He thought she was a rather cute little girl and he could only imagine Matthew's pride in her. But just as she jumped very high and ended up falling to her knees, her older sister entered the stables.

"Cissy!" Cynethryn scolded. "Mama has been looking everywhere for you!"

As Brencis struggled to her feet, Cynethryn grabbed her hand and began to yank her along. But the little sister balked and tried to pull away.

"Nay!" she said. "I do not want to leave yet! I have to help feed the horses!"

Cynethryn frowned. "Cissy, Mama says you must come."

"I do not want to go!"

"If you are bad, I will tell Papa!"

That brought Brencis to a halt and, in that moment, Trenton could see the fear the child had of her father. But he could also see that Cynethryn was more than willing to use that threat against her little sister, a rather severe and unhappy threat from child to child. Considering that the children must have known what their father was capable of, Trenton found it surprising that Cynethryn would say such a thing.

"Your father is not here right now," he said, watching two pairs of big blue eyes turn to him. "But your sister is right, Lady Brencis. You must not behave so. The horses will be fed, have no fear. And thank you for giving Dewi your treats. I am sure he is grateful."

Brencis was crestfallen that she wouldn't be able to help feed the horses. Looking like a whipped dog, she looked to her sister with a pathetic expression on her face.

"I will come," she said sadly. Then, she looked to Trenton. "Will you come, too?"

Before Trenton could reply, Cynethryn spoke. "Nay," she said quickly, her attention turning to Trenton. "You will not come. Only Brencis."

Trenton met the child's gaze, sensing a good deal of hardness in one so young. Last night, the child had been rather quiet, so he hadn't spoken to her much at all. But this morning, he could see what the smoke and noise of the hall had drowned out – this child was no wilting violet. She had iron in her blood and he sensed that she was wary of him.

"I have no intention of coming," he said evenly. "I am not finished with Dewi, but I thank you for your kind invitation all the same."

Brencis simply looked depressed as Cynethryn yanked her along, pulling her out of the stable and into the muddy stable yard.

Trenton watched the pair go, wondering if Cynethryn was always so firm or if that was purely for his benefit. Somehow, he didn't think so. He could see the rigidity in her. Perhaps it was her nature, brought on by a brutal father, or perhaps it was something else. Trenton couldn't imagine one of Matthew Wellesbourne's grandchildren to be so hard. But then again, she was the product of an unusually cruel father. Although Trenton went through life showing limited concern for those he wasn't close to, he couldn't help but feel concern for the little girl with the hard manner.

Something in her eyes had his interest.

But he didn't linger on it. Just as he was about to turn away, he caught sight of Lysabel entering the stable yard and running straight into her daughters. Suddenly, he wasn't so concerned with tending Dewi as Lysabel now filled his field of vision, and he watched as she gently scolded Brencis. He could tell by her body language that she wasn't happy with her youngest child, and Brencis was starting to weep. She began rubbing her eyes as Lysabel bent over and kissed her on the head.

At that point, Trenton felt as if he should perhaps defend the child or, at the very least, let her mother know that she had been trying to be helpful. Leaving his horse sucking down the oats, he left the stable and headed for the trio in the center of the stable yard.

"Greetings, Lady de Wilde," he said pleasantly. "It is a fine morning."

Startled by his appearance, Lysabel turned to him with both surprise and pleasure on her face. "Good morn to you, Trenton," she said. "You are up very early."

He smiled at her words, drinking in the sight of her and feeling his heart flutter, just a little. "I have never known anything else," he said. "There are times that I do not sleep at all and simply greet the morning as the night fades away. In fact, your youngest daughter is up early, too. She was very helpful to me this morning as I tended my horse."

Lysabel's attention moved between Brencis and Trenton. "I see," she said, although she didn't sound particularly pleased. Finally, she sighed. "Cissy is consumed by horses. She rises early nearly every morning to help with the feedings. I have told her that it is an unseemly task for a young girl, but she does not wish to listen."

Trenton's gaze moved to the little girl, still in the grip of her older sister. "There is nothing wrong with loving horses," he said. "I love them myself and, in fact, they seem to love her. My warhorse took her treat quite calmly, which means he understands she loves him. Horses know these things."

As Lysabel looked doubtful, Brencis' face lit up. "They do?" she said. "Does he really know I love him? I do, you know."

Trenton's grin broadened. "Of course he knows," he said. "But I will still tell you not to go near him unless I am around. He is not a pet, my lady. You must be careful around him."

Brencis nodded eagerly, but he could see that she probably didn't mean it. As he tried to think of a way to convince her again to never go near the animal without him around, Lysabel gestured towards the manse.

"Take her inside, Cinny," she said. "Wash her face and hands."

Cynethryn didn't move right away; she glanced at Trenton first. "Aren't you coming, Mama?"

Lysabel nodded. "Of course I am," she said. "Go, now. I will come in a moment."

Now, Cynethryn's gaze moved to Trenton full-on, her blue eyes cold and appraising. Trenton simply looked back at the child, neutrally, until she finally turned away and pulled her younger sister with her. The adults watched the pair walk away before Lysabel turned to Trenton.

"I am sorry if Cissy was a nuisance this morning," she said. "She loves horses so that I fear she will make a nuisance of herself in any case."

Trenton wasn't thinking so much about Brencis as he was about Cynethryn and the threatening way she'd been looking at him. "She did not make a nuisance of herself," he said. Then, he scratched his neck in a reluctant gesture. "But she did feed my warhorse pears whilst I was not around, and that horse is violent. He has been known to stomp men to death, so you must stress to her not to go near the horse for her own safety."

Lysabel's eyes widened. "God's Bones," she breathed. "Of course I will tell her. Thank you for warning me."

He simply nodded, his gaze moving over her in the early morning light. He still couldn't believe that in all the years he'd known the woman, he'd never realized how beautiful she was.

He'd been a fool.

"No harm done," he said, pretending to turn back for the stable when what he was really doing was working up the courage to continue the conversation while not seeming too eager about it. "In truth, Brencis reminded me of something. There is a village to the north. I passed through it on my way here."

Lysabel nodded. "Ilchester."

"Ilchester," he repeated. "I was planning on visiting the village and I wondered if you and your daughters would like to come along."

Lysabel smiled. "That would be lovely," she said. "Why do you need to visit the village? Mayhap, I can direct you to the proper merchant."

"I am not quite sure yet."

It was a cryptic answer, but a truthful one. He had no idea; he simply wanted to do something with Lysabel, and he didn't want to leave her daughters behind, so he thought a trip into the village would give them a chance to spend time together. Perhaps the older one might look less like she wanted to slit his throat if she came to know him. But Lysabel didn't have to know that; he watched as she laughed softly at his vague reply.

"In that case, how can I refuse?" she said. Then, she sobered somewhat. "In fact, I was hoping to ask a favor of you today, Trenton."

"Anything. What is it?"

Now it was her turn to appear reluctant. "In speaking of my father last night, it occurred to me that I have not seen him in some time," she said. "I have a great urge to visit my parents and I was wondering – if you do not have other plans to attend to – if you could escort us to Wellesbourne Castle for a visit."

He dipped his head gallantly. "It would be my pleasure, Lady de Wilde," he said. "When would you like to go?"

"Is tomorrow too soon?"

He shook his head. "It is not," he said. "But I should like to form a proper escort. Who is your man in charge of the soldiers at Stretford?"

"His name is Markus de Aston," she said. "From the Oakhampton de Astons. He has served my husband for several years and, to be truthful, he has no great love for Benoit. However, as I told you, Markus only knows that Benoit has left and nothing more."

Trenton took that into consideration. "And I will make sure that is all he knows," he said. "It might be good if you could introduce me to the man and tell him what we are planning so he does not have to take orders from a complete stranger."

Lysabel agreed. "He surely saw you last night in the feasting hall, as he was present," she said. "But I will make sure he knows that he is expected to take orders from you."

With that, she smiled at Trenton and turned to leave the stable yard. He was on her heels, following her, looking forward to the trip to Wellesbourne perhaps more than he should have. It would take at least two or three days to reach Wellesbourne Castle.

Two or three days of being with Lysabel.

He could think of nothing else he'd rather do.

CHAPTER FIVE

Sir Markus de Aston was a high caliber knight, a support for the Sheriff of Ilchester's position, who had come through Matthew Wellesbourne, Earl of Hereford, by way of the de Nerra family of Erith Castle in Cumbria. From the Somersetshire de Aston family, Markus was tall, muscular, with reddish-blond hair, and rather good-looking, and he had come to Stretford Castle because Wellesbourne had enough knights and Matthew thought he was doing a good turn by sending such an excellent knight to serve his son-in-law.

But he'd sent Markus into a hellish situation, something the young knight had been forced to endure for a few years. But the main issue with Markus was that, having come from Wellesbourne, he was somewhat protective and partial to Lysabel, as Matthew's daughter. Watching her suffer with a bastard of a husband when there was nothing he could do about it had turned him into a stiff, rather embittered man.

As a man of emotion, the only way to save himself was to harden his natural tendencies. And now, with Trenton's presence, he didn't seem any less hard. In fact, the mere suggestion that he go against what he believed Benoit would want hardened him even further.

He knew what his liege was capable of.

Lysabel had introduced the young knight to Trenton and explained that he would be forming an escort to take her and her daughters to Wellesbourne Castle. That suggestion alone was going against anything Benoit would agree to, and Markus naturally balked.

"We cannot go," he said flatly. "Lord Benoit will return at any time and he would be displeased to see that his family had gone to Wellesbourne without his permission. I am sorry, but you cannot go, Lady de Wilde."

In truth, Lysabel had expected a refusal, but not so quickly or so firmly. They had gathered to discuss the request in the same solar where Trenton and Lysabel had their lovely conversation the night before, a solar where all of the riches of the de Wilde coffers were on display. Trenton was standing by the door as Lysabel and Markus stood over near the big table, cluttered with Benoit's things. It was a stark reminder of the lie that Trenton and Lysabel were perpetuating, leaving things as if the man would be returning any day. Therefore, it was no wonder that Markus rejected the suggestion of traveling to Wellesbourne Castle.

It was not what the lord would want.

Hearing Markus' staunch denial, Lysabel knew she had to tread carefully. Markus was very much a man who carried out his lord's wishes, whether or not he agreed with him. But Lysabel also knew that there had been many a time when Markus hadn't agreed with Benoit, and it was to the man who at times had showed consideration for other factors that she aimed her plea.

"Markus," she said patiently. "I realize you are only doing what you believe is in my best interest, but you must look at it from my perspective. I've not seen my parents in a very long time and Wellesbourne Castles is only a two-day ride from here. While I am waiting for my husband to return, I would like to visit my parents, whom I love very much. They have not seen their granddaughters in almost a year. Would you deny my father his joy in seeing his granddaughters?"

Markus faced her, his manner firm but bordering on angry. "My lady, if Lord Benoit returns home and you are not here, it will not go well for either of us," he said. He eyed Trenton a moment before lowering his voice. "Must I make this plain in front of a stranger?"

Lysabel didn't like that Trenton was being called a stranger. "He is not a stranger," she said. "I told you who he was. I have known him my entire life. You may speak freely in front of him."

Markus' gaze settled on the woman. It was clear that he was mulling over her answer. All he knew was that an unfamiliar knight had arrived the previous evening and, today, he was being told this man would be escorting Lord Benoit's wife and children to Wellesbourne. Nay, he didn't like that at all.

"My lady, forgive me, but although you may know him, I do not," he said, trying to be patient. "It is my responsibility to tend to the welfare of you and your children while Lord Benoit is away. I cannot, in good conscience, turn your safety over to a knight I do not know. I am sorry if you do not understand that."

Lysabel was not only becoming embarrassed, she was becoming angry. "*My* safety," she snorted quietly. "You only care for it when my husband is not here. When he is here, you look the other way like everyone else. Your words are empty to me, Markus, so pretend not as if my safety is truly your concern. Your only concern is Benoit's reaction if he was to return and discover I was gone."

Markus straightened up, eyeing the woman whose well-aimed tongue had hit him where it hurt – his integrity. It was the very thing he'd wrestled with since the day he assumed his post at Stretford and realized very quickly that he served a man who beat his wife, among other infractions. And it wasn't an occasional thing; it was frequent, resulting in a woman who was broken and bruised most of the time. When he wasn't beating her, he was out whoring, or robbing from his vassals, or any number of unsavory things.

Nay, Markus didn't any of it, but he turned a deaf ear to it because there was nothing he could do. Benoit de Wilde was his liege and his duty was to serve the man. In that respect, he supposed his words to the lady were, indeed, hollow. Hollow in so many things.

But he had no choice.

"Mayhap that is true, my lady," he said. "If your husband were to discover I let you go to Wellesbourne Castle, then there would be hell to pay for the both of us."

Lysabel looked at him a moment before turning to Trenton. Standing back in the shadows of the room, he was simply listening to everything going on very carefully. She was looking for some manner of direction in his expression but he gave her none. Frustrated, she was about to do what she swore to him that she wouldn't do – she wanted Markus' cooperation but he wasn't going to give it to her unless he knew the truth, and perhaps not even then.

But she had to try.

"I want you to listen to me, Markus, and listen carefully," she said. "And I want your oath as a knight that what I tell you will never leave your lips. Will you do this?"

He hesitated a moment. "Aye, my lady."

"Then swear it."

"I swear upon my oath that I shall not repeat what you tell me."

"And I will swear to you that what I tell you is the truth. I will make this vow before God."

"As you say, my lady."

With a heavy sigh, she looked at Trenton again, who by now had an expression on his face that suggested concern. He had an idea of what she was going to say, but he didn't stop her; perhaps he, too, understood that such an illusion couldn't be kept from those in command. It was clear that Markus' loyalties were with Benoit regardless of how he personally felt about the man. That being the case, he would continue to be loyal to him and Lysabel would continue to be a prisoner with the ghost of Benoit de Wilde hanging over her, in death as he did in life. As long as Markus believed Benoit would return, he would continue to carry out his duties as his lord would want him to.

Therefore, Trenton kept silent as Lysabel continued.

"The last night that Benoit was seen here at Stretford was a terrible night," she said quietly. "Do you remember that night, Markus? You must be honest."

It was clear from Markus' expression that he did, indeed, remember that evening. It was the first time he lowered his gaze.

"Aye, my lady."

"You heard me screaming."

Markus sighed faintly. "Aye, my lady."

"But you did nothing to help me." When Markus simply kept his gaze averted, unable to look at her, Lysabel continued. "I know you could not act against Benoit, Markus. I understand that. If anyone was to help me, it had to *be* me. Twelve years of beatings was too much for me to take. Markus, that night was the last night Benoit beat me or ever shall beat me. He is dead."

Markus' head shot up, his eyes widening. "Dead?" he hissed. "What? *How?*"

Lysabel was quiet for a moment. It was her turn to look away, knowing what she was about to say to the dedicated knight. But she felt strongly that she had to.

It had to be this way.

"The shattered window," she murmured. "Do you remember it?"

He nodded, looking at her with extreme shock. "Aye, my lady."

"Benoit was beating me with his fists and... and the window became broken," she said, knowing she was about to lie about the whole situation because she didn't want Markus to know that the man standing a few feet away had killed his liege. It was better this way. "I killed Benoit with the broken glass. I wrapped him in a cloak so he would not bleed everywhere, stuffed him into the wardrobe, and told you that he had left and I did not know where he had gone. I killed him because if I did not, I knew he was going to kill me."

Markus had gone from extreme shock to extreme disbelief. "You... *you* killed him, my lady?"

"Aye. And I must go to Wellesbourne Castle to discuss this with my father. I need his counsel."

Markus' mouth was hanging open and when he realized that, he shut it quickly. He tore his gaze from Lysabel, looking to Trenton, who was still standing near the door like a massive, silent sentinel. He hadn't moved a muscle. His gaze moved back to Lysabel.

"Clearly, your friend de Russe knows of this," he said, struggling with the news. "You told him?"

"I removed the body," Trenton said. He could no longer remain silent and when both Lysabel and Markus looked at him, he stepped from the shadows. "I removed it and disposed of it. No one will ever find it."

That part was the truth, but Markus was still wrought with disbelief and the longer he looked at Trenton, the more suspicious he became.

"*How* did you know about it?" he demanded. "You only arrived yesterday. This cannot be a coincidence."

The man was smarter than Trenton had given him credit for, but he knew Lysabel had lied to Markus for a reason. He understood. Before he found himself defending himself against a very angry Markus, however, he sought to ease the man. If he couldn't ease him, then Markus de Aston could very well find himself gone the same way Benoit had gone. Trenton wasn't beyond disposing of the man simply to keep a secret safe, but more than that, he had to protect Lysabel in this situation.

Things were about to get nasty.

"It is, I assure you," he said, half-truth, half-lie. "I came to Stretford to visit Lady Lysabel, whom I have known since she was born. She has told me what her husband did to her and it was my pleasure to dispose of his body. Your hands may be tied to help the lady because you serve her husband, but I know no such restraints. The man deserved to die for what he has done to the lady and if you do not believe so, then I invite you to tell me to my face."

It was as challenge, thrown down between two fairly seasoned knights, only Markus had no idea what Trenton did for a living. So in this instance, it was more like a lion challenging a guard dog. The dog had teeth, and knew how to use them, but the lion had claws that would gut the dog before he even realized what had happened.

The suspicion in the room turned into something appraising and unfriendly.

But Markus wasn't stupid and he wasn't reckless. He knew the big knight was taller and heavier than he was, and from the look of the man, suspected he was more than deadly. He wasn't going to willingly enter into a confrontation with him, even if had been challenged, mostly because he happened to agree with him. But he was still stunned by the entire situation and his gaze returned to Lysabel.

"Tell me that this is not a plot of some kind with de Russe," he said seriously. "Tell me this wasn't something that was planned."

Lysabel shook her head. "I swear to you that this is not a plot of any kind. What happened with Benoit... it was nothing that I had planned. It simply happened."

"And you swear to me upon your children's lives that Benoit de Wilde is dead?"

"I swear to you with all that and more. He is dead."

With that, all the air seemed to leave Markus as he hissed, exhaling until there was nothing left. He turned away from Lysabel to compose himself, struggling with the news he'd been given.

"My God," he breathed. "He is truly dead?"

Lysabel watched him closely. "He is," she said. "Thank God, he is. And now I must go to my father and ask him what I should do. That is why I must go to Wellesbourne Castle, Markus. I want you to remain here and ensure that Stretford Castle is run smoothly and normally, and that everyone believes Benoit will return at some point. Until my father tells me what to do, it must be that way. Do you understand?"

Markus ended up over by the windows that overlooked part of the bailey beyond. After a moment, he took a deep breath and turned to her.

"I want to go with you to Wellesbourne," he said. "Your father gifted me to Benoit, if you recall. I must know what he wishes for me to do now… now that Benoit will not return. Will you allow me to go with you, my lady?"

Lysabel nodded. "I will," she said, "providing that you take your orders from Trenton. Not only is he the son and heir to the Duke of Warminster, but he is an earl by title. He is the Earl of Westbury, so by rank alone, you must take orders from him, Markus. Is that clear?"

Markus' gaze moved in Trenton's direction. "De Russe," he muttered as if suddenly recognizing the name. "Warminster. I do not know why I have not made the connection before now. Gaston de Russe is your father?"

"He is."

"Then I will willingly follow your command, my lord."

Trenton simply nodded, pleased to see that he wasn't about to have a fight on his hands with Benoit's irate knight. In fact, the man seemed rather dazed by the news and now was rather submissive with everything explained to him. He recalled Lysabel telling him that Markus had no great love for Benoit, and that was clear in the man's manner. Serving the man had only been a duty. With that understanding, Trenton was eager to move forward with their intentions. That's what this meeting was about, after all.

"Then prepare an escort of men for Wellesbourne Castle," Trenton told him. "I will trust you to select the best thirty men you have. The lady wishes to leave on the morrow, so make haste to arm and supply the escort. We will depart at dawn."

Markus nodded sharply and made his way to the door, quitting the chamber without another word as he went about his duties. It seemed as if, perhaps, he needed to be alone to think of what he'd been told, or at least that was the sense that Trenton got. He went to shut the door behind the man, turning his attention to Lysabel when they were finally alone in the chamber.

"You only told him part of the truth," he said quietly. "Do you not trust him to know all of it?"

Lysabel looked at him. "I do not want him to know your role in the situation," she said. "Markus is trustworthy, but I can see he is already wary of you. And you heard him – he wanted to know if it was some kind of plot between us. I will tell him the truth at some point, but not now. I... I do not want him looking at you as a killer, Trenton."

He regarded her carefully. "But I am," he muttered. "Do you not know what I have been doing all of these years for the king, Lysabel? When I came for Benoit, that was not the first time I'd carried out orders such as that. It is what I do for Henry – if he has enemies, it is my duty to eliminate them. Whatever the king wishes, I carry it out. Shall I go on?"

She turned away. "Nay," she said firmly. "And I do not care what you do for Henry. All I know is that you saved me, and I loathe that anyone would look at the situation any differently."

He smiled at the thought. "So you did it so spare my reputation?" he asked. "It is noble of you, but unnecessary. My reputation is what it is. One more death will not break me."

Lysabel shrugged. "To me, you will always have my utmost gratitude and respect. And I do not want anyone to think otherwise of you."

Trenton thought that was most flattering, in truth. She wanted to protect what others thought of him, and that was rather endearing of her.

"I've never had a lady come to my defense before," he said. "Stop it or you will swell my head. Is it possible you find me attractive now and not my brother?"

It was a leading tease and he had no idea why he said it, only that he wanted to see her reaction. Was he looking for some kind of encouragement? Some sign that he was making her feel warm and giddy, just as she was making him feel the same? It was reckless, and he knew it, but he truthfully didn't care.

Idiot!

But Lysabel fought off a grin. "I am *not* coming to your defense," she said. "And I told you that your brother is the only one who has ever had my attention."

"You do not like me better than Dane, not even a little?"

She rolled her eyes and turned away from him, but she was smiling now. "Stop pestering me, Trenton de Russe," she said. "I have work to do."

He saw her grinning as she left the chamber and he watched her go, standing in the doorway as she headed down the corridor to the mural stairs that led to the upper floors. But she paused before she took that first step, throwing him a look that was both humorous and, he thought, rather flirtatious. Then, she stuck her tongue out at him and bolted up the stairs, leaving him laughing softly.

And I find you most attractive, sweet Lysabel, against my better judgement...

CHAPTER SIX

BRENCIS WASN'T A happy traveler.

Riding in the wagon hurt her belly, and her mother wouldn't let her walk with the soldiers, so she was very upset about the entire situation. Trenton could hear her weeping, complaining to her mother, and he could hear Lysabel's soft, gentle tone, trying to calm her child. But Brencis wouldn't be soothed. They were barely a day out of Stretford, and already, it was a long journey.

As Trenton and Dewi plodded along, Trenton couldn't help but notice that his horse seemed distracted. Usually, the big black warhorse was the first one on an escort, refusing to let any other horse get in front of him, but over the past few hours, the horse seemed to want to slow down, or turn around even, and Trenton couldn't figure out why the horse was behaving in such a way. Twice, he'd had to slap the horse on his big neck to force him to stop swinging his head around, as if he were trying to turn about. Dewi could be a quirky creature even in the best of times, but this was something beyond what he normally did.

As Trenton tried to figure out his fickle beast, Markus rode off to his right astride a leggy gray stallion. The knight had formed the escort party perfectly and since their discussion in the solar, he'd been completely cooperative. Obedient to a fault, even. Trenton wasn't sure he trusted the man, but he didn't make his mistrust obvious. He simply kept an eye on him. If he had any questions or commands, they were immediately relayed to Markus, who ensured they were carried out. His efficiency was beyond question.

Trenton had quickly discovered that Markus was the only knight Benoit had. The rest of the men were simply soldiers. There were several sergeants, men who seemed rather rough around the edges, and then the rank and file soldiers, and Trenton had no idea where Benoit obtained those men. From what Trenton had seen, they were barely one level above animals themselves, uneducated and unrefined men, but they did what Markus ordered them to do and that was all Trenton cared about.

Still, he couldn't help but think that a man was often defined by the men who served him, and with the exception of Markus, Benoit's soldiers were most definitely a reflection of their ugly, brutal master.

And this is what Lysabel had been exposed to all of these years.

He'd only spoken briefly to her last night during the feast, as she'd only stopped by to supervise the meal in the midst of her packing. And in the darkness of the early morning, he'd loaded her and her daughters into a wagon because he thought that would be easier for them to ride in, and they set out on the road north.

The wagon bed was covered with straw and then a layer of blankets for comfort, and there were pillows to ease their ride as well, so it wasn't completely uncomfortable, but Brencis was having a difficult time with it. It was into the afternoon now and Trenton could still hear her grumbling and, on occasion, wailing. Finally, he decided to go back and have a look for himself.

Maybe he could help soothe the savage beastie.

Brencis was miserable and didn't care who knew it. When Trenton approached the wagon as it lurched along the road and undoubtedly hit every hole in its path, he could see that Cynethryn was hanging over the side of the wagon, appearing utterly bored and unhappy, while Brencis sat across her mother's lap as Lysabel tried to soothe her. As soon as she saw Trenton approach, however, she seemed to come alive. As he came near the wagon, she practically launched herself from her mother's lap and rushed to the side of the wagon.

"Can I ride with you?" she begged. "I do not want to ride in the wagon any longer! It makes my belly hurt!"

She was nearly falling out of the wagon in her haste, so he reined Dewi next to the moving wagon, trying to keep her from spilling out and hurting herself. Lysabel was also grabbing at her, getting a good grip on her skirt, but Brencis didn't seem to care. She was far more interested in Dewi as the big horse came close. As her mother and Trenton tried to keep her from falling, she reached out with both arms to pet Dewi on his shiny black neck.

"Beautiful Dewi," she crooned. "You are my friend. I have missed you!"

Dewi was muzzled so there was no chance of him snapping at the child, but he twisted his big neck so that his muzzle was rubbing up against her. In fact, he seemed very interested in her, and her attention, and it began to occur to Trenton that perhaps the reason why his horse had been so distracted was because his treat-giver had been wailing and upset. Dewi was a smart animal and had quite a memory. Even so, Trenton was somewhat surprised to realize that Dewi was about as interested in Brencis as Brencis was in Dewi.

"Cissy," Lysabel tugged on her daughter's skirt. "Sit down. You may not ride with Sir Trenton."

But Brencis wasn't going to give up. She tried to put her arms around Dewi's neck even though they wouldn't go even half the way around.

"I love him," she crooned, kissing the horse's neck and laying her cheek on his soft fur. "He loves me, too. Can I please ride with you, Sir Trenton? *Please?*"

Trenton didn't think it was a very good idea, considering how violent and sometimes skittish the horse could be. But he was coming to feel some sympathy for the little girl who was so in love with horses.

"He is not a riding horse, my lady," he said. "He is bred for battle, and can be difficult at times. I would hate for you to be hurt."

Brencis was stroking the horse between the eyes, running her fingers through the mane between his ears.

"He will not hurt me," she said confidently. "He wants me to ride with you."

Trenton cocked an eyebrow. "Is that so?"

"It is."

"How do you know?"

She looked at him seriously. "He has told me so."

Trenton simply nodded his head, glancing at Lysabel, who was looking rather apologetic. "I am sorry she has been such a nuisance," she said. "She has not traveled well this entire trip. Praise God it will not be a long one."

Trenton fought off a grin. "The village of Cirencester is up ahead," he said. "I was thinking that we should find you and your daughters lodging for the night. I believe Lady Brencis could use the rest after a rough first day."

Lysabel nodded in complete agreement. "That would be appreciated," she said. "I think all three of us can use the rest. Although I love my daughter dearly, I am close to strangling her simply to quiet her."

As Brencis looked at her mother and frowned, Trenton's grin broke through. "Then I shall send men ahead to seek proper lodging," he said. "Have no fear, Lady de Wilde. You shall have peace this night."

With that, he tried to spur Dewi forward, but the horse was far too interested in Brencis, who was still petting and hugging him. In fact, Lysabel had to pull her daughter away from the warhorse so Trenton could move him forward, and even then, Dewi made his unhappiness known. Suspecting the horse simply wanted more pears from the hands of a besotted little girl gave him limited patience with the beast, and he both spurred him forward and smacked him on the rump when he didn't want to obey. Trenton was starting to think he had two disobedient children on his hands – the horse *and* Brencis.

Unhappy Dewi, and unhappy Trenton, sent Markus and another

soldier on ahead to Cirencester to scout lodgings for the women as Trenton rode the rest of the way into the village astride a warhorse that was getting quite worked up about having no pears. He tossed his head and foam from his lips splattered from his muzzle. Overhead, clouds were starting to roll in and Trenton was coming to think that there would be summer rain soon, so his decision to find shelter sooner rather than later was a sound one.

Cirencester was a dirty little village that was quite overpopulated. Arriving on the outskirts, Trenton could see that poverty was fairly rife. It was August, so it was a warm month, and half-naked children ran in the gutters, chasing each other, as dogs barked alongside, while the stench from the gutters themselves filled the air to the point of making Trenton's eyes water.

It smelled like a cesspool.

Heading deeper into town, Trenton kept an eye out for Markus, hoping the man had found something that was at least tolerable. Given the state of the village, he wasn't at all sure that would happen. Amongst the wattle and daub huts, some of them held together by nothing more than twigs and mud, Trenton eventually spied a fairly large livery and thought it might be a good place for the escort to bed down for the night, providing it was close enough to the lodging for the ladies.

Trenton turned to the nearest soldier and pointed off towards the livery, and the man understood the command and began to pass the word back through the troops. Bedding down in a livery wasn't an unusual thing for groups of men, because taverns were expensive and not designed to accommodate masses of men, so Trenton headed for the livery to pay the livery master a few coins for the privilege. The men were beginning to move into the livery yard when he caught sight of Markus, heading back in his direction.

"Well?" Trenton reined his horse to a halt. "What have you discovered?"

Markus flipped up his three-point visor, of the latest style. "There are a few taverns towards the northern end of town," he said. "A brief perusal told me that none of them were fit for Lady de Wilde, if you get my meaning, but there is one place, a smaller place off the main road, called The Greene and The Glory that does not seem to be overflowing with whores."

Trenton cocked an eyebrow. "I suppose we have little choice," he said, glancing up at the sky as dark clouds gathered. "Did you secure a room?"

"I secured three. I did not know how many you wanted."

Trenton nodded. "Wise," he said. "I shall take a room and the ladies can take another. Will you take the third or will you sleep with the men?"

Markus' gaze drifted over to the group now beginning to filter into the livery yard. "That crew?" He shook his head. "Even if there was not a third room, I would not sleep with them."

Trenton looked at them. "But they are your men."

Slowly, Marcus shook his head. "Make no mistake, my lord," he said, lowering his voice. "They are de Wilde's men. They think like him and they behave like him. It is like having an army of misfits."

Trenton had suspected much the same thing, but hearing de Aston's opinion only confirmed his observations. "As long as they obey your commands, I suppose an army of misfits is better than no army at all," he said. "Take Lady de Wilde and her daughters to the tavern. I will be along shortly."

Markus nodded sharply and headed towards the wagon, which was just rolling by at this point. He spoke to the two men driving the team, pointing down the road to the northern end of the town. Just as the wagon began to pick up speed, Trenton could hear someone calling his name.

"Sir Trenton!" It was Brencis. "Can I come with you to the stables, please? Sir Trenton!"

It would have been very easy not to hear her plea, but Trenton couldn't seem to ignore the child. She was sweet, and eager, and her all-consuming love for horses was somehow growing on him. He knew she probably wanted to see the other horses in the stable and he honestly couldn't think of a reason to deny her. She wouldn't be much trouble, he didn't think, as he settled Dewi into a stall. He could handle one little girl. With a sigh, perhaps one of resignation, he reined Dewi over towards the wagon.

When Markus saw him coming, he uttered commands to the men driving the team, and the wagon lurched to a halt. Brencis was standing on the edge, waving Trenton over, and he simply reined Dewi next to the wagon bed and scooped her up with one enormous arm. His focus was on Lysabel.

"I will see you at the tavern," he told her. "Brencis and I have a horse to settle."

Words of denial were on Lysabel's lips, but she couldn't bring herself to utter them. Brencis was giddy with delight and Trenton didn't seem too annoyed at her request, so she simply smiled and nodded her head, knowing that any such refusals at this point would only see a hysterical daughter. As the wagon proceeded forward once again, Lysabel's last glimpse of Trenton and Brencis was as the man settled the little girl across his lap and held tightly to her.

But Brencis wasn't going anywhere. She was exactly where she wanted to be and nearly delirious with delight as she was permitted to ride in front of Trenton astride his big warhorse. She held tight to the arm that was around her, holding her steady as they entered the livery yard where the men were gathering. A few words from Trenton had the men moving over to the north side of the yard and away from the corral with horses in it, and he proceeded to enter the livery itself, a great stone structure with a heavily-thatched roof.

The livery inside was far less busy than outside. In fact, there were only a few animals in the cool, quiet interior and as Trenton entered, a round man in well-mended clothing approached him.

"Lodgings for your horse tonight, my lord?" he asked.

Trenton nodded. "My horse and a few others," he said, gesturing towards the gang of men outside the livery. "Those are my men and they may need to seek a roof over their heads if the rains come, so I will pay you for the privilege. Most of the men are on foot but there are a few mounted soldiers, and we will need to feed those animals as well."

The livery man nodded, eyeing Dewi, whose head was nearly as long as the man's body. "He's a big one, my lord," he commented. "Since he's muzzled, I'll assume he bites?"

"Quite happily."

"Will you unmuzzle him so I can feed him?"

Trenton lifted Brencis up and handed her over to the livery man, who quickly took the child and set her to her feet. "Aye," Trenton replied as he dismounted. "As long as you feed him, he shouldn't snap at you, but be advised that he has a foul temper at times. Brush him and water him, too."

The livery man simply nodded. "I've been in business for thirty years," he said. "I've seen plenty of foul beasts come through here."

Trenton smiled, but it was without humor. "I can only imagine how true that is," he said, removing a glove so he could extract coins from his coin purse. He pulled out several, placing them in the man's palm. "Just be cautious around my horse and you should survive intact."

The man looked at the coins in his hand; it was a good deal of money. "Thank you, my lord," he said sincerely. "Put your horse over here."

He was indicating a particularly warm and cozy corner with a small window for ventilation. As Trenton led Dewi over to the corner that smelled heavily of hay, the livery man followed along, unstrapping the enormous saddle and pulling it free of the horse. It ended up slung over the side of the stall as Trenton pulled his horse into the warm, dry area and removed his bridle, tying a rope into the halter he wore to secure him. He glanced around, looking for Brencis, who seemed to have strangely disappeared. So once the rope was secure and the livery man was pouring water into the horse's bucket, he left the stall to hunt down the child.

It didn't take him long to find her.

She was standing in a stall next to the entrance with a small white pony, hugging the animal and whispering to it. Trenton could hear her as he came up, and she was telling the pony much of the same things she had said to Dewi, only the pony was far more docile. As he came to the edge of the stall, a smile on his lips, she petted the pony's face and scratched his velvety nose, kissing the animal between the eyes.

"I see you've found a new best friend," Trenton said, leaning against the post of the stall. "Dewi will think he has been jilted."

Brencis looked at him, beaming. "I saw her when we came into the stable," she said. "She looks so tiny and alone here. Where is her mummy?"

Trenton peered at the pony, noting the whiskers and the faint white dusting of hair around the muzzle. "This is not a young horse," he said. "She is older. See the white whiskers?"

Brencis looked at what he was pointing to. "Oh," she said simply. "She *looks* young."

"She is small."

"I love her very much."

"I am sure she appreciates that."

Brencis continued to hug and pet the pony, who was really very tolerant of the little girl fawning all over her. Trenton wondered how he was going to pull her away from the little thing without causing a battle.

"We should find your mother now," he said. "You can come with me in the morning to visit the pony again when I come to collect Dewi."

Brencis' face fell but she didn't argue. She simply looked at the pony with that terrible longing as one does when leaving something one very badly wants. In fact, Trenton had to look away because, more and more, he was becoming sympathetic to Brencis and her undying love of horses. It was really very sweet to witness, such innocent joy in something so simple. But it was more than that – this child, who had grown up with such a cruel father, still found the ability to love. As he stood there, waiting for her to separate herself from her instant best friend, the livery man came up beside him.

"I see she's found Snowdrop," he said.

Both Trenton and Brencis looked at the man. "Snowdrop?" Brencis said. "What's that?"

The livery man pointed at the little white pony. "It's her name," he said. "Snowdrop because of the white snowdrop flower."

Brencis looked to the little pony in delight, resuming her hugging and petting. Trenton scratched his neck in a reluctant gesture. "I am not entirely certain we are going to be able to leave," he muttered to the livery man. "My lady seems to be quite fond of Snowdrop."

The livery man watched as the little girl petted Snowdrop and the pony tried to nibble on her. "A man gave me the pony in payment for shoeing his palfrey," he said. "I've no real use for her. She eats my food and grows fat. Why not buy her for your daughter? I will give you an excellent price."

If Trenton could have throttled the man for saying such a thing in front of Brencis, he would have. The little girl's eyes lit up and she hugged the pony around the neck so hard that it startled the little beast.

"I will take the best care of her!" she said, tears already streaming down her face. "I want her and she has no one to love her. She will love me and I will love her. *Please...* may I have her?"

Trenton exhaled, long and slow, sensing a losing battle ahead. He knew what his answer was going to be; his only concern was in telling Lysabel that he'd purchased a pony for Brencis. He knew he shouldn't, and he further knew that she would probably become angry with him, but he thought that it was time to put poor Brencis out of her misery when it came to her love for horses. Clearly, she lived and breathed them, and this little pony needed an owner. A six-year-old owner who would love her more than anything on earth.

Besides... he was afraid to deny her. As a man who held absolutely no fear, in any arena, the fear of tears from a lonely little girl had him surrendering.

He was a fool.

Stepping into the stall, Trenton crouched in front of the weeping girl and the fat, white pony, watching for a moment as Brencis snuggled with the pony "We have a long trip ahead of us," he said. "It will be a very long trip for a pony with such little legs."

He was giving a last-ditch effort to reason with her, but Brencis was beyond reason. She only knew what she wanted.

"She is strong, I know it," she insisted, wiping the tears on her cheeks. "I will ride her the whole way. She will not be tired at all because I will be very gentle. I will not make her tired."

She sounded so very sincere and Trenton could see that nothing short of an act of God could discourage her. So much for trying to reason with her.

"Half a crown and the pony is yours," the livery man said, throwing another nail in the coffin of Trenton's decision. "I'll even throw in a bridle and a saddle for the little miss. They came with the pony."

Trenton was close to throttling the man again, who was trying hard to seal the deal, but the truth was that the decision was already made. Standing up, he sighed heavily.

"Do you have another pony?" he asked. "There are two girls. I cannot purchase a pony for one and not the other."

The livery man nodded quickly and scurried away. Trenton returned his attention to Brencis as the little girl was now petting the back of the pony, running her fingers through the white hair. He could see how delirious she was. That kind of happiness was foreign to him, so very happy that one could nearly burst with it. Trenton couldn't even remember when he'd been that happy, or *if* he'd ever been that happy, and he was wildly envious about it. Perhaps in making Brencis so happy, he was living vicariously through her.

Was there truly such happiness in all the world?

As he continued to watch Brencis and her new pony, the livery man appeared again, leading another pony, a fat brown animal that was dark all over except for her flaxen-colored mane and tail. When Trenton turned to look at the animal, the livery man had the pony walk a circle.

"This little lass belongs to my own daughter, but she doesn't ride her any longer," he said. "She's become too old for her, I fear, so Honey has no one to love her. Will your other little girl love her?"

Trenton didn't even know how to answer that, considering he'd be giving the pony to Cynethryn, who hadn't shown him much warmth since she'd known him. He simply shrugged and dug into his coin purse again, pulling out a couple of coins and handing them over to the livery man.

"Feed them and brush them, and when we leave in the morning, we shall take them both," he said. "Include the bridles and blankets and anything else that comes with them."

The livery man was thrilled, having offloaded two useless ponies for a tidy sum. As he took Honey back to her stall, Trenton turned to Brencis, who was now standing at the rear of the pony and trying to braid her tail.

"Well?" he said to her. "Did you hear all of that?"

Brencis looked up from the tail. "What?"

"You are now the proud owner of Snowdrop."

Brencis blinked. "Me?"

"You."

"She... she is mine?"

"She is yours."

Brencis stared at him a moment before dropping the tail and running to him, throwing her arms around him and squeezing him as tightly as she could. He was so tall, and she was so short, that she ended up embracing his upper thighs, but the message was clear.

"Thank you," she murmured as she hugged him. "Thank you for my pony. I love you very much."

With that, she rushed back to the white pony and hugged the horse's neck again, squeezing so much that the animal was once again startled. It was clear the pony wasn't used to all of the attention, but that was going to soon change.

Trenton was sure of it.

Little Brencis had thanked him like no one else ever had. *I love you very much.* He was certain she'd said it only because he'd given her the pony, but he was equally certain she meant every word and that fascinated him. Were there really people in the world who loved so freely and showed emotion so freely? He was seeing a good deal through the eyes of Brencis, a side of the world he'd never really seen before. His world was death and espionage, and that was something he'd learned to guard himself against. But this... this was something he'd never experienced before.

He thought he could get used to it.

"Now that you know she is yours, you will bid her a good eve," he said. "We must return to your mother and tell her what we have done."

Brencis looked at him, rather fearfully. "You will not let her give my pony back, will you?"

"Nay. It is my gift to you."

She seemed relieved. "And my father? You will not let him take it away?"

He could hear the fear in her voice and he felt a stab of rage that was unexpected. He could hardly imagine this lovely, sensitive child subjected to Benoit's horrific behavior. Shaking his head, he held out a hand to her.

"Nay, lass," he said quietly. "I will not let him take it away. Come along, now. We must go."

With the promise that the pony was hers – truly hers – Brencis separated herself from her new pet somewhat easily. Her gaze still on the white pony, she took Trenton's hand and let him take her from the stable, but she wouldn't take her eyes off the pony until she could no longer see it. Outside the livery, sunset was beginning to fall and the dark clouds overhead had obliterated the sky, and the smell of rain was in the air.

With Brencis in hand, Trenton hurriedly made his way down the road until he came to a sign that said The Greene and The Glory. A small, two-storied building was attached to it and he pushed his way inside, coming into a small common room that was crowded with people, including Lysabel, Cynethryn, and Markus.

It was warm and fragrant in the tavern, with contrasting smells of baking bread and spilled ale, and as Trenton carefully planned out what to tell Lysabel, Brencis had no such restraint. She ran to her mother, threw herself into the woman's arms, and announced that she now had a pony named Snowdrop.

With the secret out, Trenton had no choice but to confess what he'd done and plead for forgiveness if necessary. He tried to make it sound as if the pony would be thrown out into the wild had he not purchased it, making it appear as if he had little choice in the matter, but he could tell by Lysabel's expression that she didn't believe him. But he could also see that she, too, couldn't deny Brencis. The little girl finally had what she wanted and there was no curbing her excitement.

It was palpable.

When Trenton told Lysabel that he'd also purchased a pony for Cynethryn, that seemed to bring the older girl around. Hearing her name, and realizing that not only had her sister been given a pony, but she now had one as well, had her on her feet as she begged her mother to see it. As the rain from a summer storm began to fall outside, Trenton found himself leading Lysabel and both girls back to the livery where Brencis ran to Snowdrop and Cynethryn was introduced to Honey.

As Lysabel stood with Brencis, admiring her new pony while casting Trenton expressions of both joy and exasperation, Trenton stood with Cynethryn as the girl looked over her pony with disbelief.

It appeared the girl was in shock. Trenton finally turned away from Lysabel to see that Cynethryn was staring at the dark pony with her mouth hanging open. She hadn't even touched it yet.

"Do you like her, my lady?" he asked the little girl. "If you do not, I can ask the livery man if he has any others. He told me that his daughter had grown too old for Honey and that the pony had no one to love her any longer. I thought you might like to love her."

Cynethryn couldn't seem to take her eyes off the pony. "For me?" she finally asked. "She is truly for me?"

Trenton nodded. "Truly," he said. "Do you know how to ride?"

Cynethryn nodded. Then, she shook her head. And then she burst into quiet tears, something that concerned Trenton greatly.

"What is the matter?" he asked. "If you do not like her, I shall find you another one, I promise. You needn't be worried."

Cynethryn shook her head. Weeping, she finally reached out to touch the pony as if hardly believing any of it.

"I want her," she whispered tightly. "You… you gave me a pony."

"Aye. You and your sister."

"But why?"

"Because these ponies needed girls to love them."

She turned to look at him, her big blue eyes watery. "But I did not ask for a pony."

"You did not have to. I simply thought you would like one."

Cynethryn digested his answer, wiping furiously at her eyes. "I… never ask for anything because my father will not… he tells me no."

Trenton was starting to understand, just a little, why she was so stunned with the pony. It seemed to him as if she'd never received an unexpected gift in her entire life. It also gave him a clue as to why the girl had seemed so morose and grumpy. A little older than Brencis, she'd learned the harshness of life that her younger sister hadn't yet, and she had no idea that a man could actually be kind to her.

"I will not let your father take the pony away," Trenton said after a moment, giving her the same answer he'd given Brencis. "You may keep her as long as you wish. She is yours."

Cynethryn wiped away the last of her tears, using two hands to pet the pony now. Trenton thought he could see a little joy in her eyes, this stony-faced lass, until she finally looked up at him.

Slowly, a smile spread across her lips.

It was all the thanks Trenton needed.

THE SUMMER STORM was pounding overhead, with bolts of lightning lighting up the common room.

The hour was late as Trenton sat at a table near the hearth, listening to the snoring going on around him as travelers seeking shelter were sleeping around the fringes of the room. Over his head, snug and warm, Lysabel was sleeping in a big bed with her two daughters, both of them undoubtedly dreaming of their new ponies.

It had been an eventful day for them all.

Trenton's thoughts lingered on the ponies, too, and the way Lysabel had looked at him when she realized how kind and generous he'd been with her daughters. It was a look Trenton hadn't seen from her before, one that caused his heart to race. There was gratitude there, but there was also something else, and it was that something else that Trenton was currently contemplating.

He knew he shouldn't.

Staring into the flames of the low-burning fire, he was feeling a great deal of turmoil. Lysabel was a woman, newly widowed, whose husband had been a beast. Now, she was free of him and she had a chance to find a decent man. Trenton only wished that man could be him.

But it was impossible.

Even if he hadn't already been married, he wouldn't have considered himself a decent prospect for her. But in his defense, it wasn't as if he'd been careless with women – his three marriages had stemmed from actions that had been reasonable at the time. He'd married Alicia because it had been a good political match, and Iseuld because she'd been pretty and bright, and then Adela because his father had talked him into it soon after the death of Iseuld. He'd been emotionally vulnerable at the time and he'd gone along with it but, in hindsight, he shouldn't have. Adela had been the worst mistake he could have possibly made.

A mistake he couldn't fix.

Therefore, whatever longing he was developing for Lysabel was misplaced and wrong. He had no right at all to find her attractive, or hope she was seeing him as no longer the big, intimidating boy but now the powerful, handsome man. Nay, he had no right at all.

But he was hoping for all these things, nonetheless.

And he couldn't seem to think straight about it.

"Why are you still awake?"

The voice came from behind and, startled, Trenton turned to see Lysabel walking up in the darkness, wrapped up in a heavy robe. Her hair was mussed, and she looked sleepy, but there was a smile on her face. He eyed her.

"Why are *you* still awake?" he countered. "You went to bed long ago."

Her grin broadened as she sat down on a stool next to him. "I did," she agreed. "But Cissy and Cinny are so excited about the ponies that it took me a goodly long time to get them off to sleep. Now, Cinny is snoring and Cissy is kicking, so I cannot fall asleep. Besides, the travel has upset my stomach. I came down here to see if I could procure some warm milk. Maybe that will help me."

Trenton was on his feet. "I will have it brought to you," he said. "Sit right there. I will return."

Before Lysabel could stop him, he wandered into the darkened rear of the tavern and in a few moments, she could hear voices. Someone was moving about. Soon enough, Trenton reappeared and reclaimed his seat.

"The tavern keeper will bring you some," he said quietly. "But between the snoring and kicking, I am not sure it will do you any good."

Lysabel laughed softly. "I can only try," she said. Then, she took a second look at him. "You did not answer me. Why are you still awake? Is snoring and kicking keeping you awake also?"

He grinned. "Nay," he said. "I do not sleep well as it is. I never have. When I am tired enough, I shall sleep, but it will probably be for no more than an hour or two at most. Besides, we must be up at dawn if we are to make it to Wellesbourne Castle by evening tomorrow."

Lysabel nodded, her gaze moving to the flames. "I cannot believe we are almost there," she sighed. "I cannot remember the last time I was at Wellesbourne Castle. Benoit always made my father come to us; we could never leave and visit him. I am very eager to see my papa."

Trenton was watching her profile as the reflection from the flames flickered on her face. "As am I," he said. "It has been several years. It has been several years since I have seen your father or my father, in fact. It seems like forever."

She glanced at him. "When was the last time you saw your father?"

He inhaled slowly, deeply, pondering her question. "At least six years," he said. *Since my father coerced me into marrying Adela.* But why couldn't he tell her that? Somehow, he couldn't bring himself to tell the woman he was married. He didn't *feel* married. He never had, at least not to Adela. "My father and I have a rather... troubled relation-ship."

Lysabel yawned, pulling the robe closer about her body against the chill of the room. "Your father always seemed like such a kind, wise man," she said. "I know my father considers him a brother. May I ask what is so troubling with him?"

His relationship with his father wasn't something he spoke of, but with Lysabel, there wasn't any such restraint. It was easy to tell her things he kept down deep. She was easy to talk to.

"Many things, I suppose," he said. "My profession, for one. My father did not want me to serve Henry in the capacity that I do. He does not feel that it is particularly noble."

Lysabel looked at him. "I told you that I did not care what you did for Henry, and I do not," she said. "But, clearly, it is something... important. I saw that when you burst into my chamber the night you took Benoit. You and your men were swift and skilled. You are warriors."

"We are assassins," Trenton rumbled. He cast her a sidelong glance, seeing the surprise on her face. "You may as well know what I do, Lysabel. It is neither noble nor glorious. I am called the Crown's Own Agent and I do what Henry tells me to do. If he wants men brought to him, then it is my job to find them and bring them to Henry by whatever means necessary. If he wants his enemies killed, then it is my job to kill them. Have no illusions that whatever I do is great and honorable. It is not. And my father does not approve."

Lysabel tried not to show any hint of judgment as she spoke. "But... why?" she asked. "He is The Dark One, the man who betrayed King Richard at the Battle of Bosworth. I do not know much more than that, as I have never asked, but everyone knows what Gaston de Russe did. And your father feels it is his right to judge what you do?"

Trenton shrugged. "He wanted my reputation to be better than his."

"And it is not?"

"Not even close."

Lysabel could see that in that softly-uttered statement, there was some shame in Trenton's tone. It was the first time she'd seen the consummately confident knight show any hint of a reflection on his duties, perhaps even his life as a whole. Trenton was a man who seemed to keep things well-hidden and as she realized that, she wondered what other secrets he might be hiding.

It was just a feeling she had.

"Then why do you do what you do?" she asked quietly. "You are a fine knight, Trenton, and you are an earl. You can simply retire to your estate and command your army and lead a fine and noble life. Why do you serve the king in this capacity if your father finds it dishonorable?"

He looked at her then. "Because I do not find it dishonorable," he said. "I am very good at what I do. I am shaping a kingdom, Lysabel. What I do matters to the king and I am proud to serve him."

"Even as an assassin?"

"Any man in the king's army has sworn to kill and die for him. Why should my role be defined any differently than any other knight sworn to obey Henry's command?"

He had a point but, even so, he seemed rather torn. He seemed proud of his role in Henry's arsenal, but his father's disapproval was disappointing. It was a great insight into the man she'd known her entire life, but she hadn't known him well.

Until now.

She liked what she saw.

"If I have anything to say about it, I believe you to be as fine and noble as any knight I have ever seen," she said softly but firmly. "You saved me, Trenton. You saved my life and I have said it before, but I shall say it again – I will always be deeply grateful to you. I will sing your praises until I die, so in the eyes of at least one person, you are a great and noble man."

He was feeling the slightest bit embarrassed by her praise because it wasn't something he came across very much in his line of work. But he also felt warmed by it. Hers was an opinion that mattered to him.

"Then I hope I shall always be that in your eyes," he said, "and you will stop dreaming about my brother, Dane."

Lysabel burst into soft laughter as the rather serious mood between them was broken. "I told you that I do not dream about him any longer," she insisted. But she soon sobered. "Does he know what you do? For the king, I mean."

Trenton nodded. "He knows," he said. "Dane serves my father, as the captain of his army, but before he assumed that post, he and I served in Henry's army together for a time. I miss serving with my brother. I miss him a great deal."

"He did not choose to serve the king as you do?"

"He was not offered the post – I was," he said. "Besides, Dane is more at home when he has a thousand men to train and command. He has astonishing command presence."

"And you do not?"

He gave her a half-grin. "I can command thousands with ease also, but I grow quickly bored," he said. "I must have new and unusual things to keep me occupied. But I will tell you something truthfully – as much as I can command thousands with ease, I fold like a weakling to a child begging for a pony."

Lysabel started laughing. "And that is another thing," she said. "I have not yet had the opportunity to scold you for purchasing those ponies for my children. What on earth possessed you to do such a thing?"

He shrugged and looked away, but he was grinning. "I told you," he said. "Brencis begged for the pony, and then her eyes got watery, and I collapsed like a fool. How can I resist such a thing?"

Lysabel shook her head reproachfully. "Really, Trenton," she scolded softly. "When did you become so weak?"

"The day I met your daughter."

"You should know better. Have you no children of your own?"

He sobered. "Nay," he said. "My wife, Alicia, died in childbirth ten years ago. I have no children."

Lysabel sucked in her breath, a gesture of horror. "Oh, Trenton," she breathed. "I am so terribly sorry. I did not mean to show such disrespect by asking such a thing. I did not know."

His eyes glimmered weakly at her. "I know you did not," he said. "You did not offend me. It is simply a statement of fact."

Lysabel nodded, but she was still feeling terrible about it. The poor man had lost his wife and child, and she had been clumsy about it. As she tried to figure out how to make amends to the man for her tactlessness, the sleepy tavern keeper suddenly appeared and handed her warm milk in a chipped wooden cup.

Lysabel stood up to accept it, thinking she should return to her chamber now that she'd made an ass of herself and leave Trenton to his quiet evening. As the tavern keeper wandered back into the kitchens, she turned to Trenton.

"I am truly sorry about your wife and child," she said quietly. "For everything you must have gone through… there are no words to describe my sorrow for you. Forgive me for being so insensitive, my old friend."

With that, she bent over and kissed him on the forehead, leaving the common room with her warm milk in hand and disappearing up the darkened stairs.

Trenton sat there and watched her until he could see her no more, feeling her kiss on his forehead like a brand. He'd been kissed by women before, many times, but not like that. Never like that. There was so much emotion and tenderness in the kiss that his heart was still thumping because of it. That beaten, scared woman was much like her youngest daughter in that she hadn't lost the ability to feel, and feel for others especially. She fairly oozed gentleness and compassion, with eyes that bespoke of deeper emotions he couldn't hope to comprehend. He'd never experienced anything like it.

He wished she hadn't left him.

Turning his attention back to the dying flames, Trenton realized that any hope of detaching himself from Lysabel had been summarily dashed. That warm, wonderful, and beautiful woman had his attention as no woman had ever had it, and he knew now that purging her from his mind was going to be an impossibility.

And he hated himself for it.

CHAPTER SEVEN

Wellesbourne Castle
Warwickshire

WELLESBOURNE CASTLE LOOKED like a castle of legend.
Sitting on a plain and surrounded by not only a moat, but great earthworks rising up all around it in an outer ring, the white-stoned structure looked as if it were simply rising out of the ground, dominating everything within its realm. It was quite large and could be seen for miles. As soon as Trenton spied the bastion in the distance as the sun rapidly set to the west, he sent a messenger riding for Welles-bourne so they knew of their approach. In truth, he was surprised they'd made such good time considering what had gone on that day with Brencis and Cynethryn and their ponies.

It had been quite the circus.

It all started before dawn when both girls were awake and dressed, ready and waiting for him when he was prepared to head to the livery. Lysabel was awake, too, appearing tired, clearly not having gotten much sleep with the continued snoring and kicking throughout the night. But Trenton took all three of them over to the livery where the horses were already being prepared, including the two ponies.

In truth, Trenton had expected the girls to want to ride their new ponies and he was prepared. Markus had been informed of the addition to their party and he was assigned to watch over Cynethryn while Trenton took Brencis. It wasn't ideal for the only two knights in the party to be distracted with girls on ponies, but there was no way to keep them off the animals and he didn't want to trust their safety to anyone else, so he shared the duty with Markus.

They set out on the road north on a warm summer dawn, and both ponies kept up with the escort rather well until about an hour later, when they both started showing distinct signs of fatigue. Given that the ponies hadn't been ridden much, their tolerance hadn't been built up, and two hours into the ride, Trenton and Lysabel had to convince the girls to stop riding the ponies. Trenton wasn't honestly sure that Honey, Cynethryn's pony, wasn't going to drop dead of exhaustion. In fact, Trenton ordered both of the ponies heaved up into the wagon, where they both quickly laid down as Brencis and Cynethryn tended to their new pets.

But the addition of almost nine hundred pounds of animal greatly fatigued not only the wagon itself, but the wheels and the horses pulling it. That slowed their travel down considerably until midday, when Trenton had both ponies removed and simply tied them up to the rear of the wagon so they could walk. Rested, the ponies did well after that, and laying on their bellies and facing the rear of the wagon, Brencis and Cynethryn watched their prized possessions the entire trip to Wellesbourne.

And that had been the fuss and trouble that constituted their second and final day of travel.

The sun was nearly set when the party approached the outer ring of earthworks surrounding Wellesbourne Castle and men with torches were riding out to meet them. Trenton had been away from Wellesbourne for several years, but not long enough that he didn't recognize Matthew Wellesbourne when he saw the man. Astride a muscular dappled warhorse, Matthew looked ageless and strong. But he didn't see Trenton as he headed straight for the wagon carrying his daughter and granddaughters.

There was a good deal of squealing and hugging going on back in the wagon. Trenton could hear Lysabel's voice and he could also hear Matthew's surprised tone. There was much joy in their reunion. As they approached the moat with the gatehouse beyond, Trenton heard his name from Lysabel and, suddenly, Matthew was riding in his direction.

"Trenton!" he gasped, reaching out to nudge his arm. "God's Bones, is it really you?"

Trenton had his visor up, smiling wearily at his father's best friend, a man he'd known his entire life. Matthew Wellesbourne, Earl of Hereford and Baron Ettington, was something of a legend. He was a ruggedly handsome man with curly blond hair, now almost completely white, that he kept shorn close to his scalp. He had enormous blue eyes, a square jaw, and an expression that suggested there was an inherent gentleness inside of him. Given the fierceness of his reputation, that gentle expression was a ruse.

The man was positively deadly, as decades of warfare had proved.

"It is me, my lord," Trenton said, a smile playing on his lips. "It has been a very long time. I hope you have been well."

Matthew nodded. "Well enough," he said. "And you?"

"Very well, my lord."

Matthew smiled at him. He had an easy smile and an easy manner about him, something that made him very endearing to his men and allies alike, hence the "White Lord" moniker. He was the benevolent lord in all things, but once crossed, he became a viper. Trenton had always admired that about the man, how he could be so kind and generous one moment and then, as swiftly as a flame doused, could slit a man's throat with great ease. But it wasn't that he was unpredictable; in fact, he was quite predictable.

He was simply a man of many talents.

And he loved Trenton to a fault. Riding alongside, Matthew reached out and placed the forearm of his left arm on Trenton's shoulder. It could only be his forearm because years ago at the Battle of Bosworth, where England's history had been decided, Matthew had lost his left hand saving Gaston's life.

It was a selfless act that had bonded the men deeper than brothers.

Therefore, whenever Trenton saw Matthew's missing hand, he was reminded of the sacrifice. Matthew's hand for Gaston's life. It was a brotherhood that Trenton could well understand because he felt the same way about Dane, who was really only his brother through marriage, but it didn't matter. They were blood brothers as far as he was concerned, and he would gladly sacrifice a hand or any other part of his body simply so that Dane could live.

"You are looking more and more like your father," Matthew said, breaking Trenton from his train of thought. "How is life in London with Henry?"

That same question out of his own father's mouth would have not sounded so pleasant or so neutral, so Trenton appreciated that. He wasn't sure what Matthew thought of what he did for Henry but, true to form, Matthew wouldn't let his personal opinions cloud his tone or his judgment. He tended to be fair in all things.

Even so, it was a question with many answers, not the least of which was why Trenton was at Wellesbourne, leading Lysabel's escort. Given that they were going to be discussing that subject very soon, Trenton sought to get it out of the way so that Matthew could at least have some time to prepare before Lysabel brought it up. What the man was about to hear would be devastating, no matter how tactfully it was delivered.

It was only fair he know the truth.

"Henry is why you find me here, my lord," he said, lowering his voice and spurring Dewi forward. In the same motion, he indicated for Matthew to follow him, and he did, swiftly. When the two of them came alongside one another, Trenton resumed. "There is simply no delicate way to phrase this, so I will come to the point. The first thing you must know is that Lysabel and the girls are well. They are not in any danger. But the second thing you should know is that Benoit de Wilde is dead."

Matthew blinked rapidly a few times, the only indication of the astonishment and concern he felt. "*Dead?*" he repeated. "How?"

"I killed him."

"Now," MATTHEW SAID slowly and steadily. "Explain this to me so that there is no doubt in my mind as to what has happened, Trenton. Please."

Trenton knew this question would come, especially after he told Matthew of his role in Benoit's death and Matthew immediately shut his mouth and returned to the wagon bed where his daughter and granddaughters were. All the way into Wellesbourne's enormous bailey, and all the while as Matthew's wife and Lysabel's mother, Alixandrea, greeted her daughter and grandchildren, Trenton knew the question would come from Matthew and he prepared his answer. While happiness and joy of a reunion went on around him, and Alixandrea took her girls into the castle, Matthew pulled Trenton into his private solar and shut the door.

Now, the question hung in the air between them.

Trenton was ready for it.

"In order to explain to you what happened, I must tell you something that you do not know," he said. "At least, Lysabel does not think you know, so if you do not, then I am sorry to be the bearer of such news. Benoit de Wilde was a vile excuse for a human being; he beat your daughter. Henry sent me to Stretford Castle to abduct Benoit and take him to London because Benoit made the unfortunate mistake of stealing a mistress from Henry. Lysabel does not know this; I have not told her. But she does know that I killed Benoit."

Matthew was staring at him with an expression between shock and rage. But still, he held fast. He was a master at the neutral expression. But the father in him, the one who was hearing such terrible things about his child for the first time, couldn't quite hold back.

"I had heard rumor of Benoit's whoring," he finally said. "I am not totally ignorant of it."

"And you did nothing?"

For the first time, Matthew started showing some emotion. "I had only heard of the women," he said. "But the beating... my God, Trenton. Are you certain of this?"

Trenton took a deep breath. "The night we came to Stretford, we were met by a woman screaming," he said quietly. "We could hear the blows. When we burst into Benoit's chamber, it was clear he'd been beating the woman in the chamber, the woman I assumed to be his wife. It was not until Benoit was bound and gagged that I realized it was Lysabel. I was only supposed to take Benoit to Henry so that the king could decide on his punishment, but when I saw what Benoit had done to your daughter, I fully admit that I killed the man. I do not regret it."

Matthew's face had lost some of its color. After a moment, he sat heavily in the nearest chair, clearly stunned by the news. Then, in a true moment of shock, he put his hand over his face.

"God," he whispered. "God in heaven. He truly... he truly did this? He took his hands to my child?"

Trenton could hear the devastation in his voice. "Aye," he said. "It was not the first time, my lord. He has been beating her for years."

Matthew's head snapped up, tears of disbelief in his eyes. "That is not true. Please tell me that is not true."

Trenton nodded with regret. "Ask her," he said. "She told me it had been going on for years, ever since he realized he could not get his hands on any of the Wellesbourne fortune. When I asked her why she did not tell you, she said that she could not let you feel the guilt for having burdened her with such a man. She did not want you to know."

Matthew stared at him, wide-eyed, as he realized what had truly been happening with his daughter. But the more he thought on it, the more the situation began to make some sense, and after several long moments, he let out a hiss. The clues over the years began to fall into place, whether or not he wanted to admit it.

Oh, God... he didn't want to admit it!

"She was never allowed to come and visit," he finally muttered, running a hand over his cropped head. "Benoit would invite us to Stretford, but only during the times that he was agreeable. We could never simply go unannounced; we tried, once, and were told that Benoit and my daughter were not in residence. The soldiers would not let us in, so we had to turn back for home. Now... now some of this is starting to make some sense."

Trenton felt for the man. "He had to make sure that when you visited, there was no sign of what he did to your daughter," he muttered. "She was afraid to tell you, afraid you'd kill the man and suffer from the guilt of it the rest of your life. But know that I harbor no such guilt; Benoit de Wilde was an animal and I have no restraint in killing an animal that deserves it."

Matthew simply sat there for several long and painful moments, processing the situation, before returning his attention to Trenton.

"I do not even know what to say, Trenton," he said hoarsely. "I feel like a fool, like I should have known this."

Trenton shook his head. "There was no way you could have," he replied. "Your daughter did not want you to know. She evidently hid it well."

That seemed to hit Matthew particularly well, knowing she had hid her pain from him. Pain he had imposed upon her, like a prison sentence. "But I should have been more astute," he said. "Surely... surely there were signs. Signs that I evidently ignored. I cannot live with myself if that is really the truth."

Trenton reached out, putting his hand on the man's shoulder. "There was nothing you could have done," he said. "But when I saw what was happening, I took action. You saved my father's life, once. Consider the favor returned."

Matthew sighed heavily, reaching up to grasp Trenton's hand at his shoulder, holding it tightly. It was gratitude beyond words, for the man seemed incapable of speaking at the moment.

He was rattled to the bone.

"Benoit de Wilde seemed to be a very decent man when he courted Lysabel," he said after a moment, his voice hoarse with emotion. "I have always prided myself on being a good judge of character, and I honestly had no reservations about him. He was kind to Lysabel and seemed quite fond of her. But right after they were married, the requests for money began to come, and the requests for Lysabel's inheritance because he needed to expand his army. They were not unreasonable requests, but I was not prepared to give him such a great sum of money. After that... after that, communication became less frequent. Visits were friendly for the most part, but not as they had been before the marriage. When rumors of his whoring reached my ears, I confronted Benoit about them and he told me that it was none of my affair. God... I should have known it was more than that, but Lysabel never told me a thing. There was never even a hint."

Trenton could see that he was kicking himself. "You must not blame yourself, my lord," he said. "Lysabel is a strong woman, stronger than you know. She believed she could deal with the situation and that it was her cross to bear. Whatever the case, it is over with now."

Matthew nodded faintly. "Is it?" he muttered. "For me, it has just begun. I must come to terms with what I've done to my beloved daughter. And I cannot tell my wife any of this; it will kill her."

"Then what will you tell her about Benoit's death?"

"I do not know yet."

Trenton sat down in a chair opposite him. For the first time, he was seeing the age on Matthew's face. In his sixth decade, he was, in fact, an old man. But Trenton had never realized that until this moment, until the situation with his eldest child suddenly aged him. Trenton hadn't any fears that such news would take its toll on Matthew but, evidently, it had.

He could see it in the man's face.

"It is not as if his death can be hidden," Trenton said quietly. "There is no longer a Sheriff of Ilchester and Lysabel wanted me to escort her to Wellesbourne to seek your counsel. None of the Ilchester men, save Markus de Aston, know that Benoit is dead. Even Markus does not know that I killed Benoit."

That name brought Matthew's head up. "Markus?" he repeated. "I sent him to Stretford those years ago, Trenton. Surely he knew of what Benoit was doing to my daughter."

Trenton didn't want to incriminate Markus, but there wasn't much he could say to deny it. "He swore an oath to de Wilde," he said. "He kept his nose out of the man's personal business, and for good reason. A man like de Wilde could ruin a knight with just a few words, and he would be believed because he is the Sheriff of Ilchester. Markus did what he had to do in order to survive. You cannot blame him for that."

From the expression on Matthew's face, it was clear that he understood that perspective for the most part. Knights were duty-bound, and they did not question their liege. But the good and moral man in him wrestled with it.

"Mayhap," he said. "But what would have been the tipping point for him to stand up and protect an innocent woman? When my daughter is killed? Then how much would he have minded his own business?"

Trenton didn't have an answer. "I do not know," he said honestly. "What I do know is that Lysabel lied to him and told him that she killed Benoit in self-defense, presumably to protect me. All concerns of Markus de Aston aside, it is Lysabel who needs your advice in how to handle this matter."

Matthew sighed heavily and sat back in his chair, thoughts of Lysabel, Trenton, Benoit, and now Markus whirling through his head. He was trying not to feel the rage that threatened to consume him, but rather focus on his daughter and her needs. For her sake, he had to remain calm and consider the serious issues at hand.

But it was a struggle.

"It is quite a quandary, no doubt," he said. "Ilchester was a hereditary title, one passed through the males in the de Wilde family. But since he and my daughter have no sons, his girls become his heiresses."

"Then you can hold the title in trust until one of them marries and it passes to their husband?"

Matthew nodded, deep in thought. "I believe so," he said. "But I must consult with Henry on the matter. He knows that Benoit is dead?"

"He knows."

"Then I should go to London to see him. I would like you to go with me."

"It would be my honor."

Matthew paused. Now that the shock of the situation had settled, he was more aware than ever of Trenton's role in all of this. "Thank you, Trenton," he said quietly. "For all you have done... thank you."

After that, there wasn't much more to say. Trenton got the impression that the man was eager to see his daughter now, perhaps to see for himself that she was safe and whole, and to forget for a time what he'd been told.

A great deal had been discussed, and dirty business revealed, and, in truth, Trenton didn't want to talk about it anymore, not even to Matthew. He found that even telling the man what had happened to Lysabel caused his blood to boil.

And, like her father, he found that he wanted to see her.

THE FEASTING HALL of Wellesbourne Castle was a massive, two-storied thing with a minstrel's gallery against the north side of it. Great banners of the House of Wellesbourne and her allies hung from the gallery, including a banner from the House of de Russe.

Trenton had recognized the proud black and gray banner with his father's dragon on it and he'd stood there a moment, gazing up at it, and thinking of his father probably more than he'd thought of the man in a very long time. He loved his father desperately and seeing Matthew again, and knowing how close the men were, made him feel the pain of their estrangement more than ever. What was going on between them was foolish and complicated.

He wished very much that they were on speaking terms.

He tried to push aside the sorrow he was feeling as he sat in the feasting hall and watched Matthew with his two granddaughters. The girls were happy to see him; even Cynethryn, the reserved one, wasn't so reserved when it came to her grandfather. One of the first things the girls spoke of was their new ponies, pointing to Trenton and telling Matthew that Trenton had given them the ponies. While Trenton seemed embarrassed by the attention, Matthew simply laughed. He hugged his granddaughters, listening to their chatter, as Lysabel sat with her mother further down the table.

Alixandrea, Countess of Hereford, was about her daughter's size and shape, with the same lovely bronze hair that she kept pulled into a bun at the back of her head. Even though she was middle aged, there was hardly a line on her face, and when she smiled, she reminded Trenton very much of Lysabel.

They had the same smile.

The women invited Trenton to come and sit with them, but he begged off, feeling very much as if he were intruding on a family reunion. In fact, after he finished eating, he excused himself from the table with talk of seeing to Dewi. He worried for the horse when he was in an unfamiliar place.

Matthew let him go without question.

But Trenton didn't make it to the stable right away. He left the great hall and ended up in the bailey, gazing up at the clear night sky and seeing a million stars spread across the blackness, as if a great and mighty hand had taken a handful of diamonds and tossed them across the heavens.

But even as he looked up at the sky, his thoughts were on Lysabel.

He'd told Anthony, Timothy, and Adrian that he would meet them The Horn and The Crown tavern in Westbury in three weeks, and he was already about a week into that time span. Ten more days and he'd have to head to Westbury, and from Westbury he would have to return to London. He tried to imagine that time when he would leave Lysabel, but he honestly couldn't.

He was greatly distressed in that he didn't want to leave her.

Certainly, she was safe now. There was no question of that. She was with her father and he would make sure she was taken care of, always, so his original intention in going to Stretford, to see to the welfare of an old friend, had come to fruition. He'd done what he'd set out to do – to ensure Lysabel was well and safe.

But what he hadn't counted on was the door to another world that had opened to him, a world of little girls whose only goal in life was to have a pony, and a woman he'd once known as a long-legged child who had grown up into a woman of strength and beauty like he'd never seen before. It was a world of laughter, of kindness, and of all the things he'd never before experienced. He felt as if he'd been living in a cave and had suddenly emerged into a wonderful, new world.

It was a world he didn't want to leave.

Depression swamped him. He was heading for the stables, but he caught sight of Lady Audrey's garden off to the right, a walled garden named for Matthew's mother. Everyone knew that Lady Audrey's garden was a magical place, a place of peace and beauty, and Trenton found himself heading for it as if his feet had a life of their own. At the moment, he simply needed to think. Pulling open the old iron gate, which squealed appropriately as it was moved, he stepped inside.

Even though it was a fairly bright night, as the moon was nearly three-quarters, he couldn't see too terribly much in the garden, but he could certainly smell the blooms. Almost immediately to his right was a stone bench and he sat heavily, thinking of the things he wanted and the things he could never have.

This was all his life was ever going to be.

No love, no children, no heirs.

He wasn't going to have a child with Adela, mostly because she couldn't stand the sight of him and he certainly couldn't stand the sight of her, so a coupling was out of the question even though she was his wife. He had touched her one time, and one time only, and that had been on their wedding night. After that, she screamed every time he came near her and after a week of screaming, he'd left his home of Penleigh and had headed on to London.

He thought that was all he was ever going to know when it came to a woman until that night he broke into Benoit de Wilde's chamber.

Trenton's gaze trailed up to the stars again, as if he could find his answers there. Was there some invisible wisdom to help him through this, to tell him that he needed to leave Wellesbourne and forget about Lysabel Wellesbourne de Wilde? He knew what he needed to do, but after that sweet kiss Lysabel had given him last night in the tavern, he couldn't seem to do it. That small gesture had branded him.

He was still hating himself because of it.

The garden gate suddenly creaked again, catching his attention, and he turned to see Lysabel entering. *Oh, God*, he thought. A romantic, moonlit night and a woman he found increasingly hard to resist.

This wasn't going to end well.

Quickly, he stood up.

"Why is it you find me every time I'm trying to find solitude?" he scolded, although it was lightly done. "Last night in the inn, tonight in the garden. Can you read my mind so brilliantly that you know where I am going and what I am thinking, always?"

She grinned. He could see her white teeth in the moonlight. "I am sorry to disappoint you," she said. "The soldiers told me that they had seen you come in here. Am I intruding, then?"

He nodded, saw her expression fall, and then shook his head and laughed. "Of course you are not intruding," he said, gesturing to the bench. "Sit down. I was simply gazing up at the stars."

Lysabel moved towards the bench but she didn't sit. "My mother sent me here, you know," she said. "She felt bad that you left the feasting hall. She wants you to know that you are most welcome to remain."

"I know that."

"She thought you might have felt awkward because it was only family sitting at the table."

He lifted an eyebrow. "I have been told since I was a child that I *am* part of the Wellesbourne family."

She laughed softly. "You are," she said. "My mother wanted to make sure you remembered that."

"I do," he said. "Has she asked why I am here and not Benoit?"

"Nay," she said. But her gazed fixed on him for a few moments before continuing. "I know you spoke to my father this afternoon. I saw you go into the keep with him after we arrived. You told him everything, didn't you?"

Trenton couldn't decide if she sounded perturbed or relieved. "As much as I dared," he said quietly. "When we arrived, he asked right away where Benoit was, and I could not lie to him. I hope you understand that."

She nodded quickly. "I do, of course," she said. "I had hoped that it would come from me, but I understand you had no choice. All he has said to me about it is that he spoke with you, but I am sure he and I will speak more in-depth about it at some point. And I am certain he has not told my mother because she asked me where Benoit was. I told her that he was away and quickly changed the subject. She has not asked anything more."

Trenton nodded and sat down, looking up at her expectantly until she sat down, too. The bench wasn't very large which meant she was sitting rather close to him. Trenton received the distinct impression that she was sitting on the edge of the bench so that their bodies wouldn't brush against one another, because with his bulk, he was easily taking up half of it.

"You should know that my girls are already demanding to see their ponies," she said, making conversation. "They are trying to convince my father to take them out to the stables even now."

Trenton gave her a half-grin. "I am pleased that they are so happy," he said. "Besides, I know what it is like to have a new horse. It is a very exciting time."

Lysabel was looking up at the stars, nodding her head. But, in truth, she hadn't come out here at the request of her mother.

She came out here all on her own.

Oh, she'd lied to him. Quite blatantly. When she saw Trenton leave the great hall, she'd waited a short amount of time before telling her mother she needed to use the privy and fled, following Trenton's trail as he left the keep.

She had ulterior motives. She'd been watching Trenton throughout the entire meal, even sending her mother to invite him to sit with them, but he had declined. He seemed rather standoffish. They hadn't had much opportunity to talk this day because most of the focus was on the girls, the ponies, and when they'd arrived at Wellesbourne, he immediately disappeared with her father. She'd known why, and he had just confirmed it.

Still, she wondered if somehow, someway, she had displeased him. He would hardly even look at her.

Then she began to obsess over it, wondering what she could have done to upset him. Lysabel had known that once they reached Wellesbourne Castle, there would be no reason for him to remain, and she didn't want him leaving whilst upset with her. He'd done his duty – he'd come to Stretford to make sure she had recovered from Benoit's beating, and then he'd brought her on to Wellesbourne. She was coming to think that she had imposed on him too much in asking him to escort her to Wellesbourne.

She couldn't imagine any other issue.

With that in mind, she continued the conversation.

"I wanted to thank you again for escorting my daughters and me to Wellesbourne," she said. "It was very kind of you to do so."

He simply dipped his head. "It was my pleasure."

"Where will you go now?"

He turned to look at her. "I have only just gotten here," he said. "Are you throwing me out already?"

She giggled. "Of course not," she said. "But you certainly do not plan to remain here forever. I was just wondering where you were going when you departed."

He shrugged, his gaze returning to the heavens. "Back to London. Back to what the king has planned for me."

He didn't sound too enthused. Lysabel looked at him, cocking her head so she could see his face more clearly. "You do not sound as if you want to go," she said. "I thought you liked serving the king."

"I do," he said. "But… well, it has been a very long time since I have been at Wellesbourne. It reminds me of better days. Happier days."

"Are you so unhappy?"

"Not necessarily. But it does remind me of days when I had less burdens and less sorrows."

"Like your father?"

He looked at her then. "Why would you say that?"

She lifted her shoulders. "I am not certain. I suppose it was the way you said it."

His gaze lingered on her. "Then you are astute," he said. "Aye, I worry over my father. And other things."

And other things. Lysabel wasn't sure what he meant by that, but she could feel something radiating from his eyes when he looked at her. Could it be… *warmth*? Certainly, it was the warmth of an old friend, his natural concern towards her, but as she looked at him, she swore that there was something more to it.

And that realization shocked her.

Is it actually possible? She thought. *Would Trenton ever look at me as more than someone he once knew in his youth?* It had been a very long time since a man looked at her with such interest and she'd forgotten what it had felt like. It made her heart flutter and she could feel her cheeks grow warm.

God, she was ashamed to even think that a man as powerful and important as Trenton de Russe could ever look at her in such a manner. Her life was in turmoil, she was newly widowed, and she had two small children in tow. Something like that would be most unappealing to a potential husband. Moreover, she was damaged goods, and the reality of the situation was that a man like Trenton didn't want damaged goods.

It was a hugely disappointing thought.

"I am sorry for your burdens," she said, averting her gaze because her entire body was beginning to quiver with the way he was looking at her. "You have a great deal that you are responsible for and I do apologize if escorting my children and me to Wellesbourne added to them. I suppose I should not have asked you, but I knew we would be safe with you. If that was inconvenient, then I am sorry."

"Inconvenient?" he repeated. "If I thought so, I would not have done it. I enjoyed it."

"But you spent good money on two ponies."

"It was the best money I have ever spent."

"You know my children will never forget you. Any man who would buy them ponies is their friend for life."

He lifted an eyebrow. "Never forget me? Now you are making it sound as if I will never see any of you again."

She smiled. "I did not mean to," she said. "But I am equally sure we will not see you frequently in the future. You are a very busy man. But it would be nice... for the girls... if you could see them when it is convenient. You have been a great friend to them and other than my father, they've not had kind men in their lives."

Trenton was coming to think that the conversation was taking a fortuitous turn. He could either agree with her full statement, or he could contest parts of it. Especially the part about not seeing them frequently in the future. The more he looked at her, the more he knew that, against his better judgment, he was going to say something he probably shouldn't.

He should simply keep his mouth shut.

But he couldn't.

"I would like to see Cinny and Cissy often, if you will permit it," he said. "And I should also like to see you."

She looked at him, her features registering surprise. "Me? But you needn't worry about me. I will be fine. Papa will make sure of it, so you needn't trouble yourself."

"It is no trouble," he said, sensing that she didn't get his hint. "And I would not return to see how you are faring. I know you are well and safe. I would return simply for the joy of seeing you."

Lysabel's expression was one of confusion. "But... why?"

He sighed sharply and stood up from the bench. "Lysabel, you are making this most difficult," he said, sounding like he was scolding her again. "I want to come back to see you because... well, I want to see *you*. I want to talk to you, and laugh with you, and see you smile. Do you not understand my meaning?"

Now, she did, and she averted her gaze in shock. All of those thoughts she'd just had about a man like Trenton de Russe and the type of women he would want came flooding back on her, stronger than before. She understood him; aye, she did. Plainly. But it simply wasn't possible.

... was it?

"Trenton, you cannot," she whispered. "You must not say such things."

"Why not?"

Now, it was her turn to grow agitated. Standing up, she began to wring her hands. "Because... because you cannot," she said. "Please do not misunderstand... you are a magnificent man and if I could... if there was any chance... I would be most honored and delighted. But I am newly widowed. In fact, men do not even know that Benoit is dead. It would reflect terribly upon you should you show any attention towards me."

Trenton understood her point of view and he agreed with it, but something inside of him simply couldn't let it go. He should, and he knew he should, but he couldn't.

"Then you reject me on moral grounds," he said. "Not because you do not find me... appealing."

She looked at him, sharply. In spite of the shocking conversation, a smile flickered on her lips. "I remember thinking when I first saw you how handsome you had become," she said. "And I lied to you about dreaming of Dane when I was a girl. It was really you I dreamt of, though I did not want you to know it."

He flashed a smile, his teeth gleaming. "I *knew* it," he hissed. "There is no world in which my brother outshines me."

It was a moment of levity in an otherwise serious conversation. They both giggled, a nervous and giddy gesture. It was Lysabel who sobered first.

"Nay," she murmured. "He does not outshine you. In my eyes, he never has. And what you have said to me... Trenton, I shall live on it for the rest of my life. But I am not suitable for you. I am damaged, as you know. It is a shameful thing."

His smile quickly faded. "God's Bones, woman," he muttered. "You are the most perfect creature I have ever seen, inside and out. There is such strength and dignity in you. Even that night... that night I took Benoit away, I remember thinking how very strong you were in the face of everything. That is something remarkable, Lysabel. You are the most worthy woman I have ever known."

As Trenton watched, tears filled her eyes. He could see it in the moonlight. "That is the kindest thing anyone has ever said to me," she whispered. "You cannot know what it means to me to hear you say that. Even so, I have much healing to do, Trenton. I am in no position, mentally or physically, to entertain a man's attention, not even from someone as wonderful as you."

"Then let me help you," he said. He was uncomfortable with saying such things to her, but he couldn't help himself. "Let me come to visit you. Let me sit and talk to you as if there are no troubles on this earth. I cannot tell you what the past few days have meant to me. My world is filled with death and destruction, but the day I returned to Stretford, I was met with a world I'd never seen before. Little girls who want ponies, who see the world with such innocence... I have never known anything like that before and I do not want to lose sight of it."

Lysabel was overwhelmed with the conversation. She was thrilled and crushed all at the same time.

"If this had been any other circumstance," she said softly. "If Benoit had been dead a year, and everyone knew it, or if you had said this to me years ago before I knew Benoit, then I would be the most fortunate lady in all of England to have your attention. I would bask in it. But what you are suggesting... I am so afraid it would go badly for both of us."

She was right, but he wasn't going to admit it. He wasn't going to give up. With a faint sigh, he closed the gap between them, watching her recoil from him slightly, wary of his very close proximity. Reaching out, he gently took her hand and lifted it to his lips, kissing it tenderly.

"I understand your fears," he murmured. "I have no right to press my attentions. I know that. But know that I would never do anything to bring you shame or harm you, at least not maliciously. All I ask is that you let me show you how a man can be kind to you. Nothing more, nothing less. I promise I shall be discreet in every way, but you deserve to be showered with affection and kindness, Lysabel. Please do not deny me that great honor. Please let me show my affection for you."

Lysabel was swept away by his words and by his touch. When he kissed her hand again, she could feel the earth move beneath her feet. Everything felt as if it was rocking around, but it was the most wonderful feeling in the world. Trenton de Russe, that enormous and frightening knight, the one who had saved her from a fate worse than death, wanted to help her heal. He wanted to show her what it meant for a man to be kind to a woman.

God... how could she resist?

She couldn't. It was against her better judgment, but there was a huge part of her that wanted his kindness. Perhaps even needed it. In any case, she couldn't resist him. Already, she was swept up with the feelings he was creating within her and they were more powerful than she was.

"How can I deny a man who bought my children ponies?" she breathed.

He grinned. "You cannot," he said. "It was all part of my master plan."

"Was it really."

"Nay."

She believed him. Lysabel smiled at him, and he smiled in return. And suddenly, his lips were slanting over hers and his arms were going around her body. It was a kiss of enormous proportions, a kiss that was heated and sensual, delicious and naughty. It was all those things and as Lysabel fell against his warm, powerful body, all she could feel was utter surrender.

There was no resisting the man.

She didn't want to.

Any romantic kiss she'd ever been given had come from Benoit, who had no sense of gentleness. He would kiss her so hard that there had been times he'd driven her teeth into her cheek, drawing blood. She would avoid his kisses as much as he could, but with Trenton, it was as if an entirely new world had opened up. No pain, no roughness – simply warm and sensual. Very quickly, Lysabel realized that she liked it very much.

She wanted more.

She must have given Trenton a sign of her eagerness, a wordless invitation to ravage her, because his tongue licked at her, prying her lips open and invading her mouth. His hands were in her hair, holding her head steadfast as if fearful she'd pull away. Somehow, he backed her against the garden wall and that was where things grew heated.

Now, she was a captive audience.

Normally, being unable to move would have sent Lysabel into a panic, but with Trenton, she was a willing victim. His mouth moved over her chin, her neck, suckling her gently and sending bolts of excitement through her. Being that she wasn't a virgin, she knew what it meant to have a man touch her intimately, and when his big hand moved to her breasts, she didn't flinch away from him. She welcomed it.

Dear God... is this what it means to be touched by a man? Is this how it is supposed to be?

All she'd ever known with Benoit was the violence of the act, not the joy of it. Trenton gently fondled her right breast, timidly at first, but with increasing confidence when she didn't push him away. As her breath came in unsteady gasps, Lysabel reached up and unfastened the ties on her bodice. When Trenton realized what she was doing, he helped her. The ties came away and he yanked the top shoulder of her garment down, enough to expose her right breast.

His hot mouth clamped down on a tender nipple and Lysabel gasped with shock at the unadulterated pleasure of it. She shoved her hand into her mouth, biting off her cries as Trenton suckled her, his big body and imposing presence smothering her. But Lysabel had never felt safer or more cherished. For the first time in her life, she wasn't afraid of a man's touch.

It was as if she could feel for the very first time.

His hands were everywhere, touching her carefully, while his mouth seemed to nibble every bit of expose flesh it could. Lysabel was absolutely helpless against his onslaught, her hands on his broad shoulders, bracing herself so she wouldn't fall right to the ground. For certain, it was the only thing holding her upright at the moment. Her legs were as wobbly as a newborn colt's.

Somewhere in the distance, a sentry's cry roused them both from their haze of passion and Trenton's head shot up, alert for any unwanted interruptions or prying eyes. But he knew they were exposed in the garden as they were, and his enormous hands went to her face, cupping her cheeks and forcing her to look at him.

"Forgive me for taking the liberties, but I cannot help myself," he whispered, kissing her yet again. "I suppose I could say it is a foretaste of what is to come, but the truth is that I shall never get you out of my mind, not ever. Now that I have tasted you, I want all of you."

Lysabel found herself looking into his dark, glittering eyes, her heart beating so forcefully that she was certain he could hear it.

"Tonight," she whispered. "After the girls are asleep. There is a small service room in the vault, at the base of the stairs. Do you know which chamber I speak of?"

He nodded. "I do."

"I will be there."

Without another word, she fled the garden, leaving Trenton breathless and trembling. He'd never felt so aroused in his entire life.

The night was about to get interesting.

CHAPTER EIGHT

I T WAS JUST after midnight when Trenton entered the small, dimly-lit chamber at the base of the stairs to find Lysabel waiting for him.

It was a room used by the servants at times, in a section of the vault that was fairly empty, so there wasn't a good deal of traffic about. Considering the clandestine nature of their meeting, that was a good thing. For what they were about to do, they didn't need witnesses.

"The girls have gone to sleep, I take it?" Trenton asked, simply to break the timid silence.

Lysabel motioned to the door, indicating that he should shut it. He did, and bolted it, before returning his attention to her.

"They are," she said, smiling weakly. "No more kicking and snoring for me tonight, at least for the time being."

He snorted softly. "That is a good thing," he said. Then, his smile faded as he glanced around the darkened, musty room. "Lys, you did not have to invite me down here after… well, after what happened in the garden. I have no such expectations, nor would I ever suggest something more intimate than what we've already done. I do not want you to feel as if I have pushed myself upon you."

Lysabel was shaking her head before he even finished. "This is *my* suggestion, Trenton," she said. "I… I do not know why I suggested it, only that it seemed right. When you kissed me in the garden, it seemed so right and natural to me, as if it was always meant to be. I have spent my life being revolted by a man's kiss, but tonight… you changed that. One kiss, and you have changed every perception I have ever had."

It wasn't that Trenton didn't want to bed her. In fact, in the flickering light of the chamber, with one small taper throwing out golden light onto the four walls, he could see a pallet on the ground, a neat collection of blankets fashioned into a bed. He didn't know if the pallet had already been here or if Lysabel had made it. He could very easily throw her down upon it and ravage her, but he didn't want her to think that his flesh against hers was the only thing he had in mind. What he felt ran much deeper than that.

"But it was just one kiss," he said, his eyes glimmering at her. "There will be many more to come, God willing. One kiss and I do not expect you to do… this."

Lysabel's warm expression faded. Then, her features dropped entirely. "I see," she said, lowering her gaze. "Then I have made a fool of myself. I am sorry, Trenton. I did not mean for you to feel obligated when that was not what you had in mind."

He went to her, quickly. "I do not feel obligated," he assured her. "Believe me, I would like nothing better. But you seemed so hesitant in the garden that I do not want you to think that *I* expect this. I don't, you know. I am happy to do whatever you wish to do, even if it is to simply sit and talk."

Lysabel looked up at him, feeling her stomach quiver, knowing that she wanted to feel as he'd made her feel in the garden. Like a wildfire, those sensations had consumed her and she wanted to taste more, to taste something she'd never before known. It was curiosity, it was desire, but it was also something more – it was the way her heart felt when he had touched her.

Magic.

It was bold and reckless of her, but she didn't care.

"I wish for you to kiss me," she whispered.

He sighed quietly; she could hear him. "Are you certain?"

"Never more certain of anything."

Trenton didn't say another word. His arms went around her and he pulled her against his body, planting a soft, warm kiss on her mouth and feeling her succumb to him almost instantly. There was no hesitation or reservation, as if she were surrendering completely. In fact, she began to grow aggressive, wrapping her arms around his neck and snaking her tongue into his mouth because that was what he'd done to her, out in the garden. Trenton groaned, instantly aroused.

He was overwhelmed by her.

More than twice Lysabel's size, Trenton used that strength to pick her up, holding her tightly against him. He tasted her lips, her flesh, his mouth moving across her cheek to her tender earlobe. Her skin, so pale and soft, was sweet and delicious. He suckled on a tender earlobe, listening to her gasp with delight.

Lysabel was wearing a surcoat with a neckline that displayed the swell of her breasts, and Trenton's mouth moved all over her cleavage, suckling and gently licking, before returning to her mouth and kissing her deeply. As he did so, his right hand moved to her left breast, very gently cupping it. When she didn't stop him, he squeezed harder. As she'd done in the garden, Lysabel quickly unfastened the ties that held the surcoat snug on her body, shimmying as if to shake it right off her. As her mouth fused to Trenton's again, she went to work on his belted tunic.

Trenton was on fire. He helped Lysabel untie his tunic, so impatient at one point that he ended up ripping a tie when he yanked at it. His mouth was on hers, his hands on her naked flesh as he found himself making the most logical move he could think of – he had her up in his arms and moved for the pallet behind them.

Lysabel was all wrapped up around him, kissing the man as she'd never kissed anyone in her life. His masculinity, his charm, and his power had her drowning in him. For a woman who had never shown any aggression in the bedchamber, a single kiss from Trenton had changed all of that. Now, she was coming alive.

Swept away...

Trenton laid Lysabel down on the pallet, lying down right on top of her. He pulled her shift free, his big hands coming into contact with her full, sweet breasts, his mouth capturing a nipple. Lysabel groaned as he suckled her and she began reaching for his breeches. Trenton felt her fumbling and he moved to help her, pulling them down to his knees. He still had his boots on and he didn't want to stop to remove them; liquid fire in his veins was preventing him from stopping their momentum, even a little bit. But once his hose came down, and she was nude beneath him, he planted his face in between her legs and pleasured her.

Lysabel cried out softly as he licked her mercilessly. His mouth, his hands, were doing wicked things to her, things she had never experienced. The extent of Benoit's lovemaking had been hard and demanding, and at this moment, Lysabel understood what it meant to have a man love her. She never could have imagined the joy of it, and she desperately wanted to feel him within her. Trenton didn't make her wait long; his tongue had manipulated her to the verge of a release but stopped short of it. He lifted himself up over her quivering, supple body and mounted her.

Lysabel gasped as he thrust into her. Trenton was a big man and his manhood was proportionate, and she felt every inch as he drove it into her. She responded to him eagerly, her pelvis moving against his, meeting his thrusts, feeling sparks fly every time he plunged deep. Wrapping her arms around his neck, she pulled him down to her and slanted her lips over his as he continued to thrust.

She was still kissing him deeply as she climaxed for the first time in her life, and Trenton's mouth absorbed the swift pants of pleasure. As wildly aroused as he was, he kept his focus, bringing her to another climax a few minutes later. After that, he couldn't control himself and when he felt himself peaking, he didn't try to stop it. It was such a glorious orgasm that he nearly lost consciousness.

It was everything he knew it would be.

But Lysabel apparently wasn't finished. She was grinding her wet heat against him, seeking his spent manhood that was still partially engorged. Knowing what she wanted without her asking, Trenton plunged back into her wet body and felt her climax yet again. He didn't think it was possible for him to grow hard again so soon, but it was literally minutes before he was rock-hard again, thrusting into her and loving every moment of it.

He couldn't get enough of her.

It was like a dream, a little piece of heaven that he had never known to exist. A dream where he was making love to a woman he adored, and a woman who adored him in return. Lysabel was touching him everywhere, curiously and gently, and in little time he climaxed so hard that, this time, he bit his tongue.

It was the most amazing sexual experience he'd ever had.

Eventually, Trenton fell against her, his body still embedded in hers as she lay beneath him. He lay there with his arms around her, holding her fast and close, thinking on how his life was going to change from this point on. He'd been wildly attracted to Lysabel since nearly the beginning, but now there was something more involved. He'd claimed her, physically.

The intimate act between them sealed it.

In fact, he knew he loved her. He couldn't remember when he hadn't. He'd been lying to himself if he thought it was anything else other than love, so he simply lay there and held her, savoring every moment as if it was the best one he had ever lived.

It took Trenton a few minutes to realize that Lysabel had fallen asleep in his arms. The woman who didn't seem to sleep very well, or so she'd told him, was now fast asleep, warm and safe for probably the first time in her adult life. Her soft, sweet snores filled the air. With a grin, he tightened his grip around her, holding her close.

Before sunrise, they parted with kisses and soft words, and even as Trenton watched Lysabel walk away, heading up the stairs and into the main part of Wellesbourne's keep, he knew one thing: it had been the best night of his life.

And he knew he would never let her go.

CHAPTER NINE

"WHAT ARE YOU looking at?"

The question came from Alixandrea. It was a warm and bright morning, the weather excellent for almost any manner of activity. At the moment, Matthew was standing in his solar, watching something in the bailey from one of the three long lancet windows in the chamber. As his wife came near to see what he was looking at, he pointed out of the window.

"Cinny and Cissy are riding their ponies," he said. "I was attending to tasks this morning when I started to hear the laughter. Can you see them? Lys is with them, as are Trenton and William."

Smiling, Alixandrea came alongside her husband, peering from the window to see her grandchildren having a marvelous time. "They look so happy," she said. "Cissy is positively about to burst."

Matthew grinned. "William has been asking Cinny if he can ride her pony and she keeps pushing him away," he said. "I find that I do not want to work in here any longer. I want to go outside and play with my grandchildren."

Alixandrea laughed softly. "Then go," she said. "Your tasks can wait. What are you doing, anyway?"

He turned and pointed to the cluttered table behind them, full of maps and missives and any number of other things.

"As you know, Warwick Castle is a crown property since Richard Neville's death those years ago," he said. "It borders my lands to the north. Henry has sent me a missive asking if I wish to purchase the place. If I do, he will grant me the title Earl of Warwick."

Alixandrea looked at him in surprise. "Earl of Warwick?" she repeated. Then, she shook her head firmly. "That title has nothing but horrific memories attached to it, Matt. Why should you want such a thing?"

Matthew grinned. "It may have horrific memories attached to it, but it is still a powerful name," he said. "Henry is looking for money to fill his dwindling coffers, so he is trying to sell off some of these properties. I suspect I am not the only one who has been approached about purchasing crown properties. Besides, I have four sons that I must provide for. James, as my heir, will inherit the Hereford title and Wellesbourne Castle, but there are still Thomas, Daniel, and William to provide for. The Warwick lands and title would be magnificent for Thomas."

Alixandrea wasn't so sure. "Thomas Wellesbourne, Earl of Warwick?" she said. "It would make him quite proud, I am sure. And he is a good boy, so he would be a credit to the title. Does Henry want a good deal of money for it?"

Matthew shrugged. "He wants a substantial amount, but the return on it would be endless." Another happy scream from the bailey caught their attention and they both turned towards the window again. "Enough business for the day. I am going outside to ride ponies."

Alixandrea waved him on, smiling at her happy husband. But before he could quit the chamber, she called out to him.

"Matt," she said, somewhat hesitantly. "Where... where do you suppose Benoit is? Does it not seem strange that he has not come with his wife and children?"

Matthew was caught off-guard by the question and he paused. Alixandrea was the mother of his children, the most beautiful, wonderful, and trustworthy woman he knew. He'd told Trenton that he wasn't going to tell her of Benoit's death, and especially not of everything else Trenton had told him, but in looking at her, he couldn't in good conscience keep the secret from her.

Alixandrea was a reasonable, wise woman and it was possible, at some point, that he would require some of that wisdom in this situation. Retracing his steps, Matthew thought on how to tell her the truth.

"I must tell you something that cannot leave this room," he finally said. "Swear to me that you will not say anything to anyone, not even to your daughter."

Alixandrea grew serious. "Of course, Matt," she said. "What is it?"

What is it? Matthew didn't even know where to start. Reaching out, he grasped her arms gently, his right hand holding her while the stump of his left wrist rubbed against her in a comforting gesture.

"Benoit is dead," he said, watching her eyes widen. "You needn't concern yourself with the circumstances of his death, but know that he is dead. Lysabel knows this, but her men and the whole of Stretford Castle do not, and that is why she has come to Wellesbourne. She is seeking my guidance on how to proceed, but I must see Henry about this very soon. Cinny and Cissy are the heiresses to the Sheriff of Ilchester's title and wealth, but the king must know what has happened. Only then will I be able to properly guide Lys in this matter."

Alixandrea stared at him in shock, clearly struggling to absorb the news. Finally, she spoke.

"Did... did someone kill him?" she asked.

"Aye."

She let out a hissing sound and closed her eyes tightly, as if physically impacted by his answer. "I knew it," she muttered. "God forgive me, I knew it. What happened? Did he finally whore with the wrong woman and her husband killed him?"

Matthew's heart sank. "How did you know about that?"

"The whoring?" she said, as if it was the most obvious thing in the world. "I hear things, Matthew, and I have heard this for years. You did not have to tell me, but I knew. That is why I am thrilled that my daughter and grandchildren are here without that hound of a man. Lys did not deserve the disrespect Benoit showed her."

Matthew was feeling horrible, as if he hadn't protected his wife from the terrible rumors, and it only compounded his guilt where Lysabel was concerned. He'd failed his daughter, and now his wife. Furthermore, he had planned on telling Alixandrea about the beatings but from the look on her face, he didn't think she could take it. He could see how distressed she was about Benoit's behavior, something she'd never expressed until this moment. But telling her how the wretch of a man had taken his hand to their daughter... for the moment, he would spare her that horror.

"And you kept all of this buried inside you?" he asked her quietly. "Why did you not ask me about it? Why did you not say something?"

Alixandrea's eyes began to brim with tears but she fought them, blinking rapidly. "And add to your pain?" she said. "I would never do that. You were already suffering guilt at your daughter's husband's behavior and I would not add to it. But I have long suspected that you confronted him over it. Did he deny it?"

Matthew sighed heavily. "He did. Repeatedly."

Alixandrea shook her head in disgust. "Then there was nothing more you could do," she said. "But I must say that I never liked Benoit. Did you know that? I pretended otherwise, because you seemed convinced he would be a good match for Lysabel, but there was something in the man's eyes that betrayed the darkness of his soul. I saw it in the way he treated his servants and his men, yet he would be sweet and kind to our daughter. I knew he had that evil streak in him."

"And you said nothing?" he asked, incredulous.

She shook her head, feeling desperate and sad. "What could I say? You had already committed to him and I was hoping against hope that whatever wickedness was inside of him would not turn against Lys, or if it did, that she could deal with it. She is a very strong woman. I hoped... I hoped I was wrong about him."

Matthew could see that she was distraught, so he pulled her into his arms, holding her closely. "You were not wrong," he muttered. "And I have a great deal to make up to Lys. Her pain is my doing, Alix. You cannot know how that hurts me."

Alixandrea clung to him. "You could only do your best," she said. "It is Benoit who bears the shame, not you. He is truly dead, then?"

"Truly."

"Then I am overjoyed." She released him, looking into his sorrowful face. "He is gone and we have our Lys back. We must look to the future to ensure her next husband is nothing like Benoit. We have been given a second chance to give her a happy life and we must be grateful for it."

There was that wisdom he depended on her for; her outlook to the future, to hope. She was right in all things. Matthew kissed her.

"I am grateful," he said. "For Lys and for you. Now, if there is nothing more to say on the matter, I am going to go and ride ponies. I am going to enjoy this moment and be thankful for it."

Alixandrea smiled encouragingly and he kissed her one more time before quitting the chamber and heading out into the busy, dusty bailey.

Thankful, indeed.

With the sun on his face, Matthew's attention moved from his wife to the ponies, once again drawn in by more happy screams. He focused on the two small ponies trotting I circles around Trenton, while his youngest son, William, ran in circles with the ponies, grabbing at the girls and teasing them. That was where the happy screams were coming from.

William was his wild child, so full of life and delight that he reminded Matthew very much of his own long-dead brother, Luke. Luke Wellesbourne had been a redheaded force of nature, loved by the women, and passionate about life in general. He had lost his life at the Battle of Bosworth, the same battle where Matthew lost his left hand, and there wasn't a day that went by when Matthew didn't miss him.

Still, seeing William and how much he behaved, and looked, like

Luke often eased that grief of a long-dead brother. Sometimes he was even glad Luke wasn't around anymore because he was certain that between William and Luke, England would be in a good deal of trouble as the wild boys of Wellesbourne went on a rampage of wine, women, and more wine, leaving Matthew to make excuses for their behavior and pay off the irate fathers of compromised women.

But, God, he would have loved to have had the opportunity. It would have been a small price to pay for having Luke back.

"Grandfather!" Cynethryn saw Matthew and was waving him over. "Look at me! Look at my pony!"

As Matthew waved to her, William tried to teasingly grab her off the pony. "This is *my* pony!" he announced. "I am going to ride her into battle!"

Cynethryn screamed, although she was grinning. "You are a very bad man, Willie!"

Matthew started to laugh as he walked up on his daughter, who was watching the spectacle with a grin on her face. "Aye, you are a very bad man, Willie," Matthew said as he put his arm around Lysabel's shoulders. "You had better not steal that pony or Trenton might have something to say about it."

Trenton, standing in the middle of the two ponies to ensure the girls didn't get into any trouble, waved a dismissive hand at William. "Mayhap I shall buy him his own pony for his birthday," he said. "If I do, I fully expect him to ride it into battle."

William laughed. "I would crush it."

"You think well of yourself, do you?"

"Well enough to know I can outride you, de Russe. You do not frighten me."

"I should."

William tossed his head back in gleeful laughter. "Then we must have a contest," he said. "We shall have games and whoever wins shall have bragging rights. That winner shall be *me*."

"A Wellesbourne has never beaten a de Russe in anything. You shall not be the first."

William's expressions went from laughter to outraged, a rapid gesture that was too dramatic to be real. "Do I hear a challenge, my foolish lad?" he asked.

Trenton was trying not to laugh. "You hear the truth."

William stopped chasing the girls and came over to Trenton, seeing that the man was struggling with laughter. He began to laugh, pointing at him.

"You cannot even keep a straight face when you say it," he said. "I will therefore challenge you to games of my choosing. Will you accept?"

"It depends on the games."

"Afraid?"

Trenton suddenly took a step in William's direction, a threatening gesture, and William scattered, still laughing. More laughter arose from Matthew and Lysabel as William made sure to stay out of Trenton's long arm span.

"He has a healthy respect for you, Trenton," Matthew said. "But he is fierce in battle; I have seen him."

"But Trenton is bigger and stronger than little Willie," Lysabel said, teasing her youngest, pesky brother. "Trenton serves the king, and who does Willie serve?"

Matthew cast her a long look. "He serves *me*," he said. "He is part of the Wellesbourne war machine, something that even the king relies on. Trenton is a great knight, no doubt, but do not diminish your brother."

Lysabel grinned at her father but her gaze moved to Trenton, who had pulled Brencis' pony to a halt because something on the bridle was loose. After their night of passion, she found that she only had eyes for the man. When she saw him this morning as he brought the ponies out for her daughters to ride, her heart began to beat so forcefully that she swore it was going to pound right out of her chest.

She'd slept better in his arms last night than she'd ever slept in her life, and he'd awoken her to gentle kisses, telling her that it was nearly dawn. She wanted to awaken like that every morning for the rest of her life.

Lysabel had returned to her chamber just about the time her daughters were beginning to stir, and when they finally awakened, the first words out of their mouths were those begging for their ponies. Since Trenton had purchased the ponies, Lysabel sent word to him and asked for the animals to be brought forth.

In truth, Lysabel had expected to see a servant leading out the ponies, not Trenton himself, but she was quite happy to see him as he emerged into the morning pulling two little beasts behind him. He'd greeted her politely, with no hint of the intense passion they'd shared the night before, but when no one was looking, he'd winked at her. That wink had been an arrow of delight, straight into her heart, enough to make her head swim.

She winked back.

Even now, as Lysabel stood with her father and brother, she had eyes only for Trenton and it was increasingly difficult for her to focus on the conversation at hand.

"I am not diminishing my brother," she said belatedly. "I am simply stating that Trenton is older and has had more experience."

William took exception to that, facing his sister in a defiant gesture reminiscent of his Uncle Luke.

"More experience does *not* mean he is better than I am," he said. "In fact, I believe I shall challenge him to a fight. Broadswords, no armor. Man to man. Let us see who shall win!"

Matthew looked at Trenton, who was still fussing with the strap on the bridle. He didn't reply until he was finished with whatever he was doing and Brencis kicked her pony again to get it moving. As she resumed riding in a circle behind her sister, Trenton turned to William.

"Are you sure you want to do that?" he asked.

William was arrogant. "Do I detect concern? Fear, mayhap?"

Trenton grinned at the cocky knight. "You detect joy, dear Willie," he said. "Name the time and place. I shall be there."

William was back to smiling. "Now, I say," he demanded. "Go and get your sword. We shall do this *now*."

"Will," Matthew called him off, shaking his head. "Not today. Let us ride ponies today and nothing more."

Trenton held up a hand to Matthew. "It is no trouble, my lord," he said. "But you had better bring forth the swaddling, for when I am done with your son, you will need it to wipe up his tears."

Matthew started laughing; he wasn't going to get into the middle of this. "Willie, you are utterly ridiculous," he said. "I do not care what you and Trenton do, but there had better not be any blood. And if anyone cuts anything off, I will not be held responsible for what your mother does. Her wrath shall be swift."

Trenton looked at William. "The rules are established, then."

"The first man who falls to the ground loses."

"Agreed."

As William flashed him that broad grin and ran off to collect his weapon, Matthew broke away from Lysabel and made his way to Trenton, who was watching Cynethryn as the girl bounced by on her sweaty pony.

"Do not underestimate William," he muttered. "He has a hammer for a right hand and he is very fast. He is also crafty and will look for any opportunity to trip you."

Trenton cast him a long glance. "I promise I will not hurt him, my lord," he said. "But I do intend to teach him a lesson."

"If you do, then you will have succeeded where I have failed."

Trenton simply smiled at the man, his dark eyes glimmering with mirth. Shaking his head at the impetuousness of young men, Matthew turned to the girls, still riding their ponies.

"Ladies, your ponies are tired," he said. "There has been enough riding this morning. We must now tend them and let them rest."

The girls pulled their ponies to a halt. It was Brencis who was the most disappointed. "Can we ride later?" she asked anxiously.

Matthew nodded. "You can," he said. "Get off, now. We shall take the ponies back to the stable and brush them and feed them. Having an animal also means you have a responsibility to take great care of them."

Cynethryn slid off her pony but Matthew had to help Brencis down. With the disappointed girls leading their ponies, Matthew took them back towards the stables, leaving Trenton and Lysabel watching after them. After a few moments of watching them walk away, Trenton turned to Lysabel.

"It seems as if we have been abandoned," he said.

Lysabel didn't move. She just stood there, smiling at him, unsure what to say. The last time they were alone, sexual things had happened, so she tried not to stand too close to him, afraid the attraction between them would drag them into one another's arms for all to see. Already, the pull between them was very strong, like a tempest.

It was difficult to resist.

"It does seem that way," she agreed. "Thank you for bringing out the ponies earlier. When I sent word to you, I did not mean that you should bring them out. I simply meant to ask you if you could have a servant bring them forth."

He wiped off his hands, brushing them off of dust and pony hair, as he started to walk in her direction.

"It was my pleasure to bring them out," he said. "I knew I would get to see you if I did."

Her smile grew, now with pinkened cheeks at his compliment. "And so you did."

He eyed her. "I do not regret last night," he said, lowering his voice. "Know that I will look in earnest for the next such opportunity."

Now, she was flushing a bright red. "Mayhap we can meet in that little chamber again tonight," she said quietly. "I suppose I could find my way there if you can."

"Indeed, I can. I have decided that you should be touched, and touched often."

She giggled, feeling silly and giddy at his flirtation. "Really, Trenton," she scolded softly. "How bold."

"How true."

She looked at him. "I never knew you had such thoughts."

He fought off a grin. "There is much you do not know about me," he said. "I will take any opportunity to tell you. And show you. Therefore, do not be alarmed if you are walking in a dark corridor and someone reaches out to grab you. It will be me."

She snorted. "And if it is not?"

"Then I will kill him. Have I not already demonstrated that?"

The smile faded from her face as the mood grew suddenly serious. "You have."

He folded his enormous arms across his chest, his gaze lingering on her. "Then you know I mean what I say," he said. "No man shall ever raise a hand to you again, Lysabel, and no man shall ever touch you again but me. Do you believe me?"

She cocked her head, a curious gesture. "When you say that no man shall ever raise a hand to me again, I do," she said. "But what you say about no man ever touching me again but you... Trenton, that sounds as if you wish to court me."

He suddenly cleared his throat and averted his gaze, looking off towards the stables where Matthew was standing watch over his granddaughters, who were brushing down the ponies.

"If men think Benoit is alive, that is impossible," he said, knowing that this wasn't a subject he wanted to discuss with her, feeling increasingly guilty that he hadn't already. The longer he delayed, the worse it was going to be when he finally told her. "In any case, I should go retrieve my weapon while your brother is off finding his. I have a challenge to fight."

Lysabel went to him, then, standing fairly close. "You will be careful, won't you?" she said. "If my brother hurts you, I will be forced to beat him within an inch of his life."

Her close proximity had Trenton fighting off the urge to pull her into his arms again. He found that nothing felt so natural, the impulse to hold her against his body.

"You are my champion, madam," he said softly, his dark eyes twinkling. "But it will not come to that, I promise."

"You are certain?"

"Of course I am."

Forcing a smile, Lysabel put a gentle hand on his forearm, giving him a rather meaningful look before heading off to the stables where her father was. Trenton put his hand over hers as she walked away, feeling her flesh slide away from his as he watched her go. He turned to watch her, appreciating the rear view as her skirt flared out from her hips, sweeping gracefully to the ground. She had a delicious figure from what he could see.

With lingering thoughts of her tender flesh, he forced himself to focus on the task at hand, and that was destroying young William Wellesbourne, the arrogant whelp. The young knight was soon to know the meaning of pain.

He felt rather proud to know that Lysabel would be watching.

MATTHEW HAPPENED TO turn and look in the direction of his daughter and Trenton just in time to see Lysabel place a tender hand on Trenton's arm and he clearly saw when Trenton put his hand over hers.

It was more than the touch of friends.

Matthew had been married for many years. He knew how a man touched a woman; even the most innocent of touches could mean something warm and affectionate. Had Matthew not seen the way her daughter looked at Trenton last night, he might have simply thought it was nothing more than a polite gesture.

But he was coming to suspect that wasn't the case.

Last night, while he entertained Brencis and Cynethryn, Lysabel and her mother sat together in conversation, mother to daughter, and Matthew had to admit that he felt left out. He wanted to sit and talk to his daughter also, but Alixandrea had monopolized her, so he spent his time with his grandchildren, which made him very happy. But more than once, he looked over to Lysabel to see that she was looking at Trenton rather longingly.

At first, he thought he was imagining things. He caught her staring at the man not once, or twice, but at least five times through the evening. Then he'd look to Trenton to see that he was looking at Lysabel, but it was never at the same time. They always seemed to avoid one another's inquisitive stares, but when Trenton finally excused himself and quit the hall, Lysabel had watched him go with all shades of sorrow in her expression, something that had Matthew's full attention.

She'd left the hall a nominal amount of time after Trenton did and returned about a half hour later, seemingly dazed. She'd sat down with her mother again for only a couple of minutes before pleading exhaustion and excusing her and her children to bed. While Alixandrea took the three of them up to their chamber, Matthew remained in the hall, thinking that perhaps Lysabel's attention towards Trenton was nothing out of the ordinary. From the story he'd heard, Trenton had saved her life, so it was only natural she'd feel some sort of attachment to him.

Everything was normal.

At least, those thoughts were on his mind this morning as he'd been watching Trenton and the girls on their ponies as Lysabel stood off to the side. Matthew thought it was all quite innocent and friendly, with the girls screaming, William teasing, and Lysabel laughing. He was starting to think he'd imagined what he'd seen last night as his daughter and Trenton had spent their time staring at one another. But the moment he saw Lysabel touch Trenton on the arm, and Trenton putting his hand over hers, he knew instantly that his suspicions had been right. There was something going on between the pair.

And that was something he didn't want to see.

Matthew loved Trenton like a son, but the man had demons. He was also married. Matthew truly hoped that there wasn't actually anything clandestine going on, but then again, he hadn't seen his daughter or Trenton in a very long time.

Anything was possible.

But it wasn't something he would, or could, stand for. He would not let his daughter have an affair with a married man if he had anything to say about it and he had to believe that he had raised Lysabel better than that, to respect the boundaries of marriage and not to cross into another woman's territory.

Even if that woman was Adela.

Therefore, as Lysabel approached him and Trenton headed off towards the keep, Matthew returned his attention to his granddaughters, who were now starting to braid their ponies' tails. His mind was on Lysabel, and on his next move. He wasn't going to ask her outright if there was anything going on with Trenton, but he thought perhaps a bit of unsolicited fatherly advice might be in order.

For Lysabel's sake, he had to.

"Mama!" Brencis cried when she saw her mother approach. "Can we put ribbons on Snowdrop's tail?"

Lysabel looked at her father, who simply chuckled at the child. When he caught Lysabel's eye, he lifted his shoulders as he had no control over anything little girls did.

"She will get the ribbons dirty, Cissy," Lysabel said. "I do not think it is a good idea. But you may brush her tail and braid it."

Brencis frowned. "But I want to put a ribbon at the end of the braid!"

"If you cry about it, I will make you go inside this instant and sit with Grandmama."

Brencis shut her mouth, but she wasn't happy. It was clear that she had great beauty ideas for her pony. As her girls fussed over the ponies, Lysabel turned to her father.

"You do not have to watch over them any longer, Papa," she said. "I will do it."

Matthew smiled and put his arm around her shoulders, kissing her temple. "I have not seen them in a long time," he said. "It is no trouble. Besides… I have not had much of a chance to speak with you since you arrived yesterday. Your mother has been taking up all of your time."

Lysabel smiled up at her father, the man she adored most in this world. "I am here now," she said. "You have me all to yourself."

He smiled in return, his gaze drifting over her lovely face. She looked so very much like Alixandrea with a touch of his mother mixed in. She had Audrey's eyes, which he had, and so did Brencis. Big, blue, bottomless pools. But in looking at her, he saw his little girl, his first born. And all Trenton had told him came tumbling down upon him as he realized this was really the first time they had a moment to speak on what had happened, the very reason why she was here.

"It is nice to have you all to myself," he said, lowering his voice. "It has been a very long time since that was true. Lys, Trenton told me what happened with Benoit. He told me... everything."

Lysabel's smile faded. "I know," she said. "He told me. I wanted to tell you myself but you took Trenton aside before I could tell you. Papa, before you say anything, I want you to know that I was never going to tell you any of this. I knew how guilty you would feel, and how terrible, and I knew you would be moved to murder. I did not want to reduce you to that. As much as I hated Benoit, I loved you more, so please do not be angry that I did not tell you."

Matthew stared at her, hearing her selfless sacrifice. He found himself blinking rapidly to chase off the tears. "I am not angry with you, but I am sorry, Lys. So very sorry. I feel as if I have failed you."

Lysabel shook her head. "You did not," she said softly. "You did not know how this would end up, Papa. None of us did. After we were married, Benoit... changed. I could never tell you any of this, but it was true. It started after you would not give him my inheritance. After that, I could see any warmth or affection he ever had for me disappear, day by day. When Cinny was born, he was so disappointed that it was not a boy. When I was pregnant with Cissy, it was the best he had treated me in a very long time. I think he was fearful to take a hand to me and risk damaging his son, but when a girl-child was born, he became worse than ever before. But I felt strongly that it was my burden to bear."

Matthew felt sick as he listened to her speak. "I wish you had not," he muttered. "I wish you had told me."

Lysabel gave him a squeeze, unsure what more to say. Brencis and Cynethryn rushed up to Matthew and begged him for a comb for the ponies, and not a brush, and he sent them to the nearest stable servant, who went on the hunt for a comb. With the girls away, Lysabel turned to her father.

"The girls were never touched, and other than hearing what their father did to their mother, they were spared the brunt of Benoit's rages," she said. "But they, too, are healing slowly. Cinny is still very fearful of loud sounds and Cissy is afraid of the dark, so I am hoping that they will heal at Wellesbourne. I do not want to return to Stretford, Papa. May we please remain here?"

Matthew pulled her into his arms and hugged her tightly. "Of course," he whispered. "Even if you had not asked, I would have insisted. You will remain here from now on. Stretford will be but a bitter memory."

Lysabel felt so very warm and safe in her father's embrace. "Thank you," she said, feeling more comfort and peace than she had in years. "I cannot face going back there, if ever. But I must have your counsel on how to proceed regarding Benoit's death. His men do not know, except for Markus. Trenton told you that."

"He did. He also said you took the blame for Benoit's death. Why did you do that?"

Lysabel shrugged as she lowered her gaze. "I suppose I did not want Markus to think ill of Trenton," she said. "He was already suspicious enough of him. It was easier for me to tell him that I did it in self-defense. Did I do wrong?"

"Probably not. To tell Markus that Trenton had killed Benoit would more than likely only complicate the issue."

"Then what shall I do now?"

Matthew released her from his embrace but he still kept an arm around her shoulders. "I must consult with Henry about it," he said. "We will decide what's to become of the Ilchester title."

"It was Henry who sent Trenton for Benoit, in fact," she said. "Did Trenton tell you?"

Matthew nodded. "He did."

Lysabel's expression seemed to change at the mere mention of Trenton. Matthew could see something light up in her eyes. "He came with his men to take Benoit away," she said. "They burst into my bedchamber and captured Benoit. He was killed when Trenton removed him from the chamber."

"I know."

"Trenton and his men were very brave, Papa."

"I am sure they were," Matthew replied. He eyed his daughter a moment. "This was the first time you have seen Trenton in a long time, is it not?"

Lysabel nodded. "Aye," she said. "I did not even know it was him until he recognized me. I would have never known, in fact. He has changed a great deal from the last time I saw him. Have you seen him regularly?"

Matthew shook his head. "Nay," he said. "I see Gaston fairly frequently, but Trenton spends all of his time with Henry, doing Henry's bidding."

"He told me what he does for the king."

"What did he tell you?"

"That he is an assassin."

Matthew lifted his eyebrows to her honest answer. "He is all that and more," he said. "Your Uncle Gaston... well, he does not approve of what Trenton does."

"Trenton told me that, too."

"Trenton de Russe has become a very powerful man. Henry uses him like an attack dog."

She smiled. "He is nothing of the sort," she declared. "He is a kind man and my daughters think he is wonderful."

He is wonderful. In that statement, Matthew knew that Lysabel thought that Trenton was pretty wonderful, too. He could hear it in her voice, the adoration of a hero worshipper. Perhaps, that's really all it was but, in any case, Matthew felt the need to nip it in the bud. Perhaps, this was where he needed to interject some of his fatherly advice.

"Is that so?" he said casually. "Has Trenton told you what he has been doing all these years, other than carrying out Henry's orders?"

Lysabel shrugged. "Not really," she said. "He did tell me that his wife died in childbirth."

"The first wife did, aye."

She looked at him strangely. "What do you mean the first wife? He has had more than one?"

"Three. His third wife lives at Penleigh House, one of Trenton's major properties. She's a bastard daughter of the Duke of Brittany."

Lysabel stared at her father, clearly struggling with what she'd been told. "He's... he's married?"

"He is. Did he not tell you that?"

It was as if his words had a physical impact on her. As Matthew watched, a rush of color flushed Lysabel's cheeks and she stared at him for a moment before quickly looking away.

"Nay," she muttered. "He did not tell me."

Matthew eyed her as she averted her gaze, obviously shocked. She appeared nervous, even upset, and he wasn't sorry. It was clear that Trenton hadn't told her anything about Adela and Matthew realized that he was quite upset to realize that. Had Trenton been toying with her? Perhaps that thought infuriated him more than anything but before he could continue the conversation, he caught movement out of the corner of his eye.

A big knight with a tanned, hawk-like face and dark blond hair to his shoulders was heading in his direction from the walls of Welles-bourne. Matthew noticed the captain of his army, Sir Ransom "Ranse" de Troyes, and when de Troyes lifted a hand to him, Matthew waved back.

"Come," he said to Lysabel, hoping to change the subject away from Trenton. "I want you to meet someone."

But Lysabel dug her heels in. "Not now," she said, her voice sounding strangely tight. "I... I must go into the keep, Papa. Will you bring the girls in when they are finished?"

She pulled away from Matthew before he could stop her. "Of course," he said. "What is the matter, Lys?"

Lysabel was moving away from him quickly, her head lowered. "Nothing," she said. "I am simply tired, I suppose. I will see you later."

With that, she darted off towards the keep, leaving Matthew looking after her, thinking the impact of Trenton's marriage had rattled her greatly. That told him that, indeed, there was something between the two of them and Trenton had clearly been dishonest about it. But he was prevented from stewing about it as de Troyes approached and the subject turned to a small escort party from the north, riding through the village of Wellesbourne.

Since Wellesbourne was on a major road from Warwick to the south, that kind of thing wasn't unusual, but Matthew liked to know who was coming and going, and de Troyes delivered a smart report. It was almost enough to cause Matthew to forget about Lysabel and Trenton, but not quite.

Even as he made his way to the battlements to see the party passing through, Lord Bedworth he thought, his thoughts lingered on his daughter. He hated upsetting her so, but if Trenton had, indeed, been untruthful with her, then it was better she know the truth about him now rather than later.

But Trenton was going to get an earful from him the next time he saw him.

CHAPTER TEN

THERE WAS A fight going on outside, but Lysabel didn't want any part of it. Sitting on the window seat with a view that looked off to the north, over towards the village, all she could feel was deep and abiding sorrow.

Trenton was married.

She could hardly believe it. He'd saved her from Benoit, then had come back to ensure she was well, and then he'd escorted her to Wellesbourne Castle as if he didn't have a responsibility in the world. And then, last night... God, last night he'd said such things to her, sweet and romantic things, things she'd never heard in her life, and then he'd made love to her in a way she'd never imagined possible. He'd made her feel safe, and warm, and adored.

But it had all been a lie.

Lysabel couldn't tell her father any of it. Given how he felt about the entire situation with Benoit, he was more than likely to take Trenton's head off if he knew the man had toyed with her, so Lysabel vowed to keep her mouth shut about the entire situation. There was too much embarrassment on her part, anyway. She didn't want her father to know she'd been so gullible.

But, God... *it hurt.*

Therefore, she decided she wouldn't see him anymore. She would remain in her chamber until he left Wellesbourne and after that, she never wanted to hear his name again. And the ponies... he had purchased them for her daughters and she clearly could not return the gifts because her girls were already so attached to them. So that being the case, she would have to give him money for them. She didn't have a lot, as Benoit never saw fit to give her any real money, but she would give Trenton what she had and be done with it.

Lysabel felt stupid weeping tears over the man, but in her defense, he'd made her feel safe and warm and wanted. His touch had awakened something in her, something she'd hoped to explore, but that was not to be.

It was so disappointing.

Instead of dreaming of their future together, she found herself searching her baggage for her coin purse so she could pay him for the ponies. She finally came across it, pulling out a single gold coin, the only one she had, and she'd had it for years. She didn't know how much Trenton had paid for the ponies, so the gold coin should be enough to repay him and then some.

With the gold coin placed upon the tabletop, she would wait until his battle with William was over before sending the money with a servant. Wringing her hands, and periodically wiping at the tears that would escape her eyes now and again, Lysabel made her way over to the bed and laid down, staring up at the ceiling.

In truth, there was something more than Trenton's betrayal on her mind.

It was a betrayal all her own.

A deception of unfathomable proportions was happening at this very moment. It was something that had been in the back of her mind for a couple of weeks now, ever since her menses had failed to show. But she'd put the thought out of her mind, and prayed every day that her cycle would come, but God was not listening to her.

As the days passed, Lysabel suspected that she was with child, but when she started feeling poorly in the evenings, as she did the night at the tavern when she and Trenton had shared that lovely conversation, she was fairly certain of it. The same God who had sent Trenton to save her was now cursing her with everlasting memories of Benoit.

Her thoughts shifted to the child in her belly, a child conceived the night that Benoit had been killed. The screaming that all of Stretford had heard, and that Trenton had heard, had been Benoit punching her into submission because he had come to her for sex and she had told him that she was too tired.

That had been the catalyst.

First, he'd hit her with a closed fist in the face that had sent her to the ground, and half-unconscious, she'd tried to crawl away. He'd fallen on top of her, right there on the floor, and had tried to toss her skirts up. When she resisted and begged, pleading with him not to do it, he'd slapped her several times, as hard as he could, and she'd ended up on her back, struggling to defend herself as he'd thrown her skirts up completely and cursed her for denying him his husbandly rights.

After that, it had all been a blur, something she'd endured more times than she could count. Lysabel had never known intercourse to be anything other than rough and painful, but with Trenton, it had been a beautiful and emotional thing. Perhaps that's why she'd lured him to the small chamber in the storage vault – because she wanted to know what intimacy between a man and a woman was really meant to be like.

Now, she knew.

Even so, she couldn't help but ponder the irony of bearing a child from her dead husband. That vicious, painful act had come to fruition, and the night Benoit was killed, another life was sparked within her.

Perhaps it was Benoit's final revenge.

But she'd kept it all from Trenton. It wasn't as if it was any of his business, truly, but last night when she'd taken him into her bed, it was a dirty trick she'd played on the man. She should have been honest with him. Perhaps if he'd know of her suspicions, he wouldn't have touched her, but that wasn't what *she* wanted. She'd wanted him to touch her. It had been a hunger she couldn't deny, something she'd put her heart and soul into, and now she was paying the price because Trenton de Russe was a man she could never have.

Now, that dirty trick had been turned against her.

As Lysabel lay there and pondered the situation, she was coming to think that Trenton already being married was perhaps for the best, for both of them. She had no right to be angry with him, after all.

She was just as guilty as he was.

With resignation and disappointment in her heart, she pushed herself off the bed and ran a comb through her hair, re-braiding it and pinning it. There was a polished bronze mirror on the table against the wall and she picked it up, eyeing herself and smoothing at her hair. With the hell she'd endured for so long, she often found herself looking for the positive in any given situation, even this one. The positive was that Trenton had made her feel things she'd never felt before, and she was grateful. He'd made her feel alive, and that told her that Benoit hadn't killed all that was soft and emotional within her.

He hadn't killed her ability to love.

Picking up the gold coin, she took a deep breath and departed the chamber, closing the door softly behind her.

It was time to end it.

WILLIAM DIDN'T STAY on his feet long.

The very fast, very arrogant knight may have been a trickster, confident he could send Trenton to the ground through careful planning and swift timing, but Trenton was on to his game.

At the onset of their challenge, William had literally run circles around Trenton, trying to wear him out and make him dizzy, making him more vulnerable to the attack William was planning. He tried to confuse the man by using swift movements with his sword, leaning one way and then going the other, and through it all, Trenton simply fended off the strikes William did manage to throw at him and nothing more. He didn't make any offensive moves. In fact, he was waiting for William to tire himself out and at the rate he was going, it wasn't long in coming.

The moment William actually stopped all of his fancy footwork, laughing at Trenton and taunting him, Trenton pretended to strike out at him, which caught William off-guard. He very nearly tripped over his own feet in his haste to get away, and it gave Trenton the window he needed to kick William in the back of his left knee, sending the knight to both knees. Then Trenton lashed out a big boot and shoved him over, kicking him right into the dirt. As the gathering crowd of soldiers roared with laughter, William Wellesbourne was swiftly brought down.

Trenton assumed that was the end of it, but that was his mistake. With a grin on his face, he bent over William and offered him a hand to pull him up. William pretended to accept it, but he yanked on Trenton so hard that the man nearly went down, and would have had it not been for the fact that he was simply too big for William to pull over. But William managed to get to his knees and ram Trenton from the side, sending him off-balance and onto his back.

After that, it turned into a wrestling match.

Neither one was throwing punches; they were simply trying to dominate each other. Trenton had the size and strength on William, but William was as wily as a fox. He refused to be pinned, even when Trenton shoved his face into the dirt. On and on it went, with soldiers and knights standing around, laughing, including Markus and Matthew's captain, Ranse. They were having a good time at the expense of William, and Trenton to a certain extent, as the two of them wrestled each other like a couple of wildcats.

Eventually, Trenton ended up on top of William, with the young knight on his belly, pinned in an awkward position. At this point, Matthew had turned his granddaughters over to a trusted servant and wandered out to the bailey to see what was going on. When he saw Trenton with William shoved into the dirt, he put a hand over his mouth to cover his laughter. That was most definitely not the position

William had been hoping for. When Trenton caught a glimpse of Matthew, and his expression, he twisted William's arm behind his back even further.

"School is in session, Willie," he said, loud enough so that Matthew could hear. "It is time for you to learn your lesson. Tell me that a de Russe is always better than a Wellesbourne. Say it!"

William howled as Trenton twisted his arm, not enough to break it, but enough to hurt. "Never!" he cried. "Tear my arms off, but I shall never say it!"

Trenton was grinning as he tightened his grip and William began to squirm. "I *will* tear your arm off if you do not say it."

"I won't! You're a brute, Trenton de Russe. You cannot make me say it!"

Now, Trenton couldn't stop the laughter. "You are dead wrong, little lad," he said, twisting his arm a little more. "Say it and I shall end your pain."

William's face was turning red. "Never!" he said. "Do your worst, but I will not say it!"

By now, the men standing around were having a good laugh at William's expense, including Matthew, who decided to end his son's pain. He walked up on the pair, bending over so he could look his son in the face.

"Willie, a very big man is trying to snap your arm in two," he said. "If I were you, I would simply say what he wants you to say and be done with it."

William was starting to become humiliated. "I will not," he said. "If he is going to break my arm, then he should get on with it!"

Matthew looked at Trenton, a smirk on his face. "I believe he is surrendering."

"I am *not!*" William spat.

Matthew shook his head at his son's foolishness. "Trenton, I would consider it a personal favor if you did not break his arm. I have need of him from time to time."

In an instant, Trenton let William go and leapt to his feet, staying far enough away from William that should the man try to retaliate, he was out of arm's length. William pushed himself out of the dirt, eyeing Trenton, but that ever-present smile flickered on his lips. Trenton could see by looking at him that there were no real hard feelings, even if Trenton had humiliated him just a bit.

"Another time, de Russe," he said, rubbing his right arm, the one Trenton had twisted. "I will get you another time when you least expect it."

Trenton grinned. "You are welcome to try," he said. "But there never was a Wellesbourne that could best a de Russe, and you shall not be the first."

William pointed at him with a rather mischievous smirk on his lips as he walked away, taking his sword from a soldier who happened to have picked it up out of the dirt. Matthew followed his son, putting a fatherly hand on his shoulder as they headed off. With the spectacle over, the crowd started to disband and Trenton headed for the knight who was holding his sword, also picked up out of the dirt. Ranse de Troyes lifted the weapon, hilt first, to Trenton.

"An excellent spectacle, my lord," de Troyes said. "I have often wanted to do that myself to William, but the fact that I serve his father makes beating the son rather precarious."

Trenton laughed softly as he took his sword from the man. He didn't really know him, but he'd seen him around the castle in the time he'd been there. His was a new face at Wellesbourne, at least to Trenton.

"We have not yet met formally, but your praise is appreciated and appropriate, so I can tell that you are a man of taste," he said, watching de Troyes grin. "In case you have not yet been told, I am Trenton de Russe."

"Trenton de Russe, Earl of Westbury," Markus put in. He was standing a few feet away. "Westbury's father is the Duke of Warminster."

Trenton waved him off. "I do not go by Westbury," he said. "De Russe is my preference."

Ranse dipped his head respectfully. "Ransom de Troyes, my lord," he said. "I have heard stories of you from your time here at Welles-bourne Castle. I have heard that there wasn't a man here who could best you, and I see that rumor holds true with young William."

Trenton snorted. "As you have heard the threats, Willie intends to do all he can to dispel that rumor," he said. "If you see him sneaking up behind me with a hammer, I hope you will warn me."

Ranse laughed. "Indeed I will, my lord," he said. "Now, if you will excuse me, I fear I have been away from my duties long enough."

With that, he headed back to the gatehouse. Trenton held up his sword, seeing if it suffered any damage during his bout with William, as he spoke to Markus.

"He seemed amiable enough," he said.

Markus nodded. "We both came to Wellesbourne at nearly the same time," he said. "I was unfortunate enough to be sent to Stretford whilst Ranse remained here. He is an excellent knight, having fostered and trained at Canterbury."

"De Lohr?"

"Aye."

"He is a good man."

Trenton was about to say more when he caught sight of Lysabel standing several feet away. She was politely waiting for him to end his conversation without interrupting, and he immediately excused himself from Markus and made his way over to her.

"How long have you been standing there?" he asked pleasantly.

But Lysabel didn't smile in return, nor did her manner reflect any warmness. In fact, she answered him rather coolly.

"Long enough to see you beat my brother into the ground," she said. "He has deserved that for a long time."

Trenton sensed her mood but he wasn't sure why. "He will forget whatever humiliation there was in an hour," he said. "He will be back at me tomorrow, challenging me again, I am sure."

"Mayhap."

There was a pause and Trenton was increasingly aware of the somber mood she was in but he didn't want to ask outright what her trouble was. If she wanted him to know what the matter was, she would tell him. Or, so he assumed. He continued on as if nothing was amiss.

"Where are your daughters?" he asked. "I expected them to overpower your father and take their ponies back. I cannot imagine they would let those little animals rest so easily."

Lysabel looked at him. "Since my father had charge of them, I am sure they are well, wherever they are." Then, she extended her closed fist to him. "Here."

Trenton couldn't see what it was that she had folded up in her palm, so he extended his open palm and she deposited a dull gold coin into it. He looked at her in surprise.

"What is this for?" he asked.

"The ponies."

He frowned. "What do you mean?"

"I mean that I am paying you for them."

He was greatly confused by now. "But why?"

Lysabel didn't hesitate. "Because I am sure your wife would not like you to spend money on children that are not your own," she said. "Mayhap it is better if you return to London now, Trenton. There is no reason for you to remain here."

Wife.

Trenton felt as if he'd been punched in the gut; all of the air got sucked out of him. By God, she knew! Someone had told her that which he should have told her himself and he could see by the expression on her face that she was furious with him. *Nay... not simply furious.*

Hateful.

His first reaction was to fall to her feet and plead forgiveness, but he fought it. If there was any hope in salvaging this, and he prayed there was, then he needed to remain calm and rational. He had to say everything he needed to say before she walked out of his life forever.

He had a lot of explaining to do.

"May we go into the garden and speak of this?" he asked.

Lysabel shook her head, taking a step away from him. "Are you married?"

"It seems to me that you already know the answer to that question."

"I want to hear it from you."

"I am."

She sighed sharply, rocked by the truth from his mouth. "Then there is nothing to speak of," she said evenly. "Last night, you spoke of kindness and caring, and you led me to believe that you wanted to court me. But I have since discovered that to be untruthful. There is nothing more to say, Trenton. Thank you for what you did for me when you removed Benoit, but your task is finished now. You may leave."

His heart sank. She was stiff and unyielding, unwilling to even extend him the slightest courtesy, but he didn't blame her. He didn't deserve it. He should have told her the truth last night at the very least, but his selfishness had prevented it. Something foolish and giddy that had caused him to withhold information because he didn't want to spoil that lovely relationship they had been building. He had wanted to live in a fantasy world and he had.

But now, it was going to cost him.

"I am sorry I did not tell you," he said, hoping she would listen to him before she walked away. "I have no excuse other than I did not want to tell you. What I told you last night was not a lie, Lysabel. You *are* the most perfect creature I have ever seen, and I wanted to be close to that perfection. And what we shared, just the two of us, was beyond compare. I wanted to know something I'd never known before – the laughter, the witty repartee, the expression on your face when you look at me that makes my belly quivery like a giddy squire. I have never known that with anyone and I suppose I wanted to live in that world with you, where only the two of us and your children exist. It is such a beautiful world and I did not want to lose it."

Lysabel was looking away from him. She knew she should walk away, but she couldn't bring herself to do it. Like Trenton, she had wanted to live in a fantasy world where no one else existed. She'd caught a glimpse of it and she wanted it very badly. But there was so much grief in her heart at the moment that she hardly knew where to begin.

"That does not excuse what you have done," she said. "You have made me a party to stealing another woman's husband and that his shameful. You used sweet words and lies to coerce me and I shall never forgive you for it. You made me believe that I was special."

"You *are*," he insisted softly, feeling desperate when he had no right to. "You are more special and wonderful than anything I have ever known. If an explanation will do any good, then I shall gladly give you one. My father forced me to marry Adela six years ago and since that time, she has lived in Penleigh House without me. I have been home only twice. She hates the sight of me and I hate the sight of her, and I forget that I am even married. I hate that I am. It is a marriage in name only, so when I realized I felt something for you, it was so very easy to forget that I have a wife. I wish I did not; God in heaven, I wish that more than anything on earth and I am so very sorry that I pulled you into that deception. But I am not sorry for what I feel for you."

Tears were in Lysabel's eyes, trickling down her cheeks as she quickly wiped them away. "You should have told me."

"I know. Believe me, I know. But I couldn't, and the more time passed, the harder it became to be truthful."

Lysabel sighed heavily, finally turning to look at him and seeing how anxious he appeared. She'd never seen that expression on his face before, the consummately controlled knight. It was enough to cause her to believe that he was truly repentant, but it still wasn't good enough, because she had a volley of ammunition to fire at him. What was blooming between them was about to be destroyed for good.

"It does not matter," she finally said. "Nothing matters any longer. You see, I have a secret of my own. I have not been truthful with you, either. The night you came to Stretford and killed Benoit was the night I conceived his child under brutal circumstances. I should have told you of it last night, when we became close, but I didn't. Like you, I wanted to share something I'd never known before, so in that sense, I am as guilty as you are. We have both lied to one another. Go back to London and forget you ever knew me, Trenton. It will be better for us both that way."

He stared at her, his features pale and slack. "Oh… Lys," he finally sighed. "I am so sorry."

"So am I."

"But it does not change my feelings."

She looked at him, sharply. "Do you not understand?" she snapped. "This is Benoit's child."

"I understand."

She was starting to become frustrated. "You are married, and I am pregnant with a dead man's child. Those are two things that cannot be overcome, no matter how much you pretend otherwise. You should be furious at me."

"Yet, I am not."

"Are you mad?"

Trenton remained cool. "Not at all," he said. "But I want you to tell me something."

"What?"

"Look at me and tell me how you have felt about me since we left each other this morning. Forget about this moment in time and the anguish you feel; tell me what you felt for me as I was making love to you."

Her frustrated movements came to a halt as she met his gaze, that murky gray color that was like looking into the eye of a storm. There was a tempest raging in those orbs, and as much as she tried to look away, she couldn't.

"Why?" she finally asked, tears welling again. "What good will that do?"

Trenton reached out and took her hand, even as she tried to pull away. He placed the gold coin in her right palm and folded her fingers over it, giving her back her money.

"Please tell me," he whispered. "If they are to be the last words I ever hear from you, then make them something to remember. Please."

Her lower lip began to tremble and she finally tore her gaze away, blinking rapidly to try and dispel the tears. But it was a losing battle.

"I do not want to speak of this," she said. "It will only bring us both pain."

He sighed sharply. "I want to explain something to you about me, since all truths are between us," he said. "I have been married three times. As you know, my first wife died in childbirth. She was a sweet girl and I loved her, but like a fool, I never told her. My second wife was murdered before we ever had the chance to develop feelings for one another, and my third wife... you already know the situation with her. I never believed I was careless with women, but it seems that way. One cannot deny one's own record. Therefore, I will tell you this – I knew early on that I was attracted to you and, at this moment, I wholly adore you. I am certain that it is turning in to love, and if it is, I swear I would not keep from telling you every day. The reality is that I am married to a woman who hates me, a woman I never see. The reality is that she does not have my heart – except for my first wife, no one ever has. I do not give it readily or easily but, at this moment, I could give you my heart and soul and everything else, and I would not regret one moment of it. Lysabel, for the first time in my life, I know I could be happy. Married or not, I will love you for the rest of your life and never be sorry."

Lysabel closed her eyes tightly, her hand at her throat as if she were in physical pain. In truth, she was; she'd never heard such beautiful and tragic words in her entire life. The problem was that she believed him.

She believed every word.

"Words of such beauty," she said. "I have waited my entire life to hear such words. But they are empty."

He shook his head. "They are filled with my heart. Does that mean nothing to you?"

"It means everything to me. But you cannot promise me a respectable relationship or even a marriage. What you are asking... do you know what you are asking of me?"

He looked rather ill. "Aye," he said after a moment. "I know."

"You want me to be your... your concubine. Your mistress. Is that fair to me?"

He shook his head. "Nay," he said hoarsely. "It is not fair to you. In fact, it is horrible of me. I know that. But I cannot help what I feel for you."

Lysabel studied his face, the genuine sorrow there. He may have omitted the truth about his marriage until confronted, but once the truth was out, he'd been more than open with her. Perhaps it was only desperation, but she didn't sense that he was trying to manipulate her. He was simply trying to explain himself now that he was forced to. Like a child who was caught stealing, he was forced to confess.

Perhaps it was time for a confession of her own.

"When Benoit first came to court me, I was fond of him," she said. "He was handsome, and kind in the beginning, and I was flattered. He never told me he loved me but he showed affection for me, and that was enough. It was like... like the warmth from a summer day – pleasant, welcoming. That was what I felt for Benoit – pleasant and welcoming. It was never anything more because I simply never felt that way about him. But with marriage, one does not expect love. But when his behavior changed, it was no longer pleasant. It was a nightmare. I have spent twelve years in a nightmare, Trenton, and it is something I never thought I would awaken from until you came. Last night, I felt as if I had finally opened my eyes for the first time to see what the world had in store for me, and it was something I'd never seen before. You wanted to know how I feel? Now, you know."

Trenton couldn't tell if she was softening to him. "This is not a good situation for either of us," he said quietly. "I know what I am asking of you. I know you consider the child you carry to be a burden, but I do not. It is a part of you and therefore welcome. If finding another marriage is something that you wish, then I will not stand in your way. It will kill me, but I will wish you the very best. I understand that marriage is the honorable thing to do, and I cannot offer you that. But what I can offer you is me, as I am, for the rest of our lives. I will purchase a beautiful home just for us and the children, and we can live there in peace and happiness, looking at each day like a gift and each night like a treasure. We are both looking for that perfect world to live in. Let me build it with you."

It was the most wonderful thing Lysabel had ever heard. All of the hurt and disappointment she'd felt at discovering his marriage was fading, replaced by joy that was washing over her tenfold. Was it possible he wanted to build this perfect life with her, as he'd described? It was such a big decision and one she didn't take lightly... but, God, she wanted to believe in him.

"I want to," she said quietly. "Trenton, please know that I want nothing more. But I must... think. What you are asking of me is too big of a decision for me to simply give in to it, no matter how much I want to. There is not only me to consider, but Cinny and Cissy and the child I carry. You will be assuming responsibility for four people. It is not just me."

"And I will love them as if they are my own flesh and blood."

She sighed faintly, seeing the sincerity in his expression. "I know," she murmured. "But what of our families? What of my father and your father? Sure this is not something either one of them will approve of."

Trenton lifted his eyebrows with regret. "I have spent my life doing things my father does not approve of," he said. "One more thing will not matter."

"But it *does* matter to me," she said. "I am not sure how my father is going to react to this, Trenton. It could very well ruin your relationship with him as well as mine."

Trenton nodded in agreement. "I realize that," he said. "But I also know that our fathers love us. They want us to be happy. We are adults and we are permitted to make our own choices in life. We must live our lives for us, not for them."

"That is not entirely true and you know it," she scolded softly. "You are your father's heir. You will inherit the dukedom when he passes on. What does that make me?"

He smiled. "It makes you a very important woman," he said. "I can offer you everything but marriage, Lysabel. But only you can decide if the price you will pay is worth it. I have already made my decision. But I will abide by whatever you decide."

She looked at him, his downtrodden expression. "Will you?" she whispered. "I wonder."

"I swear I will."

"If that is true, then you must let me speak to my father first. I value his advice."

Trenton didn't look all too happy. "I suspect he will not be pleased with any of this."

Lysabel knew that. "But he must know. It is not as if we could keep it from him."

They were prevented from finishing their conversation by Cynethryn and Brencis, who suddenly came bolting out of the stable area with an old servant on their heels. Both Lysabel and Trenton turned to see the girls running in their direction, squealing and shouting, heading straight for them. While Cynethryn ran to her mother, Brencis crashed into Trenton and latched on to his hand, tugging at it.

"The ponies are rested!" she announced. "Can we ride them again? Please?"

She was literally hanging on Trenton's hand and he grinned as he looked to Lysabel.

"Well, Mummy?" he asked. "What say you?"

Lysabel gave her daughters a wry expression. "As if I have any say at all," she said. "If the ponies are rested, and Sir Trenton says that it is all right, then you may ride them again."

More squealing and jubilation as the girls began running back to the stable. The old servant who had been following them around threw up his hands in exasperation and trotted after them, leaving Trenton and Lysabel grinning.

"Well?" Trenton said again as he turned to her. "I suppose it is time to ride ponies again."

It was his way of telling her he'd said all he'd needed to say. Now, it was time for both of them to make some decisions. Therefore, Lysabel simply nodded and, together, they followed the girls and the harried servant back towards the stables. They couldn't help but think this was a glimpse of the perfect life they'd both been speaking of.

His duties for the king be damned. This was the perfect life Trenton had always been looking for and he knew for a fact that he would be quite happy to supervise pony rides all the rest of his days.

CHAPTER ELEVEN

Two days later

"P APA?" LYSABEL RAPPED on her father's open solar door. "Are you busy?"

Planted in a big chair and wallowing in the residual smoke from the previous night's fire, Matthew had been looking over a map of Warwick boundaries when his daughter knocked on the door. Immediately, he waved Lysabel in.

"I am never too busy for you," he said. "In fact, I was hoping someone might come and visit me. With Cinny and Cissy riding their ponies all day long, they do not come to see me. I am a lonely man."

Lysabel laughed softly. "You can always go outside and ride ponies with them."

Matthew shrugged. "I did," he said. "I took them in the meadows around Wellesbourne yesterday, but I cannot play all of the time. There are a few things around here that require my attention."

Lysabel could see all of the maps and documents spread out in front of him. She pulled up a cushioned chair, looking at everything.

"Why all the maps?" she asked, pointing. "What are you looking at?"

Matthew looked down at the large map of Warwickshire, with little marks on it he'd made with his quill. He pulled the bank of tallow candles closer so they could both see better.

"Warwick lands," he said. "With Warwick Castle now belonging to the king, Henry is hoping to make some money from me."

Lysabel looked at the lines drawn, outlining the shire she'd grown up in. "Why? Does he want you to buy Warwick?"

Matthew nodded. "That is exactly what he wants," he said. "I am thinking on it, too. It would be a grand legacy for Thomas."

Lysabel thought of her younger brother, a man who was dark-haired and dark-eyed, unlike the rest of the blue-eyed Wellesbourne brood. "And how is Tommy?" she asked. "I've not seen him in a very long time."

Matthew sat back in his chair, his attention on her. "No one has seen *you* in a very long time," he said, smiling. "Tommy and Rosamunde and James and the rest of your siblings have been here from time to time and, of course, I cannot seem to rid myself of Willie, but they all miss you. They will be happy to know you have come home to stay."

Lysabel smiled also, but it was a weak gesture. She'd come to her father with a great deal on her mind and she wasn't quite sure how to bring it up.

All of this – conversation about her siblings and small talk on what her father was doing in his solar – was a stalling tactic. For the past two days, she'd tried to come up with a way to discuss the situation of her and Trenton with her father, but anything she could think of sounded cheap and ridiculous. She didn't want to sound like a foolish, love-struck girl.

Now, she was struggling, afraid she would lose her courage and leave before she spoke her mind.

She had to bring up the subject, somehow.

"And what of Uncle Mark and Uncle John?" she asked. "Are they well, too? I cannot remember when last I saw either of them."

Matthew nodded. "They are well," he said. "You know that your Uncle John commands my outpost at Kington and your Uncle Mark now occupies Rosehill Manor near London. That used to belong to

Aunt Livia years ago. Do you remember her?"

Lysabel's smile turned real. "That old bird with the shrill voice," she said. "She used to terrify me as a child. All I remember is her hugging me and somehow, my face always ended up in her bosom. It was horrifying."

Matthew laughed, low in his throat. "She never had children, you know," he said. "All she wanted was grandnieces and nephews, and when you were born, she never forgave me for not naming you after her. She had to settle for Rosamunde bearing her name as a middle name."

Lysabel snorted. "She left a goodly inheritance to Rosamunde as her namesake."

"But she left you Rosehill, as my firstborn."

"How fortunate. I get the house, but Rosamunde gets the money."

Matthew simply shook his head, grinning. "I am fortunate that all of my children will have large inheritances or dowries," he said. "You, your sisters, your brothers, and, of course, there's Audrey. She has been well provided for even if he has been in a convent for the past twenty years."

Lysabel reflected on her eldest sister, who was actually her father's bastard, born nine years before Lysabel was born. In truth, Audrey hadn't spent much time with her siblings, as Audrey's mother had her own family and kept Audrey with her, but Lysabel remembered a polite young woman who looked exactly like her father. Audrey had never married and instead had chosen to join the cloister, which was where she remained today.

"As long as she is happy, that is all that matters, isn't it, Papa?" Lysabel said, rather leadingly. She saw an opportunity to broach the subject she'd been so very afraid to bring up. "I think that as long as your children are happy, that should be the most important thing."

Matthew leaned back in his chair, putting his hand behind his head. "That is all I have ever wanted for my children," he said. "If Audrey is happy praying all day, then that is her choice."

"I agree."

He looked at her. "Now that... well, now that Benoit is gone, what would make *you* happy, Lys?" he asked. "Have you thought about it? A fine husband, mayhap? A great house and great prestige?"

He couldn't have asked a more perfect question and Lysabel knew she had to speak her mind. It was now or never. She wanted him to respect her unorthodox choice, so she knew she needed to sound firm and reasonable about it.

At least, she would try to.

"I am glad you have asked me," she said. "Truly, Papa, I never thought I would be happy in my lifetime. Of course, I was happy when I was a child. I love you and Mama, and we had a wonderful life here at Wellesbourne. I even loved it when I fostered at Kenilworth. I had a grand time there. And in the beginning with Benoit, I wasn't unhappy, but I wasn't thrilled, either. I suppose I was merely content. But when the trouble started, any hope for happiness was gone. It was like that for so very long."

Matthew's expression softened. "I know," he said quietly. "Though I cannot change the past, know I will do all I can to ensure your future is as happy as it can be."

Lysabel gazed at her father, into those blue eyes she knew so well. "I know it will be happy," she said. "Papa... do you think that when a man and woman care for each other, that nothing else should matter?"

He shrugged. "Unfortunately, there are things that do matter, even if a man and woman love each other," he said. "Your question does not have an easy answer."

Lysabel sighed and lowered her gaze, thinking on what to say next. It was like playing a chess game; for every move he made, she had to counter until she got her point across in a way that didn't have her father crawling the walls.

She wasn't sure that was possible.

"I must tell you something and you must promise not to interrupt me," she said after a moment. "I have thought very hard about this subject and I must ask you to let me speak my mind before you give me your opinion. Will you do this for me?"

Matthew nodded. "Of course I will. What is on your mind, Lys?"

She swallowed hard before continuing. "You told me that Trenton was married, and he is," she said. "But I asked him about his marriage and he told me that it is in name only. Adela is his third wife, and his father forced him into the marriage, and she hates Trenton. He does not live with her, he does not see her. That is why he remains in London with Henry, I think, because he has no real home to go to. Something like that is not fair, Papa. It is not fair to him that his father forced him into such a terrible marriage. Don't you think so?"

Matthew was listening to her with a good deal of suspicion, having an idea where this conversation was going. He could feel himself tensing.

"Gaston did what he felt was best for Trenton at the time," he said quietly, "just as I did what I felt was best for you at the time when I pledged you to Benoit."

Lysabel jumped on that statement. "Then fathers *can* be wrong," she said. "You were wrong about Benoit and Uncle Gaston was wrong about Adela."

"We are not perfect, Lys. We can only do what we feel is right."

Lysabel took a deep breath, preparing for her final onslaught, but tears filled her eyes and she couldn't chase them away. "Papa, I want to be happy," she said as the tears began to fall. "Trenton has made me so very happy. Better still, he has made the girls happy. He is kind and patient and sweet, everything a man should be. He makes me happy, Papa. Is that so very wrong?"

Matthew was blindsided by her tears, coming from his daughter who not once during the time she was married to Benoit had broken down in front of her father, which would have been a hint to her miserable life. But here and now, she was in tears, the first real sign that Matthew had seen of her true feelings on her marriage to Benoit and her hope for something better. It was like a dagger to his heart but, considering the subject matter, he was struggling to remain on an even keel.

"It is not wrong for an old friend to make you happy," he said, trying to stay away from anything romantic. "I am glad he makes you and the girls happy. Trenton is a great friend."

But Lysabel shook her head, almost violently. "Nay," she said. "*Not* a friend. As a man, as a companion, and as a lover. He has found happiness with me and I with him, and even though he is married, he wants to make a life with me because we make each other happy. Even if you do not agree with me, I want you to at least accept my choice. I adore Trenton, Papa, and I want to be happy. I deserve it."

Matthew watched her wipe at her tears, struggling to compose herself. God, he hated to see her cry and he felt a tremendous amount of guilt with it. This was his doing, her misery, so a large part of him wanted to agree with her. Anything to see her happy and ease his guilt.

But the logical side of him couldn't agree. Not even a little bit.

"Aye, you do deserve it," he finally said. "And you do not think you could be happy with someone who could offer you a respectable marriage?"

She sniffled, now wiping at her nose. "Mayhap," she said. "But I do not want anyone else."

He tried to be gentle. "But you have fallen for the first man to show you some kindness, Lys. Trenton has been very kind to you so it is natural that you should feel something for him."

Lysabel looked at him. "I am not a fool," she said. "I would not fall for a man simply because he was kind to me. There is more to it than that."

"And it is not something you could find with a decent man?"

She frowned. "Trenton *is* decent," she said. "I know what he does for the king and I know his father does not approve, but he told me he feels as if he is making a difference and that is why he serves Henry in that capacity. He likes it. Who are you to judge the man for what he feels strongly about?"

She was growing agitated, but Matthew remained calm. He didn't want to fight with her. "I can only judge him based on his history," he said. "Trenton is a killer, Lys. You know this."

"And what are you? You are a great knight who has killed many men."

"But what I do is different. I kill men in battle, or because they threaten me or my family or my way of life. Trenton kills because he is commanded to kill, ruthlessly. The men he kills are not his enemies, but Henry's."

She didn't like what he was saying. "If Henry commanded you to kill one of his enemies tomorrow, would you deny him?"

"Not necessarily," he said honestly.

"Then why is what Trenton does so terrible?"

Matthew sighed heavily; she couldn't understand what he was trying to tell her and that was beginning to frustrate him.

"It is my duty, as your father, to protect you," he said. "I failed with Benoit but I shall not fail in the future. And it is my opinion that any romantic relationship with Trenton is not only hazardous, but immoral because the man is married. You can justify it any way you wish and tell me that he is unhappy in his marriage, but he is offering you nothing, Lysabel. He is offering you the position of being his mistress and when he tires of you, he will find someone else to fill that role. Are your morals so destroyed by Benoit's treatment that you do not know what is right or wrong any longer?"

Lysabel stared at her father. "Is that what you think? That I no longer know what is right and what is wrong?"

Matthew could see the hurt in her eyes. "What else am I to think?" he asked. "That you would shame your family and yourself so terribly, what else am I to think, Lysabel? Do you think any of us will be able to hold our heads up when you become Trenton's whore? Your shame is shame for the entire family."

He couldn't have done more damage had he beat her with his fists, for the feelings she had were the same. *Whore.* That's what he'd called her, but even that word didn't dampen her feelings in the matter. Verging on hurt, angry tears, Lysabel swallowed the lump in her throat.

"I cannot help what I feel," she said hoarsely. "It has nothing to do with what is right or what is wrong, or knowingly bringing shame upon my family. I feel what is in my heart."

Matthew wasn't convinced she was thinking clearly and it only frustrated him.

"You are vulnerable and Trenton has preyed upon that," he said. "And what about your daughters? When it comes time to find them proper husbands, do you think any decent family is going to permit their sons to marry the daughters of a woman who is the mistress to an earl? Stop thinking of yourself and think of Cissy and Cinny. Think of what you are condemning them to."

Lysabel couldn't listen to him any longer. She stood up, turning towards the door. "I think you are being cruel and unjust," she said. "You say that you want me happy, but that is not entirely true. You only want me happy so long as I am doing what you want me to do, and that is selfish."

Matthew stood up, too. "That is not true," he said quietly. "I want you to be happy, but I want you to realize the price for this happiness with Trenton."

She paused by the door, her jaw ticking. "Forgive me for not trusting you, Papa," she said. "The happiness you condemned me to was my hell for twelve years. You will forgive me for wanting to choose my own happiness from now on. Even if you do not approve of it, I ask that you not interfere. It is my choice now. You lost that leverage the first day Benoit beat me unconscious."

With that, she yanked the door open, leaving Matthew feeling sick to his stomach. Slowly, he sank back into his chair. Was she right? Had he lost that right to choose what was best for her when he so badly misjudged Benoit? All he wanted to do was protect her, to make sure she didn't make another mistake that would ruin her life, this time ruining her reputation. But she wouldn't listen to him this time.

In fact, he doubted she would listen to anyone except the one person who had convinced her that her life as a mistress would be far better than anything else she'd known so far. He loved Trenton like a son but, at this point, they were more like adversaries. And like any good warrior, Matthew knew how to handle an adversary.

He would have to do what needed to be done in order to save his daughter.

He'd have to go to the source.

Rising from his chair once more, he went on the hunt for Trenton.

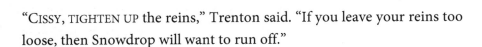

"CISSY, TIGHTEN UP the reins," Trenton said. "If you leave your reins too loose, then Snowdrop will want to run off."

Brencis and Cynethryn were in the area near the stables once again, an open area where soldiers usually trained or gathered, but it had become the pony area because Trenton wouldn't take the girls outside of the walls while they were still learning how to ride. He and Matthew and several soldiers, including Markus, had taken them out once in the meadows, and Brencis had ended up on her arse. That had frightened both Matthew and Trenton, so now the girls only rode inside and on mostly level ground until they could become more skilled.

All skill-learning aside, they were having the time of their lives. Cynethryn was actually much more adept at riding her pony than Brencis was, who didn't quite have the coordination and grace that her sister did. While William, who had forgiven Trenton enough for his humiliation that he was now participating in the pony training, remained with Brencis so the little girl wouldn't fall off again, Trenton set up a very small barrier and started jumping Cynethryn over it.

For Trenton, it had been bonding time to spend with the little girl who had been quite sullen and standoffish when they'd first met. Since the day he'd purchased the pony for her, he'd watched the child come out of her shell. She was still rather serious at times, but she laughed and talked with him now, whereas before, she wouldn't. Trenton was coming to think she was simply a serious child in general, but at least now there was a smile on her face from time to time. And she was quite proud of learning how to jump her pony over the little barrier, a pride that grew as Trenton praised her.

"Trenton," William said as he tended to Brencis. "What say that you and I put up some larger barriers and jump our horses over them? Let us see who can jump the highest."

Trenton rolled his eyes. "Is everything a contest with you?" he asked. "First the swords, now this. Are you eager to be beaten again, Willie?"

William laughed. "I have three older brothers," he said. "We are Wellesbournes. Competing with each other for domination is simply something we do. Ask my father."

Trenton shook his head. "I have never seen your father demand that his sons compete against each other."

"He does not. In fact, he discourages us. But there is something inside of us that begs us to triumph over one another. Call it the victory spirit!"

"I call it exhausting."

"Then you will not pit your horse against mine? Afraid you might lose?"

Trenton cast him a wry expression. "My horse is not built for jumping," he said. "I would not force him to do it. Besides, if that is the only way you can assert dominance over me, then go ahead. I will simply give you the victory."

"You hurt my feelings, depriving me of my chance to beat you fairly."

Trenton faced him, balled fists on his hips. "I am going to hurt your body if you do not stop harassing me," he said. "Go, now. Pay attention to your niece before she falls off and breaks something. And if that happens, know my retribution shall be swift."

William simply grinned at him, that cheeky gesture that prevented

Trenton from truly becoming angry with him, and returned his attention to Brencis. Trenton turned back to Cynethryn, who had stopped her pony and was looking at the pony's feet. Trenton went to her.

"Is something wrong?" he asked.

Cynethryn climbed down from her pony all by herself and crouched down, looking at the pony's legs. "I think she is hurt."

"Why do you say that?"

"Because she limps."

Trenton took the pony by the reins and walked her in a circle to see if he could verify Cynethryn's observations. As soon as the pony started to move, he could see a definitive limp and he pulled the pony to a halt, crouching down beside it and running a practiced hand over the legs. Cynethryn stood next to him, greatly concerned.

"Is she hurt?" she asked. "Did I hurt my pony?"

Trenton could feel a slightly swollen tendon in the right front leg. "She is not used to being ridden so much," he said. "Her leg is injured, but not badly. She will need to rest it for a few days."

Cynethryn's face fell as she went to pet her pony. "I did not mean to hurt her."

Trenton could see how upset she was. "You did not," he said kindly. "She simply needs to become accustomed to being ridden again. She will rest and then you will take her out again when she is well, and it should build up her strength."

Cynethryn nodded, watching her sister as she trotted by on her fat, white pony. "We should take her back to the stable," she said sadly. "What shall we do for her leg?"

Trenton, with his well-controlled emotions, was having a difficult time not feeling great sympathy for the little girl whose out-of-shape pony had sprained a fetlock. He wasn't used to showing compassion, in any form, but the introduction of Cynethryn and Brencis, not to mention Lysabel, had tugged at those usually-tight emotions so that they were spilling out all over the place. That heart of his, usually so hard, had numerous cracks in it now that were only growing deeper and wider. Handing the reins over to the child, he started to head for the stable.

"Not to worry, sweetling," he said quietly. "I will help you tend your pony and while she is mending, we will find you another pony to ride. Would that make you happy?"

Cynethryn looked at him in surprise. "You... you *would*?"

"Of course," he said. "Come along, now. Let's fix your pony."

Cynethryn was looking at him the same way she had when he'd first bought her the pony – incredulous that a man should go out of his way to be kind to her. She nodded and took her pony's reins, pulling the animal along.

"You... you are certain she will be well again?" she asked him.

He nodded. "I am certain."

"I will not lose her?"

He looked at her, feeling his heart tug, just a little more. He could hear the fear of uncertainty in her voice, probably the same uncertainty she'd suffered from her entire life. An unpredictable and violent father had seen to that. He could only imagine how little joy the girl had been given in life, and now that she found it, she was terrified to lose it.

"You will not lose her," he said. "I promise."

That seemed to ease Cynethryn considerably. She wanted to trust him and he was slowly building that trust. As the pair resumed their walk towards the stables, Trenton heard someone call his name.

Pausing, he turned to see Matthew heading in his direction. The man had to pass by Brencis and William, and he paused a moment to say a few words to Brencis, which left her smiling. Matthew continued on, his gaze moving between Cynethryn and Trenton.

"What?" he said. "Is it time for the pony ride to be over already?"

Trenton pointed to the front right leg of the animal. "I am afraid there has been too much activity for Cinny's pony," he said. "Her leg is a little swollen. Nothing a few days of rest won't cure."

Matthew bent over the pony, feeling up both front legs as Trenton had done. "Ah," he said as he felt the slight bump in the right fetlock. "I see. Certainly nothing that cannot be healed."

Now that her grandfather had said the same thing Trenton had, Cynethryn was feeling much better. "Will you help, Grandfather?" she asked.

Matthew nodded. "Of course I will," he said. "Take the pony into the stable and tell the stable master than you must have a poultice for your pony. He will know what to do. I must speak with Trenton for a moment, but I will be there shortly."

Happy, Cynethryn led her pony over towards the stables. When she was out of earshot, Matthew turned to Trenton.

"Do you have a moment for me?" he asked. "I wish to speak with you."

Trenton nodded. "Of course, my lord," he said. "Would you like to speak here or someplace more private?"

Matthew looked around. "There is no one nearby, save Willie," he said. "And I can keep an eye on him should he come too close. What I have to say to you is not for his ears."

"My lord?"

Matthew looked at him, fixing him in the eye. He came right to the point. "Lys came to see me," he said. "She tells me that you and she wish to have a life together."

Trenton didn't change his expression but, inside, he was starting to tense up. He could just see by Matthew's expression what the man thought about everything.

It wasn't good.

Trenton and Lysabel had spent the past two days avoiding speaking on the very subject that Matthew had now broached. Trenton had told her that he would await her decision on the matter, so he didn't want to pressure her, but he also knew that, at some point, she would speak to Matthew. She had told him she would.

Therefore, he wasn't particularly surprised by Matthew's words, but he did brace himself for the man's reaction. He was prepared for an argument, or worse. The past few days had taught him a good deal about what he felt for Lysabel, and it was something beyond mere attraction.

He realized it was love.

In that respect, he, too, had a good deal to say to Matthew.

"Are you *sure* you would not like to speak of this someplace more private?" Trenton said.

Matthew shook his head. "If we are out here for all to see, I cannot lose my temper and neither can you," he said. "This is the perfect place."

Trenton nodded shortly. "Very well," he said. "I am prepared to answer any questions you may have."

Matthew paused, his expression bordering on displeased but he was trying to keep himself from sinking into that pit. He was trying to stay rational.

"Questions," he muttered. "I have many questions, in fact. Is it true you want my daughter to become your mistress?"

Trenton hesitated. "That is not a term I would use for Lysabel."

"Oh?" Matthew said with a hint of sarcasm. "Then what would you call her? A courtesan? A concubine? Trenton, I am trying very hard to be understanding here but, unfortunately, my daughter is involved and I cannot be unbiased about this. Just what, exactly, do you have in mind for my daughter?"

The conversation was off to a rocky start and Trenton was starting to feel scolded. "My lord, you know I am married," he said. "You also know I am married to a woman of my father's choosing, a woman who cannot stand the sight of me. All she wanted was the de Russe money and titles. She lives at Penleigh Manor and entertains her Breton friends and, I would suspect, lovers if she has a mind to. She views our marriage as a prison, something keeping her trapped, and she makes no secret of her disrespect for it."

Matthew threw up his hand to prevent him from explaining himself further. "And?" he said, trying not to snap. "You seek solace with my daughter?"

"I have fallen in love with your daughter."

That brought Matthew to an instant halt. He stared at Trenton a moment before letting out a hissing sigh, closing his eyes as if to ward off those very words.

I am in love with your daughter.

The situation just got more complicated.

"Christ," he muttered. "Trenton, this cannot be. You cannot love her."

"Why not? You do."

Matthew's head snapped to him. "Because I am her father," he said. "You do not have the same attachment to her that I do."

Trenton shrugged. "That does not mean I cannot love her," he said. "Your daughter is a strong, wise, and beautiful woman. How can I not fall in love with those qualities?"

Matthew's jaw tightened. As the seconds ticked away, the more rage and despair he was feeling. Reaching out, he grabbed Trenton by the arm.

"I want you to listen to me and listen well," he rumbled. "You and my daughter are not love-struck children. You are adults, and you know how the world works. Trenton, I know you have a horrible marriage, but just because you have been unlucky in your relationships, do not condemn Lysabel to the same. She's already suffered through the indignities of Benoit, and now you want her to suffer through the indignities of becoming your whore? And what of Cissy and Cinny? What are you condemning them to? Do you know what people will say? They will call them the children of that mistress, the one who lives openly with the Earl of Westbury. They will accuse my daughter of terrible morals and assume her daughters have the same, so when it comes time for them to marry, not a decent family in England will have them. Is that what you wish for them?"

Trenton had stiffened during the course of Matthew's speech and now stood gazing at the man with a taut expression and ticking jaw.

Nothing Matthew said was untrue and he knew that, but to hear it laid out so brutally was difficult for him to swallow. But, still, he held his ground, ground that for all of his tenacity, he could feel slipping away.

All of this was slipping away.

God, please don't let it slip away!

"Of course I do not," he said. "And their mother's lover will be the Duke of Warminster, a prestigious position. I will command the finest husbands for both girls."

Matthew shook his head, exasperated. "You are not thinking clearly, Trenton," he said. "Think with your mind, not your heart. I think it is better for her to be the wife of a lowly knight than the concubine of a duke."

"And I do not."

"At least marriage will make her honorable, which is something she will not have should she be your kept woman."

Trenton's brow furrowed. "You make it sound so dirty, as if I only want her for a possession," he said. "I told you that I love her and I meant it. Why is it wrong for me to want to be with her?"

"It is not wrong," he said. "Except that you have a wife. Whether or not your father forced you into marriage is not the issue. The issue is that you *are* married, whether or not you want to be. You are living in a world of make-believe if you think you can take Lysabel as your concubine and no one will judge either of you for it."

Trenton was growing increasingly distressed. "I know people will judge," he said. "They judge me even now. *You* judge me even now. That's what this is all about, isn't it? You share my father's prejudice against me."

Matthew dropped his hand from Trenton's arm. He wasn't going to lie to the man's face about it.

"It is true that your duties for the king are not something I would do," he said. "That does not mean I judge you for it, but you are correct in stating that I do not want an assassin for my daughter. Even if it is you."

Trenton lifted a dark eyebrow. "I fully intend to resign my post," he said. "I have other properties I can retire to. I will take Lysabel and the girls, and we shall live there in happiness and love. That is something none of us has ever known."

"But *they* will eventually," Matthew stressed. "They will know the happiness of a family, and with a man who can be a husband and father to them. You cannot be either of those."

In that statement, Trenton saw an opportunity to press his case even more. Matthew was bringing up another man, *any* man, who would be both a husband and father to Lysabel and her girls. It was a faceless, nameless man who threatened everything Trenton wanted.

But it wouldn't just be the three of them at some point; soon, there would be a fourth.

"Any man you find for Lysabel and the girls will be taking on an instant family," Trenton said. "Lysabel is pregnant; did you know that? The night I killed Benoit was the night her child was conceived. It was conceived in the most brutal way possible. I am more than willing to overlook her pregnancy. I do not care in the least and I will love that child as if it were my very own. Do you really think you can find a decent man to take Lysabel, her two girls, and an infant? It is not as if she doesn't come with great wealth or titles, you know. She has much to offer, but to a discerning man, her liabilities will outweigh her assets and any other man will simply be desperate for what she has to offer. Is that what you want? Another Benoit who is just looking for an opportunity to dig his claws into the Wellesbourne name?"

Matthew looked at him in shock as he finished what was a rather strong tirade. Lysabel hadn't told him of the child in her belly and he was not only feeling foolish about it, he was feeling a great deal of astonishment. What Trenton said wasn't unreasonable; a woman and two small girls was one thing, but now with the added burden of an infant, it would be increasingly difficult to find her a desirable husband. Most men simply weren't that accepting, and it would be far worse if that baby was a girl. A son, a man could assume as his own, but three girls...

It complicated the situation.

Still, Matthew couldn't give in to Trenton's argument.

"Pregnancy or no pregnancy, it does not change the situation," he said. "Trenton, listen to me. If you love Lysabel as you say you do, then you will not want to condemn her to a world of shame. Of course she has fallen for you; you saved her from Benoit. It is natural that she feels something for you. But when the shock of Benoit's passing fades away, she will realize that she jumped from one bad situation to another if she goes with you. As her father, I must protect her. Even from you."

Trenton could see that Matthew was coming to the heart of his opinion on the situation and Trenton could feel everything slipping away from him faster than before. Even the pregnancy revelation hadn't swayed the man. And if that didn't do it, nothing would.

He could feel his heart beginning to pound.

"Then what are you saying?" he finally asked. "Are you telling me that there is nothing I can say to change your mind?"

Matthew was firm, but there was sorrow in his eyes as he spoke. This wasn't any easier for him than it was for Trenton, but he had to do what he felt was right.

"Nay, there is nothing you can say," he said quietly. "I am asking you to leave, Trenton. I want you to go. Lysabel deserves better than what you are offering her, and I want you to leave and never come back to Wellesbourne as long as she is here. If you do not leave voluntarily, I will have you escorted out."

Trenton knew he would, too. Rather than rise to the man's threat, he did something he'd never done before – he began to plead.

"Please do not ask me to do that," he said, his voice hoarse. "I do not want to leave her or the girls. I love them, Uncle Matthew. I cannot leave behind something I love."

It was rare when he called Matthew by the name he'd called him when he was young. It was indicative of his level of emotion and Matthew, a naturally emotional man, was fighting off the extreme pain of this decision.

But he knew it was for the best.

"I cannot approve or condone what you are asking," he said. "Trenton, I love you as much as if you were my own son, but at this moment, you are a threat to Lysabel and her future happiness. If you love her, then you will let her go. You will put her future over your wants, and if you do not do that, then you are not the man I thought you were."

That which was slipping away from Trenton was now gone. Trenton could feel it. He ran a weary hand over his face, struggling to keep his composure, made worse when Brencis shouted to him as William took the girl over the tiny barrier he'd made for Cynethryn's pony. His gaze was on Brencis and that happy little face, now something he was destined never to see again.

It was tearing his heart out.

"You want me to leave her?" he asked, pointing to Brencis. He had a lump in his throat. "How can I leave her? She has a love for life that I shall never have, and it is glorious. And Cynethryn... she is such a serious child and she is now coming to warm to me. It is one of my best accomplishments, gaining her trust. And Lys... the woman is glory personified. And you are asking me to leave this all behind, Uncle Matthew? Are you truly asking me to do this?"

Matthew could hear the pain and it ripped at him, like great claws. He hated seeing Trenton so shattered, but he could not go back on his request.

He *would* not.

"They were never yours to begin with," he whispered. "Trenton, you cannot ask me to approve of what you want. In your heart, I think you know how wrong it is but you are blinded by this infatuation you have with Lys and her girls."

Trenton's head snapped to him. "It is *not* an infatuation," he said, his eyes blazing. "I love them. I have told you that. How dare you diminish my feelings?"

Matthew hung his head for a moment. He didn't want a battle but if they continued this conversation, that was going to happen.

"I will say this one more time and this will be the end of it," he said. "If you love my daughter, then you will let her have the life she deserves in an honorable marriage, not a life as an earl's mistress. It is a cheap and tawdry thing you are asking and while there is breath left in my body, I will never approve of such a thing. You are unsuitable for her in so many ways, only you do not see that through your own selfishness. I want you to gather your things and go, Trenton. I will give you an hour. You will not speak to Lys or the girls before you go, and I will remain with you until you ride from these gates. Is this in any way unclear?"

"And if I refuse?"

"Then this will get ugly. Do you truly want Lys to see that?"

He didn't. The longer Trenton looked at Matthew, the more he realized that this was really over. The life he wanted for him and Lysabel had slipped through his fingers, dashed to pieces by a man who only saw the morality of the situation, not the heart of it. He couldn't fight Matthew, nor would he, so the only thing he could do was obey the man.

But, God, it was killing him.

"I do not," he muttered, feeling dead and hollow inside. "But I will say this; you have always been the wise and understanding one, but I see now that you have lost those qualities. Since I am not allowed to speak to Lys, what will you tell her? That you ordered me away?"

Matthew was honest. "I will tell her that you have gone and why. If it makes you feel any better, I will shoulder the burden in this situation. I will tell her that I forced you to leave."

It didn't make him feel any better to hear that, and he didn't like the idea of leaving and not being able to tell Lysabel farewell, but he could see by Matthew's face that no amount of pleading would change the man's mind.

"I see," he said. "When you tell her that, you can also tell her that you have put your pride above her own happiness. Make sure she knows that."

Matthew had heard the same thing from Lysabel, but he wasn't going to respond to Trenton. In truth, there was nothing more to say.

And his heart was breaking.

In silence, Matthew followed Trenton as the man went to the knight's quarters to collect his property, and then back to the stables where Dewi was having a lovely nap. As Dewi was brought out and saddled, Cynethryn was still in the stables, watching a groom put a mustard poultice on her pony's leg, and she smiled at Trenton and her grandfather when she caught sight of them.

Matthew smiled, but Trenton was focused on Dewi, too distraught to even look at the little girl who was now looking at him quite curiously. She was still looking at him as he mounted his steed and thundered off in the direction of the gatehouse.

The last anyone saw of Trenton, he was riding from the gates and disappearing into the village beyond.

When Matthew told Lysabel the truth behind Trenton's departure a few hours later, she wept uncontrollably.

CHAPTER TWELVE

Deverill Castle
Wiltshire

THEY CALLED HIM The Dark One.

Gaston de Russe, Duke of Warminster, was a larger-than-life warrior who had fought more battles in his lifetime than most. He came from a long line of warriors, for the House of de Russe had come over with William the Conqueror in days long past, and the name de Russe stood for power, talent, and intimidation.

That reputation still held true.

Gaston had been married at a young age to a cold and unpleasant woman, and that marriage had produced Trenton. When he married his current wife, Remington, he acquired her son, Dane Stoneley, whom he adopted after the death of Dane's father. But Gaston and Remington had produced seven more children – twins Adeliza and Arica, Cort, Matthieu, Boden, Gage, and Gilliana. He had six sons and three daughters to carry on the de Russe name, and they had obliged him for the most part by producing grandchildren – Adeliza and Arica had both married fine men and had eleven children between them, while Matthieu had married a few years back and had four sons.

But the rest of the de Russe sons weren't so obliging.

Dane had been married once before but had lost his wife to a fever many years ago, while Cort, Boden, and Gage seemed to think they didn't have to marry, ever. Then, there was Trenton, who had been unlucky in the three marriages he'd had. His current marriage in particular was something that had been bad for Gaston's relationship with his eldest son and that, coupled by other complex issues, had kept Trenton away from Deverill Castle for six long years.

It was something Gaston had stopped agonizing over a long time ago, but something he'd never gotten over. He still hurt for his son and missed him every day.

But life went on.

Seated in his large, paneled solar, the one that overlooked his wife's tranquil garden but also had windows facing the bailey should he need to see the comings and goings of the castle, Gaston was in the process of examining his map of Wiltshire and Dorset because he'd received a missive from the king offering him some local crown properties at a good price. While Gaston was always looking to expand his empire, the property he really wanted was in Dorset.

Sherbourne Castle was a magnificent castle with rich lands attached to it, and he had hoped to purchase the castle and use it as a bargaining chip to lure one of his sons into a marriage. But as he pored over the maps, his son, Cort, appeared in the doorway with the news of a new arrival.

"Da," Cort sounded breathless, having run all the way from the gatehouse. "You will never believe who has come."

Gaston looked up at his son; he was his first son with Remington, an enormous man with copper curls to his shoulders and eyes the color of the sea. In fact, he looked astonishingly like his mother all the way down to her pale, freckled skin, only on Cort, Remington's coloring and Gaston's massive build made him look like a god.

Cort de Russe was all shades of delicious.

And he had no shortage of women throwing themselves at his feet. It was something he was quite proud over. One look at that beautiful, curly hair and those flashing eyes, and women were butter in his hands.

At twenty years and nine, it was time for the man to settle down, but he was squirrelly when it came to allowing his father to broker a marriage for him. In fact, it was with Cort in mind that Gaston wanted to purchase Sherbourne. Even his cheeky, egotistical son couldn't pass up on an opportunity like that.

Or, so Gaston hoped.

But those thoughts were pushed aside as the very man he'd been considering was now standing rather excitedly in his solar. Cort had an excitable personality, passionate in everything he did, so to see the man twitching with glee wasn't anything unusual. A smile played on his lips as Gaston sat back in his chair.

"Tell me, Cort," he said. "Who could possibly be visiting me to-day?"

Cort didn't sense that his father was taking him seriously, but he knew the moment he spoke, his father would. He was so excited that he simply couldn't be gentle about it.

"Trenton is here," he said.

As Cort knew, the smile vanished from Gaston's face and a look of astonishment washed over him. "Trenton?" he repeated. "*Here?*"

Cort nodded eagerly. "Come, Da," he said. "He is at the gatehouse."

Gaston shot to his feet. But something kept Gaston from running. His heart was pounding and eagerness surged through him, but he didn't go. He'd long since stopped running to Trenton because he'd realized long ago that if Trenton wanted to see him, Trenton would come to him. He was finished going after a son who only rejected him when he came too close.

Slowly, he sat back down.

"If Trenton wishes to see me, tell him where to find me," he told Cort. "You had better go tell your mother now."

Cort was puzzled but he did what he was told. The relationship between his oldest brother and his father had been contentious over the years, so he didn't try to second-guess either of them and he didn't get involved. He'd learned long ago that whatever went on between those two was better left for them to work out alone.

As Cort headed off to tell his mother the news before returning to the gatehouse, Gaston returned to the maps in front of him, but his mind wasn't on his business. He was feigning it was, but it wasn't. His mind was on Trenton and his visit. He felt so much anxiety that it was difficult for him to focus on anything.

Why had Trenton come?

As much as he pretended not to keep track of his eldest son, the truth was that he did. He had a home in London where his cousin, Patrick, resided and Patrick saw Trenton quite frequently. Patrick commanded the small army kept based at Braidwood House, situated on the banks of the Thames just to the east of the Tower of London. Whenever Trenton was at Greenwich, he would visit Patrick, a man who had suffered a good deal of trials and tribulations in his life. Somehow, Trenton felt a kindred spirit with Patrick because the man understood what it was to suffer. He also wasn't as judgmental as Gaston was. Therefore, Trenton trusted him, and Patrick told Gaston what he could of the man.

But Gaston knew it wasn't all of it.

As he waited for Trenton to show himself, Gaston's gaze moved back to the map of Wiltshire and parts of Dorset and Somerset. He noted Trenton's properties of Westbury, Penleigh, and the hunting lodge at Hawkridge. Gaston had given those to Trenton, as his heir, hoping those things would ease whatever rockiness was between them, but gifts and titles hadn't solved a thing.

He honestly wasn't sure anything ever would.

Ever since Trenton had been a young man, there had been long periods of separation, and a mother who hated the sight her son's father and tried to poison Trenton against him. Even though the years had seen father and son repair the damage for the most part, Gaston always thought there might have been some part of Trenton that still believed his mother, that still resented a father who had been away so much.

Mistakes he'd made with Trenton that he hadn't made with his other children. Perhaps that was why Gaston had a soft spot for his eldest son, the lad who had gone through more tribulations than most. And then, there was his work for Henry...

That was something Gaston tried not to think about. When Trenton had taken the post with Henry, Gaston had given him his opinion on the dishonorable nature of it, but it hadn't swayed Trenton. The man was convinced he'd be doing great and important things for Henry when the truth was that he was simply Henry's attack dog. Everyone knew it. Everyone in England feared Trenton in a way they'd never feared Gaston, mostly because when Gaston moved, it was with an army, and one knew what was coming. But with Trenton, he moved in stealth, with his band of trusted men, and one never knew what was coming until it was too late.

Gaston had always wanted something better for his son than what he had been dealt, but it seemed as if that wasn't meant to be.

Truthfully, Gaston had no idea how long he sat there and reminisced about Trenton's life and where he'd gone wrong. He lost all track of time as he pondered his eldest. When next he realized, a massive figure was suddenly standing in his solar doorway and he looked up to see Trenton standing there in full armor.

Never had Gaston seen a prouder, or more welcome, sight.

His boy had come home.

"Trenton," he said, realizing there was a lump in his throat. "I... I was told you had arrived. It is good to see you, lad."

Trenton stood there, looking at his father, his features pale and his expression tight. There was tension in the air, tension created by separation and the fragility of the relationship between them. But there was also relief in the air, relief that they were once again in the same room, men who loved each other, but men whom the years had damaged. Trenton finally spoke.

"Father," he greeted. "Am I welcome?"

Gaston stood up and came around his table. "Of course you are," he said. "You are always welcome here."

Trenton didn't say anything for a moment. In spite of what his father said, he wasn't sure if he felt welcome or not. That tension between them was turning into awkwardness. His gaze was on his father, realizing that the man looked very tired. He'd never seen him look so tired and he felt a stab of sorrow that he'd stayed away for so long, his father had gotten old in that time. In fact, it was rather shocking to see him this way.

In Trenton's mind, his father had always been the biggest, most powerful man in the entire world. They shared the same height – six inches over six feet – and they both had the same nearly-black hair and gray eyes. Their builds were also very similar and their weight had always been close, so essentially, they were exactly the same size. But in looking at his father now, Trenton could swear the man had shrunk a little, and his dark hair had a good deal of gray in it.

Six years could certainly change a man.

"I... I've not seen mother yet," Trenton said as he took a couple of timid steps into the room. "Cort went to tell her I have arrived. And I'm told that Dane is no longer here?"

Gaston moved towards his son, his manner also timid. "Dane is still at Deverill, but he is in Warminster administering justice today," he said. "Dane has been my sheriff for a few years now, but I do plan to move him up to a newly acquired property near the Marches soon. As much as I depend on him, he cannot stay here with me forever. It is time he had his own lands to administer."

"New property?" Trenton asked, sounding politely interested. "Where is it?"

"Blackmore Castle," he said. "It runs the stretch of the Marches bordering de Lara territory, between Shrewsbury and the Trilateral castles of Trelystan, Hyssington, and Caradoc. It will be an important place in the Marches for Dane to administer and we shall be allied with de Lara along that stretch of the Marches. With de Lohr holding nearly the entire southern stretch of the Marches and de Lara and de Russe holding a stretch of the middle, it will work greatly in Henry's favor towards maintaining peace with Wales."

Trenton nodded in understanding. "Dane is deserving of such an honor," he said. "I hope to see him before he leaves."

"He is not leaving for the Marches for some time. And he should return soon from Warminster, so you will see him."

Trenton simply nodded, again, and the conversation died. As Gaston was thinking of something more to say, perhaps even ask him why he'd come, Trenton turned for the door and Gaston seriously wondered if the man was about to leave. But instead, he closed it and threw the bolt.

That brought Gaston's curiosity. As he stood there, he watched Trenton remove his helm, revealing his damp, dark hair, and set his helm to the nearest table. He seemed quite pensive, his head lowered as he made his way towards Gaston, seemingly pondering something that was on his mind. Gaston could just tell by looking at him that something was weighing heavily upon him.

But Gaston was not prepared when Trenton lifted his eyes to him and there were tears pooling in the muddy depths.

"Da," he said hoarsely. "I need your help. I do not know where else to turn."

Gaston was shocked; terrified was more like it. "What is it?" he asked, reaching out to grasp his son by the arms. "Trenton, in the name of God, what has happened?"

Trenton was trying to compose himself enough so that he could speak without weeping. Angrily, he wiped at his eyes, but the tears wouldn't seem to stop. He was so overwrought that he simply couldn't control his emotions any longer. A two-day ride from Wellesbourne, straight through, had left him exhausted and fragile. He'd had all that time to think about Lysabel, and Matthew, and the horrible ending they'd suffered. With a heavy sigh, he plopped onto the chair behind him.

"Forgive me for my display," he said, trying to assure his father that he wasn't going to fall apart. "I am not sure where to start, so it is best to start at the beginning."

Gaston didn't let go of him. There was a stool behind him and he grabbed around for it, pulling it forward so he could set his bulk upon it. He was still so astonished that his son, his proud and powerful son, had been driven to tears that he was positive something catastrophic had happened.

"Speak, lad," he said quietly, encouragingly. "Tell me what has happened."

Trenton took a deep breath, steadying himself, but when he looked at his father, he felt very emotional. Years of separation, of hard feelings, of his father's disapproval didn't seem to matter at the moment. All he knew was that he needed help and, in spite of everything, his father was the one man he could depend on, no matter what.

"In July, Henry sent me to the home of Benoit de Wilde, Sheriff of Ilchester," he said. "As my men and I were entering the grounds of the castle, we heard a woman screaming. She was being beaten. We made our way into Benoit's chamber and found both him and the woman he had been beating. Purely by chance, I recognized the woman and it was Lysabel Wellesbourne. De Wilde had beaten her bloody."

Gaston's face was a mask of disbelief. "Lysabel Wellesbourne?" he gasped. "My God... de Wilde *bloodied* her?"

Trenton nodded. "Severely," he said. "Henry had sent me to Stretford Castle with the intention of bringing Ilchester back to him, but I did not make it that far."

"What did you do?"

"I killed him," he said simply. "When I saw it was Lysabel that he had abused, I killed him. Before you chide me on the fact, know that I do not regret it and that Uncle Matthew knows what I have done. He has thanked me for it."

Gaston's eyes were wide with the astonishment of the situation. He took a moment, pondering what he'd been told, before speaking.

"I cannot imagine I would have done any differently," he admitted. "It sounds as if you saved Lysabel's very life."

Trenton nodded. "I did," he said. "De Wilde was a vile excuse for a man, Da, not only with his wife, but with many things. That was why Henry sent me for him. You knew him, didn't you?"

Gaston nodded. "A little," he said. "We had crossed paths from time to time, and I knew he was married to Lysabel. I had also heard the rumors of his whoring, and I'd even told Matt about it, but Matt told me he would take care of it. What I'd not heard was that he abused his wife. God, I had no idea. Did Matt?"

Trenton shook his head. "Nay," he said quietly. "The news hit him hard."

Gaston sighed sympathetically. "I am sure it did," he said. "But what has you so upset, Trenton? What does de Wilde and Lysabel Wellesbourne have to do with anything?"

Trenton looked at his father, thinking that his question had so many answers. He was a little calmer now, but he wasn't any less emotional. He proceeded as carefully as he could, given the subject matter.

"Lysabel Wellesbourne has a great deal to do with everything," he said. "She has two young daughters and they will heal with time. Benoit never physically abused them, but the fear he struck into them and the cruelty he showed them were substantial. It is difficult..."

He trailed off, as if frustrated, and Gaston urged him onward. "*What* is difficult, lad?"

Trenton yanked off his heavy gloves, tossing them aside. His movements were sharp, full of frustration.

"There is simply no easy way to say this," he said. "Lysabel and I want to be together. I have never in my life, with the exception of Alicia, loved a woman. You know how devastated I was when Alicia died, and then Iseuld followed, and now Adela. Adela is the wife I did not want and a woman who has ruined whatever self-respect I ever had for myself. She makes it clear how much she hates me, and that is no way for a married man to be treated. I have not felt married since the day I took my vows with her. Yet, with Lysabel... it happened so naturally, so unexpectedly, that I was surprised by it. Overwhelmed by it, in fact. She and her daughters have shown me a side of life I never knew to exist, at least not for me, and we wish to be together. But Uncle Matthew will not allow it. I was at Wellesbourne Castle two days ago and when I told him of my love for Lysabel, he told me to leave and not come back."

Gaston was listening to his son with more astonishment than he ever thought possible. His stoic, proud, and complex son had fallen in love... not with his wife, but with another woman, a woman he'd known his entire life.

In truth, Gaston didn't know how to feel about it. He simply couldn't comprehend it. But the longer he looked into Trenton's pale face, the more he began to realize that this was no joke. It was the truth.

Trenton had found love.

Gaston put a hand to his head in disbelief.

"Oh... Trenton," he said, but it ended up coming out in one heavy sigh. "I... I do not know what to say, lad. I simply cannot believe what I am hearing."

Trenton wiped the remaining moisture from his eyes. "Why not?" he asked. "Because it is me we are talking about? Since when do I love anyone other than myself, is that it?"

Gaston was shaking his head before Trenton even finished. "That is not what I mean," he said. "I simply mean it is a great deal to absorb. This is not something I ever expected to hear from your lips, ever."

Trenton snorted, now feeling embarrassed that he'd become so emotional. He stood up from the chair and headed to a table next to the wall, one that contained a bowl full of nuts, half of them cracked with empty hulls still in the bowl, and a decanter of wine. Trenton picked up the wine and sniffed it before pouring it into a cup that still had some dregs at the bottom of it.

"I have not seen you in six years," he muttered before taking a long drink of wine. "Six long years, and when I do come to see you, I behave like a hysterical woman. Forgive me for carrying on so."

Gaston watched his boy as the man downed the rest of the cup and then poured himself another one.

"There is nothing to forgive, Trenton," he said. "Clearly, the situation has you upset, and it is understandable that it would."

Trenton downed half of the second cup and then stood there a moment, pondering the situation.

"I have been a disappointment to you my entire adult life," he said. "Here is yet another instance where I can disappoint you. I have a wife, yet I am in love with another woman. I want to live with her and make a life with her. That is the reality of it and that is why Uncle Matthew asked me to leave."

Gaston stood up, stiffly. "You have *not* been a disappointment to me your entire adult life," he said. "Trenton, you are my firstborn. I had such great dreams and hopes for you when you were born, and I still have great dreams and hopes for you. That has never changed."

Trenton looked at him. "But what of *my* hopes and dreams?" he said. "Since I am here, we may as well get this conversation out of the way. Do you know why I have stayed away for so long? Because I was tired of looking in your eyes and always seeing such disappointment. I was tired of you placing expectations on me that were not of my choosing. I had my own life to lead, but you did not seem to realize that. You wanted me to follow the path of your choosing, and I could not do it. But when you forced me into a marriage that I did not want, that was the end for me. *You* did this to me, Da. Had you not forced me into marrying Adela, the past six years more than likely would not have happened."

Gaston knew that. He'd had many years to think on that very subject, and he'd come to the same conclusion Trenton had come to.

He'd caused the rift.

"I know," he said quietly. "Believe me, Trenton, I blame myself daily for what has happened between us. But in my defense, I simply wanted something better for you than I had. I wanted a better reputation for you, a better marriage. My intentions were good even if nothing went according to plan."

"*Your* plan," Trenton pointed out. "I am not angry with you over it anymore. I have long since gotten over my resentment. But what hurts me the most is the division it caused. I tried to tell you once but you just would not listen to me."

Gaston was submissive because nothing Trenton said was untrue. If he was to make this right between them, then he would have to swallow his pride and accept the blame.

"Then what would you have me do, lad?" he asked. "You came into this chamber and asked for my help, and I am listening to you now. What help do you want from me?"

They were back to the painful subject of Lysabel and Trenton drained his cup. He could feel the alcohol coursing through his veins, loosening his tongue and feeding the emotions he was trying to keep a rein on.

"I know I am married," he said. "By the laws of God and the laws of this country, I am, and it is a sticky position that I find myself in. I simply want to be happy with the woman I love, who happens not to be my wife, and I do not think that wanting to be happy is asking too much. I do not expect Uncle Matthew's blessing, but I would at least ask that he not interfere. This is my life, and Lysabel's life, and we must live it as we see fit, for certainly, our fathers had their chances to direct us with their good guidance but in both cases, there was failure. Now, it is our turn to choose our own happiness."

Gaston sighed faintly as he turned away, heading over to the big and comfortable chair that he sat in quite often because it eased the strain on his back. He had aches and pains in his old age. The chair was positioned near the hearth, which was dark at this hour, and he sat heavily. His mind was trying to process what was happening with Trenton, but he was also hurt by his own guilt in that he had a hand in his son's misery. He could see that he'd lost Trenton's trust, and that was hard for him to take.

Leaning back in the chair, Gaston looked to his son.

"So you want to live with a woman who is not your wife," he said.

"Surely, I cannot judge you for it, because that is exactly what I did with Remington in the early days when I first met her. I was married to your mother and she was still married to Guy. I know you remember those days, Trenton, but you do not remember just how difficult they were for us. We tried to keep as much as we could from you and Dane, but much of that time was filled with tribulation."

At least his father wasn't trying to judge him; Trenton felt better with that. He knew his father was the one man who could understand his predicament, considering what he went through with Remington.

"I remember some of it," he said. "I remember when Guy abducted Remi and nearly killed Patrick. I remember Dane and I stealing an old nag of a horse and trying to help you rescue her."

Gaston smiled at the memory. "Talk of what you and Dane did still makes her angry," he said. "You stole that old horse and rode it all the way from Oxford to Yorkshire. Even though I could never tell Remi, I was very proud of you and Dane for your bravery. That took great courage."

Trenton grinned, a reluctant gesture. "Remi threatened to beat us."

"She never did."

Trenton laughed softly. "Nay, she never did, but there were many threats for many years after that. She still might try, even now."

"It was because she loved you, lad. She was afraid for you."

"I know." Trenton sobered. "She is a good woman, Da. She has been very good to me. In a sense, Lysabel reminds me of her – she, too, was abused by her husband, much as Remi was, but instead of letting it crush her, she has remained strong. So very strong. She is a very good woman and much as you could not let Remi go, I cannot let Lysabel go, either, but Uncle Matthew does not understand that."

Gaston did, indeed, understand and that, more than anything, was why he couldn't refuse him. God, he knew what it was to love a woman so much that nothing else mattered. He looked at his son intently.

"Then what do you want me to do?" he asked quietly.

"I want you to talk to him," Trenton said, going to his father and taking a knee beside his chair. "Please, Da. Talk to him and explain to him that love cannot be denied. Tell him that we do not expect his approval, but we do not want his interference. Will you do that for me?"

Gaston knew that would be the request. He knew the entire conversation was a build-up to it and, in truth, he was being put in a bad position. Trenton was his son, but he wanted something unorthodox and, some would say, immoral. Matthew was Gaston's very best friend, a man who had sacrificed his left hand so that Gaston could live, so there was a deep and unbreakable bond between them.

Years and years of battle, of camaraderie, and of life or death situations had cemented Gaston and Matthew together. Now, Gaston was being asked to convince Matthew not to interfere in his daughter's life. Matthew was supposed to look the other way when Lysabel became the mistress of a man who loved her – Gaston's own son.

God, nothing was simple any longer.

"What you ask, Trenton," Gaston said hesitantly. "You are asking me to interfere in Matt's decision regarding his own children. I would not expect him to interfere in my decisions regarding my family and I am sure he will not take kindly to me interfering with his business. Do you understand that?"

Trenton nodded. "I understand," he said. "I would not ask if it did not mean everything to me. Please, I would think you would want to do all you can to at least right some of the wrongs between us."

Gaston was only going to let Trenton browbeat him about their relationship for so long. He was willing to be submissive, and to admit his guilt, but he wasn't willing to be provoked. He would draw the line.

"Of course I do," he said. "But you are not going to make me feel as if your decision to pursue another woman is somehow my fault. This is not the tactic to use, Trenton. You are a man; accept that you want to fornicate with a woman who is not your wife. I will accept that I pushed marriage with Adela on you, but your decision with Lysabel is your very own. I have no part of that."

Trenton could see that the man had his dander up and he realized he'd gone too far. "I am sorry," he said. "It was unkind of me to say that. And I fully accept that this is my choice, and my decision, which is why I am so unwilling to let it go. I have had a taste of happiness with Lysabel and I want to know it forever. Please, Da, *help* me. Talk to Uncle Matthew. Help him to understand that happiness is sometimes more important than honor."

Gaston could hear the desperation in his son's voice, something he'd never heard before. Trenton had always been supremely confident in everything, a man who never second-guessed anything he did. He had Gaston's stubborn traits in him. Therefore, the desperation concerned Gaston because he was wondering if Trenton wasn't being reckless about this. It wasn't like the man to be impulsive.

But it was apparent that something quite serious was going on, enough to drive Trenton straight to his father after six years of separation. Either Trenton had lost his mind or he was, indeed, quite serious about Lysabel Wellesbourne, and the truth was that Gaston had no choice but to side with him. He was his heir, his flesh and blood, and he would do anything for him.

Even risk a lifelong friendship.

"If that is your wish, then I shall go to Wellesbourne," he said quietly. "Leave me, now. Go and see your mother and your siblings. Let me think on what is to come and how I shall approach Matthew with it. You're quite sure about this, Trenton?"

Trenton was nearly limp with relief, realizing that he had the ally he'd hoped for in his father. "Aye," he said. "More sure than I have ever been of anything in my life."

"You would have saved me a lot of trouble had you declared your intentions for Lysabel twenty years ago."

Trenton grinned. "Twenty years ago, she was twelve years of age and I was twenty. She was far from my mind and, I will admit, I never gave her a second glance. That was my mistake."

"Then she must have grown into a magnificent woman."

"You will see her, Da. Then you will understand."

"I am sure I will."

Trenton was still kneeling next to his father's chair and as he stood up, he kissed his father on the head before heading to the solar door and unbolting it. He felt better than he had in two days, now with hope on the horizon. Throwing open the door, the first things he came face to face with were his mother, four brothers, and a sister. Dane, Cort, Boden, Gage, Gilliana, and Remington all grinned when they saw him, and a cry of delight went up. Thrilled, Trenton roared with joy and opened his arms, and it became a giant love-fest right there in Gaston's solar doorway.

The prodigal brother had come home.

And Gaston listened to it all with a smile. It was so good to hear the chatter, the laughter. He could hear Dane, who must have just returned early from his business in the village, and he could also hear his youngest daughter, Gilliana, as she squealed when Trenton squeezed her.

Listening to the happiness going on outside of his solar made Gaston realize just how much he'd missed Trenton's presence. He'd never felt complete without his eldest son, but now, he did. He'd found that piece that was missing.

Trenton was home.

Hopefully, there would be no more separations and, perhaps, that was the predominant reason he agreed to go to Wellesbourne. He wanted to please his son, because surely one more disappointment, and Trenton might leave and never return.

It was a fear Gaston had.

He was willing to risk his best friend's devotion because of it.

CHAPTER THIRTEEN

Wellesbourne Castle

I T WAS A warm day, with a gentle breeze blowing in from the west, a sea breeze that carried the sea birds this far inland.

In Audrey's garden, Lysabel was sitting on the stone bench, the same stone bench where she and Trenton had shared the first kiss of their romantic interlude. She was watching her daughters as they followed her mother from bush to bush, clipping buds and putting long-stemmed flowers into a woven basket.

Cynethryn and Brencis seemed to be having a pleasant time, but it was a rare moment in the past two days, ever since Trenton had left abruptly. Of course, Lysabel knew why he'd gone, thanks to her father, but the girls were confused, so she had told them that Trenton had business he needed to attend to. The girls were very anxious to know when he would be returning, but that was something Lysabel couldn't answer. All she could tell them was "soon", but she was certain that wasn't the truth.

She suspected he would never come back.

Lysabel was accustomed to disappointment. She'd been suffering it most of her adult life, so this was just another disappointment in a long line of disappointments. God didn't want her to be happy; she'd already decided that. He wanted her to stay miserable because she was evidently doing penitence for some terrible sin she must have committed in her life, and she was so embittered about it that she could taste it upon her tongue.

Bitter with the sorrow that was her life.

A squeal from Brencis caught her attention and she looked over to see her mother plucking a thorn from the little girl's finger and wiping her tears away. Brencis wasn't a particularly happy girl, anyway, because a few hours after Cynethryn's pony went lame, Snowdrop turned up with a sore hip, so both ponies were tucked away in a stall, healing from too much riding by overeager girls. Lysabel took the opportunity to have the girls do other things, like tend the garden with their grandmother, but they weren't too eager about it. It didn't have the same allure as ponies.

In fact, Brencis was wailing by this point because of her pricked finger, but her grandmother gave her a kiss and turned her towards a bush with lovely pink flowers that she could tend. There were a few servants around, women who always tended the gardens, and one of them began to help Brencis cut off the pink flowers and put them in her basket. As Cynethryn rushed to cut her own pink flowers, Alixandrea wandered over to where her daughter was sitting.

"God's Bones," she muttered, pulling off her gardening gloves and wiping at the sweat on her forehead. "'Tis a warm day today."

Lysabel nodded, watching her daughters fight over the pink flowers. "It is."

It was a short answer, not impolite, but it conveyed her unwillingness to be drawn into small talk. Alixandrea eyed her daughter a moment before sitting down on the bench next to her.

As Matthew's wife and Lysabel's mother, Alixandrea knew what was wrong. All of the information had come from her husband, and none from her daughter, and she'd vowed to remain silent on the matter unless Lysabel wanted to discuss it. But as the days passed and she saw how depressed and lifeless her daughter was, she was having a difficult time holding to that vow. Lysabel was avoiding both of her parents for the most part, and Alixandrea felt sorry for the woman. She very much wanted to hear her side of it.

Perhaps it was time for a mother's understanding.

"Lys," she said as she pulled the wimple off her head, the one that was meant to keep the dust and dirt out of her hair. "Would you like to talk about it?"

"About what?"

"Your father told me what happened with Trenton. Did you think he would not?"

Lysabel shifted uncomfortably. "There is nothing to discuss," she said. "Papa has sent Trenton away. He has made his decision."

Alixandrea looked at her. "Mayhap he has," she said. "But I want to hear about the situation from you. All I have heard is your father's side of things. Will you do me the courtesy of telling me yours?"

Lysabel sighed heavily. "Why, Mama?" she asked. "Will it change things? Will it cause Papa to change his mind?"

Alixandrea could hear the distress in her child's voice. "Probably not," she said. "But I would still like to hear it from you. Will you tell me?"

Lysabel fell silent, still watching her daughters. As she sat there, her eyes began to fill with tears, which she quickly blinked away.

"Oh... Mama," she whispered. "He simply does not understand."

"What does he not understand, sweetheart?"

Lysabel wiped at her nose. "I cannot help that I have fallen in love with Trenton," she said. "He cannot help that he has fallen in love with me. I know he is married, but his wife hates him and he hates her. They should have never been married in the first place. All we want is to be happy without Papa's interference."

Alixandrea watched her daughter struggle and she was greatly sympathetic. It was essentially what her husband had told her, but without Matthew's fatherly take on the situation.

Now, she was hearing the emotional side.

"Your father only wants what is best for you, even if what is best for you does not make you happy at first," she said gently. "I think he believes it is an infatuation you have with Trenton because he saved you from your terrible life with Benoit. It is natural that you should look to Trenton as your savior, but that does not mean you love him."

Lysabel looked at her mother, incensed. "I am a grown woman," she said. "I know what love is. What I feel for Trenton was not something that suddenly appeared. It was something that grew until I realized what it was. Mama, he is kind to me and he makes me smile. He is good to Cinny and Cissy, better than their own father ever was, and at least I know that Trenton will never raise a hand to me and that is more than I can say for Benoit. I have not felt safe since I left Wellesbourne to marry Benoit."

Alixandrea's brow furrowed. "What do you mean when you say that is more than you can say for Benoit?"

Lysabel looked at her mother. "Did Papa not tell you that?"

"Tell me what?"

"That Benoit beat me."

Alixandrea stiffened, an expression of horror creeping over her features. "He did not," she said, sounding weak. "Sweet Jesus... he *beat* you?"

Lysabel looked away, hating that she now had to explain Benoit's behavior to her sweet mother. "I thought Papa told you," she said. "Benoit started beating me after he realized Papa would not give him my inheritance. I endured at least ten years of my marriage being beaten black and blue. He would beat me when he was sober, when he was drunk, or simply because he felt like it. He was beating me the night Trenton came to Stretford on the orders of Henry. The king wanted Benoit for an offense, which Trenton never told me, but instead of taking him back to Henry, Trenton killed him when he saw that the man had beaten me."

Now, Alixandrea's eyes were filling with tears and a hand went to her mouth, indicative of her shock. No, she hadn't heard any of this and in the times she had seen her daughter over the years, she never saw bruises or anything else to indicate what was going on. Her daughter never seemed particularly happy with her marriage, but she never saw the signs of abuse. Whatever signs there were had been covered well, and she was absolutely devastated.

Alixandrea's first reaction was to be furious at Matthew for not telling her, but she suppressed that instinct. This was her daughter's crisis and the focus needed to be on her. She had to assume that if Matthew didn't tell her any of this, he must have had a good reason. She knew the man too well to believe his intention in withholding the information had been anything other than to protect her from the horrors of the truth.

Taking a deep breath, Alixandrea forced herself to calm, at least as much as she was able.

"Then Trenton truly saved you, more than I realized," she said hoarsely. "I am so sorry for what Benoit did, Lys. Your father and I knew that you were not particularly happy with him, and when the visits became less and less frequent, we were deeply distressed and did not know why. But now... I suppose the situation makes a little more sense. Clearly, you were living with a monster but you never asked us for help. Why not?"

Lysabel could see the pain in her mother's eyes, the same pain she had seen in her father's when discussing Benoit. As a parent herself, she understood what it would be like to have one of her daughters abused by a husband and being powerless to stop it. In a show of sympathy for her mother, she reached out and grasped the woman's hand.

"I will tell you what I told Papa," she said. "My father would have killed Benoit. He would have felt such guilt and rage for marrying me to a man who abused me that he would have killed him, and that guilt would have weighed on him for the rest of his life. I love Papa too much to burden him with such a thing. It was better to suffer in silence... Benoit was my husband and he had every right to do whatever he pleased. There would have been nothing you could have done about it."

Alixandrea squeezed her daughter's hand tightly, a sob escaping her lips. Lysabel could see her mother breaking down and she moved closer to her on the bench, putting her arm around her mother's shoulders to comfort her.

"No tears, please," she whispered. "The girls will see and it will upset them. They are mending nicely in the wake of their father's absence."

Alixandrea nodded quickly, forcing herself to still her tears. "He never... he never touched the girls, did he?"

"Never."

Alixandrea felt some relief about that, but she was still shattered over the revelation of her daughter's treatment. But in that realization, she came to see why Lysabel would have fallen for Trenton. Literally, the man had saved her. He represented a new life and a new hope to her, in more ways than one.

"Then you are all on the path to healing," she said, squeezing her daughter's hand again. "I understand now why you hold Trenton in such regard. It makes a good deal of sense. But even so, he is not the man of your future. He has been kind to you, and he has made you feel safe and warm, but you must face the reality of his situation – he is married, Lys. Regardless of the fact that it is a bad marriage, it does not erase *the* marriage. I am not diminishing your feelings for him, but did you ever consider the long-term implications of such a relationship?"

Lysabel wasn't as defensive as she had been earlier. Holding her mother's hand, she was starting to feel comforted and even vulnerable in a sense. She knew she could be honest with her mother and the woman would be honest with her in return.

"You mean children?" she asked softly.

"Aye."

Lysabel sighed heavily. "I am pregnant now, Mama," she whispered. "It is Benoit's child, conceived the night he died during the terrible beating he dealt me. Trenton knows of this and it does not matter to him. He is willing to accept the child as his own, and love it as his own. Only a man of great honor and of noble heart could do such a thing."

Alixandrea had to close her eyes, reeling from two doses of rather serious and intense news in a short amount of time. First Benoit's abuse, and now a pregnancy. It was a struggle more than ever to hold herself together.

"A baby," she murmured.

"Aye, a baby."

"Your father did not mention this, either."

"I have not told him. Unless Trenton did, there is no way he could know."

Alixandrea was coming to think her daughter had been dealt a horrible lot in life. Lysabel had been such a bright, beautiful child, and they had always hoped for such great things for her. But the hopes of the parents had been dashed by the realities of a man Alixandrea had never liked.

In truth, she saw no point in telling her daughter her opinion of Benoit as she had told her husband. She was coming to blame herself for not saying anything those years ago, but there was no sense in looking back. It didn't matter any longer if she had an intense dislike for the man; he was dead and gone now, and Lysabel now had a chance for a much better life with a man who deserved her.

But that man wasn't Trenton de Russe.

Alixandrea was going to side with her husband in this case, now that she understood the entire situation. To allow Lysabel to go with Trenton would be to condemn her to a life that would be dishonorable at best. She couldn't allow her daughter to enter into such a relationship, but she also knew Lysabel well enough to know that to forbid her of such a thing, as Matthew had done, wasn't the way to convince her.

Alixandrea had to be more subtle than her husband had been, but she was going to get her point across.

"There is no shame in the child you carry now," she finally said. "It was conceived with your husband, who is now dead, so no man would find that shameful. But I will say something about this situation, Lys, and I will say no more, so please listen. It is important that you do."

Lysabel looked at her mother seriously. "I am listening."

Alixandrea patted her hand. "I understand that you love Trenton," she said. "We all love Trenton. I have known him for most of his life and we shall always be grateful to him for what he has done for you. He has given you the opportunity for a new hope in life, the hope of a new beginning for you and the girls. That is a remarkable thing."

Lysabel smiled timidly. "I think so, too," she said. "And I do want a new life... with him."

Alixandrea nodded. "I know, sweetheart," she said. "But I want you to think very carefully about this because it is important for you to see the situation from all sides. Will you do that?"

Lysabel nodded hesitantly. "I will try."

Alixandrea smiled sadly, her gaze intense upon her daughter. "I want you to put yourself in your father's position," she said. "He is a great man, of great standing, and he has the respect of all of England. He is the White Lord of Wellesbourne, and that is a burden that he labors to maintain every day. He has worked hard for it. Now, imagine you are your father – you have seven wonderful children. But then, your eldest daughter decides that it is in her best interest to become the mistress to a married man. Now, the reputation your father has worked so hard for is blemished by your choice. Your father has an eye on a wife for your brother, James, but because of your decision to enter into a relationship that is considered dishonorable, the family of James' potential wife rejects your father's marriage proposal. In time, the same thing happens for Thomas and William. No one wants to have the Wellesbourne name because it is tarnished. What I am saying is that your decision, although it seems to be the right one for you, can have lasting effects on the entire family. The shame will not only be yours, but all of Wellesbourne, and your father's good reputation will be lost. Is that what you wish for all of us?"

Lysabel was looking at her mother, greatly distressed. "Of course not," she said tightly. "But why can I not be happy, Mama? Why can I not be with a man of my choosing?"

Alixandrea leaned forward, kissing her daughter on the forehead. "You can be happy with a man of your choosing," she said. "But not this man. He is already taken, sweetheart. You must do what is right, for all of us."

With that, she squeezed her daughter's hand and stood up, smiling gently at her as she walked away, heading back to her granddaughters who were still fighting over the pink flowers. But one word from Alixandrea stopped them and, together, they followed her from the garden with a servant in tow.

Lysabel watched her daughters and her mother leave, her mind still lingering on what her mother had said. The woman had a way of putting things that made sense, even if Lysabel didn't want to accept it. She really couldn't argue with the logic because everything her mother said was true. Her decision to go with Trenton was a decision that would affect them all. Her father had tried to tell her that, but she didn't want to listen. She had accused him of being selfish when the truth was that she was the selfish one.

It wasn't only her life she would be ruining, but her entire family's lives.

Oh, God... must I really give Trenton up?

Lysabel hung her head, thinking of Trenton, of the life she wanted with him so badly. She could feel it slipping away, this idea of a perfect world where Trenton and her daughters were the center of it. A world of ponies and babies and joy and love... did she really have to give it all up? Had she been living in a fool's paradise, after all?

The mere thought was making her sick.

Lysabel lost track of time as she sat there, pondering the situation. The servants who had been tending to the flowers had moved to the other end of the garden, pruning and cutting, but still she sat, mourning for the life she so badly wanted. As she sat there, staring at the dirt, she heard the gate next to her open.

Casually, she turned to see Ranse de Troyes entering the garden. He spied her immediately since she was sitting so close to the garden gate and he smiled politely when their eyes met.

"My lady," he greeted. "I do not mean to disturb you, but I was looking for Lady Cynethryn and Lady Brencis."

Lysabel pointed to the southern gate. "My mother took them out of the garden that way," she said. "They left a little while ago. Why? Is there something I can help you with?"

His smile grew. "I found two ponies they can ride," he said proudly. "I heard how disappointed they were when their own ponies came up lame, so I searched the village and found two very nice ponies that they are welcome to ride."

Lysabel had to grin at him. "But they already have two ponies," she said. "Now they need two more?"

He shrugged. "It is only a loan," he said. "They can ride the ponies until their animals heal. They have been having such fun with them that it is a shame to see them so disappointed."

Lysabel laughed softly. "You are a tender heart," she said. "You must have children of your own if you are so sympathetic to them."

He shook his head. "I do not," he said, his smile fading. "At least, not a living child. My wife died in childbirth last year along with my daughter."

Lysabel's smile vanished. "I am so very sorry," she said sincerely. "I did not know. I have not been to Wellesbourne in a few years, but the last time I was here, I am not sure if you were serving my father yet or not. Forgive me for not remembering."

He waved her off, his manner easy going. "Not to worry, Lady de Wilde," he said. "I do not expect you to remember every knight under your father's command. I came into your father's service six years ago, and I believe you have come to visit Wellesbourne once during that time, but we have not been formally introduced. I am Ransom de Troyes, your father's captain."

Lysabel nodded politely, eyeing the tall man, with long, muscular arms and legs, and blond hair to his shoulders. He was a handsome man and seemingly quite friendly. She'd seen him around since her arrival, especially in the feasting hall, but she didn't know his name. It simply hadn't come up.

"And how do you like serving my father, de Troyes?" she asked.

His grin was back. "I like it a great deal," he said. "The White Lord is a fair and decent man. It has been my honor to serve him."

"Thank you."

"May I inquire to the health of your husband, Lord Benoit?"

It was an innocent and socially polite question, but one that gave Lysabel pause. It reminded her that no one, save her father and mother, Trenton, and Markus knew that Benoit was dead.

She proceeded carefully.

"He is away," she said, avoiding the question and heading for the garden gate where her mother had disappeared with her children. "If you will excuse me, I must find my daughters and if they behave themselves, they may be worthy of the ponies you have procured for them. It really was quite kind of you to do that."

Ranse watched her as she walked away. "It was my pleasure, Lady de Wilde," he said. "The ponies are in the stables when they are ready. Since Lord de Russe is no longer here, I will be pleased to watch over your daughters myself if you wish."

Lysabel forced a smile. "Your offer is very generous," she said. "I would say that it is not necessary because Willie will watch over them, but knowing my brother, he would try to steal the ponies out from under them. Mayhap you would be good enough to supervise Willie while he supervises my daughters."

Ranse laughed quietly, knowing what she said wasn't far from the truth. Sometimes William Wellesbourne was more of a child than most children he knew. Lysabel gave him a polite wave as she quickly disappeared from the garden, leaving Ranse looking after her, pondering the lovely Wellesbourne daughter for a moment before leaving the garden the way he'd come.

"CISSY AND CINNY want to know if you will take them riding again, Matt, and... what on earth are you looking at?"

Alixandrea had entered her husband's solar, having left her grandchildren with the cook, who was supplying the children with the most marvelous candied grapes. But the lure of candied grapes wasn't strong enough to deter their desires to ride ponies again, which was the predominant theme with the pair, so Alixandrea dutifully sought out her husband to ask his permission and participation.

She found him in his solar, looking most curiously from the lancet window that overlooked Audrey's garden. He didn't even hear her when she entered, nor did he turn to her when she started to speak, which was why Alixandrea asked him what had his attention. Matthew pointed from the window.

"Lysabel," he said. "I have been watching her for quite some time. I saw you talk to her. What did you say?"

Alixandrea came to stand next to him, looking from the window to see her daughter speaking with Ranse de Troyes. She avoided her husband's question.

"What is Ranse doing there?" she asked.

Matthew shook his head. "I do not know," he said. "He came into the garden a few moments ago and started talking to her. Did you speak to her about Trenton?"

Alixandrea sighed; he wasn't going to let the subject go. "I did," she said. "I told her what you told her, I am sure. I told her that although I understand her affection for Trenton, he is not the man for her. I believe that I have given her much to think about."

Matthew continued watching the pair in the garden as they conversed. "Lysabel, as always, will do what Lysabel wants to do," he said. "She was stubborn as a child and she is still stubborn."

"She takes after you."

Matthew turned to look at her with a grin. "Is that so?" he said. "You are a cheeky wench."

She laughed softly. "That is *your* misfortune," she said. Quickly, she sobered, watching her daughter stand up from the bench as she and de Troyes continued speaking. "I think you must give your daughter some time to come to terms with what her life has become. For her sake, and for yours, do not speak to her on Trenton again. Let me handle it from now on. She may be more apt to take my advice. I have some experience handling stubborn people."

Matthew chuckled, his focus returning to the garden where it appeared that the conversation between his daughter and Ranse was starting to break up.

"De Troyes is a good man," he said. "We are fortunate to have him here."

Alixandrea nodded. "He is," she said. "My heart is still broken over the death of his wife last year. They were both so excited for that baby."

Matthew nodded. "He was an excellent husband to Lady Maribel," he said. "He was quite kind and attentive to her. They were inseparable."

"I know."

At that moment, Lysabel departed from the garden, leaving de Troyes standing there, watching her go. Matthew's gaze lingered on the man for a moment as de Troyes watched Lysabel.

A thought occurred to him.

"Ranse is the kind of man that Lysabel needs," he said. "Sometimes the best medicine for a broken heart is to find something, or someone, to mend it."

Alixandrea looked at him rather strangely. "Lysabel? And Ranse?"

Matthew shrugged. "Why not?" he said. "They are nearly the same age, and we know what kind of man Ranse is. I would have no reservation betrothing my daughter to him."

Alixandrea hadn't considered Ranse as a possibility, but she realized he wasn't a bad candidate in the least. "Nor would I," she said. "But the pain of losing Trenton is still fresh with Lys. Mayhap you should wait before you put another man in her life."

Matthew's expression hardened. "And wait for Trenton to come back and steal her away?" He shook his head. "I will not wait. Although I asked Trenton to stay away, I do not believe for one moment that he really will. I fully expect him to return, and if Lysabel is betrothed or even married again, then Ranse will stand between Trenton and Lysabel. It is protection that Trenton cannot ignore."

Alixandrea pondered that scenario a moment before shaking her head. "Trenton is a killer," she said quietly. "You have said so yourself. He may very well kill Ranse to get at Lysabel. Do you really want to put Ranse in that kind of a position? It is not fair to him."

Matthew knew that, but he also wasn't willing to leave his daughter's future to fate, especially where Trenton de Russe was concerned. Ranse de Troyes would make a fine husband for her, but more than that, he was determined to put a wall between Trenton's wants and his daughter's life.

"I cannot imagine that Trenton would kill an honorable knight, a man who is legally Lysabel's husband," he said. "I would like to believe he would do the chivalrous thing and walk away. In any case, Lysabel must marry again, and Ranse is without a wife. I believe it will be a good match."

He sounded as if he was trying to talk himself into it. Alixandrea didn't respond; she'd already said everything she needed to say. Matthew's suggestion wasn't a bad one, but the timing wasn't ideal because Lysabel still felt strongly for Trenton, and surely Trenton still felt strongly for her. To put another man in the middle of the equation was risky at best, but she knew that Matthew was doing what he felt was best for their daughter.

Unfortunately, Alixandrea wasn't quite so sure.

CHAPTER FOURTEEN

Deverill Castle

THE MORNING AFTER Trenton's arrival to Deverill found him outside just after dawn, standing near the soldier barracks and watching Cort and Dane run new soldiers through a drill.

Deverill was a troop training center for crown troops, as well as Warminster troops, as Gaston had always been a trainer of men for the crown and that hadn't changed from one king to the next. The House of de Russe, historically, had a very close connection to the crown, and Gaston for the sheer length of his experience, was a trusted advisor to the king in military matters. When it came to Trenton, however, Henry didn't much care what Gaston thought of the capacity Trenton served in. Henry did as Henry wanted to do, and that was simply the way of things.

Trenton had grown up around training grounds, so watching Dane and Cort put the troops through their paces brought back many fond memories. Long ago, when he'd been quite young, he remembered his father's dear friend and general, Arik Helgeson, a tall, Viking-looking knight who had been one of the best trainers in England. The man had lost his life in an ambush years ago, something that Gaston had never quite overcome, and watching his brothers with the soldiers reminded Trenton very much of Arik and days gone by.

He'd missed them.

So, he stood on the edge of the field, waving at Cort when the man lifted a hand to him, and trying not to think of the very reason why he'd come to Deverill. He'd hardly slept the night before, with thoughts of Lysabel heavy on his mind, so he'd come to the training field to distract himself. He hadn't seen his father yet this morning, but he was certain that he would soon. His father had always been an industrious early riser. He didn't want to press the man about is plans to visit Welles-bourne, but that was certainly on his mind.

Over to his right, his brother, Dane, was bellowing out commands like a good drill sergeant, something that made Trenton smile. His gaze drifted over his brother; while Trenton had Gaston's enormous size and dark coloring, Dane took after his long-dead father for the most part. He was average in height, very well built, with his mother's eye color and a crown of cropped, blond hair. He was quite handsome, as Trenton had acknowledged when Lysabel told him that she'd dreamt of Dane in her youth. But more than that, Dane simply had something that women found irresistible.

Trenton often wished he'd had his brother's charisma. Ever since they were children, it was Dane who had taken charge of things and Dane who had been the brains of any operation. Trenton had never met a smarter man in his life. Trenton had been more of a follower in their youth, with Dane leading the charge and Trenton being the muscle. Trenton often missed those carefree days of youth with his cohort in crime, Dane.

Even now, his brother saw him lingering by the edge of the field. While Cort had simply waved to him, Dane turned command over to the nearest sergeant and headed in Trenton's direction. The brothers saw each other as often as they could, but it had been a long while since they'd last spoken. Trenton smiled as Dane ran up to him.

"So you are up early, are you?" Dane said. "Since you serve the king these days, I thought you might be a man of leisure. Up all night and sleeping all day, as it were."

Trenton snorted. "A lot you know," he said. "I'm risking my life every second of every day while you spend your time screaming at frightened men."

Dane laughed, revealing a toothy smile that looked very much like his mother's. "That is because they need to be screamed at," he said. "I realize you are an important man, but those of us without a dukedom to inherit must work for our daily bread."

Trenton simply shook his head. "You are no pauper," he said. "Da told me that he's moving you to Blackmore Castle on the Welsh Marches. A prestigious post, Brother."

Dane nodded. "It is," he said proudly. "You shall address me as Lord Blackmore from now on."

"Does that make you feel important, little man?"

Dane started laughing. "I must keep up with you, after all. Someday, you will be the duke and I shall be your lowly advisor."

"Advisor? Who told you that?"

"*Me*," Dane said, incensed. "I have no idea how you have survived this long without me. You will need my wisdom when Warminster becomes yours."

Trenton chuckled, his affectionate gaze on his brother. "That is true," he said, sobering. "I have missed you. With the great reunion last night with the family, you and I have not yet had a chance to talk, just the two of us."

Dane's smile faded. It was the first time the two of them had been alone since Trenton's arrival, and being the nosy and concerned brother he was, Dane had a million questions for him.

"I assumed you came here for an important reason," he said. "Shall we go for a walk?"

"Indeed."

Turning away from the training field, Dane and Trenton began to walk. It was like days of old, when it was just the two of them, and the bond that formed those years ago was something that had only gotten stronger over the years. Leaving the training area completely, they headed towards the main area of the bailey.

Deverill Castle had a massive outer wall that was nearly eight feet thick and the bailey had been a vast, oblong-shaped yard at one time that had been divided into sections by walls that Gaston had commissioned when he inherited the place. Portions of the castle were actually built into the wall, creating something of a mammoth structure that dominated the countryside for miles in every direction.

It was a grand structure. Trenton found himself looking at the pale gray walls, made from limestone that had been locally quarried. He was waiting for Dane to speak, because he could sense the man's curiosity and concern. As they neared an area that wasn't heavily populated with men, Dane finally broke the silence.

"Now," he said, "will you tell me what has brought you back to Deverill after six long years?"

Trenton sighed pensively. "A woman," he said simply. "Rather than get into a long, drawn-out story, suffice it to say that I have fallen in love with a woman."

Dane's brow furrowed in shock as he looked at him. "*What?*" he hissed. "What woman?"

There was a crowd of men up ahead and Trenton came to a halt, turning to face Dane where they still had some privacy.

"In July, Henry tasked me with abducting a rival who had been a thorn in his side," he said. "To make a long story short, I was sent to Stretford Castle. Do you know it?"

Dane blinked as if startled. "That is de Wilde's home."

Trenton nodded shortly. "Aye," he said. "Upon entering the grounds, I could hear a woman screaming and when we breached the house and located our target, we realized that the screaming had been coming from de Wilde's wife as he beat her. His wife turned out to be Lysabel Wellesbourne."

Dane's eyes widened; unlike Trenton, who was a rather stoic character, Dane tended to show his reactions without fear. He wasn't afraid to let anyone know what he was thinking.

"God's Bones," he gasped. "I knew she was married to the man, but I'd never heard anything like that about him. That he was a womanizer, aye. But a wife beater? Never."

Trenton gave him an expression suggesting that de Wilde's actions had been very, very bad. "When I saw what de Wilde had done to Lysabel, suffice it to say that the man didn't leave Stretford alive."

"You killed him."

"I punished him."

A smile flickered on Dane's lips. "I am proud of you," he said. "Sounds like the bastard deserved it. What did Henry say? Did he want him killed?"

Trenton shrugged. "That was not an issue. The man is dead and Henry has accepted it." He hesitated before continuing. "I have spent some time with Lysabel. At first, it was to make sure she was healing after de Wilde's beating, but very soon, I found myself... *attracted* to her. To be plain, I have fallen in love with the woman and she adores me, as well."

Dane was honestly stunned. His serious, heartless brother wasn't so heartless after all. He'd never heard those words come out of Trenton's mouth, not even with Alicia, his first wife. Trenton had loved her, Dane was sure, but he'd never really said so. It was mostly in his actions rather than his words. Therefore, the mere fact that Trenton was voicing his love for a woman was shocking.

"I do not even know what to say," Dane said after a moment. "Are... are you happy about this?"

Trenton nodded. "I have never felt like this in my entire life," he said, a glimmer of joy in his eyes. "She is beautiful and sweet, and she makes me smile. And she had two adorable daughters who have, for some reason, latched on to me as if I am something important to them. I cannot tell you how it fills my heart, Dane. It has opened up an entirely new world for me."

Dane watched Trenton's face when he spoke; he could see the happiness. But he could also see something else behind his expression, something cloudy.

"But...?" he asked. "But something is wrong."

Trenton sighed heavily; it sounded like a growl. "You know what is wrong."

Dane did. He'd been thinking it all along. "That bitch you are married to."

Trenton nodded. "Everything would be perfect but for her." He shook his head sadly. "I have never felt married to her, Dane. You know this. You know how it has been with her. She is a stranger who bears my name, a stranger who only wants the de Russe name and the Westbury money. I do not even feel welcome in my own home; I haven't since I married her. It wasn't that I was content with my terrible marriage more than I was simply resigned to it. Then I met Lysabel and all that has changed."

Now, Dane could see the sorrow. It ran deep. "What will you do?"

Trenton shook his head. "She wants to be with me and I want to be with her," he said simply. "I told Uncle Matthew what we wanted and he banished me from Wellesbourne Castle. I came to Deverill in the hopes that Da could talk to Uncle Matthew about it. I do not need the man's approval, but I would at least ask that he not interfere. We are two people who make each other happy and we wish to be together. It is as simple as that."

In spite of the way Trenton made it sound, it wasn't a simple situation at all. Dane scratched his head, thinking on a tragic situation for his brother and wishing he could do something about it.

But there was also something else on his mind, something that Trenton wasn't aware of. He hated to tell the man in the midst of all of this, but it was important that he know, now more than ever. Once Gaston was brought into the conversation, Dane felt compelled to speak on it.

"Trenton," he said, reaching out to put a hand on the man's shoulder. "I know that Da is glad to see you and it is unfortunate that it took a situation like this for you to visit, but there is something you should know about Da these days."

Trenton looked at him, curiously. "What is it?"

Dane patted him on the shoulder. "I am not even supposed to know this, but Mother confessed to me one night because she could not deal with it alone," he said. "In fact, I was going to send word to you about it but I am glad you have come to me first. It's Da – the physics think he has a cancer in his throat. He has had a bad cough this past year, something he could not shake, and two physics from London came and diagnosed him with a tumor in his throat. His health has been deteriorating."

Trenton was looking at him in horror, the first strong emotion Dane had seen on the man's face in a very long time. "My father is sick?"

Dane nodded seriously. "I am sorry, Trenton," he murmured. "Mother knows, of course, as does Cort, but no one else. Da does not even know that Cort and I know, and now you. You must not let him know that you know. It would wound his pride if he knew that his sons knew of his health issue. To him, we must always believe he is strong and invincible. He is The Dark One, after all. He has a reputation to uphold."

Trenton stared at him. Then, in a shocking move, his lower lip began to tremble and he slapped a hand over his mouth, looking at Dane with eyes that were growing moist. That reaction from Trenton brought out Dane's emotional response and he put both of his hands on him, a comforting gesture, but one that put a lump in Dane's throat. It was like a dagger to his heart to see Trenton so upset.

"Nay, Dane," Trenton said through his hand. "My father is not dying. Tell me he is not dying."

Dane's eyes were moist and he drew in a long, steadying breath. "He is getting old," he said frankly. "He will see seventy years next year, Trenton. He is not a young man any longer. That is the truth. He has lived a long and full life, and he has been very happy. You must remember that."

Trenton still had his hand over his mouth. "But he has been unhappy with me," he muttered. "I have brought him a great deal of disappointment."

Dane shook his head. "You know that is not true," he said. "He always wanted great things for you. You had to follow your own path and it was difficult for him to accept it, that's all. But he has accepted it. He is proud of you, I promise."

Trenton blinked and tears splattered onto his dark eyelashes, tears he quickly wiped away. Drawing in a long, deep breath, he labored to keep his composure.

"And I have come, asking him to ride to Wellesbourne and fight my battles for me," he said, clearly devastated. "He should not be making such a trip. He should not be burdened with this."

Dane agreed with him, but he wasn't going to say so. "But he is going to go," he said. "If you have asked it of him, he will go. And you cannot tell him not to; he will wonder why. If he knows that you know about his cancer, it will destroy him."

Trenton nodded, wiping at his nose, slowly regaining his poise. "You are correct, of course," he said. "But I feel so terrible that I have asked this of him when his health is not good. I remember thinking when I saw him last night how much he had aged, but I did not know it is because he has been ill."

Dane nodded faintly. "No one else knows, either, although I suspect Uncle Matthew might. My mother doesn't keep much from him with regards to our father."

Although he was calmer now, Trenton was feeling hollow and weak. He and his father had a turbulent relationship, but he wasn't ready to lose him. He was still that little boy who loved and admired his father greatly, and the thought of losing his father made him feel absolutely lost.

"What do I do now?" he asked. "I have asked father to intervene with Uncle Matthew and I should not have. I have a wife who lives off of my money and my name, who has taken everything from me right down to my self-respect, and when I find a woman I love, I cannot even have her. God, I wish I'd never even heard the name Adela of Brittany. It is a curse I can never be rid of."

They were all questions without answers, statements with no resolutions. With that, he touched Dane's cheek in a brotherly gesture and walked off, wandering away to contemplate what his life had become and further contemplate the very real possibility of losing his father in the near future. It was all too much to take for him and, at the moment, he needed to be alone.

It's a curse I can never be rid of.

Dane watched his brother walk away, feeling so very terrible for him. He hated to see him so distraught, with so many problems to deal with. It simply wasn't fair, and Dane wished with all his heart that he could help him.

… and perhaps he could.

Dane was brilliant, that was true, but he was also crafty. He wanted to help his brother badly enough that he would do almost anything for him, even help him with a problem that, by law and by God, the man could do nothing about.

Adela.

She was the core of the issue, that bitch who lived in Trenton's house, spent Trenton's money, and spoke horribly of the de Russe family in general. She made it no secret that she hated the family, and Dane had heard about the terrible things she'd said. So had Gaston, and Remington to a certain extent. All rumors and gossip floating around Wiltshire, the French wife of Trenton de Russe who couldn't stand anything English, especially her husband or his family.

It was a situation that had never really concerned Dane until now. Now, he felt as if his vision had cleared and could see that there was one thing standing in the way of his brother's happiness. His father was going to Wellesbourne to try and convince Matthew to allow their children to enter into a clandestine and dishonorable relationship, which would be one more thing for Adela to lament over and point out how terrible the de Russe family was. Dane wasn't going to let that happen.

For Trenton's sake, he would pay Adela a visit.

Lost in thought, Dane turned back for the training field. In the distance, he could see his younger brother, Cort, as the man ran some new troops through their paces with swordplay. Cort was animated, yelling at the men, but then calling everything to a halt so he could speak patiently with the group. Cort was a fine man, with a tremendous grasp of what was right and what was wrong. His moral compass was a strong one.

Dane needed to speak with the man.

In days of old, it was Trenton that Dane would always drag into his schemes. Dane had gotten Trenton into more trouble than he could recall but, in the end, it had bonded them like nothing else could. Partners in crime, partners in brotherhood. Now, Dane was looking for Cort to be his cohort in crime. He had Trenton's size and skill, but Dane's conniving traits. He was fearless, and even reckless, in a way Dane could never hope to be, and if anyone would be willing to help Trenton in this situation, it would be Cort.

Dane knew he could count on that.

Therefore, he pulled his younger brother away from the men and into a private corner of the yard where he explained the situation with Trenton, with Lysabel, with Matthew, and with Gaston. Before Dane had come to the conclusion of his story, Cort was already formulating a plan of action.

"You know what we have to do, don't you?" Cort asked, interrupting his brother. "We have to go to Penleigh House. We cannot stand for this any longer, Dane. We must get rid of Adela once and for all."

Dane knew that he and his brother thought very much alike, in most instances. "My thoughts exactly," he said. "This cannot go on any longer, Cort. Trenton cannot do anything about it, and Da *will* not do anything about it, so it is up to us to solve the issue once and for all, especially now that Trenton's happiness is at stake and Da is being pulled into the mess. You know he's not well enough for to deal with any of this."

Cort nodded eagerly, his copper curls glimmering. "I know." Then, he looked at Dane curiously. "So Trenton is truly in love with Lysabel de Wilde, then?"

"Wellesbourne," Dane reminded him. "She is a Wellesbourne. After hearing what Benoit de Wilde did to her, we will not mention that name again. Understood?"

Cort nodded. "I never liked him, anyway," he said. "But Trenton and Lysabel... I can hardly believe it."

"Believe it," Dane said, an eyebrow cocked. "And, unfortunately, time is of the essence. Trenton has asked Da to go to Wellesbourne Castle, and it is my assumption that he will go very soon. That means we must take care of Adela sooner rather than later."

"What did you have in mind?"

Dane shrugged. "I'm not advocating killing the woman," he said. "I may hate her for what she's done, but I cannot condone outright murder of a female. She's a greedy sort – she might respond well to a bribe to leave England and never return."

Cort's features twisted into a wry expression. "And if she takes the money and returns anyway? What then? She'll be back in his life and the problems will be compounded. We need to get *rid* of her, Dane, not simply sweep her under the rushes."

Dane couldn't disagree. "I suppose we could abduct her and hide her away in a vault somewhere, forever."

"Or we could sell her to the highest bidder," he said. "You know they still have that old slave market over in Northwic, the one that has been around since the days of Danelaw. I've heard that they still deal in slaves with men from France and beyond. They particularly like pale-skinned women in The Levant, you know."

Dane looked at his brother, a grin on his lips. "*Sell* her?"

Cort shrugged. "They'll take her away to their home across the sea and we will never hear from her again. More importantly, Trenton will never hear from her again. He will be free."

Short of murdering the woman and throwing her body into a bog, Dane thought that was as good a plan as any, for certainly, something had to be done and it had to be done now. Too much was at stake to leave it to chance or to delay.

"I suppose that is as good a choice as any," he said. "Then we ride to Penleigh House tonight, under the full moon. We will sneak into the place, abduct Adela, and be on the road to Northwic before anyone is the wiser. It will take us at least four days to get there, though. Four days with a screaming captive."

Cort didn't think that was ideal, either, but there was little choice. "I will see if I can steal some poppy powder from Da," he said. "The stuff makes him sleep. Mayhap I can get enough to keep the woman unconscious until we can get her to Northwic."

Dane sighed heavily. "Oh, we can simply keep knocking her senseless every time she comes around," he said, watching Cort grin. Reaching out, he grasped his brother by the arm. "Well, then? We're in this together?"

Cort nodded firmly. "We are," he said. "I need some adventure in my life, anyway. Training troops is boring me to tears."

Dane couldn't help but shake his head at the man. "This is not some grand adventure, Cort," he said. "We are doing this for a reason. This is serious business."

Cort never took anything too seriously. He flashed a dimpled grin at his brother to let him know that this was an adventure to him, like it or not. "I'll look at it my way and you look at it yours," he said. "In any case, we will have to make arrangements for the troops for the next few weeks. We'll have to get men to cover our duties."

Dane glanced out over the troop grounds, full of men as dust flew up into the morning air. "I will speak with the sergeants," he said. "I will not tell them where we are going, of course, but I will make sure they cover training until we return. Meanwhile, you go and pack everything we will need, including something to tie Adela up with. And get a sack for her head so no one can see her face when we transport her. We need to keep her covered up."

Cort snorted. "I will find charcoal and draw a hideous face on the sack. We will tell everyone that is what she really looks like."

Dane started to chuckle. "At least until we get to the slave market," he said. "After that, we will have to let men see her face if we are going to sell her off."

"What if she tells them that she has been abducted?"

Dane rolled his eyes. "Who are they going to believe? A hysterical female or two seasoned knights?"

Cort merely shrugged. They both knew the plan was risky at best, but for Trenton's sake, they were willing to try. Given the situation, and the misery of both Trenton and Gaston with the horror Adela had created, Dane was more than willing to risk whatever he had to in order to rid them of the Countess of Westbury once and for all.

Were the situation reversed, he knew that Trenton would do the same for him.

It was time to do what should have been done years ago. Dane and Cort were going to see to it that Adela of Brittany was never a thorn in a de Russe side ever again.

And no one would ever know the truth.

IT WAS A cool evening after a warm summer's day, and Trenton was standing out on the steps of Deverill's massive keep, gazing up at the stars.

So many stars, he thought, wondering if Lysabel was looking up in the sky at that moment. He wondered what she was doing and if Cynethryn and Brencis were back to riding their ponies. Around him, the walls of Deverill were lit up with sentries bearing torches, and the grounds were patrolled by men with big dogs. Everything was peaceful for the most part, but for Trenton, there was no peace.

He missed Lysabel dreadfully.

The evening meal had been a glorious affair of laughter and family warmth, and it had been a bright moment in an otherwise hellish day. After what Dane had told him about his father, he kept looking at Gaston to see if he could spot any sign of the cancer the physics said he had, but all he could see was a tired older man. Gaston was smiling, at times chiding Boden and Gage, who were combative with each other, but for the most part, he looked like the father he remembered. He felt like the worst son in the world for staying away so long and for holding a grudge about Adela, about other things.

He wished he could take it all back.

At the meal, Gaston announced his plans to depart for Wellesbourne on the morrow. No one really knew the circumstances for his trip, as Gaston had only confided them to Remington, but traveling to Wellesbourne was quite common for Gaston, so there were no questions as to why. In fact, Boden and Gage insisted on going with him, and Gaston relented, mostly because it was easier to permit them rather than denying them.

The younger de Russe boys were known to do what they wanted and then beg forgiveness if their father became too terribly angry about it. The Dark One, such a strict and sometimes cruel trainer of men, didn't seem to have the same standards when it came to his younger sons.

He took joy in every cheeky exploit.

With the trip set for the morrow, the meal lasted perhaps a little longer than usual, with Trenton sitting between Dane and his mother, Remington. She seemed to be the only one not particularly pleased that Gaston was going to Wellesbourne, but she didn't say so. It was more in her expression than anything else. She kept her mouth shut, watching her husband closely as the night progressed, and it was something that Trenton found his attention drawn to.

Remington had always been protective of Gaston, for as long as Trenton could remember. A deeply caring woman, he could only imagine that her caring instincts were heightened now that Gaston's health was deteriorating. Trenton found that he couldn't look at her too much because it only reminded him of his father's failing health, so when Gaston finally excused himself for bed, Trenton left the table also and wandered out of the keep to lose himself in thoughts of the present, and of the future.

He simply couldn't believe how his life had changed in a relatively short amount of time.

"I thought I would find you out here."

Trenton turned to see his mother emerging from the keep, a smile on her lovely face. He'd always thought she was just about the most beautiful woman he'd ever seen, and even in her advancing years, that hadn't changed. She was still lovely with her copper-colored curls, all wound up on top of her head, and her sea-colored eyes. He smiled weakly.

"It is cooler out here than in the hall," he said. "That place is like an oven when the days are warm."

Remington laughed softly. "It was made to keep us all warm when the weather is so cold," she said. "The circulation is bad and in warmer weather, that means the hall becomes somewhat stifling."

Trenton nodded in agreement as she came to the step next to him and looped her arm through his. He looked down at her as she gazed up at the night sky.

"It is good to be home," he told her. "I have missed it."

She smiled as she looked at him. "And we have missed you."

He smiled back at her, turning away to look up at the stars again, unaware that she was still looking at him.

"You just missed Skye and Nicolas," she continued. "They were here not long ago with some of their children. Did you now that they are now grandparents? Their eldest, Robert, has a son and he brought the infant along. Nicolas is so proud he could burst."

Trenton thought on his father's younger cousin, Nicolas, who was the brother to Patrick de Russe. Nicolas had married Skye Halsey,

Remington's younger sister, many years ago. He had always been a man of short temper, easily stirred, but he was a good knight. He lived in London with his family and had become part of Henry's diplomatic corps, oddly enough. The young knight Trenton remembered, who was so easily riled, had grown up to become a rather great communicator and excellent diplomat. It was ironic.

"I see Adrian from time to time whilst I am in London," he said. "I did hear about the grandchild. Martin, they named him. After Nicolas' father."

Remington nodded. "Boden and Gage call the baby Marty, which Adrian hates." She giggled. "The last day of their visit, Gage started calling the child Farty Marty. I thought Adrian was going to rip his head off."

Trenton laughed at the antics of his youngest brothers. "God's Bones, those two are a pair," he said. "Full of the devil."

"They remind me of you and Dane when you were younger."

"We were never *that* bad."

Remington looked at him, a twinkle in her eye. "Weren't you?" she said. "I seem to remember differently."

Trenton smirked at her, refusing to incriminate himself. He patted her hand, returning his attention to the sky as his thoughts drifted from Nicolas to his father. He felt the need to speak to Remington about it, if only to tell her that he had been told. Already, it was to be a sad conversation.

"Dane told me about my father," he said quietly, his mood sobering dramatically. "Had I known of his illness, I would have come home much sooner."

Beside him, Remington could feel her mood sobering, too. Even though she hadn't given birth to Trenton, she had always considered him her son, as Trenton considered her his mother. They had a strong bond between them, but it was a different bond than Trenton had with his father. With Remington, their bond was based on the fact that even though they weren't related by blood, they still loved and trusted one another. She respected him a good deal.

When Remington looked at Trenton, she saw Gaston as he was thirty years ago – tall, proud, big, and strong. Trenton and Gaston were so similar, in all aspects, that it was frightening at times. But it also meant they had the same stubbornness, the same fears, and nearly the same outlook on many things. Therefore, she knew that Trenton had been rocked by the news of his father's health. He was emotional like Gaston was, too.

"I am sure Dane told you that he does not want anyone to know," she said after a moment. "I have been trying to honor that, but I had a moment of weakness one day and told Dane. I know he has told Cort, and now you."

Trenton patted her hand. "I will not let my father know that I know, but I feel terrible that I asked him to go to Wellesbourne to... well, to talk to Uncle Matthew about..."

He trailed off. "Gaston told me," Remington said, seeing that Trenton wasn't particularly surprised by her admission. "I know why you have come. To be truthful, I am not surprised, Trenton. You were always a man of great feeling. I wondered how long it would be before you realized that a loveless marriage is not for you."

"It really wasn't a matter of a loveless marriage. It was simply that I fell in love with a woman and the marriage aspect did not enter my mind until I realized that it would be a complicated thing for us to be together."

Remington smiled faintly. "Lysabel Wellesbourne," she murmured. "She was such a lovely little lass. I have not seen her in years, though."

"She is still a lovely lass," Trenton said. "More so now."

Her smile faded. "And you are sure this is what you want?"

"Never more sure of anything in my life. I am just sorry that I got my father involved. Had I known of his illness, I swear I would have never asked him to intervene with Uncle Matthew."

Remington let go of him and perched on a small wall that lined the stairs. She pulled her shawl more tightly around her shoulders, looking up at the sky again, her expression distant with thought.

"Trenton, I will be honest," she said. "I do not know how much time your father has left on this earth. It could be months, it could be years. But I suppose the same could be said for any of us – none of us knows how much time we have left. But in the time we have left, we must make those days count. We must fight the good fight, and live the good life, because once we are laid to rest, we will be remembered by those deeds. I want your father to be remembered by his deeds as a man and as a father, not by the betrayal at Bosworth those years ago that seems to follow him. That is why I support him as he goes to Wellesbourne to speak to Matt on your behalf. It is important for him to accomplish important things while he still can."

Trenton had a lump in his throat as he listened to her talk. She seemed so serene and calm about it, like a woman who was resigned to the inevitable yet so very grateful for the time she had left. It was so painful to hear it, yet so beautiful at the same time. He wondered if Lysabel would ever speak so sweetly about him when his time came.

He hoped so.

"How sick *is* he?" he asked, his voice tight. "Please tell me."

Remington looked at him. "Sick," she said. "Every day, he is a little slower. He thinks I do not notice, but I do. I will tell you something that I've not told him, Trenton. I cannot bring myself to do it, not as long as he tries to keep his illness a secret. He does not want to acknowledge it, so I honor that. But I will tell you that every day that passes, and I see the man I love slow down just a little more, a little piece of me dies right along with him. On that day when I finally lose him, I shall rejoice that he is no longer suffering, but my heart will be destroyed by the loss. I cannot imagine my world without him. Still, the one thing that brings me some measure of comfort is that those who have passed before us, Arik as well as my sister, Rory, shall be waiting for him. He shall not be alone in death. To think of his reunion with Arik is the only way I can keep from falling to pieces."

Trenton closed his eyes and the tears streamed down his face, in the darkness where no one could see them. He wiped them away, hearing the grief in Remington's voice and realizing that, indeed, his father was probably sicker than Dane had led him to believe. The regret he was coming to feel at having stayed away so long was beginning to overwhelm him.

"I think that, mayhap, I shall remain at Deverill for a while," he said, taking a deep breath to compose himself. "My father may have need of me, so I will remain close."

Remington could see him wiping at his face in the darkness. "I did not tell you that to coerce you into remaining," she said. "I told you that because it is the truth."

"I know. But I cannot return to London, not now. I feel the need to repair my relationship with my father. All of the resentment and anger I felt towards him seems rather foolish now."

Remington stood up and made her way over to him, putting a gentle hand on his arm. "It will mean the world to him if you remain," she said quietly. "Mayhap, it is time to let the past go. Life is so precious, Trenton, and it flies by so quickly. When he rides to Wellesbourne, go with him. Keep watch over him. And mayhap, some of what has been damaged can begin to heal."

Trenton nodded, feeling extremely emotional as he stood there and held her hand. As he brought her hand up to his lips for an affectionate kiss, they began to hear the thunder of horses.

From where they were standing, they could see two big warhorses charging out of the stable area, heading for the gatehouse. Both Trenton and Remington watched as the horses raced by and voices began calling to the sentries at the gatehouse, who began to crank open the massive gates. Trenton, in particular, peered after the riders curiously.

"That is Dane and Cort," he said, looking to Remington. "Where do you suppose they're going?"

Remington shook her head. "Knowing those two, it could be anything," she said. Releasing Trenton, she turned for the massive entry door. "Dane lures Cort into the same misadventures that he used to lure you into, and Cort, being young and excitable, is an eager victim to Dane's mastery."

Trenton grinned, following Remington towards the entry. "Whatever he is doing this night, I am glad Dane did not try to pull me into it," he said. "Let Cort follow the man to his doom. I have followed him more times than I can count."

Remington laughed softly as she opened the door. "You are a wise man," she said. "Seek your bed and be thankful you are not out riding in the dead of night on another one of Dane's foolish escapades."

Trenton followed her in through the door, into the foyer that was lit with a dozen glowing tapers. "I intend to do just that," he said. "But you can believe I shall ask those two what they were up to come the morrow."

"If they tell you, do not tell me. I am sure that I do not want to know."

Trenton grinned as he kissed his mother good night and headed up to his chamber. Even as he headed up the narrow steps, his mind was lingering on his brothers and wondering if he should follow them just to keep them out of trouble.

He decided against it.

That night, he slept better, but he awoke before dawn with thoughts of the journey to Wellesbourne on his mind. Rising to a purple sky and cold temperatures, he made sure Dewi was prepared for the trip back to Wellesbourne and as he was in the stables, he happened to notice that neither Dane nor Cort's horses had returned.

Whatever the pair was doing, it had kept them out all night, and by the time Trenton was ready to depart with his father, younger brothers, and about fifty men-at-arms, Dane and Cort still had not returned. When he asked Remington if she wanted him to go after them, she simply rolled her eyes and shook her head. She wasn't concerned, so Trenton wasn't either, but the as the escort departed Deverill Castle, he couldn't help but wonder about the disappearance of Dane and Cort.

Whatever they were doing must have been very important, indeed.

CHAPTER FIFTEEN

Wellesbourne Castle

MATTHEW HAD SEEN the color of the banners from the approaching party and, even at a distance, he knew who it was.

He wasn't surprised.

High in his bower in the keep of Wellesbourne, he wasn't surprised that Gaston de Russe was approaching, but he was angry. Angry that the man should exhaust himself so, making the trip from Deverill Castle all the way to Wellesbourne. In hindsight, perhaps Matthew should have preemptively gone to Deverill Castle since he knew the situation with Trenton would warrant a meeting with the man's father.

He didn't need to be a soothsayer to know that.

Therefore, he watched the distant approach of the de Russe party, coming in just before sunset with a sky that was shades of deep blue, with pink clouds creating a brilliant splash of color. He loved sunsets like this, something that reminded him of the joy of life every single day, but that joy was somewhat diminished over the past few days.

He was a man in turmoil.

In the days that Trenton had been gone from Wellesbourne, Matthew had been given a lot of time to think about the situation. The truth was that he hadn't wanted to hurt Trenton. He'd known the knight his entire life and had loved him like a son, but he was a son with a good many problems and Matthew didn't want his daughter attached to a man with such demons.

That was the bottom line.

Lysabel was recovering from an abusive marriage and although Trenton had saved her from that horrible situation, and it was clear that there was a good deal of affection between them, Matthew simply couldn't allow his daughter to become the mistress to a married man no matter how much she adored him. He kept going back to that conclusion every time he tried to re-examine his decision.

Had he done the right thing?

Had he been unnecessarily cruel?

No, he didn't think so. Lysabel deserved better.

Matthew knew his refusal to condone such a thing had crushed Trenton. That had been clear in the man's face and Matthew's nature with those he loved was to be kind and generous. But he simply couldn't give his permission for Lysabel to carry on a clandestine relationship with Trenton. In his heart, he couldn't. It wasn't right and they all knew it. His daughter deserved the chance to become a wife to a fine man, and her daughters deserved a father-figure who was kind and honorable, and who didn't do the king's dirty work.

A man who didn't kill on command.

Like Gaston, Matthew held that same opinion of Trenton's service.

Matthew knew that was what Gaston was coming to discuss, among other things. It didn't matter that Gaston and Trenton had suffered a somewhat contentious and complex relationship as adults; Trenton had gone straight to his father with what had happened and Gaston, like any good parent, was coming to see what he could do to help his son, only in this case, he was coming to the home of his very best friend.

Matthew didn't know if that friendship made the situation better or worse.

"Matt?"

Matthew turned to see his wife standing behind him. Alixandrea was dressed in a flowing gown, with her hair pinned upon her head. She entered their bedchamber, a smile on her lips as she headed for her husband.

"Gaston is coming," she said quietly, "but I am guessing that you already know that."

Matthew returned her smile. "I can see his party from here," he said. "I was just going down to greet him."

Alixandrea's smile faded as she gazed up into her husband's face. "He should not have come."

"I know."

"His health…"

"I *know*, love. I know."

She sighed sadly and he kissed her on the forehead. Taking a deep breath, he moved past her, leaving Alixandrea looking after him.

"Do you think Trenton asked him to come?" she said. "If he knew Gaston was ill, surely he would not have asked it of him."

Matthew paused by the door, his fingers on the jamb. "Gaston and Trenton do not speak," he said. "I cannot imagine that even in the rare conversations they have had as of late, that Gaston has told his son of his declining health. Gaston did not even tell me about it; it was Remi who did."

Alixandrea closed the gap between them, her hands going to his shoulders in comfort. "Does he know that you know?"

Matthew's lips tightened, an emotional response to an emotional subject, pain in his heart that was strangling him. "He knows."

Alixandrea patted him on the cheek, seeing how much the situation distressed him. "Then go and greet him," she said. "I will have refreshments sent to your solar."

"Thank you, love."

Leaving his wife behind, and stewing in his own gloomy thoughts, Matthew made his way down to the entry of the keep, stepping out into the pink-sky sunset and watching as the first of the de Russe party began to filter in through the gatehouse of Wellesbourne.

The first things he noticed were two big knights charging into the bailey astride very expensive, and slightly green, warhorses. Both animals were frothing and agitated, and Matthew grinned when the blue roan animal twisted oddly and nearly dumped off his rider. It was enough for the knight to swiftly dismount, unwilling to be thrown at the end of a long trip, and Matthew approached Boden de Russe as the knight flipped up his visor.

"Damnable beast," he said, shaking his finger at the horse as if the animal could understand him. "If I hadn't spent a year's salary on you, I'd chop you up and feed you to the dogs!"

"What is the matter, Boden?" Matthew asked as he walked up. "As I recall, you told your father you could ride anything on four legs and as I further recall, it was he who bought you this horse even when he told you the bloodlines were questionable."

Boden turned to Matthew, a young man with his father's size, his father's good looks, and his mother's pale eyes. He also had her smile, which he demonstrated brightly as he hugged his father's best friend.

"Uncle Matthew," he said. "It is good to see you. And to answer your assertion, my father does not know everything. He could be wrong, you know."

"Will you tell him that to his face?"

Boden burst out laughing. "Not me," he said. "I would never tell The Dark One anything like that for fear I might come away missing teeth, or worse. Besides... if I ever want him to buy me anything again, I will have to pretend as if I appreciate this wild mount."

Matthew gave the young knight an affectionate cuff to the side of the head, grinning when the horse began to act up and ended up dragging Boden away. As Boden tried to calm the horse, Matthew continued on to the other knight, who was having better luck with a big dappled gray. Gage de Russe waved to Matthew.

"Uncle Matthew!" he called. "Look at my latest acquisition!"

He was indicating the horse, who was standing still for the most part in a rather regal pose. Matthew ran a practiced eye over the beast.

"Magnificent," he said. "Between you and your brother, it appears you got the better horse."

Gage watched Boden, older than him by a year and a half, as the man tried to calm his excited steed. "He told my father he wanted the blue roan, and my father tried to tell him that the horse's sire was mad," he said. "I have no sympathy for him."

Matthew clapped him on the shoulder. "Nor I," he said, turning to the rest of the incoming party and spying Gaston on his big, sleek stallion. "Ah. There is your father. I will send William out to you to help you settle your men."

Gage's face lit up; he and William were nearly the same age and had long been good friends. "Willie is here?"

"He is. He has just returned from my garrison at Kington Castle."

Gage nodded happily and Matthew patted him on the shoulder before making his way through the group of dismounting soldiers until he came to Gaston.

There was dust and chaos in the air all around him, of men and animals settling in after a long journey, but Matthew didn't see any of that. He only saw the enormous knight in front of him, and he took a moment to watch the man as he slowly, and wearily, dismounted his horse. Someone came to collect the animal, leading the sweaty beast off to the stables, and Matthew's heart sank as he watched Gaston's laborious movements.

This wasn't the man he knew.

Gaston was the biggest man he'd ever seen, and the strongest, but the past couple of years had seen that strength decline significantly. *A cancer*, Remington had written to Matthew. Physics from London, the best he was told, had diagnosed Gaston with a cancer in his throat, or so they suspected. The man had a cough he couldn't shake, which had apparently gone on for a year before he allowed the physics to diagnose him.

The news hadn't been good.

But no one knew, according to Remington. Gaston hadn't wanted to tell anyone, his children included, and when he realized his wife had told Matthew, he'd been upset with her, but not for long. Perhaps it was good that one person knew of his condition because, certainly, he'd never hidden anything from Matthew. He wasn't about to start now.

He needed to lean on that friendship more than ever.

But Matthew wasn't dealing well with the news. The greatest knight he'd ever known was suffering from a cancer and trying to pretend as if nothing was amiss. Gaston was proud that way and Matthew knew it. Therefore, he wouldn't insult his friend by acknowledging what they both knew – that Gaston's time on this earth was limited.

To Matthew, that made their remaining time together all the more precious.

As Matthew lingered in thoughts that were tearing at him, Gaston went through a series of heavy coughs before turning to see Matthew standing a few feet away. Once their eyes met, Matthew forced a smile and approached, reaching out a hand to Gaston. The man took it strongly.

"Gaston," Matthew said as he looked at him appreciatively. "It is very good to see you."

Gaston smiled wearily at his dearest friend. "And you," he said. "Although I had doubts that Boden would make it to Wellesbourne in one piece. Did you see his new stallion?"

Matthew grinned. "I did," he said. "It has a crazed look to its eyes."

"That is because it *is* crazed. I warned him, but he would not listen."

"So Gage tells me."

Gaston glanced over at his youngest son, who was in the process of disbanding the escort. "Gage listens to his father so he has a good horse," he said. "Boden, however, does not listen to me and if that horse dumps him on his arse, I will not lift a finger to help him."

"Some sons simply do not want to listen. I have a couple of those, too."

Gaston returned his attention to Matthew, the smile fading from his weathered face. "Speaking of sons," he said quietly. "I am sure you know why I am here."

Matthew nodded. "I know."

"May we go inside and speak?"

Matthew didn't say a word. He simply led his friend across the bailey towards the keep, laughing softly when the man scolded Boden at a distance because the horse was still dragging the knight across the dirt. Boden waved his father off, assuring him that everything was under control, and Gaston merely rolled his eyes. Clearly, his son was lying to him.

Matthew could only laugh.

Alixandrea was at the entry of Wellesbourne's tall, proud keep to greet Gaston, and he kissed her cheek and greeted her warmly. Gaston also greeted red-haired William Wellesbourne as the young man dashed past his parents on his way out to see his friends, Gage and Boden. He moved so quickly that he nearly knocked his mother down, resulting in a motherly swat to the buttocks. But William smiled that big Wellesbourne smile in response, which usually eased any anger his mother might have. As Alixandrea went to see to the refreshments, Matthew took Gaston into his well-appointed solar.

It was a chamber the two men had spent a good deal of time in over the years, and Gaston immediately began to remove what armor he could. He was in a place of comfort now, and he was exhausted from his journey, so he pulled off his helm and began to unfasten the leather straps he could get to, pulling off pieces of plate and placing them near the door.

Matthew, meanwhile, had moved to a table that contained a cut crystal decanter and several cups.

"Do you need help with that protection?" he asked.

Gaston shook his head as he pulled off the right vambrace, or forearm protection. "Nay," he said. "Just let me get some of these pieces off so I can sit down. Christ, it was a long trip."

Matthew poured the wine. Approaching Gaston with two cups, he held one out for the man. Gaston accepted the cup gratefully.

"I suppose we should get down to business," he said as he sat heavily on a cushioned chair made from a cow's hide. "And I will start by telling you what Trenton has told me. He came to Deverill a few days ago, completely unexpectedly. I have not seen my son in six years, Matt. Did you know that? Six long years."

Matthew nodded, taking a drink of the rich red wine. "He told me," he said. "He hasn't seen you since he married Adela."

Gaston took a long swig of his own wine, draining half the cup in just a couple of swallows. "It would be easy to say that if I'd known she'd drive such a wedge between us, then I would never have brokered the marriage between them, but that is not true," he said. "My relationship with Trenton was fracturing before that, even, ever since he went to serve Henry in the capacity in which he presently serves. Adela was simply the catalyst that drove in the wedge for good."

Matthew went to take a seat near Gaston, his gaze on the man. He looked pale to him, or perhaps it was his imagination talking. Knowing he was ill made him see things that weren't there.

"There is no wedge," he said patiently. "Trenton still adores you. He's still that little boy who looks up to his father and wants to please him."

But Gaston shook his head. "The wedge between Trenton and me started when he was a lad, when his mother fed him lies about me," he said. "Mari-Elle would tell him that I never wanted a child, that I did not want to be a father to him. You remember that."

"I do."

"I have always thought that there is some part of Trenton that always believed that, no matter what I did to prove otherwise."

Matthew leaned back in his chair. "I do not think so. It is his adult life that has created these problems you two seem to share."

Gaston looked at him, knowing he meant the situation with Lysabel. Now, the pleasantries were over, the small talk was finished, and the meat of the situation was upon them. Gaston drained the rest of his cup and set it down.

"Trenton has told me that he is in love with Lysabel, but you have asked him to leave her alone so that she may have a chance for a decent marriage," he said. "Is this true?"

"It is."

Gaston scratched his head, recalling everything he thought of on the journey to Wellesbourne. There was much he wanted to say to Matthew but, in truth, there was very little he *could* say. He didn't disagree with the man, for the most part. But he had a special perspective on all of this that he wanted to share.

"I will not argue the point with you, for it is your decision to make, but I want you to think back to the time when I met Remi," he said softly. "Do you recall? I was sent in to take command of Mt. Holyoak Castle, a property that belonged to her husband. Remington was married to a beast of a man, and I was married to a succubus in human form. You knew Mari-Elle, Matt. You knew the depths of her evil."

Matthew nodded, thinking back to Gaston's first wife, the cold and regal woman Gaston had been forced to marry. It had been a contract marriage, and a nightmare of a situation.

"I did," he said. "Evil was exactly what she was. She would have ruined you had you let her and, in that sense, that makes her not too different from Adela. Both you and Trenton married women who wanted nothing more from you than your name and your money."

Gaston sighed. "Adela was my doing," he muttered. "I thought she would be a good match for Trenton, providing him with French support and connections. But I ended up forcing him to marry a woman who, in reflection, is much like his own mother was."

Matthew thought he could see where the conversation was going. "Gaston, I know Trenton is miserable with her," he said. "I know this is a hellish marriage and I would not be lying if I said that with Lysabel, he seems like a changed man. That morose, serious, and sometimes humorless man transforms around Lysabel and the girls and becomes someone kind and wise and generous. My granddaughters adore him, and so does Lysabel. But you must understand that I, too, condemned my daughter to a hellish marriage with Benoit de Wilde and the worst part is that I didn't even know it. It was Trenton who had to save her from a man who had been beating her for years."

Gaston had heard all of this and he wasn't unsympathetic. "I know," he said, holding up a hand and preventing Matthew from continuing. "Let me finish my train of thought and then see if you can understand my perspective. When I met Remi, I knew she was married. I was married, also, but I had never felt married. Still, I wasn't one to take a lover, so in the beginning, there was no real romantic interest in Remi. But those feelings developed quickly and I found myself in love with a married woman. You know this, Matt, and you also know that my love for her was so strong that I tried to force the hand of the church to annul her marriage, and my marriage, so that we could be together. Therefore, if anyone understands Trenton's pain, it is I, for I went through nearly the same thing."

Matthew knew this was coming from Gaston's personal experience and he stood up, wandering over to the hearth, which was dark now as the sun was setting. He began to pick up pieces of kindling and tossing it into the fireplace.

"Gaston, if you've come to beg me to change my mind, I'm afraid that I cannot," he said. "Lysabel has gone through hell for years. Do you think I will give my approval for her to become the mistress of a man who is married? Of course I will not. It will ruin any chance she has of a decent marriage."

Gaston understood that. "I realize that," he said. "But let me ask you this – you have said yourself that Lysabel adores Trenton."

"She does."

"And Trenton adores her. They are two adults, Matt. We're not speaking of children who do not know what is best for themselves. We are speaking of two adults who deserve to be happy. If it is without marriage, then who are you to stand in their way?"

Matthew didn't reply right away. He continued to stack kindling before taking a flint and stone and sparking the birth of a blaze.

"So you are asking me to permit my daughter to become your son's whore," he said quietly, turning to look at Gaston. "Is that what you are asking me?"

Gaston shook his head. "A whore is an object, a possession," he said. "Trenton loves your daughter and that makes her far more than a possession."

"And what title would you give her?"

"An adored companion."

Matthew stood up and faced him. "If this was one of your daughters we were speaking of, I wonder if you would be so liberal."

Gaston looked away, a pensive expression on his face. He coughed a few times, something that sounded wet and rough. "I do not know," he finally said. "But we are not speaking of one of them. We are speaking of my son and your daughter, who happen to love each other. Trenton is married to a woman he despises, and the feeling is mutual. Do our children not deserve to find their happiness together? I would like to see Trenton happy just once in my lifetime. I would like to know that the pain I have caused him has been healed."

Matthew was once again reminded of Gaston's frail health. As the fire in the hearth began to blaze, he reclaimed his seat across from Gaston, his manner moody and subdued. He wasn't usually moody by nature, but being confronted with a situation he felt strongly about, and a dear friend's illness, had him off balance.

"You are asking me to condone an affair," he finally said. "Whatever feelings Trenton has for Lysabel, his intentions will never be honorable."

"What do you mean?"

"He cannot marry her. Do you not think people will know that? They will talk and her reputation will be ruined. Is that what you truly wish for Lysabel?" He threw up his hand in exasperation. "And what of my granddaughters? Do you think I can find suitable and honorable husbands for them when it comes time, knowing their mother is a concubine to a married man? Would you ruin their chances, too?"

Gaston heard the passion, the distress, in his friend's voice. "Of course not," he said. "Matt, all I am saying is that they are two people in love who should be permitted to make their own decisions. I loved a married woman, once, and I refused to let her go. Trenton has that same tenacity."

Matthew cocked an eyebrow. "What are you saying? That he is going to defy me?"

Gaston hesitated. "I am saying that love will find a way, with or without your approval."

Matthew didn't like the sound of that at all. Frustrated, he sighed heavily. "Gaston, you know I love you and you know I love Trenton, but I will not let him carry on a dishonorable relationship with my daughter. I do not want to say he is unwelcome here; I do not want to say that any de Russe is unwelcome here, but I must protect Lysabel and my granddaughters."

"From what?"

"From something that can never be!"

There was that passion in his tone again. Gaston and Matthew had never been at odds and, frankly, Gaston couldn't remember if they'd ever had an argument, but this conversation was one of the most volatile they'd ever had. Considering the subject matter, that was understandable.

"I can see your point of view, my friend," he said quietly. "But in matters of love, there is no easy answer. You think that Lysabel will forget about Trenton if they are separated, but is that really true? Would you have forgotten about Alix so easily if your love for her had been denied?"

Matthew sighed once again. "I did not fall in love with a woman who was already married," he said. "Though I fault you not for the circumstances with Remi, because surely, they were complicated to say the least, this situation is different."

"How?"

"Because it is happening to my daughter."

Gaston could see that there was no budging the man. In truth, he wasn't sure he had really been trying to. He was merely pleading Trenton's case. But he had hoped that Matthew would be a little more reasonable. Still, given that the man felt tremendous guilt for the marriage to de Wilde, it was understandable that he was extremely protective of Lysabel's future happiness.

He had to ensure his daughter found a happy and honorable life.

Not a life as the mistress of a married man.

"And it is happening to my son," Gaston said after a moment. "Your path with Alix was different, so you do not know what it means to love a woman who is legally bound to another man. You have no idea the pain of such a thing, so I do not expect you to understand. But I would hope that you would at least understand that not all things in life are clear cut, and not everything is as easy as you make it out to be."

With that, he stood up, weary and somewhat disheartened at the course of the conversation. Matthew was defensive, and probably had every right to be, but Gaston realized that he'd been looking for more understanding from the man. The White Lord of Wellesbourne was a man of great compassion and wisdom, and he'd hoped that would carry over into Trenton and Lysabel's situation. But Matthew was only seeing it from a father's perspective and nothing more.

Matthew didn't let him get very far. "Where are you going?" he asked.

"To rest."

Matthew blew out a deep breath. "Come back here," he said. "Gaston, you and I have never had harsh words between us and I do not intend to start now, but this is something too important for you to just walk away."

Gaston came to an unsteady halt somewhere over near the hearth. "What point is there in me remaining?" he said. "Your mind is made up. I cannot change it. But I will tell you that you may be headed towards heartache if you do not put love above the Wellesbourne reputation. It seems to me that is all you are truly worried about."

Matthew stood up and looked at him. "That is not true and it is not fair," he said. "I am worried for my daughter."

"You were wrong the first time you chose her a mate. Why not let her make the decision the second time?"

It was an unfair dig, but it was the truth and they both knew it. Matthew eyed him a moment. "She is still my daughter."

"And you are telling me that you know what is best for her better than she does? She is a grown woman with two children, Matt. She's no longer the foolish young maiden you evidently think she is."

"I will not let her be Trenton's whore, Gaston."

"Nobody is asking you to. They are not looking for your blessing, simply your understanding in the matter."

Matthew was starting to feel cornered and, truth be told, irritated at Gaston. It was true that he had no experience in loving a woman who was legally bound to another man, but that didn't mean he didn't know what was right and what was wrong. As he stood there, pondering how to reply, the door opened and servants appeared with trays of food and drink. Alixandrea was leading them in, smiling at her husband and his best friend.

"Gaston, I brought you mulled wine," she said gaily. "I know how much you like it."

Gaston's gaze was on Matthew. It took him a moment to reply and when he did, he turned away.

"I am not thirsty," he said. "Is there a place I may rest?"

The smile faded from Alixandrea's face. "Of course," she said. "The chamber you always use when you are here is being readied."

Without another word, Gaston lumbered through the door, heading for the stairs that led to the upper floors. When he disappeared from sight, Alixandrea turned to her husband.

"What happened?" she asked, her eyes wide.

Matthew was feeling defeated. So very defeated. He didn't like quarreling with his best friend.

"He has come on behalf of Trenton," he said. "He does not want me to interfere in Trenton and Lysabel's affair."

Alixandrea watched her husband as he went over to the wine she'd brought and started drinking from the pitcher. He didn't even take a cup. She knew how torn he was about this; she, too, was torn, but she also understood a woman's heart. She understood that Lysabel was in love for the first time in her life and she was desperate and miserable without Trenton.

"Matt," she said quietly. "I am your wife, but I am also the one who knows you best in this world. And I can be completely honest with you without being judgmental."

He looked at her. "Well? Let's hear your honestly, then."

She put her soft hand on his arm. "Your daughter is in love," she murmured. "I have tried to tell you this, but you have not been listening to me. She is in love with a man who has treated her better in just a few days than Benoit treated her in twelve years. She is not going to forget about Trenton so easily. You have mentioned betrothing her to Ranse, but even if she marries him, it will be with Trenton on her mind and in her heart, and that is not fair to her or to Ranse."

Matthew gazed into those hazel eyes he loved so well. "And you think I am wrong in this?"

Alixandrea lifted her shoulders, turning away from him. She couldn't honestly look him in the eye and tell him he was wrong.

"Nay," she said. "I know you are looking at the moral aspect of it. You are looking at Lysabel's future and the future of her girls. But you are not looking at the condition of her heart. The heart wants what the heart wants, and you cannot break that bond if it has been formed."

Matthew pondered her words. "Then what should I do?"

Alixandrea looked at him, then. "I know you do not want to do this, but you must trust your daughter to make her own decision. Trust her to make the right one. She has her father's wisdom, after all. You must give her the chance to choose her own destiny this time."

It was difficult for Matthew to accept that, but his wife was wiser than him in all things. He had to trust that she was correct. Gaston had tried to tell him the same thing, but coming from Alixandrea... now he had the two people he loved best in this world telling him the very same thing.

He didn't like losing control like this.

"Then I shall go and speak with her," he said, resignation in his voice. "I do not want my daughter to end up hating me, but she must understand that I am only thinking of her future."

Alixandrea stopped him as he tried to walk away. "Not now."

"Why not?"

"Because Trenton is here."

Matthew's eyebrows flew up. "Trenton is…?"

Alixandrea nodded, pulling him over to the chairs in front of the now-blazing hearth. "I saw him come in through the postern gate when I was in the kitchens procuring your refreshments," she said. "He must have ridden in with Gaston. Did he tell you?"

Matthew's expression tightened with displeasure. "He did not."

Alixandrea gently pushed her husband into a chair. "It is possible that he did not know," she said. "Trenton could have followed him from Deverill."

"And it is equally possible that he knew and did not want to tell me."

Alixandrea sat down next to him, holding his hand. "Mayhap he was planning to tell you," she said. "Do not think Gaston was being subversive. You know him better than that."

Matthew did, but Trenton's presence at Wellesbourne still didn't sit well. "Where did Trenton go?"

Alixandrea turned away, her gaze moving to the lancet windows of the solar as if she could see the activity beyond them.

"Lysabel is in the garden with the girls," she said. "I suspect that is where Trenton is going. Matt… stay here with me. Trust that your daughter will do the right thing, whatever that may be. Have faith that everything will work out as it should."

Matthew wasn't so certain, but he didn't argue. He kept thinking about his daughter, so vulnerable he thought, and Trenton, who wanted something very badly. Then he thought of Gaston, closer than a brother, and knew the man was hurting, too. His estranged son had come to him for help, and Matthew had shut him down. Perhaps, Gaston had some fear of losing Trenton for good over this.

It seemed that both Matthew and Gaston had fears for their children.

Lifting his wife's hand, he kissed it.

"I think I shall go to Gaston," he said. "It would seem that we have some waiting to do. You will understand when I say that I should like to wait with him, with your permission."

Alixandrea smiled at her husband. "Go to him."

Matthew kissed her hand again before letting it go, making his way from the solar and up to the chamber on the second floor, the smaller one that overlooked the bailey, where Gaston usually stayed when he visited. Matthew knocked on the old oak door, waiting in silence until it was opened and Gaston stood in the doorway. But no words were spoken between them.

No words were necessary.

They threw their arms around each other and hugged. And then, they sat and waited.

CHAPTER SIXTEEN

ANOTHER DAY, ANOTHER sunset.

Lysabel was sitting on the stone bench in the garden, watching her daughters as they chased three little bunnies through the flowers. The evening was approaching, but Lysabel just couldn't seem to summon the energy to collect her children and head into the keep. In truth, since Trenton had left Wellesbourne, she couldn't seem to summon the will to do much of anything.

The days dragged on and the nights were even worse. Her mind was filled with Trenton from one moment to the next, missing the man as she'd never missed anyone in her life. But that longing was tempered by what her mother had said, about the long-term effects that an illicit romance would have on the family. The more she thought about it, the more pressure she felt, like a great hammer beating her mother's words into her skull. Even in her sleep, they pounded into her.

Her decision to engage in an affair with Trenton would bring the entire family down.

Her father, and everything he had worked for, would be damage by her actions. Her unmarried brothers would be affected, as would her own daughters when they came of marriageable age. She couldn't condemn Cynethryn or Brencis, or even the child she carried in her belly, to a life of disadvantage because of her actions. The parting words her mother left her with were words she couldn't get out of her head.

You must do what is right, for all of us.

It had been five days since Trenton had left. Five days of anguish, and of reflection, as Lysabel could think of nothing but him. But her mother's words had her reconsidering everything. Perhaps she couldn't really be happy with a man of her choosing; perhaps she had to do the right thing, as her mother said, and sacrifice her happiness so that her family could be spared her shame.

God, she hated being a martyr.

As sunset approached and the sky began to turn shades of blue and purple, she could hear that there was something going on in the bailey on the other side of the garden wall. She could hear men and horses, meaning an escort or an army of some kind had arrived for the night. It was probably just some traveling lord seeking shelter, but Lysabel had no interest in whatever was going on. The past several days, she didn't care about much of anything.

Time passed and the sun sank further on the horizon. The girls lost the bunnies somewhere in the garden, but they found a fat orange cat that wanted to be loved, so Cynethryn picked the cat up, its long legs dangling down her body, as she headed in her mother's direction. Brencis trotted alongside, trying to pet the kitty.

"Mummy!" Cynethryn cried. "Look what I found!"

Lysabel smiled weakly as her daughter brought the cat over and put it on the bench beside her. It was a friendly kitty, and they all took a turn petting the soft orange fur.

"He is very nice," Lysabel said.

Brencis was more aggressive in showing her affection; she picked the cat up and hugged it. "I love him," she declared. "Can I take him to my chamber? Can I have him?"

"I found him!" Cynethryn said, unhappily. "He is *mine!*"

Lysabel put her hand up before a squabble could start. "I think the cat would like to have both of you loving him," she said. "I do not care if he comes inside, but make sure he is fed and goes outside when you go to sleep."

"But why does he have to go outside at night?" Brencis asked seriously. "He needs a bed to sleep on."

"He needs to go outside at night because that is when cats hunt for their dinners."

The voice came from the garden gate, which had just swung open. Lysabel, Cynethryn, and Brencis looked over to see Trenton standing in the archway, smiling wearily at the three of them. One look at Trenton and the girls screamed, rushing him in delight. He ended up picking them both up as they furiously hugged him, with Brencis hugging him so excitedly that she smacked him in the throat.

"Trenton!" the little girl squealed. "You came back, you came back!"

"Aye, I came back," Trenton said, coughing because she'd hit him in the Adam's apple. "I am back and what do I see? No ponies being ridden. Are they still lame?"

As he set the girls to their feet, Cynethryn nodded. "My pony's leg is still sore," she said sadly. "But Sir Ranse found us new ponies to ride until they get better."

Trenton put his hand on her head. "That was very nice of de Troyes," he said. "Have you ridden his ponies today?"

Brencis was hanging on to his other hand excitedly. "My pony is black and white," she said. "He tries to bite me. I do not love him as much as I love Snowdrop."

Trenton grinned at the child. "I am sure Snowdrop is happy to have your loyalty," he said. Then, his gaze trailed up to Lysabel, who was standing up by now. When their eyes met, it was as if a bolt of lightning went through him. He'd never been so glad to see anyone in his life. "Greetings, my lady."

That soft, gentle tone nearly undid Lysabel. She was already startled by his appearance, weakened beyond measure. She wanted to run to him like the girls had, but she didn't. She remained where she was, watching her girls as they fawned over the man. She thought it was very sweet, in fact, because they'd never shown their father such affection. It was nice to see that they could display such love to a man who had, in turn, been so kind to them. They wanted to love, and be loved, and Trenton gave them that opportunity.

It was one more thing to love about the man.

"Greetings," she said after a moment. "I... I did not know when you would return."

Trenton nodded, unable to take his eyes from her even though the girls were tugging on him. "I know."

"Does my father know you are here?"

He shook his head, unwilling to answer with Brencis and Cynethryn at his feet. He smiled down at the girls, giving Lysabel the hint that perhaps he couldn't speak freely in front of them. Immediately, she clapped her hands.

"Ladies," she said, softly but sternly. "Stop pulling at Sir Trenton. Go inside and wash your face and hands and once you have done that, find Grandmother and tell her you would like to help with supper."

Brencis had hold of Trenton's big fingers, dragging at him. "Will you come to sup?"

She was asking Trenton, but Lysabel answered. "You will see him later," she said. "Go, now. Do as I say."

The girls obeyed, but it took them a moment. Neither one of them would leave until Trenton promised he would see them later, and then they happily skipped away. Once they had cleared the garden and they heard the old iron gate slam, Lysabel looked at Trenton.

"Why are you here?" she asked quietly. "My father said he told you not to come back."

Trenton took a few steps towards her, his eyes glittering. "He did," he murmured. "But I cannot stay away. I love you, Lysabel. There; I've said it. I love you and I want us to be together."

His admission brought tears to her eyes. "Oh... Trenton," she gasped, her hand going to her mouth. "I love you, too. But we cannot..."

She shook her head, wiping her eyes as she trailed off. Trenton took another step in her direction. "I do not know how much time I will have before Uncle Matthew runs out here and chases me off at the tip of a sword, so I must say what I have come to say," he said quickly. "Lysabel, I want you to come away with me now. I want you to gather the girls and we are going to leave this very night."

She looked at him, wide-eyed. "Leave?" she gasped. "And go where?"

"I have other properties," he said. "I have a hunting lodge at Hawkridge, set deep in the forest north of Warminster, near Trow-bridge. It's a nice little place and we could take the girls and live there until I can secure something bigger, something worthy of you. But you would be happy at Hawkridge, I swear it."

Lysabel could see the earnest desire on his face and it cut her to the bone. He was still living in that fantasy world, but after her discussion with her mother, that world had all but dissolved for Lysabel. As much as she didn't want to admit that, in her heart, she knew it.

"Trenton," she said. "As much as I love you and as much as I want to go with you, I am afraid that I cannot."

His brow furrowed. "What do you mean?" he asked. "Why can't you go?"

Looking at him, Lysabel knew that this was going to be the most difficult thing she'd ever done in her life. He was within arm's reach; it would be so easy to grab hold of him and never let go. But her mother's words were echoing in her head, telling her that she needed to make the right choice, for everyone.

The right choice wasn't Trenton.

"Because I cannot do such a thing to my family," she murmured. "You and I have been living in a wonderful world, a world of hope and dreams, but the truth is that there is no such world. The reality is that we live in a world of consequences, and as much as it pains me to say this, my decision to go with you will jeopardize my entire family. It would be so easy to ignore them, and to be selfish, but the truth is that my choice to go with you has far-reaching implications. My father, for one; he has an excellent reputation. What will happen to him when his daughter becomes the mistress of a married man? Think of the respect he will lose."

As Trenton realized what she was saying, his eyes grew wide and confused. "But..."

She cut him off. "And my children," she said. "I know you think that simply because you will be a duke someday, that you can control their destinies, but that is not entirely true. People will look upon you with respect, but they will not want to marry their sons to the daughters of your concubine. And that is the reality of it. I cannot do that to my children, Trenton. I cannot be selfish at their expense."

Trenton's face were starting to pale as he received an answer from her that was not the one he was expecting.

"Your father told you to say all of this," he finally hissed. "He has convinced you that what we feel for one another is wicked."

Lysabel shook her head. "It was not my father," she said. "I am sure he has said to you what he has said to me, and he has only spoken about what is morally right in this situation. This is about honor, Trenton – mine, my children's, my family's, and even yours. If damaging our honor is my decision to make, then I choose not to do it. I cannot let my selfishness ruin lives."

Trenton couldn't believe what he was hearing. He put his hands to his head and turned away from her for a moment, trying to process what she was saying. The problem was that it all made sense; nothing she had said was untrue. But that wasn't what *he* wanted.

He was becoming desperate.

"If honor is what you worry over, then come with me," he muttered. "Come with me and we shall flee to France, or Aragon, or Austria. We will go where no one knows us and you will be my wife, and Cissy and Cinny will be our children. We will start a new life together."

He was grasping at the last vestiges of hope, trying to find a solution to a situation he very much wanted to end in his favor. But as much as

Lysabel wanted to, she couldn't agree with him.

"The more you beg, the more painful this is going to be," she said, tears glittering in her eyes. "I will not leave my family behind, not even for you. Think about what you are saying, Trenton. Would you really leave your father? Your mother and your brothers? I do not think you would. I know I would not. Trenton, we have shared something I have never known before and I am certain I will never know again. We have shared love and joy as God intended it. I have given you my heart and it is yours to keep, for always. But I cannot go with you. You must understand that."

Trenton's breathing was starting to come in rapid pants as he began to see the future he wanted being destroyed right before his eyes.

"God, no," he said. "Please do not tell me this. Please do not tell me that this is not something you want, too."

Lysabel took a deep breath, struggling to keep her composure. She had to look away from him, unable to stand the pain in his expression.

"I want it," she whispered. "With all my heart, I do. But it cannot be."

"Lysabel, please…"

"*Go*, Trenton. Please go. Do not make this worse by begging."

He was standing a few feet away, looking at her lowered head. His entire body was twitching with emotion, fury and disappointment and grief like he'd never known. He felt gutted, as if everything inside of him was bleeding out all over the floor, the life draining out of him as Lysabel turned her back on him. It was the worst thing he had ever experienced.

He couldn't walk away.

"If I have to beg, I will," he said hoarsely. "Anything worth having is worth fighting for, and I believe our love is worth fighting for. Don't you?"

She was starting to weep, unable to hold back the anguish. "It was something that was never meant to happen in the first place," she said tightly. "How can we fight for something that would hurt other people?

Is that the right thing to do?"

"It is what *I* want to do!"

She whirled to him, tears on her face. "Then you are fighting alone," she said, "for I will not fight for something that would hurt so many. And I cannot believe you would want to hurt others, too. I must believe that, because if you are truly so selfish, then I want nothing to do with you. Do you hear me? If you would knowingly shame everyone we love, then you are not worthy of me!"

Her last words were hissed and Trenton's head snapped back as if she'd physically slapped him. Her harsh words had just as much impact. He just stood there, staring at her, hardly able to breathe through the force of his emotion. Swallowing hard, he took a step back.

"Mayhap you are right," he rasped. "I am not worthy of you because I am willing to forsake everything simply to be with you. I do not care who I hurt, as long as we are together. If that offends you, then I am sorry. But mayhap in years to come, you will reflect kindly on a man who loved you so much that he was willing to give up everything."

With that, he turned on his heel, heading for the garden gate and feeling tears sting his eyes. But he didn't give in to them; he was too hurt and shattered for that. What he felt went beyond tears.

"Trenton," Lysabel called after him.

He paused before he came to the gate, but he didn't turn to look at her. He was afraid of what would happen if he did. "What is it?"

She didn't answer right away. Trenton remained where he was, facing the garden gate, when he heard the gravel crunch behind him. Startled to realize that she was now standing behind him, he kept his face away from her, closing his eyes tightly because he didn't want to see her. Instead, he felt a small, warm hand slip into his.

"I love you," she whispered. "Until the end of all things, I will love you and only you."

She squeezed his hand, once, and then she was gone. He heard her footfalls as she ran the other direction, heading for the small gate the led into the keep. He heard the gate open and then crash shut, the iron hinges squealing.

After that, there was complete silence in the garden except for the sounds of the bailey on the other side of the wall. The sun was down completely now and the servants had all gone inside, leaving Trenton standing alone in the dark.

It was fitting, he thought, that his love for Lysabel first started here and now, it had ended here. Only it wasn't ended; it would never be ended. He was tied to her as surely as the stars were tied to the heavens.

Covering his face, he wept.

CHAPTER SEVENTEEN

Penleigh House
12 miles northwest of Westbury

DANE AND CORT could smell the stench before they even saw the banners. But once they entered the rather unguarded courtyard of Penleigh House, a beautiful manor home that was part of Trenton's properties, they saw a collection of soldiers clustered over near the small stables and they saw the white standards with the small black crosses stitched onto them.

Dane turned to Cort in disgust.

"Bretons," he growled.

Cort had that same look of disdain on his face. "Smelly, self-righteous fools," he said. "They probably live here with her. When is the last time Da or Trenton was here, anyway?"

Dane shrugged. "I do not know," he said. Then, he looked around. "But I am sure any sentries are not de Russe. Wait – see them over by the corner of the wall? There are just two of them. Who in the hell are those bastards? This is Trenton's property – there should be de Russe men guarding the walls."

Cort was looking around, too. "There is no one guarding the walls," he said. "See how easily we entered? Utterly stupid."

Dane couldn't disagree. The came to the edge of the well-lit house, dismounting their horses and tying them off on an iron post. There was a water trough, made of stone, and the horses began to drink, but neither Dane nor Cort would stable the animals. If they were to make a swift exit, then they wanted the beasts ready to go.

It had taken them two days to reach Penleigh, and they'd ridden hard, stopping only to rest the horses. Now that they were here, their sense of outrage was magnified as they saw absolutely no de Russe trappings around the place. Penleigh House was a moated manor house that was shaped like an "L", not particularly large, with a separate kitchen yard, stables, and an area where the trades, such as tanning and smithing, took place. All of it was fairly tightly compacted together inside the moated enclosure.

It was a rich place, and evidently poorly protected. They could hear noise and music coming from within the house, and the smells of roasting meat wafted upon the air. Over to their left, the Breton group had spied them and suspicious whispers could be heard, like gasps upon the wind, and Dane turned in their direction, unsheathing his broadsword in a blatant effort to show the group that he and Cort weren't to be trifled with.

Already, there was tension in the air.

When Cort finally headed for the house, Dane was behind him, walking backwards to ensure that none of the Breton soldiers were going to try and follow. Once they reached the elaborately carved entry door, which was open, they were met by a haughty servant who spoke French, inquiring their business. Cort didn't hesitate in his answer.

"Dites à la comtesse que les frères de son mari sont là," he said sharply. *Tell the countess that her husband's brothers are here.* "Nous irons dans une chamber privèe."

The servant's eyes widened as two very big men came through the doorway, demanding to see his mistress in a private chamber. One was very big, and very dark, looking very much like his mistress' husband, so that alone told him that these men were telling the truth.

The House of de Russe had arrived.

Nervously, the servant indicated a chamber that was just off the entry and scurried away. The chamber seemed to be some kind of guard room, for it was tiny, with a hearth, a table and chair, and little else. That chamber was in stark contrast to the entry itself, which was lavishly furnished and meant to impress. Dark woods, carved and intricate, lined the walls, while overhead, Breton banners hung. There was absolutely nothing to indicate this was a de Russe property and Cort eyed Dane, who was taking it all in with disgust.

"Look at this place," Cort hissed as he entered the small chamber. "If I did not know this was Penleigh, I would think I was in Brittany."

Dane cocked an eyebrow. "Can this woman get any lower with her degradation of the de Russe name?" he muttered. "This is astonishingly shameful."

"And it has been going on for years," Cort whispered angrily. "How long has she been doing this? *How long?*"

Dane felt Cort's outrage. In fact, he had quite enough of his own. "Too long," he said. Then, he jabbed a finger at Cort. "But this is going to stop, do you hear? This will be the end of it."

Cort nodded, his jaw ticking as he pulled off a heavy glove to scratch his forehead. He was appalled with the situation; it was much worse than he imagined.

"I have a feeling we are too late with a bribe," he muttered. "She is ingrained in Penleigh like vermin on a dog. She is not going to let this go easily."

Dane was thinking the same thing but he wasn't going to voice it. The situation was repulsive in so many ways – with Adela turning Penleigh into a place in Brittany rather than the proud de Russe property that it was, and Trenton trying to block it all out by staying away and serving the king. Not that he blamed his brother; he didn't. But the man was helpless against it, with a wife and the church telling him this was to be his life. His solution was to ignore it.

But Dane's solution was to end it.

That's what brothers did for one another.

So, he went to stand by the window, plotting out what he was going to say to Adela as Cort hissed and complained. He finally put up a hand to silence the man because he didn't want Adela to hear the discord. He wanted her to think this was a friendly visit, at least for the time being.

In truth, Dane had been plotting out what he was going to say on the entire ride here. Cort thought they should simply grab her and run, but Dane wanted to be a little less obvious about it, especially since she clearly had guests. Even though the security at Penleigh was surprisingly lax, there were still Breton soldiers in the yard and unless they wanted a confrontation, whatever they did was going to have to be smooth and fast, with no screaming, and no obvious signs that they were taking the countess away.

But they were going to take the woman and run.

"What do you want?"

It was thickly-accented English that filled the chamber, and Dane and Cort turned to see Adela, Countess of Westbury, standing in the doorway.

Neither man had seen her in years, both of them remembering a rather plain, dull-looking woman. Nothing had changed. She was short, with a round body, and only average in beauty, but she was wearing a dress that was so elaborate and encrusted with jewels and pearls that it had to weigh at least fifty pounds. Her dark hair was slicked against her skull until it was gleaming, and a pearl-encrusted French hood dominated her big head. Had she had any warmth at all on that pale face, she might have been pleasant to look at, but as it was, she only looked cold and empty. They could read her hatred of everything they loved all over her.

"My lady," Dane greeted her without emotion. "We have come on important business. May be speak somewhere private?"

Adela's eyes narrowed. "What business?" she demanded. "What are you doing here, Dane de Russe? You were not invited here. I demand you leave immediately."

Dane could see that, already, this was going poorly and he wasn't going to let the woman bully him. He took a few steps, closing the gap between them.

"I would be most happy to shout our business to your guests, if that is what you prefer," he said, "and like it or not, this is a de Russe property and your husband, my brother, pays for your extravagant little habits. Why is there not a Westbury banner flying in the entry alongside the Breton colors?"

Adela eyed him most unhappily. "Get out," she hissed. "I do not want you here."

Dane's jaw ticked. "I do not care what you want," he said. "This is my brother's property, not yours. I am welcome whether or not you like it. Now, will you take us to someplace private, or will I shout your personal business for all to hear?"

Adela's round face flushed, her cheeks turning pink. She was un-used to anyone countering her commands in her own home. With a grunt of displeasure, she turned her back on Dane and Cort and began to march away. They quickly followed, making sure she didn't get away from them, as she pushed open an elaborately paneled door and entered a darkened hallway. At the other end, they could see lights glowing, and they entered what appeared to be a solar.

There was a fire in the hearth, illuminating the opulent surround-ings. Dane couldn't help but notice, casually, but Cort was less subtle about it. He was looking around with his mouth hanging open. There were fine furnishings and flashes of gold everywhere, and it became abundantly clear what Adela had been doing with Trenton's money. So far, they'd seen two rooms that were spectacularly furnished and Adela was wearing enough jewels to feed a small village for a year. As the two of them inspected the room, Adela slammed the door behind them.

"Now," she said. "What is so important that you would take me from my guests? And be swift; I have no time for your foolishness."

Dane took another look around the room, noting that one set of glass windows overlooked the courtyard where they'd come in. They were at the opposite end of the courtyard from the Breton soldiers, which was a good thing if he decided to kick out the window and take Adela with him.

He returned his attention to her.

"It is not foolishness I bring, but a business proposition," he said.

Her features tightened. "What business?"

Dane could see Cort moving in his periphery, heading to the door that Adela had just slammed with the intention of blocking her should she try to run. That gave Dane the confidence to say what he needed to say without her trying to bolt from the chamber. There was a table behind him. He sat back on it, smiling thinly at Adela's annoyed face.

"We have not seen each other in several years, Adela," he said. "You could not even be polite when you greeted me. Why must you act as if I am a stranger? I am your husband's brother."

Adela stiffened. "Did he send you here?" she demanded. "What does he want?"

"Trenton?" Dane shrugged lazily. "Nothing from you. He cannot stand the sight of you much as you cannot stand the sight of him. He doesn't care about you in the least, and I am sure the feeling is mutual. Therefore, Cort and I have come of our own accord with a business proposition."

Adela's dark-eyed gaze moved between Dane and Cort. "Clowns, both of you," she hissed. "What possible business could you have with me?"

Dane cocked an eyebrow. Now he remembered why he hated the woman so much. "You have an eye for money, like any good whore," he said. "And since you are a whore for money, my proposition has to do with paying you a good deal of it. How much would it take for you to leave Penleigh and go back to Breton where you belong?"

Her face turned a deep shade of red. "Swine," she growled. "How dare you…"

He cut her off. "You only stay with my brother, and at Penleigh, for the money," he said. He pointed to her dress. "How much did that awful thing cost? You look like a fool in it. So tell me, Adela – how much will it take for you to leave England, and my brother, and never again contact him."

Adela was so angry, so offended, that she was sweating. She turned to leave the room but saw Cort standing in front of the door, blocking her path. Realizing she was boxed in only made her angrier.

"Get out of my way," she snarled at Cort.

He grinned at her as Dane spoke. "He is not moving until you tell me your price," he said. "Everyone has a price."

Adela turned to him swiftly, backing away from Cort and heading in the direction of the hearth with its gently snapping fire. The first thing she came across was the fire poker, and she lifted it, wielding it like a sword.

"I said get out of my way," she hissed. "I shall not discuss this with you. I have every right to remain here, as the Countess of Westbury, and you cannot make me leave with your pathetic attempts."

Dane didn't move. He remained perched on the table even though he was in range of the fire poker should she decide to swing it at him.

"You married my brother because your father forced you to," he said. "Much as my father forced Trenton to marry you. It was not your doing, nor was it Trenton's, but the two of you were unfortunately thrown together. Surely you cannot be happy here."

Adela was backing away from the men, feeling extremely threatened. "That is none of your affair."

"It is a simple statement with an obvious answer."

Adela paused, looking between the two knights. "Do you truly wish to know how I feel?" she said. "I cannot stand the stink of the name de Russe on me. I cannot stand the English around me, so I pay my friends to come and stay with me. Even now, I am hosting a grand party for my friends. Do you know what we do? We toast our hatred of the English, and of my husband, as we drink the wine and eat the food that his money has provided. When I saw you had come, I was hoping that you had come to tell me of his death, but I see that I am not so fortunate. Mayhap the next time you come to me, it will be with good news such as that."

It was a vile thing to say, hatred beyond measure. It was an effort for Dane not to react to it because he would have liked nothing better than to snap the woman's neck.

"Your husband is alive and healthy," he said. "But your words tell me just how evil you truly are, Adela. I have never seen anyone with a heart as black as yours."

Adela threw up her chin. "What do I care what you think? You are interrupting my party."

Dane lifted a hand. "We do not have to," he said. "We can be quickly done with this. We want to know how much we can pay you to disappear. You are a disgrace to the House of de Russe and a shame for my brother to bear. Do you think he does not know about the men you bring to Penleigh? I am sure there are a few whore mongers among those friends you have brought into my brother's house. How many will you take to your bed tonight?"

Adela was turning red again and she lifted the poker in his direction. "You will not say such things to me!"

"Then deny it. I dare you."

She bared her teeth at him. "You are a swine," she growled. "Like your older brother, you are a disgusting excuse for a man and I loathe the sight of you. Get out of my house, do you hear? Get out and never return!"

Dane was unimpressed with her anger. "It is not your house," he said, "and if you do not name your price, you will be very sorry."

"I said get out!"

"Nay."

With a furious cry, she took a swipe at him with the poker. Dane was fast enough to grab it, yanking it from her grip. Unfortunately, the momentum of her swing, and his grab, caused her to topple over backwards and, with the weight of her dress, she wasn't able to catch herself. As Dane and Cort watched, Adela fell back into the hearth, right into the blazing flames.

It was a shocking event and she had been unable to catch herself. Unfortunately, her dress, with all of its jewels, was made of very flammable material, and she went up in an instant. Within a second, her entire skirt was in flames, tearing into her undergarments. That which wasn't in flames was seared against the flesh of her lower body, which also started to burn. Very quickly, everything but her face and arms was on fire, and Cort rushed forward to pull her out of the hearth, but Dane stopped him.

"Nay," he said, watching the woman as she was rapidly consumed with fire. "It is too late. She is already badly burned. You cannot save her."

Nor did they truly want to. Engulfed in yellow flames, Adela's screams were muffled as smoke and fire traveled down her throat. No longer able to cry out, she tried to push herself out of the hearth, but her entire body was on fire. Everything was burning. Soon enough, she could no longer move, and she simply collapsed into the hearth in a burning mess. The room began to fill with dark, black smoke, and the great tapestry above the hearth went up in flames, as did the entire side of the room. It was a shocking sight.

"Come," Dane said, realizing there was nothing they could do. "We must get out of here or we, too, shall be ash. Come!"

Cort, horrified at what he was seeing, followed his brother as the man kicked out the windows overlooking the bailey. As the two of them bailed from the chamber, the entire thing went up in flames. The wooden walls, the fabric drapery, and the tapestries made it a tinderbox. They'd barely jumped from the window before flames began shooting out of it.

With one chamber up in flames, the floor above it began to go up in smoke and flames also, and Dane and Cort backed away from the blaze as they watched the entire side of the house catch fire. The structure was not made of stone, but from wattle and daub, which was pieces of tinder-dry wood layered with things like lime and chalk, sometimes mud, but whatever the house was built with went up like a torch. On the interior, with all of the expensive woods and furnishings, and the ingredients used to treat the wood, it only made more fuel for the fire.

With their attention still on the fire that was rapidly spreading, Dane began to head towards his horse, pulling Cort along with him. They ended up running to their animals just as some of the Breton soldiers in the courtyard began to see what was going on. As they rushed for the house, Cort and Dane vaulted onto their steeds and headed for the open gatehouse, pausing to watch as the fire spread over the upper floor. They could see it through the windows, with smoke pouring out and fingers of flame licking at the walls.

The guests at Adela's party were alerted to something being very wrong as the hall deep in the house filled with smoke. Dane knew the layout of the house – beyond the entry was a large gathering room and then beyond that, a great dining hall. They could hear the screams of party guests as they tried to get clear of the heavy smoke, which was filling the house at an alarming rate. It wasn't so much that the flames were blocking their exit; it was simply that the heavy smoke was overwhelming them.

Dane and Cort continued to watch from the gatehouse as the house was overrun by the flames, and they saw one man emerge from the entry and collapse on the dirt of the courtyard with his clothing smoking. Perhaps they should have gone to help him, but considering how much hatred Adela had brought about, neither one of them made a move. Especially Dane. In his view, this was rightness served.

"Should we try to help, Dane?" Cort finally asked.

Dane didn't reply for a moment. When he did, it was to shake his head. "Nay," he muttered. "That woman wished our brother was dead. You heard her; she was hoping for it. You heard all of the vile things she said about our brother and our family. Were we burning, she would have laughed and cheered. Therefore, I will not help, not even a little. Let her evil die in those flames and consider it God's good justice."

Cort didn't disagree with him, but it was the chivalrous knight in him, the one with the strong sense of duty, that had asked the question.

Yet, the brother in him agreed with Dane completely.

Let her evil die.

They could hear screams as floors collapsed. And as the flames shot up into the night sky, they remained there until the entire top portion of the house collapsed and no one save a few Breton soldiers and the man with the smoking clothing made it out alive.

For Dane and Cort, they watched until there was nothing left to see, until Penleigh House was a giant bonfire burning brightly into the night. There was a sense of finality to it, of cleansing, and as Dane said, of justice. The wickedness and hatred that had filled the halls of Penleigh House were being purged, never to rise again. They'd come to do anything they could to save their brother from his horror of a wife, to somehow bring the tormented man some healing, but in the end, Adela's wicked actions had brought about her own demise.

And no one was sorry for it.

Before the night was out, Dane and Cort were heading to Wellesbourne Castle.

CHAPTER EIGHTEEN

Wellesbourne Castle

"MY LORD, YOU summoned me?"

Ranse was standing in Matthew's solar, arriving swiftly at his lord's summons, as Matthew knew he would.

He had a particular reason for summoning him this morning.

Trenton was still at Wellesbourne. Matthew knew that because Gaston, and Alixandrea, had told him, but Alixandrea had also told him that Lysabel had turned Trenton away when the man had begged her to run off with him. Astounded, Matthew had listened to his wife relay the tale her daughter had told her, how Trenton had begged her to leave with him, and how Lysabel, for the sake of family honor, had refused.

Truth be told, Matthew was shocked to hear it. Shocked, but deeply relieved for his daughter's sake. It was as if a massive weight had been lifted off of him. He honestly hadn't known if Lysabel would make the right choice, but it turned out she had. The right choice for her, and for all of them.

But one that broke Trenton's heart.

That's what Gaston had told him, anyway. Trenton was holed up in his father's chamber, and since the previous night had ingested at least three big pitchers of wine. As of this morning, he was sleeping off his drinking binge, which was why Matthew had summoned Ranse.

He had to move quickly in this situation. He felt rather subversive about it, but he had little choice. Better to move on with his plans to betroth Lysabel while Trenton was incapacitated, before the man sobered and perhaps made another try at convincing Lysabel to run away with him. He wasn't so sure his devastated daughter would be as strong the second time around.

Therefore, this conversation with Ranse had to take place now.

"I did," Matthew said after a moment. "Please close the door."

Ranse did as he was told, closing the solar door and then going to stand before Matthew rather formally.

Matthew's gaze moved over the man. Ranse had been with him for a few years and was a solid, dedicated, and talented knight. He was also obedient to a fault. Matthew barely had to lift a finger with Ranse around because the man anticipated him in almost everything. He was so proactive that even William, the ne'er-do-well son, had noticed and teased Ranse endlessly about it. Whenever Matthew would come around Ranse, William would start whistling to the knight as if he were a dog. He called Ranse the "guard dog" because of his obedience to Matthew, but it was all in good fun. The truth was that William admired Ranse a great deal, and as the only Wellesbourne son remaining at Wellesbourne to serve his father, he had learned quite a bit from Kenilworth Castle-trained de Troyes.

He was a good man.

Therefore, Matthew had no qualms about making him one of the family. He only hoped Ranse felt the same way.

"Ranse, you have been with me for several years now," he said after a moment. "I hope it has been as good a relationship for you as it has been for me."

Ranse nodded smartly. "It has, my lord," he said. Then, he added, "When William isn't annoying me."

Matthew started to laugh. "That cannot be helped," he said. "He annoys everyone. It is the unfortunate part of your job."

Ranse fought off a smile. "I jest with you, my lord," he said. "William is the life of Wellesbourne. Without him, it would be a sad and dull place. Present company excluded, of course."

Matthew waved him off. "I agree with you completely," he said. "Your patience with my youngest has been much appreciated. You *do* like it here, don't you?"

"Aye, my lord. It is my home." Suddenly, he looked at Matthew with some trepidation. "Are... are you considering sending me away, my lord? Is that why you are asking?"

Matthew shook his head. "Not at all," he said. "Sit down, Ranse. I must speak with you."

Quickly, Ranse found a chair and sat on it, stiffly, his gaze on Matthew still full of trepidation in spite of Matthew's reassurance that he wasn't about to send the man away. Matthew went to sit across the table from him, his expression pensive.

"What I am about to tell you must not leave this room, at least for now," he said quietly, seriously. "You must hold it in the strictest confidence. Is that clear?"

"It is, my lord."

Matthew sat forward, his hand on the table, thinking how to phrase everything. He'd been thinking about it all night but, now, the time was upon him and he had to put his thoughts into words. He proceeded carefully.

"You know that we were all greatly saddened by the passing of your wife last year," he said quietly. "Her death affected Lady Wellesbourne greatly."

Ranse's formal manner took a bit of hit, but he did nothing more than take a deep breath and force a smile. "I know, my lord," he said. "Lady Wellesbourne was at my wife's side during the birth. I have taken great comfort in the fact that she was holding my wife's hand when she passed on."

Matthew nodded, remembering that bleak point in time. Alixandrea had cried for two days afterwards. "Serving me as you have, we tend to look at you as part of the family, but the truth is that you are not; not really." He paused. "Have you thought about remarrying, Ranse?"

Ranse seemed to falter a bit. "Nay," he said honestly. "I was happy with my wife. I've no wish to replace her."

Matthew considered that. He sat back in his chair, his focus intense on Ranse. "I am asking you these questions for a reason, Ranse," he said. "There is something you should know. Benoit de Wilde is dead. The circumstances of his death are not important, but what is important is that my daughter is involved in it. The circumstances were beyond her control, believe me. As I have come to discover, de Wilde beat my daughter for years. He seriously abused her, and she is only now starting to heal. It is a good thing de Wilde is dead, for if he wasn't, I would kill him."

Ranse's eyes were filled with both shock and disgust. "The blackheart," he muttered. "I had no idea."

"No one did."

"But Lady de Wilde seems well," Ranse said, hope in his voice. "I have seen her several times since her arrival here and she seems very well."

Matthew nodded. "She is," he said. "As I said, she is healing, but I believe a strong and kind man will help her with that process, a process that no woman should have to go through alone. She is an heiress, you know. When I die, my eldest son, James, will inherit my titles and lands, but Lysabel will inherit Rosehill Manor in London. It has been in my family for many years and it is a very wealthy inheritance that includes the Syon Lordship, which is from my maternal grandmother. In any case, Lysabel brings a good deal with her to any marriage and would be a fine match for any man."

Ranse was nodding until he began to realize that Matthew might mean him. But then he thought he was imagining things because even though he was from a fine family, as the House of de Troyes was a powerful family around Bolton, north of Manchester, the fact remained that Ranse was the third son of Lord Tottington, a very powerful warlord affiliated with the Earls of Carlisle. He'd grown up having to fight for everything he had against two aggressive older brothers, which is why he loved Wellesbourne so much – he was a man all his own, without having to submit to two older brothers who only wanted to kill each other for the Tottington fortune. He'd grown up believing he was subservient to the rest of his family.

So, clearly, Lord Wellesbourne couldn't mean him.

... *could he?*

"I believe she would be, my lord," he agreed after a moment's pause. "She and her daughters would be a fine tribute to any man."

"She is pregnant with her third child. Benoit's child."

Ranse's eyebrows lifted, but only for a brief moment. "I see," he said. "But it is of no matter. The man she marries can simply raise the child as his own, better still if it is a son."

"My thoughts exactly," Matthew said. "Ranse, I would like to offer you my daughter's hand in marriage. I would like to see you become part of the Wellesbourne family, and when she inherits Rosehill, you will make a fine Lord Syon. Is there any reason why you cannot accept this offer?"

Ranse thought that he was prepared for the offer. He wasn't. In fact, he did something at that moment that, under normal circumstances, he wouldn't have done. He stood up and turned his back to Matthew, pacing away from the man, pondering the extremely generous and attractive offer he'd just been made.

He was shocked.

"Nay, there is not," he finally said, turning to look at Matthew. "But how does Lady de Wilde feel about it?"

Matthew stood up. "She does not know," he said. "I have not yet told her. I thought to seal the contract with you before telling her. She does not know you, Ranse, but you are a likable man. I know you will endear yourself to her and her children, with time. But know... know that she has some personal issues, all relating to the death of Benoit. It will take her time to overcome them, but I am certain that with your help, she can."

Ranse nodded, wondering very seriously what those issues were. "My lord, since you have asked me to marry the woman, will you tell me how Lord de Wilde died? I feel as if I have a right to know this. You said she was involved – did she kill him?"

Matthew shook his head. "Nay," he said. "Trenton de Russe killed him when he caught him beating Lysabel."

This time, Ranse couldn't keep the shock off his face. "Is *that* why de Russe escorted her to Wellesbourne?"

"Aye. He brought Lysabel home and remained to make sure she was well. He is an old family friend, you know. His concern was not unusual."

Ranse nodded quickly. "Of course not," he said. "It was quite chivalrous of him to do so."

Matthew wanted off the subject of Trenton. To tell Ranse the reality of the situation between Lysabel and Trenton might very well make the man refuse the marital contract and, in this case, Matthew felt it was important not to tell him. Lysabel had rejected Trenton, so whatever existed between them was finished. Ranse didn't need to know about something that didn't concern him.

At least, he hoped that was the case.

Alixandrea had voiced her concern about the betrothal, telling Matthew that it wasn't fair to put Ranse in the middle of the lovers, but Matthew had to believe that whatever had flared between Trenton and Lysabel was over with. His daughter had rejected the man, and if there was an ounce of honor in Trenton, he wouldn't cause trouble. Matthew was thankful that Gaston was at Wellesbourne to curb his son should the need arise.

But whatever happened, Matthew had to do what was best for his daughter.

And this was the best.

"Trenton is a good man," he said after a moment. "But the fact remains that my daughter is in need of a husband, and you are in need of wife. I realize it is a great deal to ask of a man to accept a woman, her two children, and a pregnancy, but I hope you will consider it. I can think of no better man to entrust my daughter to."

Unaware of Matthew's inner turmoil, and the real reason behind the betrothal, Ranse had no reason not to consider everything. It was true that the Syon Lordship was attractive, but the most attractive part of the deal was Lysabel herself. She was a beautiful woman and her daughters were adorable. Ranse knew he could become quite attached to them, and he thought that, perhaps, God was behind this offer of marriage because He knew how badly Ranse wanted to be a father. His one and only chance at it had ended in tragedy, and although he'd told Matthew that he hadn't considered remarrying, that wasn't entirely true. He had.

Perhaps, this offer was God making amends to him.

It was something Ranse couldn't refuse.

"I have considered it, my lord," he said. "I see no reason to refuse. I am deeply honored by your offer and most happily accept."

Matthew almost collapsed with relief. "Are you sure? You do not want more time to think about it?"

"I am sure, my lord."

Matthew sighed, very grateful for the swift decision. "Good," he said. "I am quite pleased, Ranse, and I know Lysabel will be pleased, also, when I tell her. Until then, not a word to anyone, please. I must speak to my daughter about this first."

Ranse nodded. "Of course, my lord," he said. Then, he paused a moment, hesitant when he spoke. "I know that you are aware that my father is Lord Tottington. You may also be aware that I have two older brothers who will inherit everything when my father passes away. My family has never been close, my lord. Not at all. In the time I have been at Wellesbourne Castle, I have felt closer to you and your family than I have ever felt to my own. Now, to be part of that family is truly an answer to prayer. I want to be somewhere where I belong."

Matthew smiled at the man. "You belong here," he said. "We all think a great deal of you, Ranse. When you marry Lysabel, you will officially become one of us and we are most happy to have you."

Ranse smiled at the man, a smile that bespoke of the joy in his heart. Finally, he would be someplace where people would love and respect him.

He would be home.

As Ranse left the solar and headed out to attend to his duties, it was with a joyful heart, but as Matthew remained in his solar, thinking on the contract he'd just made, it was with a heavy heart. He was thinking that, perhaps, he'd just played a dirty trick on the man; perhaps, it *wasn't* right to put Ranse in the middle of Lysabel and Trenton, as Alixandrea had suggested. Still, Matthew genuinely felt he had to do it. He had to help his daughter forget the man who had made her feel love again, and this was the best way to do it.

To give her another man to replace the one she'd lost.

Now, to tell Lysabel. It wasn't something he was looking forward to. But first, he had to tell someone else.

Gaston.

IT WAS EARLY afternoon when Gaston found Trenton in the stables, sitting on a tiny stool while soaking Snowdrop's still-sore leg with a mixture of mustard and vinegar. Gaston could smell the pungent combination as he approached the stall where both Honey and Snowdrop were tethered. Leaning over the side of the stall, he looked at what his son was doing.

"What's the matter with the pony?" he asked.

Trenton glanced up at him. His face was pale and his eyes blood-shot, indicative of the roaring headache he had as a result of his drinking binge the night before.

"She has a bowed tendon, I think," he said, returning his attention to the leg. "Cissy has not been able to ride her for several days. How did you know to find me here?"

Gaston threw a thumb towards the stable entry. "Markus is out in the yard with some de Wilde horses," he said. "He saw you come in."

"What is he doing with those horses?"

Gaston shook his head. "I do not know," he said. "It is possible he is preparing to return to Stretford Castle at some point. He must, you know. Mayhap he is just looking them over."

Trenton didn't say anything. He seemed focused on the ponies and not on anything more than that, but Gaston was sure it was a self-protection measure. Stretford meant Lysabel, and he didn't want to think about her at the moment. When the woman that a man loves rejects that love, sometimes all that is left are tasks to take the mind off such things. The wine hadn't helped him forget.

Perhaps being busy would.

Gaston knew Trenton was hurting. Even if he didn't know the man at all, his history or his heart, simply looking at him would have been enough to tell him that Trenton was a man in pain. Aside from the physical pain he'd brought on himself, of course.

There was anguish in his manner.

Unfortunately, Gaston was there to compound it.

He'd just come from Matthew, who had delivered news that was going to be devastating to Trenton. In truth, Gaston was still reeling from it and he had no idea how Trenton was going to take it. Matthew wanted to tell Trenton himself, and he'd told Gaston first so the man would know and possibly help him fend off an emotional response, but Gaston didn't think it would be wise for Matthew to deliver the news personally. He wasn't entirely sure just how in control of himself Trenton would be when he found out and he didn't want him lashing out at Matthew in his anger.

Therefore, Gaston was prepared to take the brunt of it.

There was little choice.

"I have a need to speak with you, lad, if you can spare me the time," he said. "It is important."

Trenton was fussing with the pony's leg. "Now?" he asked. "Can it not wait?"

"Nay, it cannot."

Trenton sighed. "Then what is it?"

Gaston suspected there was no chance of pulling Gaston off some place private, so he simply leaned over the side of the stall and prepared to speak in a quiet tone. But as he opened his mouth, there was a great commotion at the entry to the stable as Boden, Gage, and William came charging through, laughing and shouting at each other, going to collect their horses. Gaston stood up, facing the young knights as they charged through like bulls.

"Where are you going?" he said to Boden, who was the closest.

Boden had a rope in his hand. "Into Warwick," he said. "They are having a horse market there and we want to see their stock."

Gaston sighed heavily, leaning aback against the side of the stall. "Boden, I just bought you that blue roan not three months ago," he said. "If you want another horse, you are going to have to buy it yourself. I am not buying you another one."

Boden smiled at his father. "*You* are not buying it," he said flatly. "*Willie* is. Willie lost a bet and now he is going to buy me a horse."

Gaston waved him off and turned around, back to Trenton. "Go, then," he said. "But stay out of trouble. And no going to the taverns there. Do you hear me?"

Boden put his arm around his father's shoulders. "I hear you, you rotten old man," he said affectionately. Then, he spied Trenton with the pony. "Do you want to come with us, Trenton? I've heard there are a great many fine horses up for sale."

Trenton glanced at his younger brother. "Nay, thank you," he said. "You go ahead and spend Willie's money foolishly and leave me out of it."

Boden snorted and rushed off, rope in hand, as both William and Gage led their horses out of the stable so the grooms could prepare them. There was still a good deal of shouting and laughing going on as the de Russe brothers threatened William with something, and William vowed to punish them both. There was so much chatter flying around that it was difficult to know what, exactly, had been said, but knowing those three, it could be anything. As the shouting died away, Gaston returned his attention to Trenton.

"Your brothers have missed you," he said quietly. "Boden has always looked up to you a great deal."

Trenton simply grunted in response. "You had something important to speak to me about?"

He wasn't in the mood for small talk; that much was certain. Leaning over the side of the stall again, Gaston's gaze lingered on his eldest son.

"It is time to go home, Trenton," he said after a moment. "There is no longer any reason for you to remain here and I... I am weary. I want to go home and see your mother."

Trenton stopped what he was doing and looked up at his father, sharply. "What is wrong, Da?" he asked, standing up and looking at the man with great concern. "Are you feeling poorly?"

Gaston could see the intense worry in the man's face and, at that moment, he knew that Trenton was aware of his health woes. Remington must have told him, or perhaps Matthew had. *Someone* had. In any case, he didn't like seeing such concern for him in his son's face. It made him feel old and feeble, and not at all like himself. He waved Trenton off, irritably.

"We are not talking about me," he snapped quietly. "I am well; simply weary, but there is no longer any reason to remain here at Wellesbourne. I want you to come home with me."

Trenton studied his father a moment, trying to figure out if the man was lying to him and he really was feeling terrible, but he let it drop. He could see that his father was defensive about it.

"I am not leaving," he muttered, moving to reclaim his stool. "I will stay here for a time."

"You are not welcome here and you know it. I want you to come home with me."

Trenton stopped fumbling with the pony's leg. "Nay," he said flatly.

Gaston was starting to grow annoyed with the man. "Trenton, there is no use in you remaining," he said. "Lysabel has given you her answer. You must respect it."

"She told me what Uncle Matthew told her to say."

"He had nothing to do with it. What she told you was of her own volition."

Trenton suddenly bolted to his feet, startling the ponies as he faced his father. "And you believe that?" he demanded. "Did Matthew Wellesbourne tell you that? If he did, then he is lying. I know what he has told her."

Gaston didn't back down. "You will not call Matthew a liar," he growled. "Do you understand me? Whatever the man has done, he is not a liar, and you would do well not to accuse him of such things. What he has done is what any man would do in his position – he is protecting his daughter. Given that you have no children, mayhap you cannot understand that, but I do. You asked me to come here on your behalf and I did; against my better judgment, I did, because it was important to you. For you, I pleaded your case before my dearest friend in the world, but Matthew has stood his ground. Now, his daughter has made her decision. Stop acting like a spoiled child who did not get his way. Understand that this is a battle you have lost, Trenton. You can do no more here."

Trenton didn't like what he was hearing, even if it was the truth. "So you defend Matthew over your own flesh and blood?"

"I am not defending anyone. I am simply telling you the way of things. If you continue on this path, it will not go well for you. You will ruin the relationship between the House of de Russe and the House of Wellesbourne for your purely selfish reasons, and I will not let you do it." Gaston's jaw was ticking furiously as he faced off against his son. "Listen to me and listen carefully. Matthew has betrothed Lysabel to another man. The contract has already been agreed upon. You cannot violate it and if you try, I give Matthew permission to throw you in the vault until you come to your senses. Is this in any way unclear?"

Trenton felt as if he'd been struck. His head actually jerked back and he stared at his father in shock.

"He… he *what*?" he finally gasped. "Lysabel is to be *married*?"

Gaston's anger was tempered by the grief he saw in Trenton's eyes. He hadn't meant to shout it at the man, but Trenton's unreasonable disposition had forced him into it. Instantly, he felt himself softening by the pain he saw.

"She is," he said quietly. "Matthew feels it is best for her to get on with her life, and that does not include carrying on an affair with you. She will marry and be an honored wife and mother, not a mistress. Can you understand that, lad? It may not be the choice of the heart, but it is the right thing to do. Do not think it has given Matthew any pleasure to do this, either. He does not wish you pain."

Trenton was still staring at him, trying to comprehend what he'd been told. Unfortunately, he couldn't. He sank back onto the stool, feeling as if everything in his body had just been ripped out and smashed. Where his heart and guts used to be, there was now a big, black hole.

He was empty.

"Did she know?" he asked, his voice raspy. "Is that why… why she refused to go with me?"

Gaston shook his head. "It is my understanding that this has only come about today, so she could not have known last night," he said. "I am sure she would have told you had she known."

"*Today?*" Trenton's head came up, his bloodshot eyes glimmering with unshed tears. "This all happened today?"

"Aye."

Trenton's brow furrowed, the desperation to understand evident in his face. "But how?" he demanded. "No one has come in or out of Wellesbourne since we have been here, not even a messenger. *Who* is she pledged to?"

Gaston knew, but he wasn't sure he should tell him because it could put Ranse de Troyes in a very bad position. Trenton was a killer. Gaston knew his son was a killer, and no man withstood the rage of someone like Trenton de Russe.

"Does it matter?" he asked. "The fact remains that she is pledged. The wedding is to take place quickly, from what I understand. Come home with me, Trenton. We shall leave today. There is no reason for you to remain here and torture yourself."

"*Torture* myself?" Trenton shot back, now on his feet again. "How can you say that, Da? I love a woman who, up until yesterday, was a widow whose future, I had hoped, was with me. Now she's betrothed? How do you expect me to react to such a thing?"

"Like a man of honor," Gaston said, his voice low. "Trenton, I raised you to be a man of honor, and to linger here at Wellesbourne, now that you know Lysabel is betrothed, is not honorable. No amount of pleading with her is going to change the situation, and if you do and for some reason she decides to leave with you, it will ruin our family honor. I doubt Matthew would ever speak to me again, a man who sacrificed his left hand at Bosworth to save my life, and I would be bereft without his friendship. Is that what you want to do? Destroy me in my time of need?"

Trenton looked at him, hearing those words, and suddenly realizing his father was speaking not of Trenton, or of the situation, but of himself and his health. It was written all over his face.

And that was when Trenton started to realize that he needed to walk away.

It was as simple as that.

"Nay," he said hoarsely, looking at his father. "I would not destroy you in your time of need. I would never do that to you. But I cannot help what I feel."

Gaston could see that he was thankfully calming. He reached out, putting a hand on Trenton's shoulder. "I understand," he said. "But in this case, you must rise above it. It was not meant to be, Trenton. I need

Matthew's friendship as much as I need your love. Right now, I need you both, and to have you at odds with Matt destroys me more than you know. Matthew is doing what he feels is best for Lysabel, and I must do what I feel is best for you. Come home with me, now. I need you to."

Those pleading words were the last nail in the coffin. All of the emotion, the longing, and the anguish had reached its peak because Trenton couldn't do anything more. No amount of begging, or demanding, or rebellion was going to change the situation. But more than that, he could see that his behavior was having a serious effect on his ill father. Whatever terrible health was happening to him, Trenton didn't want to hasten it. He didn't care about his honor; that wasn't an issue.

But his father's heath was.

And that was the deciding factor.

"Very well," he said, hating those words coming out of his mouth but knowing they were necessary. "I will go home, but first I must go to The Horn and The Crown in Westbury."

"Why?"

"Because my men will be waiting for me there. I told them to. We were intending to return to London, together." He sighed heavily and turned to look at the two ponies, all wrapped up with bandages for their injuries as they munched on their oats. "I will meet them and tell them that I will be at Deverill Castle for the near future. And I will send word to Henry that I will not be returning to London. My father needs me."

Gaston was watching him carefully. "I am not asking you to leave his service."

Trenton shook his head, running a hand through his dirty, dark hair. "I know," he said, looking at his father. "But I know you are ill, Da. Dane told me and Mother confirmed it. I think you and I have spent too much time away from one another, so I would like to come home if you will let me. Let my memories of my father be that our relationship was repaired at the end of his life, so that when you finally go to your grave, it will be with the knowledge that I was a good son."

Gaston had a lump in his throat. "You *are* a good son," he said. "You have always been my pride and my joy, Trenton. I am very proud of the man you have become."

Trenton was so emotional that the tears were close to the surface. He wiped at his eyes so they wouldn't spill over. "Even though I serve Henry?"

"Even though you serve Henry."

"I love you, Da. I am sorry if I have ever disappointed you."

Gaston reached out and grabbed him behind the neck, pulling his head against his. "I love you, Trenton," he whispered against his ear, feeling his son emit a sob. "And you have never disappointed me. Let us go home now. All will be well again, I swear it."

Trenton believed him.

CHAPTER NINETEEN

S HE COULD SEE them from her mother's small solar.

With a kerchief to her nose, Lysabel watched the de Russe escort as it formed in the stable yard and spilled over into the bailey. She knew they were preparing to return home without anyone telling her. But from the window, she could see Trenton as he moved through the men and horses, making sure everything was prepared for the journey home.

A sob escaped her lips as she watched, knowing this would probably be the last time she ever saw the man. Her father had told her about the betrothal to de Troyes, and she hadn't stopped crying since. She knew what she wanted, and what she couldn't have, and it was tearing her to pieces. She finally had to turn away because watching it was too much to take. Sitting on one of her mother's cushioned chairs, she put her kerchief to her face and sobbed.

Distracted with her grief and weeping, Lysabel didn't notice her mother opening the solar door, only to stand there and watch her daughter with an expression of great sorrow on her face.

Alixandrea had just come from her husband, who had much the same expression that her daughter did, only without the tears. They were both deeply upset by the situation, but Matthew was standing by his decision. Although he felt it was best for Lysabel in the long run,

Alixandrea still wasn't certain. Most of all, she felt sorry for Ranse, who was put in a position between two lovers that he knew nothing about.

It wasn't ideal.

Matthew had told his wife that he refrained from telling Ranse about Lysabel's attachment to Trenton, thinking that it should come from his daughter if, in fact, she wanted to tell him at all. And as Alixandrea watched her daughter weep, she thought that it was perhaps time Lysabel became more acquainted with the man she was betrothed to.

The situation was bad enough without Lysabel making herself sick over it, and Alixandrea didn't want to give the woman too much time to grieve. Her life had been in enough turmoil over the past several weeks, so perhaps talking to Ranse might give her hope that a calm, peaceful life was on the horizon.

Right now, Lysabel was not only grieving Trenton's loss, but fearing the prospect of a future with a man she knew nothing about. If nothing else, speaking to Ranse might take her mind off of Trenton and the escort in the bailey, and introduce her to the man she was going to marry.

At least, Alixandrea hoped so. She had to do something, and she felt as if she'd talked to her daughter all she could about the situation. There was nothing more she could say that Lysabel hadn't already heard.

The time for talk was over.

Closing the door softly, she went in search of Ranse.

Unaware of her mother's departure, Lysabel continued to sniffle and sob. She felt as if she'd suffered through a death. Trenton was gone – and it was her doing – but the day after she refused to go with him, she was starting to have some second thoughts about it.

Perhaps, she hadn't made the right decision, after all.

Perhaps, she should take the girls and flee with Trenton, as he had suggested, and no one would ever know what had become of them. He had offered to take her someplace where no one would know them, and as the day progressed and the escort outside began to assemble, that offer was looking more and more attractive.

Uncertainties wracked her. What did it matter that her family was shamed? They would get over it. They would move on with their lives, and she would live hers with the only man she'd ever loved.

Wasn't that better than being without him?

... wasn't it?

In the midst of her mental turmoil, a knock on the solar door startled her. Wiping at her face, she turned away from the door as she spoke.

"Who is it?" she called, muffled.

"Ranse, my lady," came the voice through the door. "May I enter?"

De Troyes. Lysabel's head shot up, looking at the door as if her mortal enemy was on the other side of it. Her first reaction was to scream at him to go away, but she quickly realized that none of this was his doing. Her father was the instigator and Ranse, being that he served her father, had probably felt obligated to agree to Matthew's offer. Although she didn't know the man very well, he had been kind in their brief contact. Now, the man was to be her husband. Chasing him away wasn't going to change that.

With a heavy sigh, she wiped the last of her tears.

"Come in," she said.

The door creaked open and Ranse stepped in. Lysabel could hear him. She wasn't really looking at him but she forced herself to at least turn her head in his direction even if she couldn't bear to look at the man.

"Is there something I can do for you?" she asked, her nose stuffy from crying.

Ranse lingered by the door. "I came to ask your permission to take your daughters riding on the ponies I procured for them, my lady," he said politely. "The children are in the garden, but your mother says that they would prefer to ride and she told me to seek your permission."

He had a nice, deep voice. Soothing, even. Lysabel rubbed her eyes as she lifted her head towards the window that overlooked the bailey, hearing the noise from outside.

"The black and white pony tries to bite Cissy," she said. "She says the pony does not love her."

Back against the door, Ranse smiled. "He loves her, my lady," he said. "He simply does not know how to show it. I found the pony in a livery in town, corralled with many other horses, so I think he is used to having the other horses bite at him. It is what he knows."

Lysabel nodded, but she didn't reply. She simply sat there, leaving Ranse by the door, until the silence grew awkward. Then, she spoke.

"My father told me that you and I are to be wed," she finally said.

Ranse, who had been poised to leave the room when the silence between them grew lengthy, now paused.

"Aye, my lady," he said. Clearing his throat somewhat nervously, he took a few steps towards her. "May I say that I can think of no greater honor than to be married into the House of Wellesbourne."

Lysabel turned to look at him, giving him a second glance. As she'd noticed before, the man was handsome. He was long-limbed, but muscular, with tanned skin and angular features.

"Is that all this means to you?" she asked bluntly. "Being married into the House of Wellesbourne?"

Up until that point, Ranse had been uncomfortable and uncertain what to say to the lady, who had clearly been weeping. When Lady Wellesbourne had asked him to go to the solar to ask her about her daughters and the pony rides, he'd been disheartened to her sobbing through the door. He knew without a doubt it was because of him, and a marriage she'd clearly not wanted after the very recent death of her husband, so he was coming to feel hugely guilty in all of this.

Now, with her question, he realized that he had to say something to make his position plain, if only to alleviate some of the lady's concerns. He didn't want to start off this relationship on a bad note. He wanted to build something that he and his first wife once had – he wanted a friend, lover, and companion again.

"Nay, my lady, not at all," he said sincerely. "May… may I sit?"

Lysabel lifted her shoulders and looked away, but Ranse took it as an affirmative. There was a chair a few feet away from her and he went to it, settling his big body into it as he looked at her.

"I did not mean that to sound as if that is all I am concerned with," he said quietly. "The truth is that your father's offer was quite unexpected. And even as he spoke of it, I could not believe he meant it for me. My greatest honor will to be your husband, and a father for your children. Being part of the House of Wellesbourne is secondary to that, I assure you. I am sorry that my clumsy words did not convey that."

Lysabel turned to look at him; he seemed quite sincere and eager, in fact. In any other circumstance, she might have been happy about this, but all she could think of when she looked at him was that he wasn't Trenton.

"It is, in no way, a reflection upon you, but I am not pleased with my father's contract," she said. "I have no wish to remarry."

Ranse suspected as much. Even Matthew had told him that his daughter had some issues, so this wasn't unexpected.

"I understand," he said. "I am a stranger, so there is no reason why you should wish to marry me. Moreover, your husband's death was recent. Your father told me the circumstances, so I do not presume that you are mourning his loss."

She looked at him with some surprise. "He told you how Benoit died?"

"He did."

Lysabel's expression flickered, her eyes narrowing somewhat. "Did he tell you why?"

Ranse nodded. "I asked him, and he obliged me," he said. "My lady, please allow me to be plain – what your father told me was revolting. I am very sorry for what you had to endure at the hands of Lord de Wilde, but let me assure you that as Lady de Troyes, you would know nothing but respect and honor and gentleness. De Russe is a champion in my eyes for having killed Lord de Wilde for what he did to you and he shall always have my greatest respect because of it."

His words were kind and she wanted to believe him. In fact, it made her take another look at the man. He'd always been polite in any contact they'd ever had, and it hadn't been for show. She was coming to suspect that was simply his nature. But according to her father, he'd not told the man about Trenton because he didn't feel it was necessary. Since Ranse and Lysabel would be starting a new relationship, the ghost of Trenton hanging over it could only do harm and, in a sense, Lysabel understood. If she wanted Ranse to know about it, then she would tell him.

But the truth was that Trenton's ghost was already hanging over them, like it or not. It was smothering her, attached to her, and keeping a barrier between her and Ranse. For now, it was a barrier no man could penetrate.

Lysabel suspected it would always be that way.

"Aye," she finally said. "He is my champion, too. Were it not for Trenton, I would still be enduring my hell. Since my father told you of my past, I will not elaborate. Know that it is not something I wish to speak of, so I would appreciate it if you would not bring it up. It is a painful subject, as you can imagine."

Ranse nodded quickly. "Indeed, I can, and I will not speak of it again." His gaze lingered on her a moment, as if there was much he wanted to say, but didn't want to upset her. In truth, he wanted to comfort her. "I simply wanted you to know that our marriage will be much different. I was married before, as I mentioned to you that day in the garden, and my wife was not only my spouse, she was a great friend. I had the utmost respect for her. It is not in my nature to treat a woman as anything other than someone to be cherished and protected."

More kind words. Lysabel was almost coming to feel sorry for the man, for he had no idea that she had no interest in him. Perhaps, she should have told him the truth, but she didn't see any need. It was that dignity that Trenton had seen in her from the beginning, that woman who kept her troubles to herself to spare others the pain and suffering of them. Ranse was genuinely trying to be kind and she didn't want to tell him that all the kindness in the world wasn't going to bring him any affection on her part. Perhaps the best he could ever hope for with his new wife was a polite formality.

Her heart would always belong to another.

"You have been taught well," she said. "Did you have parents who set a good example for you, then?"

He shook his head. "Nay," he said, an ironic twist of the lips. "My mother died when I was young and my father never remarried. I have two older brothers who are constantly trying to kill each other, but as the battles were going on when I was younger, I spent much time with one of my father's knights, a man who was married to a woman for many years. They had no children, but he treated her with the greatest respect. He said women were precious and needed to be tended gently. I… I suppose that has always stayed with me, because when I married my wife, I tended her gently up until the day she died."

Lysabel could sense that the man had a tender heart and her pity for him grew. He seemed genuinely likable, and she knew her father had a good deal of faith in him, so under any other circumstances this would have been welcome match. She was truly sorry that she had no interest at all, and even sorrier that she had no choice in the matter. She feared that she would come to resent this kind, gentle knight.

"I am sorry for your wife's passing," she said. "Having given birth to two children of my own, I know what a frightening and exciting experience it can be."

"And you will know that experience again very soon, I am told," he said softly, smiling weakly when she looked at him in shock. "Aye, your father told me of the child you carry. Have no fear, I will love the babe as if he or she were my own flesh and blood."

He was too good to be true and something in Lysabel snapped. He was too kind and she felt what her father had done to him was so very wrong. They were *all* wronging him. Standing up, she made her way over to the lancet window overlooking the bailey, the one where she'd been watching Trenton form the escort. Looking from the window, she could see that they were all still there. Feeling sad, and frustrated, she turned in Ranse's direction.

"De Troyes, it seems to me that you deserve better than what this situation has brought to you," she said. "Did my father tell you *why* I have no desire to remarry?"

Ranse shook his head, but he looked at her curiously. "Other than the fact that this is all rather sudden and you do not know me?"

So that's what he thinks it is, she thought to herself. Sounds from the bailey were wafting in through the window and she turned to see Trenton as he moved among the horses that had been brought out. She could see the sun gleaming off of his dark head. Oddly enough, the more she watched him, the more she came to feel as if holding on to him would be futile.

The situation between them, for the most part, was over.

It was strange, really. There wasn't just a wall and her father separating them; there was a marriage and his wife. For the first time, she was coming to understand just how much of a barrier that was, whereas only minutes earlier, she hadn't cared. The truth was that she *did* care, and she cared enough to know that, at some point, she would want to be Lady de Russe and it was something Trenton could never give her.

To be a man's wife… she'd seen how her own parents behaved with each other, and being Lady Wellesbourne, for her mother, gave the woman a sense of pride and status. It was more than the love of a man. It was knowing he loved her enough to give her his name.

That had been the example set for her.

Perhaps now, she was coming to realize that it meant more to her than she realized. *Respect and protect* is what de Troyes had said. She could tell he'd meant it.

Then perhaps this betrothal, as her father had hoped, was the best choice, after all.

"Aye," she said belatedly to his statement. "This is all rather sudden. So much of my life has been in turmoil as of late. But… but I hope to move forward and I hope to heal. Your patience is appreciated."

Ranse stood up, a smile on his lips. "I can be as patient as you need me to be, for as long as you need me to be. May... may I call upon you again tonight to see how you are feeling?"

It was a sweet question, but everything in her screamed denial. "Not tonight, please," she said. "Tomorrow... tomorrow would be acceptable."

If he was disappointed, he didn't show it. "Thank you, my lady," he said. "Now, with your permission, I shall go to the stables and prepare those two frothing beasts for your daughters to ride."

Lysabel simply nodded. She was about to say something more, a forced polite acknowledgement, when commotion in the bailey caught her attention. Turning to the window, she could see two men charging in through the open gates, scattering soldiers and others in the bailey because they were moving so fast.

In fact, it was enough of a commotion that Ranse came to stand next to her, seeing that the bailey was in some kind of chaos because of the two reckless riders. Cocking an eyebrow of disapproval, and perhaps concern, he turned for the solar door.

"You will excuse me, my lady," he said. "It seems we have visitors."

Lysabel didn't reply. Her attention was still on the bailey, where the two knights had pulled their horses to a halt and had bailed from them, pushing through the de Russe escort until they came to Trenton. She could clearly see Trenton as he engaged the men in a discussion, but because of the armor and helms the men wore, she couldn't see who they were.

It never occurred to her that Dane de Russe and Cort de Russe had made an appearance.

CHAPTER TWENTY

"**T**RENTON!" DANE WAS shouting as he pushed through the de Russe escort in Wellesbourne's vast bailey. "*Trenton!*"

He was bellowing as men began pointing, showing him the way to where they had last seen Trenton. Dane and Cort followed the pointing fingers, shoving men and horses out of the way, until they came to Trenton and Gaston, who had been heading in their direction. They had heard the bellowing, too.

"Dane?" Gaston said, both puzzled and incredulous. He saw Cort coming up behind the man. "What are both of you doing here?"

Dane and Cort were exhausted from a very hard ride that had taken them a little over a day. Wellesbourne Castle was closer to Penleigh House than Deverill Castle was, so it was a shorter distance for them to travel, thankfully. They knew that their father and eldest brother had traveled to Wellesbourne and they were hoping they were still there, relieved to see that the men hadn't left to return to Deverill as of yet. Even though Gaston had asked the question, Dane went straight to Trenton with the answer.

The man was going to want to hear this.

"Adela is dead," Dane said. "Penleigh House burned to the ground, and her with it. She is *dead*, Trenton."

Trenton's jaw went slack. "She's *what?*" he hissed. "How do you know?"

By this time, Gaston was standing next to Trenton, having heard Dane's revelation. He grabbed Dane by the arm.

"How do you know this, Dane?" he demanded, looking between Dane and his other son. "Cort? What is going on?"

Cort was dirty and sweaty, appearing more agitated than Dane was. "We went to Penleigh," he said. "We wanted to…"

Dane threw up a hand to stop his younger brother from perhaps delivering the facts in a rush. Cort was excitable that way. For the story that needed to be told, the facts needed to be concise, and Dane was trying to do just that.

"Do not be angry, Trenton, but Cort and I left Deverill the night before you came to Wellesbourne," he said. "We headed for Penleigh House because after speaking with you about Adela… and your problem with… well, you know… I told Cort the entire story and we decided to pay Adela a visit. She had been a thorn in your side long enough and we thought – we *hoped* – that we could bribe her into disappearing."

Trenton's mouth was still hanging open. He was having a difficult time following any of what his brother was telling him. Reaching out, he grabbed Dane by both arms but it was more a gesture of support. He had to grab on to something or he would surely fall over. Dane had just told him Adela was dead and he was reeling.

Adela was dead!

"*Bribe* her?" he managed to sputter. "Dane, what are you saying? *What happened?*"

Dane could see how shaken Trenton was. He pulled at the man, pulling him out of the cluster of men and horses, as Cort went to Gaston and pulled the man along, too. They all moved in a huddle, away from the escort, until they had a moderate amount of privacy. Only then did Dane come to a halt, facing Trenton and his father once again.

"Cort and I decided something needed to be done about Adela," he said, his gaze moving between his brother's ashen face and his father's astonished one. "She was a wicked, horrible bitch when you married her, Trenton, and she's done nothing but shame you and the de Russe name since that day. You have ignored her, and Father cannot do anything about her, so we took matters into our own hands. Cort and I made plans to confront her and try to bribe her into leaving Penleigh and going back to France, never to contact you again."

"And if she did not agree to our terms, then we were going to abduct her and take her to the slave market in Northwic," Cort put in excitedly, talking over Dane. "We were going to sell her to the highest bidder so she would be taken away, never to be heard from again."

As Gaston's eyes widened, Dane punched Cort in the arm, greatly annoyed. Cort flinched and shut his mouth, and Dane continued.

"We hoped that you would think she was dead, Trenton," he said, looking at the man. "If you thought that, then mayhap Uncle Matthew would let you be with Lysabel. God knows you deserve some happiness. We wanted to give it to you."

Trenton was beyond overwhelmed. He was overcome. "You… you were going to get *rid* of her?"

"Permanently."

Trenton could see that Dane was deadly serious. "But you said she was dead," he said. "*What* happened?"

Dane nodded grimly. "Believe me, it was not our doing," he said, "because I would happily lay claim to such a thing. We went to Penleigh and Adela was having a grand party. Bretons everywhere."

"Smelly bastards," Cort growled.

Dane ignored him. "Adela was not happy to see us, as you can imagine. As we were trying to coerce her into naming her price, she became angry and picked up a fire poker. When she swung it at me, I grabbed it, and it was her own momentum that toppled her backwards into the hearth. She went up in flames and set the entire house on fire in the process. She's dead, Trenton, by her own wicked hand. We never touched her."

Trenton stared at him. Then, he slapped a hand over his mouth as if he could scarcely believe what he'd just heard. He looked at Gaston, who was looking back at him with equal shock.

"When did this happen?" Gaston finally asked.

"Two evenings ago," Dane replied. "Penleigh is in ashes. We should all return to ensure we collect what we can from the ruins, including Adela's jewels or anything else of value that hasn't already been taken. Cort and I did not stay long enough to sift through the ruins."

"But you are certain she is dead?"

"We saw her burn before our eyes, Da," Cort said, a distasteful expression on his face at the memory. "Believe me... she is dead."

Trenton was only marginally calmer at this point as he digested the information. *Adela was dead...* it was whirling around in his mind until the news finally began to settle, and then, he could only think of one thing –

He was no longer married.

Adela was dead!

"God," he hissed. "Is it true? Is it *really* true?"

Dane nodded, seeing some of the color rush back into Trenton's face. "Aye," he said, grasping the man's arm. "We went there to try and help you, Trenton. Although I find it distasteful to rejoice over a death, in this case, she brought it on herself. What happened to her was divine justice as far as I'm concerned."

Trenton's breathing started coming in short gasps and he turned towards Wellesbourne's keep. The only thing on his mind at that moment was Lysabel, and Matthew, and before he realized it, he was on the run.

Trenton headed for the keep at top speed as his brothers and father shouted behind him, begging him to stop, but there was no sense in trying to stop the man. He was blinded by the news and by the fact that he was now a free man. He knew it and he wanted Matthew Wellesbourne to know it, too.

Free!

Trenton was just reaching the entry as Ranse emerged and the two of them nearly crashed into each other. Ranse had to grab hold of Trenton to steady the man.

"My lord?" Ranse said, greatly concerned. "Is anything wrong? Can I be of assistance?"

Trenton shook his head, pulling free of the man's grip, and continuing on into the keep. Ranse watched him go with great concern and thought about going after him, but he was forced to step aside when Dane, Cort, and, finally, Gaston raced in behind him. It was step aside or be trampled. At that point, Ranse decided that whatever was going on involved the de Russe men only. If he was needed, his lord would send for him. He continued out to the stables.

Once inside the keep, Trenton made tracks right to Matthew's solar door, throwing the panel open and charging in. Matthew was there, bent over the maps on his cluttered table, but when Trenton barreled in, he was so startled that he jumped out of his chair and nearly tripped over his feet.

"Trenton!" he gasped. "God's Bones, man, what is the matter?"

Trenton ran right to him and it was then that Matthew saw the joy in his face, the light of a thousand candles lighting up his eyes and euphoria beyond words on his features.

"I'm free," he breathed heavily. "I can marry her!"

Matthew had no idea what he was talking about, but Trenton seemed extremely agitated. He grasped him to keep him steady just as Dane, Cort, and Gaston thundered into the chamber.

"What are you saying, Trenton?" Matthew asked, concerned. "You are free? I do not..."

Trenton cut him off. "Adela," he said, trying to catch his breath. "Lady de Russe. She has been killed. I am not married to her anymore. I am free to marry Lysabel!"

Everything became clear in that panting statement. Shocked and perplexed, Matthew looked to Gaston, who was just walking up on them, reaching out to peel Trenton off of Matthew.

"Lady de Russe is dead," he said simply. "He has just received the news."

Matthew stared at Gaston a moment before returning his attention to Trenton. He took one step back, and then another, and then turned back to his table. There were a million things going through his mind at the moment, not the least of which was the fact that he felt cornered. He had Gaston, Trenton, Dane, and Cort in his solar and he knew very well what they wanted. He knew the implications of this right away.

He didn't like the pressure he was feeling.

"Trenton," he finally said. "Get out. And take your brothers with you. Gaston, you will remain."

That wasn't the answer that Trenton wanted to hear and he opened his mouth to plead again, but Gaston shook his head, pushing him in the direction of the door.

"Go," he muttered. "Wait for me outside."

The expression on Trenton's face was full of apprehension but Gaston patted him reassuringly, sending him and his brothers out of the solar. Dane and Cort had to practically pull Trenton from the chamber. When they were gone and the door shut quietly, Gaston turned to Matthew.

"Adela was killed in a fire, Matt," he said. "Dane and Cort saw it happen, which is why they are here. They came to tell Trenton."

Matthew sighed as he turned around to face Gaston. "And what? He thinks that is the magic that will change this entire situation?"

Gaston lifted his big shoulders. "He is hoping that will change your mind about his relationship with Lysabel."

Matthew's gaze lingered on the man a moment, indecision written on his face. "I told you that I have made a contract with de Troyes. I am not going to break it."

That drew a reaction from Gaston. "But why not?" he asked. "Trenton is no longer encumbered and he loves your daughter. I am sure de Troyes is a good man, but Lysabel loves Trenton. It makes no sense that you would marry her to a man that she does not love, especially when

Trenton has so much more to offer."

Matthew cocked an eyebrow. "Does he?" he said. "Let us review what he has to offer, Gaston. He has been married three times, and all three wives have died. So I am to allow Lysabel to be his fourth? Moreover, I have never said anything about his occupation, not even to you, but the truth is that I agree with you. What he does for Henry is shameful. He is an assassin and you know as well as I do that he has a fearsome reputation, and not necessarily in a good way."

Gaston could see his friend's reluctance. He understood it, but it was starting to frustrate him. "But your daughter has changed him," he said, pleading on Trenton's behalf. "You said it yourself – Trenton is a changed man around her. That is what the power of love will do, Matt, and you know it as well as I do. We were both fortunate enough to marry women that we adore. Are our children not permitted to do the same?"

Matthew simply shook his head. Then, he hissed. "I hate that I am in this position," he said. "I hate that I have offered Lysabel's hand to an excellent knight with an excellent reputation, yet Trenton expects me to break that promise and turn my daughter over to him. He expects me to go back on my word to a man who has never done him any harm. And I hate that he has made you his ambassador – he knows that I cannot deny you anything. Is that fair to me?"

Gaston went over to him, putting his hand on the man's shoulder. "I know you want what is best for Lysabel," he said quietly. "And our opinions are the same when it comes to Trenton's position with Henry. But you know my son – you know that he has a true and good heart."

Matthew looked at him. "Does he?" he asked. "He was in here not a few moments ago rejoicing over the death of yet another wife. My God, Gaston, are wives so disposable to him that he has no hesitation over replacing one with another?"

Gaston's jaw ticked. "Of course not."

"My daughter has been through *hell*. What happens if Trenton tires of her? Will she be disposable, too?"

Gaston dropped his hand, looking at Matthew with a mixture of pain and sorrow. "Nay," he said evenly. "And you are being unfair. You know how Adela treated him. You know the lack of respect or decency she showed him."

Matthew calmed somewhat. "I know," he muttered, running his hand over his graying, blond hair. "I am sorry I said that. I did not mean it. But this entire situation has me deeply torn. I must do what I feel is right for Lysabel. De Troyes is a stable, honorable man. He is not an assassin for Henry. He has not had three wives. He proves his loyalty to me every day that he serves me."

"And Trenton has not proven his loyalty to you?" Gaston shot back softly. "Matt, he was with you for years, loyal to the bone. You are speaking of my son and not some knight we barely know. You know Trenton. You know he loves you. You know he is a good man. Why must you make him seem less than what he is, in front of me, no less?"

Matthew looked at him. After a moment, he simply shook his head. "I am sorry, Gaston," he said. "I truly am. I have always said that I love Trenton like a son, and I do, but not when it comes to my daughter. All I see when I look at him is a man who has had wanderlust; he has never been satisfied being in one place, or doing one thing, for too long. Trenton was always looking ahead, always moving. Even when he was married, he did not stay with his wife. He did not stay with Alicia for very long, did he? He was in London, or with you, a good deal of the time."

Gaston nodded, although it was with reluctance. Nothing Matthew said was untrue. "He was young," he said. "He was involved in his vocation. Alicia understood that."

"Did she?" Matthew asked. "That is an honest question, Gaston. Did she really? Or did she simply tolerate it and let Trenton do what he wanted to do because she was an obedient wife?"

Gaston lifted his shoulders. "I cannot know, but it is true that Trenton was away from her much of the time."

"And Iseuld?"

"He was hardly married to her at all before her father killed her."

"And now Adela." Matthew shook his head. "Gaston, I love Trenton. I do. But I love my daughter more. When it comes to Lysabel, we are speaking of my flesh and blood. My first born. How can I entrust her to someone with Trenton's history and reputation?"

Gaston was starting to feel defeated. He was coming to see that no amount of pleading was going to change Matthew's mind and for Trenton's sake, he was already devastated for it.

"So you are telling me that your excuse throughout this entire situation, the fact that Trenton was married, is not the real reason for your reluctance at all," he said. "It goes much deeper than that."

Matthew sighed sadly and averted his gaze. "Possibly."

"Would you trust Trenton with her life?"

"Without question."

"Then why not trust him as her husband?"

Matthew didn't say anything for a moment. He was weary, and confused, and torn over the entire circumstance. Slowly, he moved around his table, lowering himself wearily into his chair.

"If I do not let Lysabel marry Trenton, will it change things between us?" he finally asked.

Gaston looked at him. "Nay," he murmured. "You are still my brother. But I would be lying if I said that I would not be hurt because Trenton will be hurt. Matt, you have the power to change his life. You hold the key to his happiness and I am afraid if you do not permit him to be with the woman he loves, it *will* change him forever. I fear for him."

Matthew was feeling defeated, so very defeated. "If you were me, what would you do? If this was your daughter, and you know everything there is to know about Trenton, what would *you* do?"

Gaston hesitated. "I have never said that I do not understand your reluctance."

"That was not the question."

"I know."

Matthew leaned forward on the table. "Then you make the decision for me. If you truly feel that your son would be the best possible husband for my daughter, then you make the decision and I will abide by it, because I am tired of fighting you and the entire de Russe clan on this. I am not willing to let this situation damage my relationship with you but I fear that is what is going to happen if I continue to refuse. So to you, Gaston, I say this – *you* decide. And be honest about it – make the decision with your head and not your heart. If you feel Trenton would be a good husband for Lysabel, then decide their future."

Gaston just looked at him.

He honestly couldn't bring the words to his lips.

"WHAT DO YOU suppose they are saying?" Cort asked.

Trenton, Dane, and Cort were lingering in the foyer area outside of Matthew's solar, waiting for Gaston and Matthew to emerge. Trenton was leaning against a wall, his head bowed, and Dane was looking at the man with some concern. After a moment, he moved away from Trenton, closer to Cort, and lowered his voice.

"I do not know," he said. "But if we thought Trenton's problems were over when Penleigh burned down and took Adela with it, then we were sadly mistaken. I want you to stay here. I will return."

Cort looked at him curiously. "Where are you going?"

Dane held a hand up for the man to keep his voice down because he didn't want to stir up Trenton, who was wallowing in a mood Dane had never before seen from him. There was something painfully dark and brooding to him. Just as he opened his mouth to reply, he saw a servant move through the foyer with a tray. Upon the tray were cheese bread, fruit, and something steaming in a pitcher. He could smell it; spices of some kind. It was mulled wine.

Women liked mulled wine.

Dane had an idea.

"Stay here with Trenton," he whispered. "Do not let him leave. I will return."

Cort nodded, watching Dane head off across the foyer, following a servant as the little woman disappeared into a darkened corridor. Trenton, too, noticed Dane leaving.

"Where are you going?" he called after the man.

He caught Dane just as the man was entering the corridor. He lifted a casual hand. "The privy," he said. "Or... something. I will return shortly."

With that, he was gone, vanishing into the darkness as Trenton stood there with a frown on his face. Cort, who had been told to keep Trenton in the foyer, went to him.

"He shall return," he said, thinking to change the subject very quickly so Trenton didn't try to follow. "Would... would you like to hear of our conversation with Adela, Trenton? We spoke with her at length before the fire started. You might be interested to know what was said."

In fact, Trenton had forgotten about Dane rather quickly because Dane did what Dane wanted to do, and Trenton had learned long ago not to worry over the man. Somehow, Dane always returned in one piece, so there was never any reason to worry. But Cort's words had his attention and he turned to his younger brother.

"I saw the two of you riding from Deverill the night before we departed for Wellesbourne," he said. "I was standing with Mother on the steps to the keep and we both wondered where you and Dane were going. I suppose I know now."

Cort nodded, but it was timidly. "You are not angry with us, are you?"

Trenton shook his head, putting a hand on the young knight's shoulder. "That I should have brothers who love me so much touches me more than you can know. I owe you everything. But I want you to swear something to me."

"Anything."

"You did not kill Adela and lie to me about it, did you?"

Cort shook his head solemnly. "We did not, I swear it."

That gave Trenton some relief. Honestly, he'd wondered. He knew the hatred between his family and Adela, so anything was possible.

"That is good. But she really is dead?"

"I swear on my oath that she is. I saw her go up in flames myself."

Trenton dropped his hand, rubbing his eyes wearily. "I believe you," he said. "Now, you can tell me about the conversation you had with her."

Cort did.

DANE'S INSTINCTS WERE good.

The mulled wine was, indeed, for a woman, and as he slipped in behind the servant into a small but lavish solar, he immediately saw Lysabel seated on a chair near the window. Even though he hadn't seen the woman in years – at least ten or more – he knew it was her on sight. She was still the same bronze-haired, blue-eyed lass that he'd known as a child, only now she'd come into her own.

She was beautiful.

"Lysabel?"

His voice made her look up, startled, only to see someone she didn't instantly recognize in the chamber with her. Dane could see the fear on her face and he hastened to reassure her.

"You do not remember me," he said. "It is Dane – Dane de Russe."

A ripple of recognition rolled across Lysabel's face and her eyes widened. "Dane?" she gasped, coming towards him. "God's Bones... I did not recognize you!"

Dane grinned. "We have grown old, you and I," he said. But then he quickly added, "But you have only grown more beautiful. I did not mean to say that you were old."

Lysabel laughed and, in that instant, Dane could see what had his brother so enamored. She was stunning.

"When did we last see one another?" she said. "I think it was here, at Wellesbourne, several years ago. I do not think my oldest daughter was even born at the time. My parents' wedding anniversary celebration, wasn't it?"

Dane shrugged. "I honestly do not remember," he said, frowning. "Probably because I had too much wine for the duration of the celebration. I do not remember the days leading up to it or the days following it for the most part, but I do remember seeing you there. And your sisters, too. How are Rosamunde and Emeline?"

"Well," Lysabel said, grinning. "You had them dreaming about you, Dane. They all wanted to marry the handsome de Russe brother."

Dane puffed up. "Of course they did," he stated firmly. "All women do. Except for you... I hear that you are quite fond of Trenton."

Lysabel sobered dramatically and she quickly averted her gaze. "Did Trenton tell you that?"

"Aye."

Lysabel frowned, her good mood gone. "You will understand if this is something I do not wish to speak of to you, or to anyone else for that matter."

Dane had seen her expression before, on Trenton when he spoke of the sad ending their love story was facing. She didn't need to confirm anything. Her feelings were written all over her face.

There was anguish there.

"I understand," Dane said, "but I must speak of it. It is very important."

Lysabel closed her eyes. "Dane, please..."

He cut her off. "Lysabel, Trenton told me the entire situation," he said. "He told me that he wants to be with you and when he told your father, the man banished him."

In spite of her vow not to discuss the situation, Lysabel found that she couldn't help it. An ironic snort escaped her lips.

"Not only has my father banished Trenton," she said, "but to truly ruin our chances, he has betrothed me to another man."

Now it was Dane's turn to appear surprised. "He did?" he said. "To whom?"

Lysabel waved him off, sad and defeated. "I do not think you know him," she said. "He is a good man by all accounts, and under any other circumstances I am sure it would have been a welcome betrothal, but I am not interested."

"Who is it?"

"The captain of my father's guard. Ranse de Troyes."

Dane let that sink in. "I know him," he said. "You must remember that I am also the captain of my father's guard, and de Troyes and I have served together from time to time. And Trenton knows of this?"

"He knows of the betrothal, but I do not know if he knows who I am pledged to. I've not seen him since my father made his decision."

Now, it made sense as to why Trenton had run so fast to Matthew when he'd been told of Adela's death. He was trying to stave off Lysabel's betrothal with important information. Still, it also underscored the critical nature of the situation – people's lives were at stake, in so many ways, and Lysabel had to be told about something that could very well change the course of her life, as well.

"Listen to me," he said urgently. "There is something you should know. Trenton's wife, Adela, has been killed in a fire. He has only just been told and he went straight to your father to tell him. Even now, my father is with your father in his solar. They are discussing the situation and if you have any desire to be with my brother at all, then I would suggest you make yourself part of that conversation."

Lysabel's eyes widened and a hand flew to her mouth in a shocked gesture. "Trenton is… he is…?"

"A widower," Dane supplied softly. "And he is free to marry you."

Lysabel stared at him as she realized what he was saying. Her first instinct was that Dane was lying to her for some reason because, certainly, the timing was all too coincidental. But she knew in the same breath that Dane was an honorable knight. He was a de Russe. There would be no purpose to him lying about such a thing.

Adela was killed in a fire.

She could hardly believe it.

"Dane," she finally gasped. "Please… it this really true?"

Dane nodded. "It is. I swear it."

She stood there, seemingly dazed. "God," she breathed. "I should not rejoice in the woman's death, but…"

He cut her off, again. She had to understand his sense of urgency. "She was evil, Lysabel," he said. "Mayhap, it is a sin to be happy for her death, but I do not care – her wickedness knew no bounds. For every curse she hurled at my brother, and at the House of de Russe, she has paid for it and I am not sorry. You should not be either. Now, go to your father's solar – and *hurry*."

Lysabel didn't say anything more. She had just heard perhaps the most important information she'd heard in her entire life, and Dane was correct – there was no more time for conversation.

She had to act.

With a shriek, she fled the solar with Dane on her heels, racing down the darkened corridor until they emerged into the dimly-lit foyer. The first thing Lysabel saw was Trenton, who looked at her as if he'd seen a ghost. His expression was wide and his cheeks were pale when their eyes met. The longing in his eyes was unfathomable, but by the expression on his face, he knew that she had been told about Adela. The fact that Dane was standing with her told him everything.

Dane hadn't gone to find the privy, after all.

But Lysabel didn't stop to talk to Trenton. She rushed right past him and straight into Matthew's solar.

And that was when the real battle began.

CHAPTER TWENTY-ONE

"**P**APA!"

Lysabel burst into Matthew's solar as her father and Gaston stood somewhere over near Matthew's cluttered table. When they both turned to her in surprise, she rushed to her father, grabbing hold of the man and nearly bowling him over.

"Papa, I just heard!" she cried, throwing her arms around his neck. "Trenton is free to marry me!"

Gaston had to reach out to steady Matthew so Lysabel wouldn't topple him. She was nearly hysterical in her excitement, and Gaston turned to see that Dane, Cort, and Trenton had filtered back into the chamber after her, all of them standing in a cluster near the door.

That tense little group told Gaston everything he needed to know about Lysabel's unwelcome appearance. Clearly, Trenton had run off to tell her what had happened and Gaston was so angry at that moment that he was close to throttling the man. When Gaston looked at Trenton with an expression to kill, Dane caught a glimpse of it and captured his father's attention, shaking his head and pointing to himself. Gaston understood when Cort nodded and pointed to Dane, too. Then, it was all he could do not to beat the pair senseless.

"Get out," he growled at them. "Get out and stay out. Wait for me in the foyer and if you stray one inch, I will hunt you down and you will be very, very sorry."

Dane and Cort moved to leave, but Trenton didn't budge. His attention was on Lysabel as she threw herself at her father, and Gaston knew as he looked at the man that there was no way he was leaving voluntarily. He was closer to Lysabel than he'd been since yesterday, and he wasn't going anywhere. But Gaston tried.

"Trenton," he said quietly, trying to turn the man for the door. "Please leave. I will be with you shortly."

But Trenton held his ground. "If you want me out of here, you are going to have to physically carry me," he said, meaning every word of it. "I am staying, Da."

Gaston didn't want a fight on his hands. Shaking his head in resignation, he turned back to Matthew and Lysabel just as the woman kissed her father on the cheek, joy beyond measure on her beautiful face.

"Oh, Papa, is it not wonderful?" she gasped. "Trenton and I can now be married! You have nothing more to worry over!"

Matthew was looking at his daughter gravely. "You do not belong here, Lys," he said. "Please leave. Gaston and I are in discussion."

Her happy expression faded. "About what?" she asked, looking between her father and Gaston. "What more is there to discuss? Trenton is a widower. I am a widow. There is no reason why we cannot be married now."

Matthew removed her hands from his neck and turned her towards the door. "Please, *leave*," he said quietly. "I will seek you when I am finished here."

Suddenly, Lysabel was realizing that there was no joy or celebration in the room, certainly not to the extent that she was feeling it. Both her father and Gaston looked extremely serious and she took a step away from her father but she did not leave. She looked between the pair, men she had known and loved her entire life.

Men who held her fate in their hands.

God... why was no one being happy about this?

"Nay," she said frankly. "I will not leave. I am tired of leaving the room when my life is being decided for me. Papa, forgive me for disobeying you but, in this case, I must. Why do you both look so serious? There is nothing more to be concerned with. Trenton is no longer married. He and I can now be together. Is that not cause for celebration?"

Gaston looked at Matthew, who was looking at his daughter. "Aren't you forgetting something?" Matthew said quietly. "You are betrothed to another."

Lysabel scowled. "De Troyes?" she said, incredulous. "I hardly know the man and in no way owe him any sense of obligation. *You* made the contract, Papa, not me. I had nothing to do with it."

"It is still a contract."

"You did not even tell him the truth of it!"

"De Troyes?" Trenton suddenly spat. "Is *that* who she is betrothed to?"

Gaston threw up a hand at Trenton to keep the man silent, but all it did was anger him. He stomped his feet and turned his back to the room, marching over to the solar door and slamming it in the faces of his brothers, who were still standing there and listening in.

He didn't want an audience.

That slamming door was a rude gesture, one that nearly severed Cort's fingers when the door slammed against the jamb. While Cort shook off his stinging hand, Dane was already planning his next move.

He'd heard enough.

Dane could hear Matthew's strained voice inside the solar and he knew what he had to do. So far, Adela was dead because he'd gone to Penleigh, and now Lysabel was in her father's solar, pleading for her happiness with Trenton because Dane had fetched her. He was sticking his nose into business that didn't concern him, but it concerned Trenton, and that was enough for him. He only wanted to see the man happy and would do whatever he could to ensure it.

So what if he was acting like a nosy fishwife. He was making a damned good one. And if Trenton had any hope of being happy, then Dane had someone else to pull into the equation now. Leaving Cort standing by the solar door, he ran out into the bailey in search of the third piece to this complicated puzzle –

Ranse de Troyes.

The knight was involved in something much bigger than he realized and according to what Dane had just heard, he didn't even know it. As far as de Troyes knew, he'd received an honorable proposal of marriage and he'd accepted.

But it had been far more than that.

Dane knew Ranse. As he'd told Lysabel, he'd know the man for years, since they both served in allied armies. He was a truly noble and kind knight, well-respected by everyone, and Dane thought the man would like to know the situation for what it was. Perhaps, it would help him make an educated decision about the rest of *his* life.

No man wanted to marry a woman who was in love with another, and Dane was fairly certain that de Troyes wasn't an exception.

He had to find him.

The de Russe escort was still out in the bailey, with men milling about in confusion now that Trenton and Gaston had gone into Wellesbourne's keep. As he ran towards the group, one of the de Russe sergeants approached him.

"My lord?" he asked. "Are we to wait here for Lord de Russe?"

Dane wasn't exactly sure. He came to a halt, turning to look at the keep and knowing what was going on in the place, before finally shaking his head.

"Nay," he said. "Disband the escort and put the horses away. Send the men to the troop house to wait for further orders."

The sergeant nodded sharply. "Aye, my lord."

As he turned away, Dane stopped him. "Where is de Troyes?" he asked.

The sergeant began to look around before finally pointing to a knight who was standing at the edge of the stable, near the gatehouse.

"I do not see him," he said. "But that is Markus de Aston, one of Lady de Wilde's knights. He might know."

Dane thanked him and headed towards the tall, red-haired knight he'd indicated. When Dane came near, he caught the man's attention with a wave.

"You, there," he said. "De Aston, is it? I'm Dane de Russe. Gaston de Russe is my father. We've met before, but briefly. You served Benoit de Wilde."

Markus nodding his head, sending away the two men he'd been talking with. "Aye, my lord," he said. "It is an honor to see you again."

Dane nodded shortly. He hated to sound rushed, but time was of the essence. "Likewise," he said. "Can you direct me to de Troyes?"

Markus nodded. "I can do better than that," he said. Then, he turned to the gatehouse, with several men on the wall near it, and emitted a piercing whistle between his teeth. When a group of them turned to him, he waved an arm. "De Troyes!"

A man separated himself from the group on the wall and made haste down to the bailey. As Dane watched, a muscular man with blond hair to his shoulders quickly approached, the light of recognition in his eyes when he saw Dane.

Dane smiled in return, but he found himself taking a second look at him, sizing up Trenton's competition. Dane knew all about the man's wife dying in childbirth last year, and as Lysabel herself had said, he was a good man. It wasn't an unattractive match. As de Troyes came close, he reached out a hand to Dane.

"Dane," he said fondly, shaking the man's hand. "You are finally taking the time to talk to me, eh? You ran past me like a madman earlier."

Dane snorted. "I had business to attend to," he said. "But I am here now, and you must come with me."

Ranse did, without hesitation, leaving Markus behind. He followed Dane, who was moving at an extremely fast pace in the direction of the keep. In fact, he started to run and Ranse ran beside him, keeping pace.

There was a strange sense of urgency as they moved.

"Is something the matter?" Ranse asked. "What has happened?"

Dane wasn't sure how much to tell him, but he had to tell him something. "I have been told that you are betrothed to Lady de Wilde."

Ranse was running beside him, his long strides keeping pace with Dane's short, swift ones. "Indeed," he said. "It all happened rather suddenly."

Dane grunted. "So I have heard," he muttered. They were drawing into the shadow of the keep now, with the entry straight ahead. "There is a discussion going on now that concerns you, I am afraid. You will want to hear it."

Ranse wasn't sure what he meant. "Discussion?" he repeated. "About me?"

"Aye," Dane said.

Silence followed as they passed through the entry, heading towards the solar door where Cort was still standing. Dane noticed that the solar door was open again, but from the angle of the entry into the chamber, they could hear the discussion quite plainly. They could hear Trenton, and Matthew, and Gaston, and on occasion, Lysabel's high-pitched voice. It was clear that she was quite unhappy, as was everyone else in the chamber.

Coming just short of the open door, Dane turned to Ranse.

"Do yourself a favor, Ranse," he said softly. "*Listen.*"

Puzzled, Ranse did as he was told.

WHEN TRENTON SLAMMED the door of the chamber, he didn't notice that it bounced against the jamb and swung back open again because he was too busy pacing, too busy agonizing over what he'd just discovered. As Gaston kept an eye on Trenton, who was close to throwing a tantrum, Matthew dealt with Lysabel.

For several long moments, he didn't say anything. He was trying to organize his thoughts, trying to keep from losing his temper. As far as he was concerned, his daughter and Trenton were acting irrationally, like love-struck children. But the truth was that it wasn't difficult for him to understand that. He knew what it was to be in love, to be so mad over someone that nothing else in the world mattered. But he was trying very hard to keep it all in perspective, hoping he could make them both understand his position on the situation. The death of Trenton's wife didn't solve the problem.

He had to make them see that.

"Lysabel, I will explain the situation again so that you and Trenton both understand it," he said. "I made the contract and it is a valid one. I made it, and de Troyes accepted. I did not tell him about Trenton. I told you that I did not tell him because I did not want the memory of the man destroying any chances you and Ranse have for a pleasant life together. Ranse is a good man, with an excellent reputation, and he will be a fine and loyal husband."

Lysabel was looking at her father in horror. "But I do not want him, Papa!" she cried. "My God... do you not understand any of this? Are you so blind to anything I want or need that you are truly ignoring everything I say?"

Matthew took a deep breath. "I am trying to provide you with a stable home life, something that Trenton has never been able to establish. Ranse, however, has proven himself a steady and attentive husband. You must understand that I am trying to do what is best for you both."

"And the best for us both is marrying the woman I love to the captain of your guard so that you may keep her here, under your wing, forever?" Trenton said, his lips trembling because he was so angry. "Tell me, Uncle Matthew, do you ever intend to let her out of your sight again? Or is marrying her to de Troyes keeping her here where you have control of her, always?"

"Trenton," Gaston hissed at his son. "You will not speak to him with such disrespect."

Trenton turned to his father. "Oh?" he said, a sarcastic tinge to his voice. "And what respect has he shown me during this entire ordeal? I have been treated like the lowest form of life ever since I told him of my feelings for her. I would have done better not to be honest about it and simply steal away with her, but because I respected the man, I told him. And what has it gotten me? Betrayal and disregard. It is as if the man hates the very sight of me for loving his daughter."

Gaston couldn't disagree with him, and he turned to Matthew rather beseechingly, knowing that this situation was going to get very bad, indeed, if they didn't gain control of it.

But Matthew was looking at Trenton, not Gaston. The knight's words had given him a dose of something he hadn't been seeing – his own behavior. Matthew had always thought of himself as a fair man. That was how he'd earned the "White Lord" moniker, but in that instant, he could see that perhaps he'd been anything but fair with Trenton. With a sigh, he turned away from Lysabel and headed towards Trenton.

"Is that what you think?" he asked, his tone quiet. "Do you really think I have shown you betrayal and disregard?"

Trenton nodded without hesitation. "Haven't you?" he asked. "I was your favorite de Russe son, someone you professed to love, until I told you of my love for Lysabel. Then, it is as if I became your worst enemy. I was honest with you and you turned on me. Do you have any idea how that feels?"

Matthew lifted an eyebrow. "And do you have any idea how it feels to know that you would destroy my daughter's life, and damage the reputations of both houses, simply for your own selfish wants?" he fired back quietly. "You are not thinking of anyone other than yourself, Trenton. You do not see what your love for my daughter will do to all of us. If anyone has been betrayed, it is me. It is my family. Because you simply do not care what happens to us, so long as you get what you want."

Trenton tried not to let his words dig into him, but they did. His father had said much the same thing. They made a good deal of sense and, for the first time, Trenton was starting to see the situation from Matthew's point of view.

Had he truly been so selfish?

"If that is true, then I apologize," he said. "I deeply, sincerely apologize. But I have been unhappy with women my entire life, for the most part, and in falling for Lysabel, I saw a piece of heaven that I wanted. Is that so wrong?"

Matthew shook his head. "It is not wrong," he said. "Wanting it is not wrong. But ruining lives to get it *is* wrong. Do you understand that?"

He was right, but Trenton wasn't going to admit it. His gaze moved to Lysabel, who was standing over near her father's table, looking at him with great apprehension. His gaze lingered on her a moment before returning to Matthew.

"I do," he said. "I do understand. And I am very sorry for being so selfish. But now, I am free to marry your daughter and I beg you for her hand in marriage. I swear to you that I shall be a good husband, and a good father, and I shall provide a safe and happy home for her and for her daughters. I love them all more than words can express. Please give me that privilege, Uncle Matthew. I beseech you."

Matthew was so tired of this same plea. It was wearing him down. "And what of de Troyes? Do you simply expect me to break a perfectly honorable bargain? If I try and he refuses, there is no court that will take my side of it. I could lose more than my daughter – my reputation will be gone. A man who breaks bargains is not a man to be trusted."

"You should have never made the offer!" Lysabel cried. The tears began to fall. "You did it to put another marriage between me and Trenton, and you did it out of spite!"

Matthew turned to his daughter, who was wiping furiously at her eyes. "I did not do it out of spite," he said calmly. "I did it because I felt it was the right thing to do. Moreover, when I made the offer to de Troyes, Trenton was still a married man for all I knew."

Lysabel was trying desperately not to sob. "But he is not married now," she said. "Papa... *please*. I love him."

Matthew couldn't look at her any longer. He turned away and went to sit in his chair, rubbing at his forehead as if to rub away the tension and sorrows that had enveloped him. Trenton and Lysabel were in love, and now Trenton was free to marry. But a deal of Matthew's own making was now the biggest obstacle between them.

"To make you both happy, I must break a contract with an honorable knight," he muttered. "A man who has never done either of you harm. Are you truly asking me to be so dishonorable?"

Trenton didn't even know what to say. He was looking at Lysabel, who was weeping into her hand. His heart was broken in so many pieces that he knew he'd never be able to put it back together again if he couldn't marry her.

That was all he wanted in the world.

"And if I say yes?" he rasped.

Matthew looked up at him, pain in his eyes. There was so much pain there. Over to his left, Lysabel was sobbing softly, and in front of him stood Trenton and Gaston, two of the men he loved most in the world. One word from his lips would keep that love intact, but another word would ruin it forever. He was in a position he didn't want to be in, trying to find a balance where everyone would understand that he was only doing what he felt best. As he prepared to make a decision that would change his life forever, a soft voice near the chamber entry spoke.

"You do not have to break the contract, my lord. I will."

Matthew, Gaston, Trenton, and Lysabel looked towards the door to see Ranse standing there. His young face was serious as he stepped into the chamber, his focus solely on Matthew, as his liege.

This conversation only involved the two of them.

"You do not have to break the contract, my lord," he said again, calmly and quietly. "I will break it."

Matthew was surprised to see him. "You have heard our conversation?"

Ranse nodded, somewhat sadly. "Aye, my lord."

"How much of it?"

"Most of it, my lord."

Matthew lowered his gaze, scratching at his graying head and feeling rather badly that the man had heard things that should have been more gently delivered to him.

"Then I am sorry," he said after a moment. "You should not have had to overhear a conversation to know that we were discussing your betrothal with Lysabel."

Ranse's expression was serious. "But I am glad I heard it," he said, looking to Lysabel, who was standing near the lancet windows that overlooked the bailey. When he spoke, it was to her. "From the beginning of your father's offer, I could feel that something was off. He said you had issues to deal with, and in our discussion earlier today, that was very clear. I could tell that you were extremely dissatisfied with this betrothal and I am sorry you felt as if you could not tell me the truth."

Lysabel's sobbing had stopped, but as she looked at Ranse, she began to feel overwhelming guilt. Guilt that so sweet and fine a man had to hear the truth the way he had.

"How could I?" she asked. "I told you all that I could, all that I felt comfortable telling you. Had I told you about Trenton, it would have looked as if my father had withheld truths, but that is not why he did not tell you. He did it because he did not wish for there to be any encumbrances on the start of a new life together. Knowing I was in love with another... that would have put an immovable obstacle between us and it was not something you deserved."

Ranse nodded, appreciating her candor, but his attention moved back to Matthew. "Forgive me, my lord, but I feel as if you did not tell me the truth because you knew if you did, I would have refused your offer."

Matthew sighed faintly. "That is possible," he admitted. "But I felt it was an unnecessary burden for you, most of all."

Ranse wasn't so sure, but he didn't counter him. His gaze moved from Matthew to Trenton, who was standing back over by his father, looking pale and worn. There was anguish in every feature.

God, he knew the emotion behind such an appearance.

He knew it well.

"When my wife died, I looked much as you do now," he said. "I had just lost something that meant a great deal to me and you look as if you are about to lose the same. I do not know why Lord Wellesbourne offered me Lady de Wilde's hand instead of you, but having heard what I have, I will respectfully decline the offer. If you are worried about me standing in your way, I will not. I could not marry the lady knowing she loved another, and that is the truth. When I marry, I want my bride's full attention. I think that is only fair."

Trenton, much like Matthew and Lysabel, was coming to feel badly for de Troyes. He was honestly shocked that the man was being so agreeable about this and he felt guilty for ever thinking terrible thoughts about the man.

"I agree with you," he said. "And there is some lady, somewhere, who will be deeply honored to bear the name of Lady de Troyes, and I believe she will be very fortunate, indeed. If you are wondering why Lord Wellesbourne offered you Lady de Wilde's hand in marriage instead of me, it is because I am a man of questionable reputation. I have been married three times, my most recent wife having died in a fire two days ago. So, you see, even though I love Lysabel and she loves me, I could not marry her, and Lord Wellesbourne, as every father should, was concerned for her future and her honor. He did not want her entering into a clandestine love affair with a married man. But before you judge me, know that my marriage to my third wife was an arranged marriage and she hated the sight of me. She did all she could to dishonor the de Russe name, so it wasn't a marriage at all. It was a union of chains, and I was its prisoner. It is true that I loved a woman other than the female I had married, but it was not a dishonorable love, I assure you. It is one I will take to my grave with me, and beyond."

It was a succinct, calm explanation of the situation and coupled with what Ranse had already heard, he could put the puzzle together. He saw what had happened. Nodding his head at Trenton, to thank the man for the honest explanation, he turned back to Matthew.

"My lord, although I am greatly honored by the offer of Lady de Wilde's hand, you will understand when I say that I have reconsidered and must refuse," he said. "Last year, I lost the love of my life. It was the worst thing that could have happened to me, so I understand what de Russe is facing at this moment. He is watching his entire life slip away. I had to face the end of what I had, and there was no choice, but now *you* have the choice. You can make two people happy beyond their wildest dreams. I beg you – on behalf of one who has loved and lost – to do the right thing. Let them be together."

With that, he turned on his heel and left the solar, walking past Gaston, who put a hand of gratitude on the man's shoulder. He also walked past Dane, who smiled at him approvingly, and finally Cort, who was also smiling at him. It seemed that Ranse had done right by all of them and once he left the solar, it was Gaston who finally turned to Matthew as the man sat at his table, drained and emotional.

"Before Lysabel and Trenton came into this solar, you had given me the choice of what to do in this situation," he said, making his way to the table. Reaching out, he extended his hand to Matthew, who took it strongly. They held hands for a moment, silently reaffirming bonds of trust and love and friendship. In spite of everything, those bonds had never been stronger. "Matt, listen to me. I do not have much time left, but in the time I do have, I would like to see my son happy. Let them wed. *Please.*"

Matthew was looking up at him, fighting off the tears. Gaston had admitted what Matthew didn't want to hear, the fact that his life, at some point in the near future, would come to an end. To Matthew, it was a dying request.

He would honor it.

EPILOGUE

THERE WERE PONIES in the wedding party.

The day of the wedding had dawned bright and warm, and guests had been invited from all over England. Even the village of Wellesbourne was in the celebration mood, as Matthew had supplied barrels of wine and two large hogs for a feast. Everyone in and around Wellesbourne Castle was celebrating on this day, cheering the happy couple on the event of their marriage.

But it was an unusual wedding party already. Cynethryn and Brencis had begged to have their ponies with them, and Dewi as well, and deck them out in flowers. Trenton had given them permission for the ponies, but he knew Dewi wouldn't tolerate being primped, so he had to suffer through Brencis' sad face when he denied her permission to decorate his warhorse. He had given the girls his approval without asking Lysabel, who hadn't been around at the time. She had been in her chamber with her mother, and Remington, and Gilliana, Trenton's youngest sister, and he hadn't wanted to bother her about it. Or perhaps he simply wanted to make his first fatherly decision.

It had felt good.

Because the wedding had happened within a week of Matthew officially giving his consent, that meant that most things, including the announcements, had been rushed. News of Benoit de Wilde's death had been circulated shortly before the announcement of the remarriage of Lady de Wilde, and messengers were sent out to all of the de Russe and Wellesbourne siblings.

Unfortunately, most were unable to attend, but a few had managed – William was there, of course, as was his brother, Daniel, a rather serious knight without much of a sense of humor. He was a trainer at Kenilworth and it showed – grim, dedicated, and knightly. William had harassed him about it until Daniel slugged him, drawing blood.

William teased from a safe distance after that.

Matthieu de Russe had also been able to attend the festivities, and he had brought his wife and young sons, who were tormented by Cort and Boden and Gage. Wellesbourne Castle abounded with screaming children and taunting uncles. But it was all in great fun.

Then, of course, there were the ponies in the wedding party.

At sunset on the eighth day after Matthew gave his consent, a priest from St. Peter's church in Wellesbourne's village performed the wedding mass at the door to Wellesbourne's keep, with nearly everyone at Wellesbourne as witnesses. Trenton had never known such happiness and as he looked into Lysabel's eyes as the priest tied their hands together with a satin sash, he was genuinely choked with emotion. It would have been perfect had a series of unsavory events not interrupted what had been the most momentous moment of his life.

It had all started with Cynethryn and Brencis being led into the wedding ceremony on Honey and Snowdrop, who were no longer lame and covered in flowers that the little girls had woven into their manes and tails. William was leading Cynethryn as Boden led Brencis, with the uncles in charge of managing the girls and the animals. It sounded simple enough. They positioned the beasts next to Lysabel, who rolled her eyes when she saw the barnyard wedding guests. She laid the blame squarely on Trenton, who merely shrugged sheepishly.

But that wasn't the worst of it. Somehow, one of the ponies had a sour stomach and started to pass gas during the ceremony, which drove most of the younger knights into fits of giggles. Nothing said romance like a pony farting throughout a wedding. It was bad enough, but Gage, who was standing near the offending pony, tried to push the beast away from him. That resulted in the animal lifting its tail and dumping shite onto his feet.

Disgusted, Gage tried to move away, but ended up slipping in the shite, crashing into his brother, Matthieu, who shoved him aside and sent him onto his arse. This startled the ponies, and Lysabel grabbed Brencis as Trenton grabbed Cynethryn to prevent the ponies from dumping the girls.

After that, the animals were banished, and the girls were teary with the loss, but the ceremony proceeded without incident. Lysabel Wellesbourne de Wilde became Lady de Russe, Countess of Westbury, and farting ponies notwithstanding, Trenton had never been so proud in his entire life.

It was done.

Day moved into night, and all of Wellesbourne had joined in the wedding festivities. Even the off-duty soldiers were drunk. The castle was lit up and could be seen for miles around, and the wine and music both flowed freely. Trenton and Lysabel walked hand in hand among the guests, receiving their blessing and well-wishes, as the girls sat sleepily with Alixandrea and Remington, who ended up taking them up to bed when the hour grew late. The last Trenton saw of his mother, it was with Brencis hanging on to her neck, cuddling up to the woman.

Already, they were family.

"My girls love your mother," Lysabel said softly as she watched Remington follow Alixandrea from the hall. "She is a truly wonderful woman."

Trenton smiled, his arm around her shoulders and a cup of wine in his hand. He gave her a squeeze as his attention turned to the great hall, with its smoke and laughter and revelry going on.

"Look at Dane," he said, pointing with the hand that held the cup. "He has only been watching that gambling game. The second my mother leaves the hall, he'll rush to join it."

Lysabel giggled when, as predicted, Dane inserted himself into the middle of a gambling game over near the hearth. "He is a grown man," she said. "Are you telling me that he is still afraid of his mother?"

Trenton looked at her. "Aren't you?"

Lysabel continued laughing, conceding the point. Her gaze moved over the hall, seeing both family and friends alike enjoying themselves. Cort, William, Gage, and Boden, the troublemakers, were laughing and drinking along with Matthieu and Daniel, older brothers who weren't quite as silly and gay as the younger knights, but they were enjoying themselves nonetheless.

Markus was also there along with Trenton's men, Timothy, Adrian, and Anthony, who had come from the village of Westbury to witness the wedding at Trenton's summons. Trenton had sent a missive to The Horn and The Crown tavern, where they had been waiting for him, and they'd come on the run. He'd only spoken with them briefly when they arrived, and it had been clear that they were surprised by the wedding to Lady de Wilde.

Considering the last time they'd seen the woman was the night they'd killed her first husband, to say that they were surprised was putting it mildly. Still, when Trenton explained everything, they understood – in his quest to ensure she was safe after the harrowing events with her husband, Trenton had fallen in love with her. It was as simple as that. Perhaps that was the most shocking of all to them, that the Trenton de Russe they knew could actually show such feeling.

But it was feeling that was exceedingly obvious.

"Trenton?" Lysabel asked over the noise of the hall.

"Aye, love?"

Her gaze was lingering on Timothy and Adrian and Anthony as the men drank heartily with Markus. "When your men return to London, are you going with them?"

Trenton looked at his men, also. He'd been with them for many years, and they'd lived side by side for most of that time. He found it ironic that in the biggest adventure of his life, the one with Lysabel, they hadn't been with him at all.

But perhaps they weren't meant to be.

They were from another chapter in his life.

"I will," he said, "but only to give Henry my resignation in person."

She smiled up at him. "Are you certain?" she asked. "I do not wish for you to surrender something you love to do. You told me once that you felt as if you made a difference. That you were shaping a kingdom."

He looked down at her. "That is true, but there is more to it," he said. "I think I was hiding from something, hiding from what my life had become. I was doing what I wanted to do because there was nothing else for me. But now... now, there is so much more for me. I told your father that I would give it all up for you and I meant it. We shall retire to Deverill Castle for now, but I shall petition Henry for permission to build a new castle at Westbury, something bigger and more beautiful than you can possibly imagine. You deserve something as grand as I can give you."

She reached up, touching his face sweetly. "Only if you're certain."

"Never more certain of anything. You are what is most important to me now."

Lysabel leaned in to him for a hug and he kissed the top of her head. But as she looked at the hall, she spied her father and Gaston sitting at the very end of one of the tables, deeply involved in their conversation.

Two great knights with their empires laid out before them, and their children marrying to cement a great legacy. It was a proud and powerful dynasty they both shared, The Dark One and the White Lord. Lysabel's gaze lingered on Matthew.

"My father seems much happier the past few days," she said. "Don't you think so?"

Trenton spied the two older men also. "Aye," he said. "He is back to hugging me again. He has not done that since this whole thing started."

"He loves you," Lysabel said. "He has always loved you. I think he feels bad for the way things went, for the position he had to take. Truthfully, now that things have calmed down and everything worked in our favor, I understand what he was trying to do. It was a terribly difficult position for him, though."

Trenton nodded. "It was," he said. "In hindsight, if the same thing had happened to Cissy or Cinny, I cannot say that I would not have reacted just as your father did."

"Did you tell him that?"

"Not yet. But I will."

"Why don't you do that now? I want to see my daughters before they go to sleep. Come up when you have finished with my father and bid them a good sleep."

Trenton's gaze lingered on his father and Matthew, seeing how wrapped up in their conversation they were. He could only imagine what they were discussing; the past, their dedication to each other, and their dedication to a braver, stronger England. Perhaps, they were discussing the future. Trenton could only imagine Matthew's grief at facing a future without his very best friend, because it was a grief that Trenton suffered every single day, knowing that each day with his father was precious.

And each day might be the last.

That was why he was so glad his father was here with him now, seeing his joy as he embarked on a new life with the woman he loved. It had been a hard-fought battle, but they'd been victorious, and it was a victory for all to share. Trenton had already discussed with Lysabel the importance of spending what time he could with his father at Deverill Castle, for as long as he could. She wholeheartedly agreed.

It was something more to love her for.

"I will talk to him," he said. "But give the old men their time together. That time between them is rare and few these days. For now, I have something else to do."

"What?"

"I have a man to thank."

Lysabel knew who he meant.

Ranse de Troyes hadn't attended the wedding, or any of the festivities even though he'd been invited. He'd politely declined, instead preferring to remain at his post to ensure Wellesbourne Castle was safe and the wedding uninterrupted. It was his wedding gift to the happy couple, but Lysabel suspected there was more to it. It would have been difficult for any man to witness a marriage that should have been his, and she didn't blame him for staying away.

The man who had made this all possible.

Therefore, she smiled in understanding at Trenton's statement and kissed him before heading from the hall, following the path of her mother and mother-in-law as they'd taken her girls to bed.

Trenton watched her go, his heart fuller than he ever knew possible. A new wife, new daughters, and a baby on the way made him more content than he'd ever been. A whole new life was laid wide before him and the world was at his feet. Together, with Lysabel, he would conquer it all.

He would be the man his father had always wanted him to be.

As Trenton headed out of the hall on his way to thank de Troyes, he looked up into the brilliant night sky and remembered that on a night very similar to this one, he'd discovered the love of his life in an abused, beaten lady who, in spite of her sorrows, had never let it destroy her. Her strength and her dignity were the things legends were made of, but the adoration he felt for her was something only dreamt of.

Trenton de Russe had finally learned the meaning of what it meant to love.

CB THE END 80

Children of Trenton and Lysabel
Cynethryn
Brencis
Raphael (Rafe)
Gaston
Brandt
Matthew
Trevor
Kristienne
Lucian

The de Russe Legacy:
The White Lord of Wellesbourne
The Dark One: Dark Knight
Beast
Lord of War: Black Angel
The Iron Knight
Dark Moon

ABOUT KATHRYN LE VEQUE

Medieval Just Got Real.

KATHRYN LE VEQUE is a USA TODAY Bestselling author, an Amazon All-Star author, and a #1 bestselling, award-winning, multi-published author in Medieval Historical Romance and Historical Fiction. She has been featured in the NEW YORK TIMES and on USA TODAY's HEA blog. In March 2015, Kathryn was the featured cover story for the March issue of InD'Tale Magazine, the premier Indie author magazine. She was also a quadruple nominee (a record!) for the prestigious RONE awards for 2015.

Kathryn's Medieval Romance novels have been called 'detailed', 'highly romantic', and 'character-rich'. She crafts great adventures of love, battles, passion, and romance in the High Middle Ages. More than that, she writes for both women AND men – an unusual crossover for a romance author – and Kathryn has many male readers who enjoy her stories because of the male perspective, the action, and the adventure.

On October 29, 2015, Amazon launched Kathryn's Kindle Worlds Fan Fiction site WORLD OF DE WOLFE PACK. Please visit Kindle Worlds for Kathryn Le Veque's World of de Wolfe Pack and find many action-packed adventures written by some of the top authors in their genre using Kathryn's characters from the de Wolfe Pack series. As Kindle World's FIRST Historical Romance fan fiction world, Kathryn Le Veque's World of de Wolfe Pack will contain all of the great storytelling you have come to expect.

Kathryn loves to hear from her readers. Please find Kathryn on Facebook at Kathryn Le Veque, Author, or join her on Twitter @kathrynleveque, and don't forget to visit her website and sign up for her blog at www.kathrynleveque.com.

Please follow Kathryn on Bookbub for the latest releases and sales: bookbub.com/authors/kathryn-le-veque.

Made in the USA
Middletown, DE
12 August 2018